ANOTHER
BREATH

Gary Moreau

Yard Dog Press

Another Breath
Gary Moreau
First Edition Copyright © Gary Moreau 2019

Published by Yard Dog Press at Kindle

This is a work of fiction. Names, characters, places, and incidents are the products of the author's imagination or are used fictitiously and are not to be construed as real. Any resemblance to actual events, locales, organizations, or persons, living or dead, is entirely coincidental.

Print Version ISBN 978-1-945941-21-4
Another Breath
First Edition Copyright © Gary Moreau 2019

Yard Dog Press
710 W. Redbud Lane
Alma, AR 72921-7247

http://www.yarddogpress.com

Edited by Selina Rosen
Copy & Technical Editor Lynn Rosen
Cover art by Gary Moreau

First Print Edition September 15, 2019
Printed in the United States of America
0 9 8 7 6 5 4 3 2 1

Dedication

This book is dedicated to our wonderful family, to Amy and John, Rachel and Keenan and all the grandchildren. A special thanks to Rick Timmins, my friend, reader and advisor. Thank you, Rick.

Table of Contents

Chapter 1

The darkness was cold and damp and in its center was a dim light. Three figures squatted near the timid illumination, as if it were capable of radiating warmth. They spoke in hushed voices, but neither the soft light, nor the quiet words, reflected the nature of their discussion.

"The time has come," declared the woman in the sharkskin coat and leggings. She looked first to the man dressed in the orange of the city militia and then turned to stare at the figure who sat crouched deeper in darkness. The light reached up from the wet floor and threw ominous shadows on her face, but her eyes were bright. She raised her clenched fist. "The opportunity must be grasped! The neck of the Technocracy must be snapped from its body!" She continued to glare at the man who preferred darkness; he shifted his weight and raised his face to meet her defiant stare.

Even in the faint light it could be seen that he was different; his eyes were black emptiness, the feral eyes of an otherworldly predator. He spoke. "It was foolish of you to demand a meeting. Are you certain this dome is shielded?"

"The Leader has provided us with stolen technology. Go ahead, Citizen, attempt to contact Home."

His muscles lost tone and his eyes drifted shut, until only narrow lines of black remained. It was only a moment before he regained his posture. "Nevertheless, my absence will be missed. If you called me here simply to satisfy your urge to express inane rhetoric, I must leave at once. If you called me because you doubt me, then voice your concerns."

The man in orange extended his hands so that his palms were brought into the light, as if the light provided warmth. He gazed at the pea-sized source of light without blinking. "We all have parts to play," he said softly, "but it is those of us on Earth who will pay with our lives. Before we offer ourselves to the sacrifice, we wished to meet the Citizen who will determine the ultimate success or failure of the plan. Is this so difficult to understand?"

"You have met me. Now I will leave."

It was the woman who responded. "I've heard it said that regeneration robs a person of his humanity." Her unseen hand tightened on the handle of the knife she held at her side. "How do we know you'll remain loyal to the cause?"

1

"The very fact that we are meeting and you are still alive should be proof enough!"

"Is it?" she responded quietly. "Once we guarantee that you'll be selected as Team Leader, how do we know you'll still be willing to sacrifice all, including your life, if need be?"

The silence that followed was unbroken, but for the soft "pat" of drops of water falling through the darkness from condensation on the inner surface of the dome.

The citizen finally spoke, "Quang Lu is convinced."

"How dare you speak his name out loud."

"You told me this dome is screened."

"Have you actually spoken with the Leader?" she asked.

"No...but he has communicated with me. Have you?"

The woman said nothing.

The man continued. "So...you haven't seen him either. Should I be suspicious of your motives?"

The man in orange stood and looked down at the Citizen, who remained crouched, partially hidden by darkness. "We have nothing personal to gain and everything to lose."

"What do you have to lose? By the time this mission is completed, you and your children's children will all be dead of old age," the Citizen said derisively.

The man in orange shifted his gaze back to the woman; she did not voice an objection, so he continued. "Quang Lu has instructed us to make use of the sea-people but to allow them only their traditional weapons. We are not to leave any clue that there is involvement from within the Technocracy. It is likely that a number of those involved in the attack on Traynor will die. We don't underestimate the Technocracy, or Traynor. Traynor's death will mark the beginning, but we expect this entire cell of the Friends of the Earth will be exterminated. All of this will be done to deflect attention from you."

"Yet, you risk discovery by insisting that I come to Cisco."

"We do not die for a stranger!" the woman spat, her voice full and loud.

The Citizen arose from his squat, the fine cloth of his blouse shimmering, even in the dim light. He backed farther away from the glowing pebble.

"Are you afraid, Citizen?" she asked with a thin smile.

"No, but neither am I stupid enough to invite discovery for the sake of some sort of intuitive assessment of my loyalty. If you're satisfied, I'll

2

return to the Citizen levels. I've already been out of the circuit suspiciously long."

"I am not satisfied," declared the woman as she too stood.

"What is it that you want? How—" The infrared range of the Citizen's vision allowed him to see the approaching figures. There were four of them and they carried a heavy bundle, slung between them. The Citizen slowly lowered his right hand and began to slip his fingers into a slit in his blouse, reaching for the handle of his laser.

"We know you are armed," the woman said. "If you are loyal to the cause, as you say you are, then you have nothing to fear. If not...you will die." She waved her hand casually toward the opposite side of the dome.

The Citizen turned and saw another dozen figures approaching through the darkness. As he returned his attention to the woman, the bundle was dropped at his feet. He heard a muffled moan.

"Go ahead," she urged, "open it."

After glancing around at the circle of armed men and women, he knelt and pulled the binding tape open. The sight caught his breath. It was his friend, the one who had accompanied him on this supposed recreational visit to Cisco, unaware that he had been invited simply to provide cover. He was awake, but bound. His black eyes were wide open, nearly circular, but he couldn't speak; his lips had been sewn shut. He twisted his body and pulled at his restraints but his words were muffled, unintelligible.

The Citizen jerked when his shoulder was touched.

"Would you like to borrow this?" the woman asked.

He took the knife from her hand and used it to slice through the string that bound his friend's lips. His friend took in a gasp of breath, the ends of string still embedded in his lips.

"Lem, Mother of Life! Am I glad to see you!"

Lem Gan continued holding the knife as he returned his attention to the woman.

"Get me out of here!" his friend yelled.

He glanced back down and rested his hand gently on his friend's chest. "Just a minute—"

"Hey, what the sludge is going on? Cut me loose!"

"Quiet!" The violence of his order surprised his friend as well as himself. "Please," he added more softly, "give me a moment while I straighten this out." Again he looked to the woman. "What is the meaning of this atrocity? I demand an immediate explanation."

"My pleasure," she responded coolly. "As you said, there is no ultimate proof of your loyalty, but you can make a statement with your actions before these witnesses. If you succeed with your mission, many

Citizens will die, but even a greater number of Unders will die. It's a sacrifice we are willing to make for freedom from the Technocracy. The Earth will recover, if it is given a chance."

"What the sludge is she talking about, Lem? Get me the hell out of here! Lem!"

The woman dressed in sharkskin motioned with her hand and one of the men in the circle stepped forward to stuff a rag in the captive's mouth. As he renewed his hopeless struggle to escape, Lem Gan withdrew his hand from contact with his friend's body.

"You will make the first symbolic sacrifice," the woman said. "Use the knife to kill your friend."

"Symbolic? Just a minute here!" He started to stand, but two pairs of hands pushed down on his shoulders; he was forced to continue kneeling next to his friend, who had stopped struggling and was now staring up at him.

The woman glared as she spoke. "There will be much death, friends and family will die! We must be prepared, not only to sacrifice ourselves, but also those we love. Are you dedicated to our purpose?"

Lem slowly lowered his gaze, toward the knife he held in his hand. "But...he is like a brother to me."

"Be honest. He is more than your brother. He is your lover. The Leader has informed us. What is your decision?"

Lem looked past the knife. "You don't understand. He can't be regenerated. His memories aren't stored. He's first generation. He will be truly dead. Body and matrix dead."

"Welcome to our world, Citizen."

Lem's eyes met those of his lover. The man began to buck and twist, but there was no escape; he became perfectly still. He was trying to say something when Lem clamped his hand over his lover's face, covering his eyes. The skin of his face was slick with sweat; he managed to pull away as Lem lowered the blade and sliced across his neck. The cut was too superficial; though it bled freely, he survived. Lem began stabbing. Wild with rage, he jabbed the blade into his lover's chest and abdomen. His hand was warm with blood, but even then he did not stop, until the woman grabbed hold of his arm.

"Enough!" she yelled.

Horrified, a measure of sanity returned to Lem. He stood and backed away, finally tearing his gaze away from the bag that contained his dead lover. He threw the knife onto the dark, wet floor and rubbed his hands on his blouse, staining it with blood.

4

"Very good, Citizen," the woman said without emotion. "We will leave you now. I've received word that the thruster-craft has lifted from the Cisco pad and will return with Pie Traynor within the next twenty-four hours. He will be our responsibility. With his death, you'll be chosen to replace him as mission commander. You'll be escorted outside this bubble, into another. Once there, you'll receive a non-lethal wound. Friends in the city militia will stay with you and claim they've rescued you. You'll tell the authorities that you and your friend came to the under city to buy slave sex. You'll tell them that you didn't see your assailants. The body of your friend will be dumped where it'll be found. You will not mention the sea-people. Do not forget to reward your rescuers. Do you have any questions?"

The Citizen took a deep breath as he stared into a shallow puddle of cold water at his feet. He shook his head and didn't raise his eyes until the man dressed in the orange of the city militia led him out of the dome. Lem Gan wasn't afraid; he longed for pain and injury.

Chapter 2

Pie Traynor studied the two-millimeter, red-brown seed that nestled in the crease of his palm. He looked down at the book on the counter and carefully took hold of the corner of a page to turn it. Despite his care, another piece of the edge crumbled away. The ancient paper had discolored and become brittle, as if it had been baked in an oven. The print was faint, not much darker than the paper itself. He read again about the redwood forests and tried to make out the pictures of the magnificent trees, never having had the opportunity to see them in person before the Death took everything.

He smiled and touched the seed with the tip of his index finger, a speck of latent life that could become a giant redwood, if it were given a chance. It wouldn't have been possible without Roxanne's expertise. The meager scraps of genetic material had been so fragmented. That was one aspect of her that had survived every regeneration; in every iteration, she was brilliant.

He leaned back in his chair and stared at the blank overhead as he thought about her. It was amazing how much of her personality was passed down through her genome. If she knew...he shivered as an onslaught of memories cascaded through the mental barriers he'd constructed. It happened sometimes.

He rubbed his face. She was the ninth. He remembered every one of them. He remembered telling the first Roxanne that she'd been regenerated. That had been an unmitigated disaster. She was so damn strong willed. And then there was the time the information filters failed and she learned about her first self, the one who had married Jack Nichols. She had killed herself five times, died of natural causes twice and had deserted him once. The pain of each of her deaths was fresh in his mind. He refused to allow himself the relief of using a chemical blocking agent. Remembering was the price he demanded of himself. But, was it enough to justify....

He shifted to a more comfortable position. He nodded in agreement with himself. This time it would be different. He'd made the same pledge to each of the prior Roxannes, but this time it would be different. He would not desert her. He would see this through to the end. They would face death together.

He shivered with dread. The crisis was approaching. He could feel it. The room seemed to be closing in on him. He felt trapped.

He shifted again in his seat and fought to control the panic. His heart felt like it was beating too hard, each squeeze an uncomfortable thud in his chest. He took a series of deep breaths, until a sense of control returned.

He refocused on the seed. He should've waited for her before harvesting the last batch but, after all, it'd been his project since long before this version of her existed. Besides, she was sleeping. The justifications did little to appease his conscience. He dropped the tiny seed into the cryogenic cylinder and sealed it.

The cylinder was only a half-meter long and ten centimeters in diameter, but it contained a potential forest. He was reluctant to part with it. He had no further specimen on which to even attempt a genetic reconstruction; the redwood fragments had been the last and most difficult, and now it was done.

He touched the control pad; the cylinder was lowered through a slot in the floor and then out of sight. It moved along its mechanical path until it was secured to a launching rail deep in the darkness of a mountain cave, to take its place alongside hundreds of similar projectiles, each with its own special cargo of frozen seeds. There was nothing more to do except wait and hope. How long? Another thousand years? Two thousand?

He rested his elbow on the edge of the laboratory table, his balled-up hands supporting his head as they pushed up against his cheeks. It was over. The sense of satisfaction was shallow and the sense of disappointment completely unexpected. Perhaps a lasting sense of accomplishment would come only after the seeds were delivered and the Earth was ready to accept them...if there would ever be such a time, he added to himself. He slammed his fists onto the table.

"House, time," he demanded.

"17:36," the house replied in its pleasant baritone.

Roxanne had told him she'd like to meet the man behind that voice. He smiled. Always teasing.

It was still an hour until dusk. He started rocking back and forth in his chair; the feeling was coming. He tried the deep breathing technique again and pounded his fists on his thighs in rhythm with his rocking. He knew there was enough air and knew that there was nothing wrong with his lungs, but the knowledge was sterile and his claustrophobia virulent.

He abruptly stood, knocking the chair over backward and, instead of the up-tube, ran toward the stairs. When he reached the top level of his egg-shaped house, he stumbled forward, his feet as insensitive as bricks.

He had to do something! He was dying! He couldn't breathe! He had to escape.

He broke into a sprint. The friction soles of his suit squeaked with each stride, as he ran round and round. His lips and tongue prickled with a thousand needles. He couldn't feel his face. He was running to escape the touch of his own shadow. He stumbled and fell. He slid across the smooth floor on his back and came to an abrupt stop with his head against the wall. The wall was cool against his ear and he could hear a sound. If his imagination would've permitted, it could have been grains of sand scraping against a window, or fine drops of rain lightly tapping on a metal roof, but his mind could not sustain the lie.

He pushed away from the wall and crawled toward the center of the empty room. His head hung down and his body drooped, causing his shoulder blades to protrude as sharp ridges on his back.

"House, chair!" he commanded, and the house obeyed.

A chair arose, its form pushed upward from the substance of the floor. He pulled himself into the resilient cup of the chair and leaned his head back, with his black citizen eyes focused on the overhead dome and his mouth partially open.

"House, north panel transparent."

A quarter of the dome turned clear to reveal a seething black madness. His breathing quieted as he watched the small, obscene movements of countless insects piled one atop another. They were constantly crawling, relentlessly seeking as they fed upon the occasional leakage from the house and, more often than not, on one another. It was if they had congealed into a single, boiling monster with an insatiable appetite. The loathsome sight of a billion flickering specks of reflected light mesmerized him.

"House, west transparent, south transparent, east, north, west, south...."

The house pulsed with the stroboscopic horror show, running round and round the dome, faster and faster until....

"Pie!"

His commands ceased at the calling of his name. He tipped his head back until the upside down figure of a woman came into view. His eyes scanned her nude body. He noted for the thousandth time the fine shape of her legs and thighs, and her dark pubic recess. Although her waist retained a pleasing slimness, her breasts no longer held the firmness of youth. Her hair was no longer a vibrant red but, instead, had faded with streaks of gray. A fan of fine lines extended outward from her eyes and deep creases were etched into her cheeks, the imprint of uncountable smiles, but she was not smiling now; her brow was furrowed with concern.

"House, dome opaque," she ordered quietly.

Her nakedness had not lost the ability to make his heart race with desire, but he didn't speak of this. Instead he said, "Why don't you attend to your face? Even if you persist until death with your idiosyncratic objections to regeneration, at least you could attend to your appearance."

She didn't give credence to his question by answering it. She knew him too well.

"House, chair," she said and walked over to him.

A second chair arose next to his but, instead of sitting on it, she took an extra step and settled onto his lap, a sensuous act in itself.

"Pie," she said wistfully, "you didn't sleep with me again today."

He hugged her against himself, savoring her closeness, but said nothing; it was a fact.

She continued. "It's getting worse, isn't it? You had another attack, didn't you?"

He looked into her green eyes and studied her face. It was not the lines of age he saw; he saw her beauty, her lips, still luscious with what appeared to be a constant smile. Her face was a pleasure to behold, made beyond beautiful by the person she was, his wife, his loving, brilliant, strong-willed wife.

"Roxy...I'm sorry. I didn't mean anything by what I said. It's just...I feel trapped. I feel like this house is collapsing around me, squeezing the life out of me. I need to get outside so I can breathe."

"Pie." She held his face with her hands and stared into the blackness of his eyes. Her fierce gaze and desperate intensity evaporated as rapidly as it had arisen. Her grip became light and her determination ebbed.

"I wish I could see your eyes, your real eyes," she said.

"You know very well this is simply an adaptation to avoid sun blindness."

"So you say. You never go outside in daylight. What's the—"

"Do you really want to go there, again?"

"No. I'm worried," she said in a small voice. "What's happening to us?"

"Happening? Nothing is happening."

Tears welled up to shimmer along the lower lids of her eyes. "Don't, my love," she murmured. "I deserve the truth."

"I am telling you the truth."

"Pie, this is me you're talking to. What is it that you want? To set some kind of record? To be the human who claims he's breathed the most

10

breaths? Isn't our life enough to satisfy you? Are you so terrified of death that you can't let go of the illusion that you live on and on?"

He wanted to respond, wanted to reassure her, but could not. His silence told its own tale.

"We made a vow to each other," she said, "to live life to its end, together. I can make it on my own. I don't need you but…I want you. I really, really want you. Don't leave me."

"I won't leave you," he said, but turned his face away from her.

Forty-two years, where had it gone? It seemed like only yesterday that he'd witnessed her body being harvested from the regeneration chamber. Beautiful and the equivalent of being in her mid-twenties. She was always beautiful, no matter her age. With assist, she had learned rapidly. She'd been fed a false story, with plenty of fake corroborating evidence that her family had died in an airship crash, that she was the only survivor and had suffered a head injury. But, it had been up to him to win her love, each time she had regenerated.

"You do remember your promise, don't you?" she asked.

He looked back to her. "Remember?"

"Pie, don't pretend to be obtuse." She kissed him. Her lips were soft and warm.

He held her against him. "Of course I remember. You are the most important person in my life."

"So, are you talking about your current life or one of those false lives you seem to believe are also yours?"

"Stop it, Roxy."

"How old are you, Pie?"

He sighed. "You know damn well how old I am."

"And how old would that be?"

"All right, if you insist in getting into this…again. I'm a little over two thousand years old."

She pounced on his words, her passion unslaked by time and repetition. "You are no one but yourself! You are the victim of a heinous lie."

The words were so familiar he could have said them with her, and knew from repetition what came next.

"You are not two thousand years old," she said. "When we met, you were a twenty-eight year old clone filled with the scars and prejudices of those who went before you, of those who died. You are not them." She brushed her fingers through his still thick, but silvery gray hair. "I love you, but I swear I will never regenerate. My poor dear, who knows how many memories you've had to assimilate? False memories. It's no wonder you're confused."

His face was blank, as if he were deaf to her words, but he was not indifferent to her presence; he savored the feel of her nearness. He loved her, but to let life burn itself out, for no reason at all? That made no sense. He lifted her effortlessly; age had not stolen his strength and could not diminish his size. He lowered her into the cup chair she had called up and then walked to the edge of the dome. He leaned against the cool surface and rested his head against his forearm.

She said nothing as she studied him.

Finally he spoke. "What kind of a cruel joke is it to provide a being with a sense of individuality and an intense drive to survive, but then make death inevitable?"

"Are you talking about God here, or is it perhaps evolutionary, a side effect linked to survival of the species?"

"I refuse to submit."

He had said it. The words were out and could not be recalled. There was silence, a beating silence that made his head ring as if it were shouting in his ears. "I'm sorry." He added so softly, it might have only been a thought. He straightened and returned to the cup chairs where he kneeled before Roxanne. Her eyes were closed, her face directed toward the opalescent dome. He sat on his heels and watched her; she was motionless except for the rhythmic movements of respiration.

"Roxy?"

There was no response.

"Roxy, you can regenerate with me. We don't have to go through the Technocracy and Mitchell Mason. You know I have enough credits to pay for regeneration for both of us. There is a private facility in Cago. We don't have to go to Home."

She turned her head to face him and then opened her eyes, as if she were capable of only one action at a time. She looked into his face, a face dominated by a prominent nose, and then to his modified eyes; his black eyebrows were turning bushy and coarse.

"I finished loading the last seeds. I hope you aren't angry with me," he said to break the silence.

"I could give a shit about the seeds."

"How can you say that? It's been our life's work and that's another reason. The Earth isn't ready. We need to live until we can ensure that the reseeding will be a success. To witness the fact that our efforts were not in vain."

"The hell we do! That's not the reason for my life. That's only what we do, or did anyway. Us, you and me, that's the reason for my life. You want us to choose death and then call it life. It won't be us, Pie. It'll be two other people that look like us. I should've known." She brought her hands up to cover her face. "I should have known." Tears leaked down her cheeks.

He tentatively extended his hand to rest it on her abdomen, a feathery touch, but she twisted away. She wiped at her tears, but more came to take their place. Despite her tears, it was anger that overwhelmed the tumultuous emotions that washed through her.

"I should have known all along," she said bitterly. "You kept us isolated on this mountain top all these years, not because you wanted to break with the Technocracy, but because you were afraid. You knew all along you'd go back to them. Didn't you!"

He withdrew from her and rocked back on his heels.

She continued. "Don't you even have the guts to admit it? You are an addict! You are addicted to the lie of regeneration to quiet your own fear of death. How many others lovers have your predecessors deserted in their futile run from death? How many lovers have been sacrificed to this illusion of life ever after?"

He said nothing.

"Well?" she persisted.

"I'm not leaving you," he answered quietly. "I just want to regenerate. I want both of us to."

"'Just regenerate'. You haven'0t heard a damn thing I've said. You've lied to me! You've never heard a thing I've said!"

He stared at the floor and breathed an unconscious sigh. "I feel like I've lived for a long time and I trust the feeling. It feels real."

He returned his focus to her, but she refused to meet his gaze. He picked up her hand, but it remained passive in his grip, lifeless. He laid it back on the arm of the chair, as if it were fragile, and then pushed to his feet.

"House, temperature outside," he said.

"Two point two degrees Celsius," the house replied.

"Will you go out with me tonight?" he asked.

She did not answer or move.

"Will you?"

She gazed up at him. He was such a huge man it was difficult to think of him as vulnerable, but he was.

"Answer me," he demanded without heat.

13

"I don't think so, Pie." Her voice was so quiet, he could barely hear her.

As if to compensate he raised his. "Do what you want! Just sit there. I'm going outside."

"So go."

He rubbed his eyes. They burned with the fatigue.

"House, temperature outside."

"One point three degrees Celsius."

He turned away and walked across the room to the down-tube. He floated downward, past the laboratory and library level, past living and dining, to the docking level, with only storage below, buried in the rock of the mountainside. He opened a cabinet and took out a one-piece thermal suit made especially for him, big enough to fit his giant frame. He slipped it on, sliding his arms and hands into the glove-tipped sleeves and then sealing it. At this altitude the temperature was dropping rapidly but he was still cutting it close. He didn't care; he had to get escape the house and see the sky.

He stepped into the lock and after the inner door closed. He hesitated. It was the thought of insects that made him pause, even though he knew they were gone for the night.

"House, temperature?"

"Minus one degree Celsius."

Good enough. He opened the outer door to the barren landscape, the rocks and gravel of an arid high mountain slope. His boots crunched on the gravel as he walked along the path, with starlight sparkling off his silvery suit with each movement. The walkway had been carved out of the cliff face of his mountainside hideaway. He glanced back at his mountain hideaway, a giant, white egg, with craggy rock rising around it, as if the mountain had reached up and grabbed hold of it.

The air was thin and biting cold, but that was forgotten when he looked up at the deep purple of the night sky, pierced by countless, bright flecks of starlight. The moon would be rising soon. He walked along the path toward the precipice where the path ended. He edged around an outcropping of granite onto a narrow ledge; the white dome of his house passed from view. There he stopped and stood with his back pressed against the base of the jutting rock that soared above him.

To the west he could see the next range of peaks, back lit by the flickering light of gigantic ozone generators. The artificial lightning produced by the enormous Vandergraph generators was too far away for him to hear the crackling and sizzling of superheated air. His mind drifted back to his youth and memories of silent heat lightening flashing against a distant horizon. It was demoralizing that the efforts to regenerate the ozone layer had produced so little benefit. It was not long before aura borealis began snaking its way across the night sky, curtains of blue and green, obscuring the Milky Way.

The wind was picking up, whistling through crevices and whipping along the ledge on which he stood. The sharp, cold air pricked at his cheeks and he pulled the face shield up so that only his eyes were exposed. He stood on the narrow mountain ledge, a solitary and silvery figure in the starlight.

"To hell with it," he said out loud. "To hell with it!" he yelled and could hear the echo of his voice reverberate from the canyon.

From his mountain refuge, the world was beautiful in its rough-edged wildness, but it was far from friendly. It was as if mother Earth had turned hostile and was now showing only its teeth.

He looked down into the inky blackness just beyond the rim of the ledge. It seemed lifeless, but he knew the insects were down there, gathered in enormous clumps in cracks and under overhangs, preserving their heat, not dead, just waiting.

He wondered again what it would feel like if he jumped. He imagined the air would become a thick cushion, pushing past his arms and legs. He wondered if he would change his mind while falling, too late, and wondered what it would feel like to get crushed against the rocks below. He took a step forward to stand on the very edge of the abyss. His knees felt like water and his stomach felt hollow while he flirted with the urge to jump; it was both frightening and exhilarating.

Chapter 3

Pie was staring into the fathomless void, frozen into immobility. Suddenly, a blunt-nosed craft arose from the darkness, so close he could have hit it with a stone. The surprise made him teeter on the verge, his arms whirling like windmill blades to keep his balance. He staggered back against the rock wall, his heart squeezing wildly as it rushed to push the adrenaline surge through every artery.

The craft hung motionless in the air; its stubby wings and squat fuselage were a mat black, barely visible in starlight, reflecting the blues and green of the aurora borealis. The high-pitched whine of its jets was hidden by the wailing gusts of mountain wind.

"God damn it," Pie said under his breath, still shaking from the nearness of death. Then rage sent a second throbbing burst of energy coursing through his body. "You son of a bitch!" he yelled. "You can hang out there forever!" He edged away from the thruster-craft and, after he had rounded the granite outcropping, began jogging along the pathway to the house.

He was still breathless from the high-altitude exertion when he exited the up-tube to enter the living area of the egg house. He rested, slightly bent at the waist, propping himself up with his hands on his knees; he was no longer young.

"Roxy," he said and then drew in another breath. "There's a thruster craft out there in the rift."

She raised her eyebrows in answer.

He stood to his full height and walked over to where she was sitting.

"Didn't you hear me?" he asked. "There's a thruster-craft in the rift."

"I know."

"What do you know?" he asked.

"The house scanners have been tracking it for over an hour. Its probable origin is Cisco City and there is one person aboard."

He dropped into the second cup-chair; the burst of energy had left a heavy weariness in its wake. He supported his chin in the palm of his hand and stared at Roxanne without allowing a blink.

"Why didn't you tell me?" he asked.

"Why should I? You've obviously decided to renew your relationship with the Technocracy. Well, here's your chance."

"Why are you doing this? Why are you making things so impossible? You know how I feel about—"

"No, I don't know how you feel anymore. You've changed. You're becoming one of them...or maybe you always were." Her voice trailed off and she hung her head.

He leaned over to raise her face toward his, but she twisted away.

"All right!" he growled. "If that's what you want."

"Shut up!" She glared up at him. "You know what I want."

"Notification," the house said in its rich baritone, "the thruster-craft Colt, piloted by Citizen Jericho Zinc, is attempting to establish a link."

"House, block," Pie ordered.

"Aren't you going to invite the Citizen in?" she asked, her mouth shaped by a lopsided smile. "Isn't that what you really want?"

"No, that's not what I want. I want you. Why are you being so stubborn? Just because I want to regenerate, doesn't mean my feelings for you have changed. Are you afraid, once I'm young again, I won't want you anymore?"

"You make me sick."

"I make you sick? You are the sick one. Otherwise you wouldn't embrace this pathological fear of regeneration. Why do you resist?"

"I'm not resisting anymore." She raised her head. "House, prepare to accept the Colt."

"Why?" Pie whispered. "First you pull me one way, then you push me another. What do you really want?"

"If you don't know by now, you never will."

They felt the distant vibration of the long dormant, landing pad, sliding out from its slot in the cliff, and then there was stillness.

"This is all your doing," Pie said as he pointed a finger at her. "I don't know any Jericho Zinc. Do you?"

"Spare me, Pie. If this is some kind of warped attempt at displaying jealously, it doesn't impress me. This is what you want, to re-engage with the Technocracy. You could have countermanded the order."

They sat in silence.

Pie began to fidget as he watched her, and finally spoke. "Roxy, put something on, will you? Casual nudity might no longer be in vogue. A lot can change in forty years."

She laughed harshly; it was forced and grated on Pie's ears. "You amuse me. Are you afraid someone will see my breasts? You don't own me. I want you but I don't need you. If I must, I'll make it on my own."

"Citizen Zinc requesting entrance to the lock," the house said.

"Granted," Roxanne replied.

They looked toward the stairwell and the up-tube adjacent to it, not knowing which Zinc would choose.

She stood and began walking toward the up-tube, a thin smile on her face. "Someone needs to greet our guest," she said lightly.

Zinc arrived via the up-tube and stepped forward. Roxanne stopped in mid-stride.

A young man stood there. The chalk-white skin of his face was stark against his thick mane of bright, orange hair and kelly-green eyebrows. He had the black eyes of a Citizen. He swaggered into the dome and smiled; his green lips parted to reveal green teeth that were unnaturally sharp, as sharp as those of any carnivore. He wore an oversized blouse of shimmering violet, with yellow stripes running up the sleeves, and loose fitting canary-yellow pants. His link was hidden beneath the fullness of one of his sleeves.

His gaze was fixed on Roxanne. He looked at her, up and down, emphasizing Roxanne's nakedness, and then turned to Pie. "Now I see what has kept you hidden away for so long." He laughed easily as he returned his gaze to Roxanne.

"You little punk," Roxanne began, "if you don't wipe that insolent smile off your face I'll rip your arms off and jam them down throat."

"Whoa, and she has fire. I like that in a woman, even an old one."

Pie walked over to stand beside Roxanne. He could see she was about to attack but in this case simple ferocity would not suffice. He stepped forward to position his massive body in front of Roxanne, screening her from the stranger's view. The air around the man was thick with the scent of a floral perfume.

Pie looked back over his shoulder. Roxanne's cheeks were flushed with anger and her hands were balled into fists.

"Roxy, let me handle this...please." He refocused his attention on their visitor.

Zinc spoke. "Such gallantry, but then...I'm a gentleman as well. I wouldn't have hurt her, much." He looked up at the giant who confronted him. "My, you are a big brut aren't you?"

"You son of a bitch. You nearly knocked me off the cliff. Say what you want and get the hell out!"

"I was told your manners were that of a barbarian and, by the way, I do appreciate those quaint terms you use."

"You'll appreciate more than that if you're not out of here in one minute." Pie's voice matched the snarl on his face.

The man ignored Pie's threat. "I've come all the way from Home, at considerable inconvenience, I might add, solely to speak with that illustrious citizen, the great and only Pie Traynor, who could've saved me all this aggravation if he'd only been wearing his link."

Pie grabbed hold of the man by the shoulders, squeezing with his fingertips until the man began to squirm from pain. Suddenly, with the quickness of a well-trained youth, he pivoted out of Pie's grip and pulled Pie forward. He slid his hip into Pie's abdomen and knocked Pie's legs out from under him with a sweeping kick. The unexpected series of moves caused Pie to fall hard onto his chest and strike his head solidly against the floor. He was momentarily dazed. Roxanne hurried to his side and knelt down to see his face, her forehead creased with worry and shared pain.

The visitor folded his arms across his chest and stepped farther into the room, keeping his eyes on the prone body of Pie, who moaned and then pushed himself up, onto his elbows.

"It looks like I haven't come any too soon," Zinc said. "The way you move and look are a disgrace. You're in desperate need of regeneration." He shifted his gaze back to Roxanne and smiled. "Now, the woman, that's a different story. I can appreciate an older woman." His voice oozed with obscene innuendo. He flopped onto a cup-chair, casually dangling his leg over the arm.

Pie forced himself to his feet. He was weak and unsteady from the blow to his head and rampant fatigue. He staggered as he walked over to where the youth sat. Roxanne stood next to Pie; she wasn't about to be intimidated by this or any man.

"Who the hell are you?" Pie demanded, pointing his finger at the man as if it were a weapon.

"Citizen Jericho Zinc, at your service." He waved his hand in a careless salute.

"Did Mason send you?"

"He did ask me to stop by and see how you were doing."

Pie turned to Roxanne. "Go below."

"No."

"She doesn't mind very well. She doesn't even look like a citizen," Zinc observed.

"I assure you she is," Pie said.

"If you say so. I've heard the story. Citizen Wiley—"

"My name is Ferrari," Roxanne said.

"Is it? Why don't you stay?"

"What story are you talking about?" she asked.

"Interesting," Zinc said with a grin.

She looked to Pie.

"Go below, please," Pie repeated.

"Please?" Zinc chuckled. "Such a nice way to put it and from one of the original Citizens. Are you afraid of me, or is it that your afraid of what I have to say, old man?"

Pie raised his fist, but the man held up his hands, palm out, and looked away with a smile, as if it were all just a good-natured joke. "Don't take everything so seriously. The honorable First Citizen, Mitchell Mason, has a message for you."

"He is anything but honorable. If Mason sent you, then he can go to hell too."

Zinc continued. "As I was saying, First Citizen Mason thinks you'd be interested to know that a message probe has just been returned to Home by the Star Grazer Hawking. It was sent by Jacky Nichols." He paused. "You do remember Jacky Nichols, don't you? The son of Jack Nichols and—"

"Shut up," Pie said and took a step closer.

Despite Pie's nearly overwhelming desire to crush the foppish man with his bare hands, Jericho's words held him in place. He clenched and unclenched his fists while he continued his icy stare.

"You're lying. Jacky's dead," Pie said.

Zinc looked up and smiled. "Nope. I don't think so. It seems the natives, the Blues, right? Anyway, they're not nearly as primitive as you reported."

The name triggered memories of that distant planet and his last voyage, a mission to explore the planetary system of Angkor in the hope of finding another planet suitable for colonization. Angkor was the pivotal star of the Grand Procession: Procyon to Mesa to Rigil Kentaurus, onto Myphid, around Angkor, and then back on a parabolic arc to Holy, then Iceland, followed by Capella and around Sol in a long arc to begin the procession all over again, never stopping. The starship crews had known about the existence of the planet, Angkor-3, for more than a thousand years, but it had never occurred to them to share that information with the Technocracy. Pie snorted with perverse amusement.

"You find that funny? I guess it is, in a way. Perhaps you aren't senile...yet. Nichol's capsule contained information that suggests that these so-called, primitive natives have developed true immortality."

"Impossible." Pie shook his head. "They are primitive."

"Did you say 'they'? Isn't it true that you actually had contact with only one native?"

It wasn't as if Jacky and he hadn't searched for others, but there'd been an equipment malfunction...was it possible? Pie shook his head. There was nothing to suggest an advanced civilization.

21

"The great Pie Traynor, explorer to the stars, legend among legends in the cylinders of Home, establishes another milestone, the biggest blunder in the history of mankind. How does that make you feel?" He watched Pie closely, searching for more signs of self-doubt, a faint smirk curling his lips.

Pie's mind bounced from one thought to another. "Flow, Pie," he murmured to himself. If this arrogant person was a sample of current human culture, then the pendulum had swung once again toward sensualism and self-gratification. Then his thoughts returned to the Angkor-3 and the alien he had tried to talk with. How could he have made such a gross error? It seemed impossible.

"What exactly did Jacky report?" Pie asked.

"So, I have succeeded in tweaking your curiosity."

"What do you want, Zinc?" Pie demanded.

"I want nothing," the man answered lightly, "but First Citizen Mason seems to think you are an indispensable component of a revisit team." He looked up at the dome; the powder-white skin of his face was ghostly against the mass of orange hair that surrounded it. "I have no idea why," he mused, as he pulled his index finger along the arm of the chair with his black fingernail slicing into it as if it were marshmallow soft, instead of perma-foam. He lowered his gaze until his vacant black eyes met those of Pie.

"Get the hell out of here," Pie rumbled ominously. "You've delivered your message. Get the hell out of here."

"I'll leave when I choose to and not a second before...old man." He clicked his thumbnail against the nail of his index finger, as if they were teeth. "Unlike you, I always succeed."

Pie leaned forward and jerked Zinc to his feet with such force that the man was momentarily suspended in air, but he regained his feet with the grace of a cat.

Pie did not loosen his grip while he pulled him toward the down-tube.

"If this is Mason's way of asking me to accept a mission, you can tell him to go to hell and make sure he takes you with him! Is my answer clear?" Pie shoved him roughly into the tube and followed after him.

Zinc slid out of the tube and quickly stepped aside to avoid Pie's arrival. Zinc fluffed his orange hair with his long black nails and then strolled over to the lock. The inner door swished open at his silent command. Before entering the lock, he turned back to face Pie.

"There is one more thing. While I was being so rudely man-handled, I gave you a little something to remember me by." He nodded toward Pie's chest.

Pie looked down and saw a small prick of blood standing on the silver of his suit.

"What the hell did you do?"

"Really? A citizen with your vast experience needs to ask? It's a poison. Don't bother trying to combat it. Too late. It's had more than enough time to disperse and bind."

Pie reached out to grab the man by the neck but he danced aside.

"Ah, ah, ah," Zinc admonished with a shake of his finger. "I am your only hope. The aircraft is mine. You either go with me as pilot, or you don't go at all." His green lips took on the shape of a smile. "It just isn't fair, is it?" He warily walked around Pie and entered the lock, but then turned to face Pie. "Citizen Mason said you might be reluctant to return to Home and left it up to me to convince you. Said I could use whatever method I thought best. You need to make a decision. You can return with me to Home and regenerate, or you can stay here and in thirty-six hours you'll be dead. Have I convinced you? I sincerely hope so, after all you are one of the originals."

"There is another choice," Pie replied.

"Do I sense a threat to my well-being?" Zinc asked with a theatrical frown. "I can't allow that." He pulled out a laser pistol from his loose sleeve and leveled it at Pie's chest. First Citizen Mason told me you don't keep any weapons here. How you've survived this long is a mystery to me."

Pie stood still, while his mind raced to find a solution. Zinc continued to talk, savoring Pie's humiliation.

"In a way you're right. You do have a third option. You can die now if you'd like. I'm sure Roxanne would appreciate the pleasure of fucking a vigorous, young man. She'd forget all about you, after I've shown her a few tricks I've learned."

Pie felt his control slipping; rage threatened to drown out his rationality.

Zinc was pleased that he'd succeeded in pushing Pie to the limit, but it had been almost too easy. "I think it's time for me to leave," he said. "I can see you're upset and you do have an important decision to make. I'll be lifting off in eight hours. If I wait any longer there won't be enough time to deliver you to Home, alive that is. It would be just another wasted effort and that wouldn't be fair...to me." He linked into the house and, when he shut the inner lock, the outer opened.

Pie continued to stare at the closed lock with rigid frustration. Roxanne exited the tube and encircled his waist with her arms.

"I was listening," she said with a sob. "I'm so sorry. I didn't know. Please, please," she begged. "I'm so sorry. I killed us, didn't I? Please forgive—" Her voice was choked off by sorrow.

Pie didn't respond for a moment. When he did, he was calm. He loosened Roxanne's arms so he could turn and hold her. He pulled her firmly against himself and she wrapped her arms around him.

"It's okay, Roxy," he said quietly. "It's going to be all right."

Her tears beaded on the silver of his suit and rolled off in tiny droplets. "I didn't mean it," she mumbled. "I didn't mean those things I said. I...I was just angry and hurt...and afraid I was going to lose you."

Pie stroked her hair with one hand as he held her with the other, stroking and petting until she quieted.

"Are you going to be all right?" Pie asked softly.

She didn't answer, keeping her face hidden against his chest.

"Have you ever heard of Jericho Zinc before?" Pie asked.

"No," Roxanne managed in a whisper.

"Me either. He must be a first regeneration." He leaned away from her to peel his suit open and inspect his wound. It looked innocent enough, a puncture surrounded by a circle of dried blood, just above his left nipple.

Roxanne looked upward at the spot of blood. She reached up and touched it with a fingertip. "Does it hurt?"

"It doesn't hurt at all."

"Do you think he was telling the truth? Maybe he was bluffing." she said, unable to keep hope from her voice.

Pie was slow to respond. He recalled other times when poison was a common method used to kill.

"He's telling the truth. I'll be better prepared next time. I should've suspected treachery when I saw the man's outrageous costume. Damn it!" he swore softly. "I should've recognized the signs," he mumbled to himself as his distracted stare rested on Roxanne's face. "Come. We must prepare to go."

He took her hand in his own and started toward the up-tube, but she pulled her hand from his grip. He stopped and turned back to her; her skin was pale, bringing out the red highlights of her hair. He returned to stand near her and gently took hold of both her hands.

"What is it, Roxy?"

"I'm not going."

"Didn't you hear that maniac? I must regenerate. I have no choice."

She lowered her face. "No," she said softly, resigned. "You don't, but I do. I'm not going with you."

He lifted her fingers to his lips and kissed them. "Roxy, we can come back. We'll be back in less than a month."

"No, you go. I'll wait here."

"You can't stay here by yourself!" he said more loudly than he'd intended.

She took a deep breath and raised her face to his. "I'm staying, Pie."

This was the Roxanne he knew very well. He tried to think of a way to change her mind, short of kidnapping her.

"You go," she continued. "I'll be all right here, but you must hurry. There isn't much time. The house has an adequate supply of hydrocarbon base. I won't starve. I won't freeze. We have the nuclear power plant for backup power, if I should need it. It'll last a month, right?"

"It's good for a few thousand years."

"Well, I won't need it for that long. I'll be okay." She pulled at him. "Come. We must get you ready."

Instead of leading him down to storage, she lead him to the up-tube and slid out of the tube at the level of their living quarters. He followed her lead. She again took hold of his hand. "Come, my darling," she whispered and drew him along with her to their sleeping pad; her intentions were obvious. Pie slipped off his silvery suit and joined her on the pad, gathering her into his arms.

"Do you love me?" she asked softly.

"Of course I do."

"Then tell me. I want to hear it. I need to hear it."

He nuzzled his face into her hair, breathing in the sweetness of her. "I love you," he declared. "I love you. I love you."

"I love you too, Pie," she whispered.

He felt the soft warmth of her skin against his. A measure of peace returned to them as they lay there in each other's embrace. For a time, they simply held each other, flesh against flesh. Later came the culmination, and then release.

While they held each other Roxanne spoke. "Who is Jacky Nichols? I think Zinc said his father was Jack Nichols. It's so weird. I feel like I know both of them but nothing comes. Who are they, Pie?"

Pie was quiet as he thought of what to say. He had all the computer matrix software blocked. There was no way she could ever access information on either of them.

"I asked you a question."

"Jack was my best friend and Jacky was his son."

"To be accurate, he wasn't actually your friend. He was someone else's friend. You just think he was your friend."

25

Pie had to smile. There was no give in this woman.

"A sappy smile is no answer. What do you know about them?"

He paused as he thought. He'd been down this road with other Roxannes and it had always led to disaster. A partial truth was better than nothing.

"I'm waiting," she said.

"Not much. He took his wife and two kids and they moved to Mars to study the crashed Slan starship and then…he, his wife and their daughter, Jacky's sister, disappeared. It was a long, long time ago. Jacky stayed on Mars and claimed to know nothing about their disappearance. Ultimately he became an out-ship driver and was part of my team when we explored Angkor-3. He decided to stay. I tried my damndest to convince him to leave with me, but he stayed behind. Stubborn runs strongly in his family genes. Both sides."

"It's so odd." She paused. "It feels like I know him but I don't remember anything about him or even a reason for that feeling. You must have known his mother."

"Yes, she was a very special woman." Pie hugged Roxanne against him and savored the feel of her body pressed against his. His Roxanne, not Jack's. He forced the thought away.

"Why did that creep call me Roxanne Wiley? Who is Roxanne Wiley?"

"Who the hell knows?"

"I've been thinking."

Pie tensed, preparing himself for the worst.

"If Mitchell Mason wants you to do something, why doesn't he just whip up another copy of you? As really creepy as this sounds, there might be a hundred variations of you running around out there."

Pie relaxed and rolled onto his back, pulling her on top of him. "Do you know how old I am?"

"Damn it, Pie. Really? Twice in the same day?"

"No, I mean this variation of me, the real me, as you put it."

"I imagine you're around sixty, just like me. Never thought to ask. You always say two-thousand or some other ridiculous number."

"I'm two-hundred and seventy-one years old."

"Bullshit."

"I'm serious."

"Oh, I get it." She tried to pull away but he held her tight. "You've had a hell of a lot more genetic modification than just your eyes. Are you still even human?" She again tried to roll off him. "This has been one hell of a day of fucking surprises."

He continued to hold her tight. "No…wait. Give me a chance, will you? It's true my aging has been slowed, but the main reason I am so old is that I spent about 200 years in cryogenic stasis while traveling to Angkor-3 and back. My memories from the mission to Angkor-3 haven't been harvested. In this case, I am truly myself. Unique. Make you happy?"

"If circumstances weren't as they are, I'd consider this a golden opportunity to improve your understanding of life and death, but…it's not. What's going to happen, Pie?"

"I'm going to have a stern talk with Jericho Zinc, then confront Mason, and then come home to you."

"Are you going to hurt Zinc?"

"Maybe."

"You have my permission."

Pie smiled as he studied her serious face, beautiful green eyes, such a joy, and knowing the woman behind that face was beyond joy. "My, my. You are pissed off."

"The man who returns won't be you. He might look like you and talk like you, but he won't be you. You—" Her voice caught. "You, my darling, will be dead. I want Zinc to pay for…for killing you."

He hugged her against his bare chest and felt the warmth of her tears. "None of that. We will see. When I get back, we can talk about it. Will you be okay while I'm gone?"

"I've told you this many times. I don't need you to take care of me, Pie Traynor. I am fully capable of taking care of myself."

Pie nodded. "I know." Typical Roxy. Some things never change regardless of regeneration, thank God. "When I get back, let's take a tour of the cities. We can search for new plants. I'm sure we'll find some. What do you say?"

She held him more tightly. "It sounds wonderful."

"I mean it," he declared. "If worse comes to worse and I need to regenerate, nothing can muddle my memory of you. You are part of everything. You are as much a part of me, as I am of myself."

She kissed him on the cheek, just a brush of her lips.

He rolled onto his side so that she slipped off, onto the pad next to him. Finally, he pulled himself away from her warmth, and then withdrew even from that contact and stood.

"It's time," he announced grimly.

She reluctantly stood and led the way to the down-tube. They descended to the lowest level of the egg house, buried within the stone that held it. They slid out of the tube into a small, round room. The room contained only one object, an antique chest with an ornate, gold clasp. It was made of real wood, the most rare of the rare.

They stood before the chest, arm in arm. They had vowed never to open it again, never to put on their links, but Pie would need to, if he was to return to Home.

"Well, you were planning on regenerating anyway," she said, unable to keep reproach from her voice.

He pressed his lips together; he no longer had a response. He turned away from the trunk and placed his thumb against a barely noticeable indentation in the wall. A door clicked and opened wide to reveal rows of dangerous looking objects. He took one from the rack and a box of shells.

"Those are guns," she said. "You've had guns in our house."

"They've been in the house for many, many years. If I'm to believe you, I'm not the one who put them here."

He fed shells into a clip and pushed the clip into the handle of the gun. Her gaze was fixed on the object, malevolent in its gunmetal blue sheen.

He continued. "It was naïve of me not to have been prepared. There has been much violence in the history of mankind. This is an ancient weapon, a Walther PPK. This is a cryo-stassis cabinet. The bullets and gun are in perfect working order. The bullets are special, armor piercing. That means if someone is attacking with a laser and hides behind something reflective, too bad. You simply aim this gun at where they are and fire. The projectile will penetrate. Here." He held it out toward her. "You'll have an advantage if anyone should try to harm you, a vital advantage."

"I don't want to touch that thing." She took a step away.

"I understand. However, you must be prepared."

"Prepared for what?"

"For everything, until I get back. For creeps like Jericho Zinc. There is a learning module in the library. Use it so that muscle memory will be fixed and you'll be proficient in its use." He held the gun out to her again. "Take it."

She shook her head.

"I don't often ask you to do something for me. I'm asking you now."

She reluctantly took hold of the gun and let the weight of it pull her arm down to her side.

"Thank you, Roxy."

He chose another handgun for itself, a massive handgun, suitable for his big hands, an ancient Smith and Wesson model 29 and an ample amount of ammunition. He put the weapon in a holster and fastened it around his waist.

He then turned to kneel before the trunk; the clasp opened with a crisp, metallic "clink". After he raised the lid, Roxanne stepped forward and they both stared into the nearly empty trunk; it contained their links, two dull-black cylinders with irregular bulges on their surfaces. One was the size of Pie's forearm. The smaller one was Roxanne's. But, it was not size alone that distinguished them, once worn they were imprinted forever; they could never be shared. She had only worn hers for a matter of weeks before she took it off and had never put it on again. For Pie, it was a different matter entirely; it felt unnatural not to be wearing it.

The only other object in the chest was Pie's diamond knife with its black ceramic handle. The blade had been made from a giant natural diamond found in the asteroid belt and was worth a fortune. It had been treated with molecular titanium so that it was not brittle and its edge was molecular sharp. It was shaped like a Bowie knife and had been given to him by a Roxanne from long ago.

Pie reached up and grabbed Roxanne's wrist, squeezing it painfully tight. "Come with me! Please!"

She looked down at the black eyes that gazed up at her and then glanced away. Wordless, she shook her head.

Pie gradually let his grip loosen, but still held her arm for a moment, before finally turning back to the trunk. "So be it," he muttered and reached in to lift out the link. Without pausing, he clamped it around his right forearm and felt the fiery pain of neural integration. His fingers spread and a fine sheen of sweat gathered on his brow. Information flowed, incoherent, chaotic. After a few moments, the onslaught slowed and his vision returned. He was online, once again within the electronic fold of the Technocracy.

The skill of control returned quickly. He was aware of the thruster-craft on the pad outside the dome and knew to the second when it was scheduled to lift. One by one, and then in groups, he shut down information channels, until only the tingling in his arm verified that the link was functioning. A feeling of tremendous power coursed through him and with it came an upwelling of ecstasy.

He was giddy and slightly dazed when he turned to look up at Roxanne. She was holding her hand over her mouth. Reason returned. Guilt and sorrow began to sour the unjustified rush of pleasure that flooded through him. He reached out for her, but she backed away and then ran to the up-tube, disappearing into its mouth.

He took hold of the edge of the trunk and reached in to retrieve his knife in its special carbon fiber sheath. He buckled it onto his left forearm and walked to the up-tube. He exited at the laboratory level and pulled on a new thermal suit; the right sleeve bulged with the bulk of his link but his knife was hidden.

When he lifted to their personal living level, Roxanne was waiting for him. She was wearing a white gown. It molded itself to the womanly curves of her body and returned vibrancy to the red tones in her hair.

He walked over to her. At his first touch she jerked, but did not pull away. He held her with his left arm. He knew she could feel the sheath and knife handle pressing against her but better that than the right forearm and the link; that arm he kept as his side. He continued the embrace until her rigidness melted and she returned his warmth with her own.

"Roxy, I'm dying. I have no choice. You know that."

She did not answer.

"Do you want me to stay here and die? Because if—"

"I don't want you to die. We've had such good times, haven't we? I loved my life with you. I love you…and, I'll miss you for the rest of my life. It'll be a void that nothing can fill."

"Don't talk like that. I'll be back soon. You don't have to stay here. I'm not asking you to regenerate. Just come with me."

"I don't want to, Pie. I don't want to witness…. We've had wonderful years here together, and I'm grateful for that." Her arms tightened. "I love you so much, Pie. I want you to know that."

"I love you too, Roxy. We'll have many more years together. Right?"

She was quiet.

"Right?"

"Yes," she replied softly, her voice distant, "many more years."

"That's more like it." Information appeared in his mind. The power beam to the thruster-craft was beginning to build.

"Roxy…I have to go now, but I will return. I promise on my love for you, but I need your help."

"Sure…I'll help you."

They walked down the stairs, hand-in-hand, to the lock that led to barren mountain escarpment.

Once there, she turned and clung to him. "I…love…." her voice caught with grief.

"I love you. Be safe. I'll be back before you know it." He kissed the top her head, and then, with his left hand, raised her face to his and kissed her forehead, and then softly touched his lips to her closed eyelids, tasting the salt of her tears. Finally, their lips met.

A message intruded into Pie's mind via the link. "Traynor, in two minutes I'm out of here. Stay if you want. You'd make good bug food."

It was as if Roxanne could hear Pie's mind. She pulled away from him and gave him a gentle shove toward the lock.

His voice was a rough knot in his throat. He turned, unable to speak, and entered the lock, keeping his back to her until the door slid shut. He stepped out, into the night, and felt the sting of mountain air on his cheeks; it was still cold, but it was warming. Dawn was not far away. He walked to the cliff edge and then stepped down, onto the smooth surface of the landing pad. The black silhouette of the thruster-craft sat perched before him, its stubby wings and barrel-shaped engines clearly visible. The entry port to the ship was closed.

He linked into the ship to open it, but encountered a block. "Damn it, Zinc, open the port!"

"I'm sorry. I hadn't noticed that you decided to join me."

"The hell you hadn't," Pie muttered to himself. The portal remained shut. "Listen, Zinc, you little shitass, open the damn port, and I mean now!"

"Patience. I've never met a man who was more anxious to desert his home and woman. I wonder why?"

Pie could hear Zinc's laughter as clearly as if they were standing face to face, but the portal did slide open. The boarding ramp extended with a distant whine, "bumping" when it met the deck. After he had walked a few steps up the incline, he was able to see his egg-shaped house again. He stopped. Roxanne was standing outside the lock, her white gown rippling in the breeze, bright, even in starlight. She was too far away for him to see her face clearly. She raised her arm and waved. She looked small and vulnerable against the huge whiteness of the house, backed by the saw-toothed shadows of the rugged mountain, so alone.

As he raised his arm to answer her wave, a mind message interrupted his thoughts. "Traynor, I don't have all night. I'm not going to risk bugs clogging the engines. Either get in or get out. I'm lifting in thirty seconds."

The thrusters began to whine and then scream as they sucked in the thin, mountain air. After one last glance, Pie turned and entered the ship.

Chapter 4

When the portal shut behind Pie, silence returned instantly. The interior of the ship was dimly lit with cold, blue light. As in all ships of the Technocracy, there was no visible instrumentation; everything was controlled via the link. He could see the orange hair of Jericho Zinc, above the upper edge of the pilot's seat, and began to walk toward the co-pilot's seat. When the ship suddenly lurched as it jumped into the sky, he was thrown to the deck and struck his ribs against the edge of a thruster casing.

Jericho laughed when he heard the thud and swiveled in his seat. "Before you do anything rash, old man, you should recall that I have a complete lock on this craft. If anything should happen to me...well, I guess you might as well have died back there with your woman."

Pie's breath returned and he crawled onto his knees. He resisted the impulse to charge at the man and punch his green, smiling teeth down his throat. Instead, he began a chain of communication with Home. He was one of the originals and had been involved in the early construction of the matrix. He knew backdoors in the system that no one remembered, other than possibly Mitchell Mason.

Taking hold of the edge of the casing, he pulled himself stiffly to his feet. He walked to the front of the ship, supporting his bruised ribs with his left hand and settled onto the seat across from Jericho. By now, the craft was at altitude and had begun to accelerate toward the south.

Zinc spoke. "My instruments detect that you're carrying a heavy metal object." A compartment flipped open in front of Pie. "I don't know what it is but, to be prudent, put it in the there." He indicated the compartment.

Pie removed his Smith and Wesson and complied with the command.

Zinc stared at the object. "What the hell is that? It looks pretty nasty but what does it do?"

"It shoots projectiles."

"Projectiles? What next, old man? Do you have a bow and arrow in your pocket?" He laughed at his witticism and repeated it. "Bow and arrow."

"No," Pie answered.

Pie studied the man silently, but Jericho liked the sound of his own voice. "So, you are one of the original Citizens. You must have seen a hell of a lot but, in all honesty, you're not nearly the man I was led to believe

33

you were. I can only surmise that you'll need my protection all the way, until I deliver you to Home." He slapped Pie lightly on the shoulder, still smiling, and then leaned back in his seat. "Now, tell me the truth, doesn't that make you feel better, old man?"

Pie said nothing, showed nothing, just watched.

Zinc continued. "You can dump that attitude. You're no better than me. You just left your lover all alone, stranded, way out here in the wilderness. I'll tell you what, and this is a promise, after I deliver you to Mason, I'm going to come back and visit your lady friend." The idea grew as he spoke. "Yes...she should be good and ready by then." He winked at Pie. "You know what I mean?"

Zinc tipped his head back and laughed. At the moment he extended his neck, Pie completed his complex exchange with Home. Pie now controlled the craft, through Home matrix.

The diamond blade was so sharp and the movement so quick, Jericho hardly felt it slice across his throat, not even having time for surprise as blood gushed from his neck and gurgled out of his mouth. The grisly, red grin of a cut hemorrhaged away his life and he collapsed, slack against the backrest.

Pie dragged his body to the portal and then returned to the co-pilot's seat. After he strapped in and opened the portal, he tipped the aircraft on its side so that Jericho's body slid out and began its long fall to Earth. His carcass would provide an unexpected feast for the hoard of insects that would settle on it. Within twenty minutes, there would be nothing left of Jericho Zinc except a disjointed skeleton and a scattering of artifacts.

Pie closed the portal and attempted to contact Roxanne, but she had reactivated the house block against communication. There was no backdoor to his system. "Damn it!" he swore to himself, but there was nothing he could do. He considered turning the craft around and returning to the egg-house. He couldn't shake the image of her standing all alone and waving. He almost gave the command but then settled back in the seat. What good would that do? He would die and she would still be alone.

He wiped the diamond blade on his suit leg and then stared at it. Far sharper than a razor, sharper than anything. He brought the blade upward to touch the point to his chest, feeling a tiny pinch as it sliced through his suit and pricked his skin. A drop of warm liquid ran down his chest. A shiver ran down his spine, he could do it. It would be easy, but then the moment passed. He slid the blade back into the carbon fiber sheath on his forearm.

He took a deep and unsteady breath and the slowly released it. He was utterly exhausted. The cabin was warm and the seat comfortable. He drifted off to sleep and didn't awaken until his link reported that the city was within fifty kilometers. He called up a visual display, preferring that to a mental image, which would have temporarily replaced his vision. To lose sight was to be vulnerable and that was one feeling he could not tolerate. His vulnerability during his recent encounter with Zinc had been one time too many.

In the darkness ahead, he saw a faint light that quickly grew until it looked like phosphorescent powder had been spilled across the lower reaches of Mount Boardman; it trailed off toward the sea and the remains of the old city of San Francisco, at least as much of it as remained above sea level. But, beyond the splash of light was absolute blackness; there were no outlying communities. Cisco City passed under the stubby wings of the thruster craft. The landing platform was beyond the reach of insects, forty kilometers out to sea.

Pie remembered long ago hearing the recorded broadcast of a man's cry of terror when the thrusters became clogged with insect bodies, and then the silence. What was his name again? Pie wondered, and then it came to him, Blas Uribe. Why did it seem like these distant memories were returning with such force? Were they really his, or someone else's, as Roxanne insisted? He tried again to contact her but had no success.

It was not long before the craft began its descent. At the exact moment of contact with the landing pad, his link confirmed touchdown. He terminated the power beam and began analyzing the surveillance data being transmitted from Home. Everything was as expected, peaceful and under control.

Chapter 5

Pie sat in the co-pilot's seat without making an effort to stand. It was quiet, except for an occasional "ping" as the thrusters cooled. He was aware of the attempts by the pad manager to contact him, but he brushed the communication aside and sealed the channel. His mind drifted on the surface of a restless doze, seeing visions of Roxanne contaminated by macabre flashes of Jericho Zinc.

Suddenly, he was awake; time was passing. He pushed himself to his feet and made his way to the portal, rubbing his face to bring himself to full alertness. It had been nearly forty years since he'd been among humans. He was dreading the contact, even if they were only Unders. He checked the blade secured in its sheath on his left forearm and the heavy handgun seated in a holster strapped to his right hip.

When the lock "swished" open, the manager and his assistant were caught off guard, with their backs to the thruster craft while they leaned on a rail, staring out to sea. They turned in unison, mimicking identical twins in their iridescent, lime-green suits that covered all their skin, including their hands; smoke-gray helmets hid their faces. Pie strolled down the ramp and they rushed to greet him, surrendering the dignity of their position.

When they reached the base of the ramp, they stopped and bowed deeply at the waist, keeping their eyes downcast, toward the grating at their feet and the frothy sea twenty meters below. Pie skirted the pair without offering greeting or recognition. He began walking toward the squat, observation building, dwarfed by the thirty story city-tower of the landing port, but it wasn't the constructions of man that drew him forward, it was the sun. It had been forty years since he'd walked beneath a daytime sky. Only when far out to sea was it safe.

The mauve clouds were fringed with magenta and pierced by shafts of bright light, the spokes of a celestial wheel. It was more magnificent than his memory told him it would be. Perhaps such majestic beauty was of too grand a scale for the mind to hold for more than a moment at a time. He was transfixed by the evolving sunrise, unaware of the two Unders who stood a few respectful steps behind him. They shifted their weight from foot to foot and glanced at one another with uncertainty.

37

Finally, the manager could bear the wait no longer; eyes directed at his feet, he ventured to speak, in a nearly inaudible voice. "Citizen, is everything satisfactory?"

Traynor became aware of the Unders really for the first time and turned to confront them. He studied them openly with his inscrutable, black eyes.

The manager's sense of misfortune arose another notch and he felt compelled to speak again. "Citizen, I live to serve...if you but ask." When Traynor still failed to respond, he added in a quaking voice, "Is the other Citizen staying on board? We were informed there would be two."

"There is no other Citizen," Pie answered, and the man asked no more. Traynor looked over the heads of the two men and saw another figure, standing near one of the landing struts of the thruster-craft. This person wore the clothing of the sea-people; tanned shark hide covered all but the inner surface of his arms and legs. His black hair was long and loose and blew freely in the ocean breeze. He was carrying the white shaft of a bone spear. A sharkskin mask, with tiny slits to protect his eyes from the harsh radiation, hung carelessly, arrogantly, from around his neck. His dark eyes met those of Traynor and he did not look away.

Pie felt a sharp sting on his right hand and looked down, thinking of poison darts, but it was only an insect, blown off course and far out to sea. He watched the multi-legged insect with fascination as its thorax began to bulge and turn pink with ingested blood.

When the manager noticed, he was aghast and jumped forward to swat the offending bug from Pie's hand. The moment he stood in front of Pie, he straightened fully, and then toppled forward, causing Pie to stumble back a step from the unexpected contact. The man clutched once at Traynor's arm and collapsed onto the grating with the shaft of the bone-spear protruding from his back. Pie quickly squatted and moved to the side, hunting for the Sea-Under, but he was gone.

The assistant manager remained motionless, fixed to the spot, his eyes pinned on the dead body of his colleague; bright red blood was seeping out of the lime-green suit.

As Pie swept his vision along the perimeters of the pad, he uplinked with Home and called for information. The shark-man had not run. Instead, he was climbing along the infrastructure that supported the landing pad, working his way toward Pie's current position. The assistant manager was still standing bolt upright, his back to the thruster-ship.

"Get down, you idiot!" Pie yelled, but the man didn't move, didn't even seem to hear.

Pie wanted this assassin. By now it was obvious that he was the intended target, not the Under who had caught the spear in the center of his back. Yet, it was unprovoked. What could the Sea-Under possibly have to gain? Pie wondered while he worked his way back to the observation building. To persist in the attack was beyond courage, it was suicidal.

Traynor flattened against the side of the building and then jumped. His fingers caught the lip of the roof, already hot in the morning sun, and he pulled himself up and over the edge. Staying on his stomach, he shimmied forward until he could look down on the grating of the pad. After a moment, he spotted movement beneath the grating, a shadowy figure advancing a few meters at a time and then pausing, to become as still as the structure itself, just another shadow.

Pie watched the man's progress, until he saw hands grip the rail along the rim of the pad. The top of the man's head appeared and then his swarthy face. He was close enough that Pie could see his dark eyes shifting, back and forth, searching for his prey. In a single, fluid movement, the shark man slithered onto the deck and ducked behind a winch housing, pausing a moment, before scampering across the deck to hide among dull-brown, supply drums, adjacent to the observation building.

Pie lost sight of the man, but his link with Home kept him informed. The assassin was pressed hard against the other side of the building on which Pie was hiding.

With sure, quiet movements, Pie worked his way over to the roof edge, directly above the man. He drew his diamond knife and tensed, preparing to jump and render the man helpless before he could defend himself. He didn't want to kill him; he wanted to talk with him.

A ruby-red beam snapped into existence. Streaking out of the sky at the speed of light, it touched the hidden man. The sudden light and blast of the explosion triggered Pie's tense muscles, causing him to spring forward. He barely managed to catch himself. Looking down, he saw unidentifiable pieces of smoldering flesh and, through the grating, a pink tinge to the rhythmic waves. The dorsal fin of a shark sliced through the water's surface, the ultimate survivor now that man had been pushed aside.

Pie rolled onto his back. "Who ordered that beam?" he demanded via his link.

"This is Citizen Evans from Home Control, on duty and ever alert."

"Citizen, if you ever, ever, act on my behalf again without consulting me first, you had better start running because I promise I'll come for you."

"I was following established protocol."

"Listen, you asshole, I'm not part of your protocol. If you doubt what I've said, or if you question my sincerity, contact that piece of shit Mitchell Mason."

"A simple thanks would do." The response was followed by an immediate off link, not allowing Pie the final word.

Pie looked up at the sky overhead. Sunlight and blue sky always seemed to bring death but, even amid thoughts of death, the beauty could not be denied. He drew in a shaky breath and released it, along with his anger and tension. After a moment more, he dropped from the roof onto the deck.

A small crowd of Unders had gathered around the fallen manager. He walked toward them and when they noticed his approach they parted, heads bowed, eyes downcast. He stopped near the body, still lying as it had fallen.

"I'm ready to go to the city," Pie announced, uncertain which of the identically dressed Unders was the assistant manager.

An Under to Pie's left answered. "Citizen, I will notify the captain you are coming."

"Never mind that. Just tell me which bay the boat is in. I'll take care of it from there," Pie said curtly.

"Citizen, it will be as you wish. It's our finest boat. It is our desire—"

"Yeah, that's great. What bay is it in?"

"It's in bay six, down and to the left. I'll show—"

Pie held out his arm and the man nearly tripped on his own feet as he tried to halt in mid-stride.

"I'll find it myself," Pie said and glanced again at the dead man and then at the gathering of Unders. He couldn't even imagine the expressions hidden behind the gray of their helmets. It had been a mistake to remain hidden away for so many years.

"I offer my condolences to you on the death of your manager," Pie said. "I did not know him, but he must have had unusually good qualities to have held his position." He turned to the assistant manager. "You are now manager and you will choose the new assistant."

The man bowed deeply at the waist. "Citizen, you are most generous. Thank you."

Pie turned away, with the Under still caught in a bow, and walked briskly down the side ramp. It wasn't far to the gangway of the boat. He paused when he saw it. The finest? The wedge-shaped boat was cradled in a lift. Rectangles of steel patches spotted a hull that was streaked with deep gouges and the front viewing-port was abraded to opacity. When he was adjacent to the entry hatch, he rapped on it with his knuckles.

Within seconds the hatch began to "whine" and "screech", as if it were ripping itself open and then, with one last ear-piercing cry, came to a stop. The captain stuck her head out the hatch and saw the feline eyes of a Citizen staring back at her. She crawled out the hatch to stand on the gangway.

Pie could not help but stare at her. She was wearing a multicolored, knit garment. It appeared to be a "one of a kind" outfit, of all things. She assumed the pose of self-effacement.

"You may leave," Pie said. "I'll pilot the boat."

She started to open her mouth, but then shut it.

"You were about to say something," Pie stated. "What was it?"

The Under woman reached out and touched the hull of the ship, as if it could feel her touch.

"I asked you a question," Pie said.

"Citizen," the woman began, "I've made certain modifications to the 'Titanic'."

"The what?" An involuntary smile tugged at the corners of Pie's mouth.

"It's named after a great ship called the 'Titanic'. The pad historian told me it was an unsinkable ship from ancient times, from before the Death, and that's what my ship is, unsinkable."

While Pie studied the woman, her eyes met his. Despite her bright enthusiasm, her eyes were already dulled by the cotton haze of cataracts and, when he looked at her hands, the skin was blotchy with dark patches and scattered crusts.

Under his scrutiny, she dropped her gaze. When she spoke her voice was so soft, the breeze threatened to take her words out to sea, even though they were only two paces apart. "It's a good ship. I've tended to her and she's cared for me. I've needed to make changes to keep her running. Excuse me for saying so, Citizen, but I doubt even you can pilot her without my help."

"What's your name?"

"Citizen, my name is Eva-64."

"Well, Eva-64, you've convinced me. I'm not sure I'd even want to pilot the 'Titanic' by myself. Let's shove off."

"I promise I'll serve you to perfection. I live to serve."

"Very nice, but all I'm asking is that you get me to Cisco City and I'd like to leave now." He took hold of the hand bar and slipped through the round portal, immediately followed by Eva-64, who flipped a switch as soon as she passed through, causing the hatch to begin its painful closure.

Pie linked into Pad Control and then felt the bump as the boat began to be lowered into the sea. Eva hurried forward and took her position in the pilot's seat, which was covered by a red and blue striped, hand-woven blanket. There were simple line drawings of ships and fish across the normally blank control module, but there were even more remarkable alterations; there was a wheel attached to a rod and another knob-tipped rod, both of which pierced the deck.

"Where is your control module?" Pie asked.

"Broken."

"Then how—"

There was a jolt when the craft smacked against the sea and then it began to roll in the waves. Pie staggered forward to the co-pilot's seat. He attempted to link into the boat, but found nothing; it was dead. It was a trap! He reached for his gun, but then felt a surge of power as the craft plowed through the waves and onto the open sea. He kept his hand on the butt of the gun, but didn't draw it; instead, he watched Eva while she moved the knob-tipped pole and turned the wheel. As the boat picked up speed, the rocking settled into a more gentle motion.

"Eva-64."

"Citizen?" She smiled with confidence.

"The matrix in this craft is dead."

"That is true. I've made adjustments so that it can be managed without the matrix."

"Why?"

She laughed. "Citizen, the matrix and control module were both broken. I used my hands and my mind and now captains from all over come to see my 'Titanic'."

He let his hand relax, but remained wary. Memories came out of hiding. Long ago he'd driven a land vehicle with such devices. "Why haven't the Citizens from Cisco fixed the matrix?"

"They don't fix anything. It's up to us to make things work and it's not easy. What with the sea scum stealing parts off the boats and even making off with pieces of the pad itself." She shook her head in frustration and disbelief.

"I don't understand. Why don't you, or the Citizens, put a stop to these destructive renegades?"

This time Eva turned fully to face Pie, searching for signs that he was toying with her, but he seemed earnest. "Citizen, may I ask a question?"

Pie nodded.

"Is this a test?"

"No, of course not. I've been...out of touch for a while."

She nodded with sudden understanding and admiration. "You've been out to the stars."

He paused before answering. "You could say that. Now answer my question. Why are the sea-people not suppressed?"

"The High Mayor of Cisco City has directed us not to harm them. They provide food from the sea for the city...and even for the pad."

"What about the hydrocarbon reserves? Can't that be used to manufacture food?"

"I do not know all things."

"No...I suppose not."

They sat in silence, feeling the ocean and the craft work out a nearly regular rhythm of heaves and rolls.

"May I steer for a while?" he asked.

She hesitated before answering. "Citizen, you can do as you wish."

"I'm asking your permission. After all, the 'Titanic' is obviously your boat."

She smiled. "In that case, I'd be honored, but I must warn you. Do not touch this stick," she pointed to the rod topped with an amber ball, "or this lever, or this knob."

Pie leaned forward and saw another small rod, projecting from the control module to her right and, next to it, an amber ball was attached directly to the surface of the panel.

"Agreed."

He took her seat, still comfortably warm from her body heat, and grasped the wheel tightly with both hands. She stood behind him, with one hand on the seat to keep her balance.

"Citizen, ease up a bit. It's not that hard to steer."

Pie relaxed his shoulders and arms, and finally his hands.

"Now if you turn the wheel to the left, the ship goes to the left, and to the right, it goes right."

"Of course," Pie agreed as he peered forward, through a crystal-clear plate that had been welded into the opaque, forward viewing-window. It was a lens-shaped piece so he could see a wide view of the green-blue ocean as it rose and fell in front of the craft. The ocean was the last bastion of the old balance; it alone retained the capacity to renew the atmosphere. Mankind's only stroke of luck was that they had managed to preserve the oceans and the life that lived there. He strained forward as he tried to sight land.

"How do you know which direction to go in?" Pie asked.

She didn't answer until he turned his head toward her. Reluctantly, she pulled a circular object from the sash of her suit and handed it to him; one never knew what a Citizen would decide to keep. He twisted it and watched the needle always move to point in the same direction.

He handed it back to her and smiled with satisfaction. "It's a compass."

Her surprise made her forget her manners. "You know about compasses?"

"Yes, but more important, if I had decided to take your boat you were going to send me out to sea without your compass, weren't you?"

She looked down for a moment, as if searching for her answer on the foot-worn deck. "You Citizens always know where you are anyway. Isn't that true?"

"Yes, I guess it is. I'm sure you would never have risked losing your ship.' Out of the corner of his vision, he saw her begin to relax again. He uplinked with Home to verify their position and direction.

As the voyage neared completion, the skin on his hands began to tighten and moisture gathered on his forehead, as if his face were radiating heat. He looked at his hands; even in the dim light of the boat, they had a rosy color.

As if she could read his thoughts she spoke, "Citizen, your new-eyes may protect your vision from radiation, but your skin has no such protection. It was foolish of you to stand out there exposed to the sun...but I understand it."

Pie turned to her and studied her with his black eyes. "Yes, I'm sure you do. You know, you've got some cancerous changes in your skin."

She nodded soberly.

"And you have cataracts."

"Yes...sometimes I have to see and can't wear the dark glasses."

"Have these problems attended to," he ordered.

"Citizen, I will...when my turn comes."

Pie was silent for a moment. He uplinked with the landing pad and connected to the new manager. When he had finished, he turned back to Eva. "Your time has come. When you return to the pad, report to the clinic."

"Thank you," she whispered.

Pie continued to pilot the craft. Sea level had risen twenty feet, altering the coastline. Between the fires and rising sea, little remained of the original city. Cisco City had been built on the bones of the old city. There were no skyscrapers; white bubbles were piled one atop another, like the roe of a gigantic fish. The umbilical cord of microwave energy was a taut rope of bright light, which rose upward from the center of the city. The energy originated from solar collectors in space, and the collectors were controlled by Home. It was because of this energy monopoly that Home dominated the cities, in fact, all of Earth.

The terrain around the city was green, but closer inspection would have revealed a stubble of waxy grass that grew during the early morning and was eaten bare by noon, and possibly an occasional scrubby bush called rock-plant. As they drew closer, the black clouds of swarming insects could be seen hanging over the pearly city, seeking entrance, devouring any organic material they could reach.

"Well, Eva," Pie said, "I think it's time for you to take over and I thank you for the experience."

She slid into the seat as he shifted back to the co-pilot's. She was intent as she steered her boat toward an underwater tunnel and then submerged, with the ocean washing over the viewing port as the craft dipped beneath the waves. She stared into the dark water, pierced by the single shaft of a navigation light, searching for clues to guide the submerged boat. Pie sat silently at her side, not wanting to disturb her concentration, even for a moment. The seconds dragged on and then a faint, blurry light appeared. The light grew as the craft arose to the surface. Less than a minute later, the water washed off the viewing port and the boat was bobbing on top of the surfacing pond. Eva reached for a switch under the panel and the barely noticeable "hum" of the engines fell silent.

Pie heard the sharp "clank" of a metal gaff snagging the craft so that it could be towed the final distance. The boat bumped against the dock and movement stopped. He stood and stretched, before turning to walk to the hatch.

"Citizen?"

He looked back to Eva, who had remained in her seat.

"Citizen, I don't mean to be out of line, but you seem...different. I guess I just want to wish you luck and, sometime, if there's a chance, I'd like to teach you all about my boat." She bowed her head.

"It would be my pleasure. And my wish for you is that this ship be even more unsinkable than the original. Remember to attend to your health needs when you return to the pad. I'll be checking to make certain you are attended to." He smiled, but she didn't look up.

He slapped the switch to the lock and it began its "screech" of opening.

Gary Moreau

Chapter 6

Pie slid out of the boat and stepped onto a wide concrete dock that stretched to the rear of the cavern. The humid air smelled of fish and the salty sea. The surface of the pond sparkled with the reflection of artificial daylight, beamed down from the cavern roof. He watched as the "Titanic" slipped beneath the water, causing the surface to flash with a wake of "V" shaped waves that expanded as they traversed the pond. Only then did he turn his attention to the gaily-dressed Unders who had gathered to greet him.

A rotund man stood before him, his hands moving as if they had a life of their own. He wore a multi-layered dress, which jiggled with each movement, revealing brief glimpses of scarlet beneath an outer glimmering of royal blue. He presumed to speak. "Citizen, as Low Mayor of Cisco City, I have the privilege to welcome you to our great city, City of a Thousand Bubbles, City of the Bay to the Oak, City of the Golden Gaze." He bowed and his bevy of attendants followed his lead.

Traynor stepped forward and pulled the man upright. The Mayor's eyes opened widely as he stared upward at the towering Citizen. Pie nodded his head to the left, where a complement of city militia stood at attention, holding tubes in their hands that were obviously weapons.

"Are these guards here to protect me?" Pie asked. "Or is it you from me?"

The Mayor did not even dare glance in the direction of the militia. He licked his lips. "Guards?"

Keeping one hand bunched in the Mayor's dress, Pie waved his other arm in an arc, indicating the security force, starkly visible in their pumpkin-orange uniforms against the shadowy wall of the cavern.

"Those armed persons. Didn't you notice them?"

"Well...yes," the Mayor stammered, "well...of course, I...." His eyes shifted toward the others in his entourage, but all he saw were the tops of bowed heads. He looked back to Pie.

"I'm waiting." Pie said.

"Citizen, there are disruptive elements."

"And just who are these disruptive elements?"

"They call themselves the Friends of the Earth." His hands hung limp, as if they had died.

"Friends of the Earth, huh? They don't sound all that bad."

47

"They are."

"What are those guards holding in their hands?" Pie asked.

The Mayor mumbled a reply.

"Again, this time so I hear it."

"Citizen, they are bolt-guns. We make them ourselves," he added with a trace of pride.

"Since when have Unders been allowed to carry weapons?"

The Mayor looked up with genuine surprise. "Citizen, we've been allowed weapons since before I was born. Ask the High Mayor."

Pie's grip loosened and his lips became slack as his head listed slightly. The Mayor had seen that look before. The entire group began to edge away.

Pie had fully uplinked, into the surveillance and energy patterns of the city. Numerous bubbles, particularly in the lower levels, showed up as defects, not dark, just not at all. If it weren't for the surrounding functioning bubbles they would have been completely invisible. As he searched upward, the percentage of functioning bubbles increased until, in the upper most levels, Citizen territory, all the bubbles were accounted for and functioning. He synthesized an overall picture of the city; it was a picture of advanced decay. The city was rotting from below.

He downlinked and returned to seeing with his own eyes. The Mayor and his group were standing ten meters away, nearly against the sharp-edged shadows of the cave wall.

Pie pointed at the Mayor with his link-incrusted forearm. "You."

The Mayor's hands began to tremble.

"Take me to the up-tube."

The man did not move.

"Now!"

The Mayor shuffled forward and Pie began to stride along the dock, toward the rear wall. After taking a few steps, he stopped and pivoted to face the Mayor, still ten meters back and walking as if his feet were sticking with each step.

"Mayor, do you propose to guide me from behind?"

The Mayor rolled his eyes without realizing it, but he did quicken his pace and began leading the way. As they passed the line of guards, Pie glanced at the blue-gray tubes they were holding, each was fitted with a semicircle at one end to brace the weapon against a shoulder. There was something about one of the orange-suited guards ahead. He was perspiring and seemed to be breathing too fast.

One did not live for two thousand without learning to trust one's instincts. Pie gripped the butt of his pistol and as soon as they passed the man, he turned. The man was raising his bolt gun but Pie was quicker; the blast of the forty-four-caliber handgun was deafening. All the guards ducked and crouched, except one. He toppled forward onto the concrete, hiding the wound ripped into his chest.

Pie studied each of the other guards and saw fear but did not detect another threat. While keeping the remaining guards in sight, he reached down and pulled the Mayor to his feet. He dragged the Mayor along toward the rear of the cavern. None of the guards had the temerity to follow.

With the cavern wall to his back, he finally turned his attention to the Mayor. "What the hell is going on?"

The mayor was quaking in his grasp and was pale enough that he was beginning to sway and would soon pass out. It was time to get to safer ground.

"Where's the up-tube?"

With a trembling hand the mayor pointed toward a nearby door.

Pie accessed the circuit and the door swung open to reveal a small, windowless room.

"What the hell is this?" Pie demanded. "It sure as hell isn't an up-tube."

The Mayor cleared his throat. "It's a levator."

"Where's the up-tube?"

"The up-tube quit functioning years ago."

"I see. How does this…levator work?"

"A cable raises and lowers the compartment."

Pie smiled. An elevator. How odd.

"Is it safe?" Pie asked.

"Citizen, it is," the Mayor declared earnestly. "I guarantee it."

"Yes, you will, because you're going to join me."

The Mayor's complexion paled yet another shade and he grasped his stomach. He dropped to his knees and began retching but little came up. When Pie judged the mayor had finished, he lifted the mayor to his feet and escorted him into the elevator.

The mayor turned to Pie, his voice flat and soft, "Citizen, the levator does not go above the Under City. A hallway on the hundred and seventy-third level leads to the High City. You don't need me…please."

"Oh come along. I like company. You'll enjoy it. But I want you to stop on a level below." During Pie's surveillance he had noted that the top level of the Under City was absent from the data pool. It was probably paranoid of him, he decided, but after the last few hours he trusted no one, certainly not the Mayor.

The Mayor nodded and touched the number board on the wall of the room. Pie momentarily felt his weight increase as the lift accelerated toward the hundred and seventy-second level. He glanced over at the Mayor, who was standing in a rear corner.

"You look worried, Mayor. Is there a reason to be worried?"

The Mayor listlessly shook his head, but refused to meet Pie's eyes.

Pie linked into surveillance and verified their destination. When the lift began to slow, he raised the Smith and Wesson. The Mayor groaned. Pie turned at the sound. The Mayor had fainted and was sprawled on the floor, his dress riding up around his waist.

The lift came to a stop and the door spread open. Pie slipped out of the little room and stood pressed against the wall. The door slid shut. This was supposed to be a functioning level. There should be light but the hallway was completely dark. He shifted his vision into the infrared and began to creep along the hallway, but stopped at the first sign of movement; a small animal scurried on down the corridor, a rat.

He paused and leaned against the wall of the hallway. His thoughts turned to Roxanne, remembering her, a solitary figure in the white gown. He shook his head and refocused his concentration. He'd been away too long; the skills and habits of an experienced operative had become rusty from disuse.

He accessed the original floor plan for this area and located an emergency stairwell. As he crept down the hall, he brushed his fingertips along the wall, until he felt the rectangular indentation of a hand plate, the control unit for the stairwell door. He attempted an uplink, but there was no matrix activity.

After carefully inspecting the passage, Pie reluctantly raised the Smith and Wesson and fired into the locking mechanism. The sound of the big gun reverberated down the passage. He waited for his vision to recover from the bright flash of the gun and for his ears to recover from the blast. When he was ready, he pulled the door open. He again searched up and down the hallway for signs of anyone approaching, but saw nothing.

It was dark in the stairwell. The air was stale and dry, sealed away for centuries. He climbed the steep stairway, until a breeze touched his neck. He looked over his shoulder and saw the reddish heat signature of a face, climbing up the stairs behind him. Pie took a few more quick steps and reached the landing. He holstered his gun and withdrew to a corner of the landing, hidden in complete darkness to await the stranger who was stalking him.

The figure paused near the top of the stairwell and extended an arm, as if holding something in his hand. With the advantage of surprise and strength, he grabbed the person's extended arm and threw him to the floor. The stranger's body landed hard, with a gush of air forcefully expelled from his mouth. Something clattered its way down the steps. Pie used the stalker's arm as a painful lever to maintain control. While he held the man's face pressed against the landing floor, he drew his diamond knife from its sheath. He touched the blade to the exposed neck of his captive.

"If you try to escape, or call for help," Pie whispered, "I will kill you." He was startled to hear a woman's voice answer.

"Do what you will!" she cried out as loudly as she could with her mouth pressed against the floor. "You kill the Earth! What is one more small death?" she added bitterly.

"Are you insane?" Pie asked, astounded by the woman's willingness to be martyred for a cause that made no sense.

"It's not me," she said, her voice still muffled. "You are the insane one. You and all your kind, sapping the Earth of its life to feed your pleasures and your perverted, multiple existences. You are an abomination," she growled, "kill me, or have the decency to kill yourself!"

"Shut up! I have some questions."

She managed to twist her face to the side. "He's here! He's here!" she screamed. It echoed down the darkness of the stairwell.

Pie struck her on the head with the heavy handle of his knife, knocking her unconscious.

When he glanced back down the stairwell, he saw another figure climbing up the stairway. Looking directly at the figure, Pie said conversationally, "No one tells me what to do, certainly not when to kill."

The person paused. While the assassin tried to decide how best to proceed, Pie stood and pushed against the door that lead to the hallway of the next level. It was locked and this matrix was dead as well. He drew his gun and blasted the lock, immediately swinging the door inward and then crouching as he entered.

The upper level corridor was as dark as the one below. Pie looked first to the left and saw the heat of numerous individuals running toward him. When he looked to the right, he saw only two individuals standing between him and the passageway that led to a functioning Citizen bubble. He returned his attention to those who were rushing toward him and emptied his Smith and Wesson into the assailants. He saw the first rank fall. Those behind flattened against the walls or dove to the floor. A quick look to his right revealed that the two figures there had not moved, apparently stunned by the massive blasts and flashes of light from the handgun.

Pie holstered the now useless weapon and drew his diamond knife. Those he had stopped with his gun had regained their courage. Pie heard the slapping of running feet against the corridor floor and saw his shadow as light was thrown onto his position. Pie also began to run, away from his pursuers and directly at the two figures standing in his way. He yelled and whooped as he swung the knife out in front. He looked like a giant lethal madman as he charged, which he was, but the two sea-people who stood in his way took no more than half a step back; they didn't lack courage, or devotion to their cause, whatever it was. Pie was impressed in a distant part of his mind, but all of his active thoughts were consumed with the blossoming of warrior mentality.

When within arm's reach, all three men swung their weapons. A "swish" of air cut past Pie's face, but Pie's knife struck flesh and bone and passed through it. One of the men fell to the corridor floor, writhing and moaning as he grasped the stump of his severed arm. As Pie turned to parry the sword being swung by the other man, he was fractionally too slow and the blade severed the little and ring fingers from his left hand. He struck the sword with his knife, slicing through the steel.

Pie had no time. Within seconds the group of attackers from farther down the passage would be upon him. The remaining attacker backed away, waiting for reinforcements, but Pie lunged forward. Ignoring the pain of his severed fingers, he jerked the man off balance and wrapped his injured hand around the man's neck, while continuing to hold the knife in his right hand. Pie's own blood made the grip slippery but he managed to pull the man around in front of him, to use the man as a human shield. He backed down the hallway, dragging the man along with brute strength, holding him up while he struggled to break free.

"Tell them to back off or I'll slice your head off!" Pie yelled in the man's ear, loud enough for the pursuers to hear as well. The attackers slowed to a fast walk while one shouted at them to attack.

Pie decided to chance a partial uplink as he dragged his captive down the passage. "Cisco Control, this is Citizen Traynor. I need assistance on level one-seven-three."

"This is Cisco Control. We've been following your progress via your link. We don't have any remote weapons in your vicinity. Proceed down the corridor. A portal will open."

"How far?"

"From your current location, about twenty-five meters. My advice is that you run like hell."

"I didn't ask for your fucking advice," Traynor snarled verbally, as well as through his link and returned his full awareness to the passage.

The attackers were advancing in a line across the wide hallway. Their swords were in their scabbards, but they were holding bone spears above their heads, in a throwing position.

It was not far now. Pie estimated the end of the corridor was no more than twenty meters away. Suddenly, he felt an impact on his hostage and the man stopped struggling; he became dead weight in Pie's grip. Then another blow stuck the man and another. A shaft whisked past Pie's ear. Another pierced the limp hostage's abdomen and passed far enough through to slice into Pie's flank. Pie continued to backpedal, until he was against a wall and could retreat no farther.

As the attackers rushed forward, a new light flooded onto them; a portal had opened a few steps to Pie's left. Pie heaved the dead man at them and dived through the opening, somersaulting as he hit the floor to break his fall. He came to his knees and brought the knife up but the first pursuer to jump through the doorway was instantly liquefied by a sonic curtain that had been activated the moment Pie had cleared it. Before another suicidal gesture could be attempted, the portal "swished" shut.

Pie quickly glanced around with his knife held out in front. Blood dripped from his other hand where the fingers had been amputated. There were nearly a dozen Unders, all standing in place, staring at Pie and the grisly violence that had followed his entrance. When he looked to his right he saw a pretty Under-woman; her face and pale-yellow dress were spattered with blood, about all that remained of his pursuer.

Pie stood, still holding his knife, though he could detect no evidence of impending attack from this group.

The woman ran, her gown rustling with her quick stride. When Pie pivoted, the other Unders also ran, as if the mere touch of his vision carried death. He watched them scatter, until he was alone. He took a moment to attend to his hand, sending neural messages to the arteries, slowing the bleeding to a dribble, and then damped the pain signals from both his hand and his side. When he straightened, he felt a stiffness in his side. He gingerly pulled open the rent in his suit, dark with blood, and observed a slash that extended through his skin and into muscle. Blood was running from the wound but it didn't appear to be arterial. He used his knife to cut away a pant leg and tied it around his abdomen to put pressure on the flank wound.

He reloaded his handgun and then he uplinked to locate an up-tube; it was at the far end of a walkway. While he walked along the broad walkway, he surveyed his surroundings; it was a major dome. It was even possible to think of it as a small village from the distant past, captured in a bubble of time. The lower reaches of the dome were hidden by buildings, and the roof by artificial sunlight. He'd been similar bubbles before. At "night" there would be a twinkling of lights in the distant ceiling, simulating stars in a cloudless summer night.

The eaves and doorframes of the quaint shops were decorated with a scrollwork of elaborate vines and fantastic flowers, cheerful in their Easter-egg colors, but most of the doors were without decoration, proudly displaying a simulated wood grain. Word of his approach spread through the village. Although he saw no door closing, he heard them, a series of "bangs" advancing ahead of him along the deserted walkway. He saw no brave souls, no reckless teens, not even a curious face peeking from behind the artificial shrubs that lined the flat rooftops.

These were tame Unders, accustomed to tight control and unquestioning obedience. They were allowed to live in apartments above their shops. In return they produced clothing, simple machines, and handcrafted decorations. Citizens took what they wanted as fair payment They lived without fear of hunger, their families safe from the violence and uncertainty that swirled through the Under City.

Many of these Unders never ventured beyond the confines of their own bubble, except for a rare holiday in the arboretum. Most cities preserved a small slice of pre-Death earth in an arboretum and Cisco City's park was particularly inviting, one of the finest. He smiled with a fond remembrance of other visits when he had searched for new species to bring back to his egg-house. They called the arboretum the Forest of Giants, not knowing that it didn't refer to the tall trees. If they had ever dug deeper into the soil of the bowl-shaped space, they would have found row after row of seats. Only a handful of remaining citizens would recognize it as the name of a baseball team and know that the arboretum had been their stadium. And even fewer would remember that it had been the original refuge of those who had survived at the Stanford-San Jose Bubble.

The plastic floor, its sheen long erased by the scuffing of an untold number of feet, abruptly changed to marble as he approached a circular courtyard. At the center of the courtyard, a wide column arose and disappeared into the glaring light of the daytime "sun". It was unguarded. There was no need; the only key to gain entrance was through a matrix link.

Pie linked into the matrix and the door slid open. He had almost expected to see another one of those jury-rigged lifts but was pleasantly surprised to find a fully functioning tube. He stepped in and ascended.

When he neared the top of the shaft, he touched the side of the tube and his ascent slowed, until he was hanging in front of an exit. He glided forward and a portal opened to reveal the interior of a Citizen bubble. Although much smaller than the bubble he'd walked through, it too had the feel of openness. Glittering streamers were suspended from above, hiding the bubble's inner surface; they twisted and twirled in a floral scented breeze, chiming with an exotic "tinkling" as they brushed against one another.

A short distance into the circular room, a woman reclined on a divan, her head topped by a metallic-gold scalp. On closer further inspection, Pie decided it was actually her skull. She wore a livid, purple gown, which parted at the waist to reveal shiny, golden breasts, capped by scarlet nipples. Her eyes were the black cat-eyes of a Citizen. Standing on either side of her were silver-haired men, also with black eyes, wearing short, purple jerkins and gold tights that left nothing to the imagination.

While Pie studied them, they stared in return and saw a massive man with dried blood on his tattered, silvery suit, the material of the right leg torn away to reveal the musculature of a massively powerful leg. They did not fail to notice the missing fingers on his left hand, or his right hand, causally resting on the holstered handle of what appeared to be a weapon. He smelled of sweat and blood. At his approach, the two men raised black sticks, like a fisherman would hold a rod, lightening-sticks.

Pie inspected the men more closely. They were not really Citizens; they had simply stained the whites of their eyes and were wearing black lenses over their corneas.

"Welcome, Citizen Traynor," the woman said, speaking in a stilted voice, as if it were beneath her to move her lips. She shifted her leg, clearing a small space on the bone-white divan, and patted it with her hand, as if calling a pet.

Pie remained where he was and continued to survey the room. The item that surprised him the most was a crystal bowl sitting in the middle of a marble table; it contained grapes, oranges, and apples, and they appeared to be real.

He returned his attention to the woman. "Why was I attacked? How is it even possible that a Citizen can be attacked in a city of our own making?"

Her golden lashes that curled above and below black slits for eyes fluttered. Her mouth opened in mock surprise, revealing the reflection of golden teeth. She closed her scarlet lips and stretched them into a smile before answering.

"My, you are primitive aren't you?" she said in a breathy voice. "Where is Jericho?"

"He couldn't make it."

"Oh...I was so looking forward to seeing him again," she said petulantly, pouting her lower lip. "He is so much fun. Don't you agree?"

Pie walked toward her and the attendants lowered their staffs until they pointed at Pie's head.

Pie paused again, this time only two strides from the reclining woman. "Listen, you bitch, whoever you are, if these gigolos of yours make one more move, I will personally dispose of them."

She brought the back of her hand up to her mouth to hide a smile.

"Who are you?" Pie demanded.

She lowered her hand. "I'm Caro Slin, High Mayor of Cisco City, your official greeter, and I certainly didn't expect such hostility. Why I—"

"Where are the others?"

"How many greeters do you want, Citizen? You got me, the High Mayor, what more could you want? Do you think we've nothing else to do? We shoulder a heavy responsibility, running this great city."

"And doing a piss poor job of it!" He pointed with his injured hand. "While you sit up here eating fruit and playing your silly games, the city is rotting beneath you." He walked over to the bowl of fruit and pinched a grape. "It's real."

"Of course it is. Help yourself. Wherever have you been, dear boy?"

"I'm not your boy and this is not your city. Anarchists and assassins control it. Who are they and what do they want?"

"You've only been here a few minutes and you're already the biggest bore I've ever met. Pie Traynor, Citizen among Citizens," she made a laughing noise. "If Jericho Zinc were here I'd show you a real man."

She sighed and stretched her arms, twisting them sensuously, and her gown fell open to reveal her nakedness. It did not have its intended effect.

She continued, unaware of her failure. "It is only through our beneficence that the Unders thrive."

"You are useless. Parasites on the community below. Why haven't you used your technology to discover and exploit new resources or make repairs? You disgust me."

"I disgust you?" this time honestly astonished. She pulled her gown back around to cover her nakedness. "You, a filthy, stinking animal, without a shred of grace or refinement, can stand there and criticize me? You ignorant bastard son of a bitch!" Her breath was coming in gasps.

She quieted her breathing and regained her composure. "For your information, there are Citizens assigned to that very task, but there is time. You should know that better than any of us. Who has had more time than you? There is always plenty of time."

She brushed her hand along the surface of the divan, drawing Pie's attention to her golden fingernails, at least three inches long and as sharp as daggers. She couldn't even wipe herself without risking a fatal injury, Pie surmised, and was amused by the absurdity of it all.

"So, you can smile," she said in a throaty whisper, and then spoke a word to one of her attendants. The man bowed and returned a moment later with a small bottle containing a milky fluid. Pie eyed the bottle suspiciously.

The man approached Pie with the bottle and pulled out the crystalline stopper. Pie drew the diamond knife and held it so the attendant would be sure to see it.

"That's far enough," Pie said and the man halted at once.

The golden woman laughed. "So suspicious! It's only a little bottle of fragrance and believe me you could use it. You stink. It's rather revolting." She wrinkled her nose. "Come here," she said coyly, and then added, "but do try to keep that icky blood from getting on my gown, will you?"

"I want only one thing from you," Pie replied. "I want the commuter-ship prepped so I can get the hell out of here."

She sat up, like a snake uncoiling. "You smell like an animal. You act like an animal. I can only presume you are an animal...or an Under." Her eyes narrowed and lips tightened. "You're not beyond time. You're old. It'll be a pleasure to be rid of you. The comm-ship will be ready in one hour."

She stood and turned her back to Pie. Her attendants stumbled over one another as they hurried to gain their proper positions at her side. A portal opened for them and they disappeared from sight.

A moment after they were gone, Pie walked around the circumference of the bubble; it was empty. He returned to the divan and sat heavily on the edge, not sure he could stand again if his life depended on it. The sharp pain in his hand and aching in his side were breaking through the neural block he'd constructed. He uplinked with Home Control.

"This is Traynor. Monitor the comm-ship being prepped for me and awaken me in one hour."

"This is Home Control. We have you, Citizen Traynor, and I must tell you. We so enjoyed sharing in your skirmish with the Unders. It was quite entertaining."

"Entertaining? Men and women died."

"They were only Unders."

"Only Unders? You—" Pie paused and shook his head in disgust. "Wake me in one hour. Do you think you can manage that?"

"No reason to be insulting, Citizen Traynor."

He shut down the link and attempted to contact Roxanne, but the block was still in place. The thought of returning to her was soothing. He dragged his legs onto the divan and fell asleep.

Chapter 7

Joshua Mason, son of First Citizen Mitchel Mason, paced the anteroom in small circles, while beyond the closed door a conversation was taking place.

"You got to be it last time."

"I beg to differ. I remember it distinctly. It's my turn."

"No, it isn't. It's mine."

"It's mine!"

"No, it's mine!"

"You always get your way."

"You do!"

"Shh, he's coming."

"All right then, but I get to be it next time and don't you forget it."

The walls of the room were unsettling, decorated with a scribbling of colors without perceptible form. A red haired boy with exuberant freckles and a pug nose, and another boy with dark eyes and long lashes, sat on child-sized chairs on a raised platform, both with expectant attention focused on the doorway. The door opened, and a full-sized human turned sideways and crouched to successfully pass through the small doorway, no larger than that of child's playhouse. The man's skin was covered by thick, short hair, giving the appearance of well-groomed fur. His bodysuit was white with pink polka dots.

Citizen Joshua Mason was followed into the reception chamber by an Under. The Under immediately dropped to his knees and bowed his head. It was a perplexing moment of unknown protocol, but Joshua was not about to demonstrate subservience to the New People. After all, his father was the First Citizen of the Technocracy.

The boys stared open-mouthed at the Citizen and then began giggling, slapping their thighs and rocking back and forth.

"I do not think this is a proper attitude to display when receiving an official envoy of Home," Joshua stated soberly.

The boys turned to face one another, screwing their expressions into exaggerated, but feigned, repentance.

Joshua continued. "I was instructed to report to the Grand Wizard at this location in order to complete the arrangements. Which one of you is the Grand Wizard?"

"I am," the redhead replied.

"Then proceed."

"Present your credentials."

"What? This is ridiculous! You know damn well who I am. I've been kept waiting for twenty-four hours with no explanation, confined to a room that would've been too small for a dwarf; given a bed that was barely large enough to even function as a chair. I am outraged! I do not intend to play any silly games with you."

"You don't?" asked the darker-skinned boy with evident disappointment.

Joshua lowered his gaze to the back of the Under who knelt before him. The mission was important, worth inconvenience and even humiliation, to a point. He raised his face, but was forced to remain slumped in order to avoid the ceiling. He forced himself to smile and then spoke. "I'd like to suggest that differences between our cultures has resulted in an inauspicious and undiplomatic inauguration of our negotiations. I recommend, in a spirit of cooperation, that we renew our efforts to communicate."

"Okay," the redhead replied.

Joshua waited, but the boys just stared at him. He cleared his throat. "Good, well...I'm glad we resolved that misunderstanding. As I understand the agreement, two of your people will join the team that is preparing to re-visit the planet inhabited by an alien race we call the Blues. In exchange for the use of our starship, crew and expertise, you will forgive recent debts incurred by the Citizen Grand Wizard, Mitchell Mason, and—"

They started laughing and squirming in their chairs. The olive-skinned boy slipped off his chair and started rolling back and forth on the platform, holding his stomach while he continued to laugh.

"Stop it!" Stiff and indignant, Joshua glared at the two little people. "Stop it, I say!"

The smile deserted the face of the redhead; his small, milk teeth were hidden by a somber gathering of his facial features. "Whoa there, Mister Citizen." He pressed his tiny thumb against his jumper-covered chest. "Are you ordering me, the Grand Wizard, not to laugh? Can this be true?"

"Well...I...." Joshua expelled his breath.

The darker skinned boy continued to lie on his stomach, facing the furry Citizen. His smiling face was propped up with his small hands, while he kicked his legs up and down with apparent abandon.

"Why are you making this so difficult?" Joshua asked earnestly.

"Why are you?" the "Grand Wizard" replied.

"Me?" Joshua's elliptical, black eyes opened wider.

The smile returned to the freckle-filled face. "I wish you could stick to the point. Are all Citizens afflicted with a short attention span?"

"Look. I'm doing the best I can to—"

"I know. I know. I'm so sorry your best is so poor. But, you aren't New, not New at all. What can one expect?"

Before Joshua could continue, he needed to remind himself of the urgency of success. "As I was saying, in addition to providing credits to pay for the out-ship and train, you will provide the consumable elements of the mission."

The "Grand Wizard" covered his mouth with both hands, one atop the other, and then slowly lowered them. "You mean...you're going to eat us?" Both boys renewed their giggling.

"No! That's ridiculous. I'm referring to—" Joshua's attention was drawn to a green tube, circled with bands of magenta, that slithered out of a hole in the wall. It was thicker than a man's arm and continued to slide out of the hole until it was revealed to be a full ten-meters long. The leading end was round and it slithered like a snake. While still on his knees, the Under began to scoot away from the "snake".

Joshua felt similarly vulnerable; never expecting he'd need a weapon, and not wishing to offend, he'd brought none. He attempted an uplink with Home as he backed against the wall, but the shield around the city denied him access to the Technocracy.

The "snake" began to curl around the kneeling Under, wrapping him in coils, pinning his arms against his body. The Under lost his balance and tipped over, onto the floor. He whimpered, but did not ask for help.

Joshua tore his attention away from the "snake" and glared at the two boys, who had crawled to the edge of the platform to watch.

"Do something!" Joshua yelled.

The red-haired boy laughed. "It's only one of Jacques' animate-sculptures. It won't hurt him."

The lips of the Under took on a purple hue before the "snake" released its death grip and slithered away to reenter the hole in the wall. The Under-man took a deep gasp of air and then pushed himself up to a sitting position without complaint, apparently unharmed. The boys lost interest in the Under and returned their attention to Joshua.

"You know what?" the "Grand Wizard" said. "There's someone you should meet. There's a certain family resemblance. Don't you think so, Toddy?"

The darker-skinned boy looked to his partner, but said nothing.

The "Grand Wizard" continued. "Jacques won't mind, after all, his work was based on my successful transplantation of an interspecies codon in rats."

"I don't know. Jacques—"

"Don't argue!" the redheaded boy said. "I'm the Grand Wizard, remember?"

"What's going on?" Joshua asked warily.

"Citizen," the Grand Wizard said, "I'm going to show you something special."

"My only desire is to conclude our negotiations and lift for Home with the New People you've selected for the mission."

"Don't offend me, Citizen. I might back out altogether. What would you do then?" He stood on his pudgy, little legs and, as he walked toward the scribbled wall, a small door appeared, leading to an equally small passage. He stopped at the entrance and looked to Toddy, who shrugged and walked over to join the "Grand Wizard". The redhead turned his gaze to Joshua.

"I can't possibly fit through that doorway," Joshua declared.

"Don't be so dense, Citizen." The boy jumped and his hand passed through the apparent solid wall above the door. "It's only an illusion. Come on now." He urged Joshua to follow, gesturing with his hand, "Come on. That's a good boy."

The two New People entered the passage and Joshua reluctantly followed, holding his hands out in front. He stepped through the plane of the wall and immediately struck his forehead on something solid. There was only darkness. He raised his hand to feel the growing lump on his forehead. It hurt. He remained still; he didn't want to risk striking his head again. The giggling of the boys seemed to be coming from somewhere near.

"Citizen, are you lost?" Toddy asked.

A little hand tugged on the leg of his bodysuit, but he resisted.

"Come on, Citizen, you can't stay in the wall forever. We won't let you hit yourself on another head-bonker. We promise."

"You mean, you did that on purpose?" Joshua asked.

"No-o-o, Citizen. Everyone is entitled to a mistake, even a Grand Wizard. The head-bonkers are just there to ensure that the Unders don't forget their place, but you're not an Under, are you, Citizen?"

One of the boys began tugging on Joshua's pant leg again. He relented and got down on his hands and knees. When his head was low enough, he was able to see down the passage and found himself face to face with the smiling redhead.

"You bastard," Joshua said.

"Well...no. I didn't have a mother or a father. Your claim is impossible. Now, come on. Stand up."

"Hell no."

"Don't you trust me?" Toddy asked. "You're going to hurt my feelings. Oh, I get it. You're getting in the mood of things."

Both Toddy and the "Grand Wizard" laughed. They held hands as they skipped farther down the passageway with Joshua crawling laboriously behind them, finding no alternate but to accept his current predicament. He vowed to himself that he would never return to New Berlin again; even if Mitchel Mason was his father, he'd have to find someone else next time, if there ever was a next time.

Joshua crawled into a room and was about to stand, but froze in place; his attention was riveted on a large, furry animal with red eyes and a bulging cranium. The animal withdrew its lips, revealing the yellow teeth of a predator and began a deep-throated growl. Joshua did not dare let his attention drift from the carnivore; there was intelligence in the eyes that were staring out of the distorted skull.

"I can see you're impressed." The "Wizard" chuckled, an adult-like sound coming from a "child". "What you don't know is that Jacques not only created this new species—and this is really incredible—it breeds true."

The short-furred Citizen and the longhaired beast continued to stare at one another, both on all fours.

"You look so much alike, I think he wants to be your friend. Don't you agree?" Toddy asked.

Joshua said nothing.

"Hey, Citizen. Oh, Citizen, can you hear me?" Toddy asked.

Joshua nodded. He knew what it was now. It was a wolf, distorted to the point of frightening ugliness, a monstrosity. He shivered with renewed fear.

"Jacques calls it a werewolf. Brilliant, I'll have to give him that, but I provided the inspiration that—" The redhead turned around. "Hello, Jilla."

The blond-haired girl walked nonchalantly between Joshua and the werewolf and confronted the two boys, her tiny hands planted firmly on her hips. "I see. The wizard game again, is it? Who gave you permission to interfere? This is Jacques' and my project."

The redheaded boy bowed his head.

"Willy, must you always be such a bad boy? I'm going to file a formal complaint with your family and yours too, Toddy."

The olive-skinned boy frowned. "Oh, Jilla. It was Willy's idea."

"Leave."

The two boys walked past the werewolf without a sideward glance, their eyes directed at the floor, and disappeared down the passage.

Jilla turned to face the Citizen, who was still crouched on his hands and knees, but less afraid of the beast; there was something at work here.

"Citizen Joshua Mason, my name is Jilla LineBFD/LineDHB. Come with me." She walked toward the passage, which expanded to the height of a normal-sized human but, when he didn't follow, she stopped. "Aren't you coming?"

Joshua nodded toward the beast that continued to stare at him with its red eyes.

"Are you mute or something? Speak up. The werewolf won't hurt you. It's in another room. The closeness is just an illusion. The wolf knows it. I'm surprised you don't. Now get up from that ludicrous position and act your age." She turned and began walking down the passage.

Although reassured, Joshua kept the werewolf in sight until he was fully into the passage and, even then, nervously glanced over his shoulder, half expecting to see the beast stalking him. When they reentered the scribble-walled chamber, a blond boy was waiting for them with an Under-woman kneeling at one side and an Under-man at the other.

"So, Jilla, you found him with the werewolves. What do you have to say for yourself, Citizen? I left unequivocal instructions for you to remain in your room."

"What the hell is going on here?" Joshua was indignant, but his fur effectively hid the heat of his anger.

The boy smiled, displaying dimples in his plump cheeks. "They are only in their forties and it was rather cute, wasn't it, Jilla? The wizard game again?"

She smiled and nodded.

"Cute!" Joshua yelled. "I'll tell you cute. You can stuff it up your ass! I don't care what you're willing to provide for the mission. In all my twenty centuries of life I've never been treated with such little regard."

"Twenty centuries?" Jilla said and met Jacques' gaze, both of them with big smiles spread across their faces.

Joshua turned from them and walked toward the wall, but there was no door. He started running his hands across the surface, searching for a hidden opening.

"Lose something, Citizen?" Jilla asked sweetly.

He turned to them, his hairy hands clenched into fists.

"Doesn't have much of a sense of humor does he?" Jilla asked Jacques. "Is this typical?"

Jacques nodded. "I'm afraid so. It's not too late to cancel."

Joshua walked over to stand between the blond cherubs, towering over the little "boy".

"If I didn't know better," Jilla said, "I'd think this old-style human was threatening you."

Joshua turned to confront the dainty "girl". "I've come here in good faith to negotiate the details and you've been treating me like an Under."

"Has a lot of spunk anyway," Jilla observed. "Maybe you're being treated like an Under because you look like an Under, except hairier, and act like an Under. Did you ever think of that?"

"Go on, enjoy your childish insults. I want to talk with your leader. We'll see how this works out."

"Mitchell Mason's deal is with my family, not the New People as a whole. While you were having fun, Jacques concluded the negotiations with First Citizen Mason."

"Fun? You are crazy!"

"Were you injured?" Jilla asked. "Other than that tiny bump on your forehead? Was anything hurt besides your over-inflated sense of importance? You are here to transport us to Home, nothing else."

"But…why—"

"Why you?" Jilla's smile widened. "I asked for you, son of the great First Citizen. We are important."

Joshua continued his black-eyed stare.

"Haven't you wasted enough time?" Jacques asked. "We're ready."

"You can go to hell! Open a God damned door and I mean now!"

A small passage opened in the scribbled wall. Joshua got down onto his hands and knees and entered the passage. As he crawled, it gradually became smaller, until he was forced onto his stomach to scoot ahead. The walls continued to collapse; he was wedged tight, unable to move forward or back. The air quickly became stale and thin. He attempted an uplink, but the shield was still in place.

"Citizen." It was Jilla's little-girl voice.

"What the hell are you doing?" Joshua paused to sip a little more air. "I can't breathe!" Pause. "You bitch! You'll pay when…." He had no more breath.

"He is so rude," Jacques said.

"True," Jilla replied. "If we had more time we could train him properly but we do want to get going."

"What do you want?" Joshua rasped.

"I want you to apologize for your rude behavior," Jilla said.

"I apologize!" His fur began to mat from perspiration and his breathing quickened as the air lost its oxygen. He was dying. "I apologize!"

"Do you mean it?"

"I apologize, please."

"Well…that is an improvement," Jilla said.

"Yes," Jacques agreed, "and we really should make some allowance for his upbringing."

The tunnel expanded, until Joshua could have stood, but he continued to lie on his stomach, his muscles quivering and weak.

The cherubs walked forward to stand over the Citizen.

"Get up, Citizen. You have work to do," Jilla said and turned to the Unders. "Help him up." Without waiting to see her orders carried out, she joined Jacques and together they strolled on down the passage.

The Unders grabbed Joshua's arms and assisted him to his feet. He almost thanked them, before realizing they were only Unders. When they exited the tunnel, the two New People were already seated in a diminutive car, which had runners along each side and handles on the roof. The Unders mounted the car, with their feet on the runners and their hands grasping a handhold. Both looked back to Joshua, who grumbled, but walked forward to take his position, clinging to the outside of the car.

The car accelerated, picking up speed as it hurtled down the passage of polished stone. Joshua strained as he clutched at his handhold, unaccustomed to such raw exposure to danger without a hint of safety features.

The car suddenly decelerated, and then stopped, causing Joshua's hands to be torn free from where he gripped the roof rail. He plunged forward and tumbled to the stone floor, finally sliding on his stomach to a stop.

The two New People exited the car and walked over to look down at Joshua.

"You certainly are a clumsy fellow," Jilla declared. "Even our Unders know enough to be prepared for a stop." She shook her head and her blonde ringlets danced. "So sad."

Joshua slowly climbed to his feet and rubbed his palms on his soiled body suit. The knees of the suit were ripped open, revealing abraded fur, pink with blood.

"You did that on purpose," Joshua said through gritted teeth. "You are vicious, cruel people."

"As Jilla already told you, we had no idea you were so weak and uncoordinated."

66

"You injured me on purpose. There'll come a time when you'll regret the way you've treated me."

"Oh my," Jacques said. "What a paranoid suggestion. We would never put you at risk on purpose. We would have made you walk. Now, now, keep that primeval anger under control." He turned to Jilla. "Do you think he's mentally unbalanced?"

"It's possible." She turned to Joshua. "We don't really need you. All we need is the comm-ship. You can remain here if you'd like."

Joshua straightened to his full height and crossed his arms as he confronted the two "children", but they ignored him and skipped away, hand in hand, to enter an up-tube. Joshua stepped forward to inspect the small tube; the tube in which he'd descended from the landing pad had been much larger.

One of the Unders coughed.

Joshua turned toward the man. "Do you have something to say?"

The Under bowed his head and mumbled.

"Speak louder!"

The Under-man cringed and brought his arms up protectively in front of him.

"Just tell me what you have to say." Joshua said. "I'm not going to hurt you."

"They...." He looked at the tube opening that the New People had entered. "They don't like us to talk. They say we are dumb animals."

"Val," the Under-woman warned, "they'll be angry if we don't hurry."

He nodded soberly. "Be careful, Citizen. They—"

"Val!"

"What were you about to say?" Joshua asked.

The man bowed his head. "Nothing. We must hurry."

The Under walked toward the wall and a second, larger tube appeared. He stepped back and waited for Joshua to go first. When Joshua walked past he tried to regain eye contact with the Under, but the Under kept his eyes downcast.

When Joshua exited the tube onto the landing pad, Jilla was waiting; her were lips tightly compressed while she was tapping her little foot on the stone. Joshua ignored her to focus on his ship. It was, in his opinion, the only thing of beauty the Technocracy had ever created: a comm-ship, a true rocket ship, sleek, gradually tapering to a sharp point, sitting upright on fins that flared gracefully from the ship's body.

"Did you forget why we're here?" Jilla asked petulantly.

Joshua turned to face her, but again looked over her head, this time through the curtain of air that surrounded and protected the pad. The sharp-edged peaks of the Sierra Nevada Range seemed close enough to touch, white-gray granite without a trace of snow.

"Citizen!"

Joshua returned his attention to the blond-haired "girl".

"I don't know, Jilla," Jacques said. "Maybe they just can't help it." The fair-skinned boy looked up at the furry Citizen. "Are you ready now?" he asked, carefully enunciating each word.

"Quite ready."

"Wonderful! See, Jilla, you just need to speak slowly, that's all."

Joshua activated the entry tube. It "whirred" as it extended from the side of the up-ship and then elbowed toward the pad. It was satisfying to be in control again, to be online with the Technocracy, to have the ship respond to his commands. He was the first to enter the tube, making the two little people wait.

When they exited into the cabin, Joshua swiveled in his seat to face the New People. The two Unders stood behind them.

"What are the Unders doing here?" Joshua asked with surprise.

"Surely you don't expect us to travel without our Unders?" Jacques replied.

"Does First Citizen Mason know about this?" Joshua asked.

"Who cares?" Jilla said without concern.

"Jilla."

"All right, Jacques." She focused on Joshua. "First Citizen Mason is much more reasonable than you. Why aren't you more like him? Did you lose something in the gene transfer?"

"Jilla, remember, they share the genes of two people, a mother and a father."

"Yes, I know. Bizarre. Kind of gross when you think about it. First Citizen Mason said that we should bring whatever we need. Did you load our personal capsules?"

"They're on board," Joshua replied, "but I do doubt he expected you to bring Unders as part of your baggage."

"Enough of this prattle, Citizen. Let us be off and let us all hope your performance is not an indication of how the rest of the mission will proceed. This is a first for the New People and its success or failure carries with it serious consequences. First Citizen Mason understands. It's a pity you don't. Don't you agree, Jacques?"

"Yes, I do agree, Jilla."

The up-ship seats were shaped like flowers and the "petals" wrapped themselves over the passengers, enclosing them in the protection of a womb-like cocoon. The pilot, Citizen Joshua Mason, couldn't see, but that wasn't necessary; he monitored the ship through his link, "seeing" much more than could be seen with mortal eyes. If pressed, he would've been forced to admit that it was the matrix that flew the ship, that he was nothing more than a fail-safe, but to him it felt like he was the pilot.

It was with pleasure that Joshua activated the comm-ship, causing pellets of kerosene and oxygen to enter the spark chamber and explode, blasting the ship upward in a steady stream of explosions too closely spaced to be perceived as anything more than a steady roar of naked power.

The needle-nosed comm-ship streaked into the cloudless sky above the honeycombed Mount Whitney, the one and only home of the New People. It shot upward on a column of billowing white, a sight as ancient as space exploration itself, automatically switching from kerosene to hydrogen pellets once above the atmosphere.

Chapter 8

Pie awakened with visions of razor-sharp fingernails slashing at him from the dark. He sat up to rid himself of the nightmare that still clung to him and leaned forward to hold his head in his uninjured hand. The discomfort lessened.

"Home, how long have I been asleep?"

"Two hours and twenty-seven minutes."

He pounded his fist into the divan, but its softness absorbed the blow, taking with it any satisfaction. "What the hell is happening up there? Incompetent—"

"Relax, Citizen, you have plenty of time. The first commuter-ship was a cargo ship and already fully loaded. It made no sense to unload it and, besides, who in their right mind would ride aboard a cargo ship? Know what I mean?"

"No, I don't know what you mean. God damn it!" Traynor yelled, though it would have been heard at Home just as well if he had only thought it. "I want Mitchell Mason online and I want him now!"

"I wish I could." The communication ended.

Pie stood and felt momentarily light-headed. He checked the load in his handgun and walked to the rear of the bubble. When he reached the closed doorway, he ordered it open, but it did not budge.

"As you wish," he said out loud and fired the gun into the hinges and then the handle. The flimsy alloy tore away in chunks with each blast. He reloaded and then kicked the door; it fell inward with a "shush" of air as it sailed to the floor. Simultaneous with his entry into the wide passage, a door opened on both side and a half dozen men holding lightening-sticks, filed out to form a tight line of bodies across the width of the corridor.

The golden Citizen slipped through a crack in the line. "You have done enough damage. You have none of the higher qualities, no grace, no beauty."

Pie began striding toward her but stopped when the Unders raised their sticks to a striking position. They held them pointed at him, but there was shuffling of feet, fleeting glances, and quick breaths.

"If you take one more step," the High Mayor said, "I swear I'll order my men to fry you to a crisp, original Citizen or not. I'm so disappointed in you. I thought it would be exciting to fuck an original Citizen, but you're not exciting. You're not even mildly interesting. You're appalling."

"Get the ship ready. Now!"

A half-smile traced her lips. "You're in luck, Citizen Traynor. The cargo ship hasn't lifted yet."

A third passage opened. Pie uplinked and found it to be just as she stated, an entryway to the spaceport. He walked toward it, maintaining a loose link as he searched for signs of treachery but, finding none, he entered the new passage.

Before the door slid shut behind him, the mayor yelled, "Have a nice trip!"

The corridor was well lit by light-lines embedded in the walls, just beneath the coved ceiling. It was empty and he walked it briskly, ignoring the ache in his side. When he reached the end, the door opened, revealing a comm-ship terminal. Three Citizens were present, dressed in clown colors and standing near the side of the circular bay. They watched him with interest.

The only sound was Pie's feet as they "clicked" on the black, marble floor of the rotunda. He ignored them and walked toward a row of silvery, transport pods. Without pausing, he climbed through the oval opening of the leading pod and lay down. His eyes saw the diffuse lighting of the high, domed ceiling, but his mind was occupied as he consulted his link to confirm that the ship was ready.

"He does stink," one of the Citizens proclaimed loudly and laughed.

Another added, "The sad thing is, he probably won't even notice." They seemed to think that was quite funny.

The canopy of the pod closed; it accelerated and then dived into a tunnel. An uncontrollable flash of heat arose in his cheeks. It wasn't the words; it was the laughter that always seemed capable of having its way with his self-esteem.

"Damn Mason, damn Jericho, and damn this whole rotten city!" he cursed to himself as he hurtled through darkness.

When the pod approached the ship, it rapidly decelerated and came to a stop. He crawled out, onto the polished stone floor of the small entry chamber and rode the lift to the entry dock. He uplinked with the ship. The moment the lock opened, he was assaulted by the stench of poorly preserved fish. He paused for a moment, but he had no time to waste.

Despite the oily surfaces and dead-fish odor, the ship was fully functional. The pilot's chair was slick. He reluctantly settled onto it and protective petals closed around him. The launch door dilated and Pie activated the engines. The ship responded, roaring into the sky, incinerating a hole in the cloud of insects that had gathered above the launch pad. With the silo sterilized by the rocket's blast, the launch door constricted until the now empty pad was again sealed.

Pie waited for the heavy hand of acceleration to lift and monitored the ship's performance. It was on course and streaking through the thin purple of the rarefied upper atmosphere before he lessened his attention.

"Home, this is Citizen Traynor aboard the comm-ship Cisco 257B, assume control."

"Citizen, this is Home. We have you."

Pie downgraded the link and released himself from the fatty surfaces of the pilot's seat. A sickening image occurred to him, he imagined he was hurtling through space, entombed in the stomach of a decomposing whale. He gagged and, as saliva flooded his mouth, breathed deeply to suppress the urge to vomit, tasting bitter bile on the back of his tongue. With the onset of weightlessness, pale-yellow droplets of oil began to float through the ship, despite the air scrubbers. He cut a square out of his ragged suit and tied it over his nose and mouth in the fashion of a bandanna; it was a futile attempt to keep the oil out of his lungs.

They must really be having a good laugh in Cisco. He could imagine the golden bitch, scarlet lips stretched wide as she brayed of her superiority. By now, most of Home must know of the practical joke as well, but it was more than a joke; the purity of the air aboard a spacecraft was no laughing matter.

It didn't make sense; nothing made sense. It was as if he'd just returned from a deep mission and had not readjusted to current society. Perhaps this was true, he reluctantly admitted to himself, perhaps he hadn't readjusted to society when he'd returned from his last mission, maybe he'd only adjusted to living in isolation with Roxanne. Roxanne, despite numerous attempts, he'd been unable to contact her.

Pie pushed the jumble of unfinished thoughts aside and activated the long-view screen, seeing Home for the first time in over four decades. It was a massive structure, filling more than fifty kilometers of cubic space, blocking out the bright points of starlight with its innumerable, spinning arms. It had no particular shape. Its cylinders were attached to one another without obvious order, like a black-limbed, cancerous growth, and somewhere, deep within its web, was the Prime Cylinder. The Prime Cylinder was the entirety of Home when Pie first saw it, so many hundreds of years ago. The simple beauty was lost in the complexity and was made manageable only by the invention of the matrix quantum computer. Hundreds of thousands lived their entire lives within the mutated, octopus construction, Citizens and Unders alike. Most had never even seen Earth despite its proximity; it was irrelevant.

Traynor turned his thoughts to Mitchell Mason, director of Home since the beginning, since Copper Mountain and, if not a friend, at least an ally against time and the changes it wrought. No one could flow better than Mason. What was he now? Desperate enough to sacrifice their relationship, or had he finally succumbed to the terminal stages of egomania? Whichever it was, he'd gone too far this time.

His mind continued to drift. He recalled the sight of Roxanne, standing alone as she waved good-by, and remembered her white gown against the white of the house and gray of the mountain granite. Then his memory took another turn; it reminded him of a broken vow. He quickly suppressed the thought.

His fatigue slipped past his thoughts and took him into a restless sleep. The petals of the chair closed protectively around him for deceleration. When weightlessness returned, he was released and floated over to the exit hatch, impatient while he waited for the magnetic beam of the docking cylinder to pull the ship the final distance.

"Cisco 257B, this is Home Control, docking is complete."

Chapter 9

Pie's sense of smell had accommodated somewhat to the stench but, when fresh air flooded through the open lock, the fishy odor's ability to offend was renewed. He gagged and held his breath until he reached the disembarkation passage.

After he had passed through the lock, he entered a truncated cone, rimmed with seats fitted to gimbals. The drum began to rotate, swinging Pie's seat, and allowing the seat to ascend the slope of the cone. A chime sounded, indicating that the rotational speed of the cone had matched that of the cylinder, and a hatch slid open, revealing a gray corridor that stretched the length of the cylinder.

There were two Unders standing on either side of the entry, dressed in fluffy, feathery yellow but, when Pie set foot on the corridor, he didn't look to the sides; he looked up. It was a relatively small cylinder and he could easily see the heads and arms of other figures as they walked the corridor opposite his, straight overhead.

The odor of the ship had permeated Pie's tattered suit and was traveling along with him, like an aura of bad luck. While Pie stood still, gazing overhead, the Unders tightened their mouths and worked to keep expression from their faces. When Pie strode past them, he didn't even notice the Unders' valiant attempt at good manners: his eyes were now fixed on the lock at the far end of the corridor and his mind was on Mitchell Mason.

He traversed more than a dozen cylinders on his way to the Prime Cylinder, riding the cones up or down, depending on the size of the next cylinder and twice swimming through drums of weightlessness at branching intersections. On his way, he passed comically dressed Citizens, who seemed to be grinning in a knowing way, unaware of their own absurdities. They knew, Pie decided, they all knew and were laughing at him. He disciplined himself to keep his eyes straight ahead and marched past them, but could not help but hear the tittering laughter at his back.

It was with relief that he sighted the burnished entry-cone of Prime. When he finally stood beside it, he paused to admire its smoothness, unblemished by time. Memories arose, of his first voyage into space. He had been too big for a scramjet and never road the rail. It was not until comm-ships were developed that his dream to travel into space came true. He brushed his fingertips across the smooth surface. The titanium alloy wasn't used anymore, but it was holding up well, as well as any new-steel. The thought caused him to smile: he was still susceptible to juvenile pride, even susceptible to loyalty for inanimate objects.

He ordered this last entry lock to open and was about to step forward with such habit and certainly that he nearly collided with the portal when it failed to respond.

He uplinked. "Mason, you wanted me and now you've got me. Take the block off this portal, or I'll blast my way in." He placed his hand on the handgun. With his armor piecing shells, he probably could puncture the titanium but it was an empty threat; he'd never be so fool-hearty as to fire this handgun in space. Mason knew this as well.

"Hello, Pie. I understand you've arrived." The words were even and unhurried, untouched by Pie's agitation. "I can see you actually are carrying that God forsaken cannon."

"Mitch, damn you—"

"A moment please. I know we have matters to discuss, but I'm currently concluding very delicate negotiations that could shape the entire future of the Project. I'm not exaggerating. You'll have to wait."

"What kind of negotiations and with whom?"

"We'll have time to talk and I'll answer all your questions, but surely you can wait one more hour. Your cabin is as you left it. Why don't you go there?"

"There's a block on the entry portal."

"I'm sorry. That was to have been modified for you. After all, it's your home too."

The portal slid open.

"That's bullshit," Pie groused.

"Now, Pie, you'll get your chance. You have my word on it."

"Your word isn't worth jack shit."

"It's so refreshing to talk with someone who isn't simply awed by my person and position. I'm sure you'll feel much better, once you've had a chance to rest and clean up."

"Mitch...." Pie held his thoughts in check.

"Yes?"

"As I'm sure you know, I don't have much time left—don't even try to deny it. If you're not available soon, I have a feeling I'm going to lose control and come looking for you, and that could be very destructive."

"Such an attitude. Isn't that sad? Flow, Pie."

Pie did not return the Citizen courtesy, but the emptiness of his link signaled that Mason had terminated the connection.

When Pie entered the wide corridor of the Prime Cylinder, he found it to be deserted. He looked up and saw no one. It was so different from the last time he had walked this hall. It had been bustling with Citizens, but now it seemed ghostly, as if he were the sole living occupant of the giant cylinder.

He turned at the first intersection. The side hall seemed to disappear as it curved upward in the distance ahead. The sound of his footsteps was magnified by the quiet. When he reached his cabin door, he stopped. He had stood just like this so many times in the past. He refused to recognize the feelings, but this small cabin, deep in the bowels of Home, seemed more like his real home than the egg-house he had created high in the Cascade Mountains. Thoughts of Roxanne boiled to the forefront of his mind.

"Soon," he vowed.

The door slid open at his command. For an original Citizen, it was a Spartan cabin, but adequate where room was at a premium. He entered and the portal slid closed behind him. With habit not requiring thought, he activated his safeguards. For the first time since he'd left Roxanne, he felt secure.

To the right was his sleeping pad, held off the deck by extensions from the wall, to the left a desk and an easy chair, and in the rear was his personal hygiene closet. The walls were Wedgwood-blue and plain but, if he desired, he could call up a scenic vision and the walls would seem to melt away. He activated a forest scene and it was as if he were standing under the canopy of tall trees. He could even hear their leaves rustling in an imaginary wind.

He dropped the holstered Smith and Wesson onto the desktop and, ignoring his personal filth, lay down on the sleeping pad. The pad warmed and oozed to support his body, searching for tension to ease with a finger-like massage. As he lay on the bunk, his gaze wandered about forest scene, until he noticed a detail that he'd never seen before: the initials of two lovers were carved into a tree trunk, held within the shape of a heart. It was a sign from another time but he was touched by this simple declaration of love. On impulse, he slipped his diamond knife from its sheath and scratched a heart into the bulkhead next to his pad and then added RW + PT in the center of the heart. He smiled, and felt more than a little embarrassed by his sentimentality.

His thoughts were interrupted by a fit of coughing that brought the taste of fish into his mouth, a not so subtle reminder that his current body was ill as well as injured. Still, it was neither the developing pneumonia, nor his wounds that forced him out of his cozy pad; it was thought of the poison. He made himself stand and stripped off his suit, having to peel it away from his side; the dried blood made the material stick as if it had been glued. He completed his undressing, placing his knife on the desk next to the handgun. His hand was beginning to throb again as he walked over to his personal closet.

He stepped into the cleansing cabinet and chose warm water. The fine spray ran in hot rivulets down his back, down his buttocks and thighs, turning the water pink at his feet. There was pleasure in feeling the warm water caress away the filth and he stood there in a mindless state, aware only of water and heat. He accidently brushed his hand across his flank and felt the ridge of the gash. He wasn't concerned; this body only had to last a few more hours.

While the evaporator dried him, his thoughts turned to the assassins who had tried to kill him. It seemed inexplicable. The Technocracy had been established with the dual purposes of saving the Earth and preserving mankind. How could things have gotten so twisted in their minds that they blamed the Citizens for the state of the Earth? Were they insane? Certainly they were fanatics. He was still occupied with the problem when he settled into his chair.

He activated his holo-screen and it materialized. It was bordered by the rough bark of an old oak that appeared to be growing directly behind it. He attempted to access the ozone production program, but was blocked. He knew other ways, long forgotten pathways. Only thirty-seven percent of ozone generating plants were functional and no new generators had been built for over two hundred years. The current ozone concentration in the high atmosphere was only seven percent of pre-Death levels, down one percent. Down!

"Question. Has the further depletion of ozone been studied?"

"The analysis was undertaken by Citizen Ennis Kirchner in the year 3665," the sexless voice of the Home matrix replied.

Pie called the report onto the screen and was stunned by what it revealed. It was as if his entire life had been nothing more than a quixotic charade. The microwave energy beams that Home broadcast to the cities of Earth were destroying ozone faster than it could be produced. The report concluded with the recommendation that the energy beams be phased out.

Where was Citizen Kirchner now? Pie wondered and instituted a search program. Kirchner's personnel file was marked inactive, in the year 3666, inactive, dead. He could find no evidence that Kirchner had regenerated. He was apparently both body and matrix dead.

Was Mason aware of this report? It was hard to believe that he didn't know about it, but it was equally difficult to believe that he did know about it and hadn't acted. Mason had been a stalwart force in the survival of mankind. He had been instrumental in preserving the human species and had led the fight to establish Home, a visionary, relentless in his dedication to the Project. His only major failure had been that debacle of the starship Pinnacle, gone forever and undoubtedly long dead. Is it possible Mason had changed that much?

How could I have missed it? Pie wondered. If it was true, what reason was there to continue? Only Roxanne. He shook his head with regret. Sadness pulled painfully inside his chest.

"Pie, this is Mitch. Are you ready?"

"Yes, Mitch...I'm ready."

Pie made a copy of his findings, a marble-sized red pellet, which he dropped into a cup in the arm of the chair. He opened a wardrobe door and found it stocked with a wide assortment of colorful suits. He avoided them and chose a black one, strapping his knife to his forearm before pulling down the sleeve. He checked to make certain his gun was loaded and slid it into the holster. If he found it unavoidable, he would attack, even if his target was Mitchell Mason, even if it meant catastrophic decompression of the Prime Cylinder.

Before stepping into the corridor, he made one last attempt to contact Roxanne, but the egg-house maintained its block. He thought a message to her anyway. "Soon, Roxy, I'll be back with you."

Pie walked to Mason's cabin. The corridors remained empty, a deathly stillness that caused Pie to glance over his shoulder and then above. He stopped twenty paces in front of the doorway to Mason's suite of rooms. The door was wider than he recalled. The symbol of the Technocracy was emblazoned across it: the Earth with the Prime Cylinder in front of it, eclipsing it, and around the circumference, seven red disks, symbolic of the seven colonies, as anonymous as a set of juggler's balls: Procyon, Mesa, Rigil Kentaurus, Myphid, Holy, Iceland and Capella. Each name brought memories to mind; he, of all humanity, was the sole person to have visited them all. It was a Ptolemaic view of humanity's domain, but accurate to an extent. If the colonies could be considered to owe allegiance to anything, it was to Home, certainly not the Earth, but it was a big "if".

The door slid open, rising into the ceiling. Pie entered and paused. The portly figure of Mitchell Mason lounged in an old fashioned, over- stuffed chair in an otherwise empty room. He was wearing a baby-blue body suit that was covered by a scarlet robe. Joshua was usually with him, but not this time. The room was senselessly large, twenty meters deep and thirty meters wide, but this waste was nothing compared to the revelations Pie had stumbled across.

"Why?" Pie asked. The question was close to a cry. His vision blurred and he hated himself for feeling the emotion, and even more, for being unable to hide it.

"I guess that is the key question," Mason rumbled, the tone seemed to imply warmth and concern. He raised his bushy eyebrows in an otherwise patrician face.

Pie's intellect caught up with his emotions; there was grave danger here. As the pain of betrayal faded, it was replaced by hardness. His nose was congested with almost-tears, but the feeling was gone. They studied each other. Mason was smiling while he slouched in the chair, causing his paunch to protrude even farther; it was the veritable picture of sloppiness and vulnerability, but it was not the truth.

While Pie stood just inside the doorway he was taken by a fit of coughing.

"That's a nasty cough you have there, my friend. From your appearance, with that antique cannon strapped to your side, I surmise that you think I had something to do with that childish prank with the comm-ship, but I swear I didn't. Come here," Mason added, and pointed to his left where a second chair appeared, as if conjured out of air.

Pie didn't miss the point, a subtle display of control, of new tricks, suggesting there were others. He began walking toward the seated man, cautiously, as one might approach a wild animal, but Mason didn't squirm; he didn't fidget or reveal any evidence of concern. Pie rested his hand on the butt of the handgun, but his thoughts were focused on the knife up his sleeve, feint and attack. No scanner could detect the diamond knife; it was unique. He stopped a few strides away.

Mason pointed at the chair.

"I'll stand," Pie said.

"Suit yourself." With the eyes of a Cheshire cat, black slits set in a fleshy face, Mason studied the big man who stood before him.

There was silence until Pie could wait no longer.

"Mason, if you wanted to speak with me, why did you send that asshole? Why did you feel it was necessary to kill me?"

Mason leaned toward Pie and appeared earnest, his brows arched, his forehead furrowed. "Zinc was somewhat abrasive, and note, I use the word 'was'. Our monitors indicated that he became inactive somewhere over old Oregon. I'm not surprised, nor do I blame you. I warned him not to push you, but he was so impetuous. And I sure as hell didn't tell him to kill you. That was his idea. Well...I'm sure he deserved it. If we need to, we can always regenerate another."

"I will kill him every time I run across him."

"I can understand your anger but the reason I sent him was because I knew if I simply asked you to return to Home, you would've refused. Do you deny that?"

Pie remained still and said nothing.

"You don't think I'd actually poison you, do you?" Mason chuckled and shook his head. "I guess you do, from that look on your face. Come on, Pie. You know me better than that. I would never harm a friend."

"I'm not sure I do know you anymore, Mitch."

"You look so serious. Bend, don't break. I'm about to offer an opportunity any operative would beg to have. And who do I choose? My old friend, Pie Traynor. What do you think of that?"

"You only want me for my memories."

"That's kind of harsh. Oh, I get it. Don't worry. I'll punish those newbie Citizens who treated you with so little respect. We take care of each other."

"Keep it, Mitch. I'm going to regenerate and get the hell out of here. This place and all I've worked for, all we've worked for, is nothing more than a sham, and you damn well know it. You know the Technocracy is actually preventing the Earth from achieving any sort of recovery, yet you do nothing, except feed yourself and build Home bigger and bigger. What's the point, Mitchell? What are you living for?"

"Now that sounds familiar. Isn't it amazing how alike all the Roxanne's are? I'll grant you, the original Roxanne contributed much to the project but, basically, she was a pain in the ass. All of them really."

"Did you have her killed?"

"Again? How many times do I have to tell you? I gather you're talking about the original Roxanne and that bastard of a husband, Jack Nichols. How many times have you asked me that? God I'm glad he's not around and no, I didn't kill them. Don't have a clue what happened to them."

"Why do you keep living, Mitchell?"

Mason leaned back in his chair and took a deep breath before refocusing on Pie. "I guess you're running short of reasons. You can borrow mine, if you want. I'm curious about what's going to happen next."

"Bullshit. You love the feeling of power, are addicted to it. Controlling others is what gets you off, always has."

Mason ignored Pie's accusation, brushing it away with a wave of his hand, as if it wasn't even important enough to discuss. "Pie, I need you. There aren't many Citizens I can trust."

"I bet. What makes you think you can trust me?"

"Did you know there are only seven of us left from the time of Copper Mountain?"

"No."

"All right, all right. How about this? Can you honestly tell me you wouldn't like another look at the Blues? As I'm sure Zinc informed you, Jacky sent a probe that has just been returned by the Starship Hawking. Wouldn't you at least like to review the information he sent us?"

Pie looked away.

Mason smiled broadly and settled back, snuggling comfortably into his chair.

Pie returned his attention to Mason. "Are you aware of an analysis of the microwave beams by a Citizen named Kirchner?"

"Kirchner...no, I can't recall anyone by that name."

"You lying bastard. We're burning away the atmosphere with those microwave energy beams. Where are you getting the water for the out-ship trains? I suppose you've also stopped mining Europa for water and are now stealing it from Earth."

"You're so argumentative. What did that woman do to you this time?"

"Answer me, damn it!"

"All right, Pie. Take a breath and settle down. The Earth has plenty of water. A few million tons now and then won't make any difference. Mining Europa is too expensive, inefficient."

"You're supposed to be our leader, the guardian of the Project."

He tried to see past the black ellipses that served as eyes, to see the man inside, but saw nothing. "What happened to you, Mitch?"

"The only thing that happened is that I succeeded. I saved humanity. As for the Earth, I don't recall that as being part of the project."

Pie was stunned by the admission.

"Anything else?" Mason asked.

"You...you're a sociopathic narcissist. You didn't save humanity. We all did, and especially Roxanne. And you damn well know the ultimate victory was to be the recovery of the Earth."

"If you say so."

"The cities are falling into terminal disrepair, rotting with corruption, but then...corruption has even found its way here. Hasn't it, Mitch? A group of Unders tried to kill me. Did you know that?"

"Crackpots."

"No, not crackpots. It was organized. They nearly succeeded. They risked certain death to attack me. They were dedicated to their cause and brave."

"Brave? An Under?"

"Stop it, Mason. You know damn well that the only difference is our access to the matrix. You are the one who created an underclass."

"There's only so much to go around. We can't promise regeneration to everyone," Mason said.

"One of the anarchists mentioned the Friends of the Earth. What do you know about them?"

"Well, that sounds like us."

"You're no friend of the Earth and not my friend either."

"Friend, colleague, old time acquaintance. They're all the same."

"The hell they are. I never realized how twisted you've become."

Mason remained as he was, his face devoid of expression.

Pie lowered his head and slowly moved it from side to side. "This is sick. This is really sick. I almost wish...."

Mason picked up the unfinished thought. "Wished the assassins had succeeded? Yes, that is your problem. In a sense, most of our contemporaries ultimately committed suicide. Most simply allowed death to catch up with them by failing to remove themselves from harm's way. True, I could have brought them back but what's the point? They'd just do it again. Even you, standing on the edge of that cliff night after night. It was plain what your thoughts were."

"What gives you the right to spy on me?"

"We watch over all our Citizens, just like a mother watches over her children. In fact, you might even say, I saved your life by bringing you Home. And let's talk about leadership. Who are you to bellyache about leadership? I've lived and strived for the Project every planet-year, year in and year out, but you? You return from a deep voyage, with many years simply skipped over while suspended in stasis, and stay here less than a month before running off to your little hideaway in the mountains, playing with your seeds and living the fantasy that you're some kind of Johnny Appleseed, as if that crap hole of a planet will ever be ready, and living with that...person, Roxanne whatever last name you gave her this time."

"Leave her out of it!"

"All right, no need to get so touchy. Bend, Pie."

"You asshole, I'm regenerating and getting the hell out of here. I know where there is at least one person I can trust and who loves—"

"I love you, Pie."

"You don't even know the meaning of the word."

Mason remained seated his hands folded in his lap. "Well, if you're referring to your current Roxanne plaything, I'm afraid I have some bad news for you. It seems she decided to take a dive off that cliff you seem so attracted to."

Pie felt like he was shrinking. The room looked as if it were moving away from him. It wasn't possible. "No!" His voice sounded small to his own ears, like it was coming from far away. "What did you do? You sick bastard!"

"Me? Nope. Afraid not. Did you say something that clued her in?"

Pie paused and then continued. "God damned Zinc. But I had blocks on any search."

"Come on, Pie. You know her better than I. Do you think your blocks would stand up if she decided to find a work around? Smart woman."

"No! No! No!" With each denial, he took another stiff-legged step toward Mason.

"Visual on," Mason ordered.

Pie froze. Out of the corner of his eyes he saw the flickering of movement. Slowly, he turned his head. It was Roxanne, standing on the ledge, with the wind blowing her white gown in swirls around her. She looked up, as if knowing that Pie was watching. He did not see anger in her face, only immense sadness, and then she spread out her arms, as if she were about to fly, and dove off the ledge. The image froze.

"I can show you her landing, if you'd like. I guess it qualifies more as a crash than a landing. Spectacular. She was fearless and decisive. I'll grant her that. Typical Roxanne."

Pie collapsed to his knees and knelt with his face in his hands. He trembled and cried without dignity, without concern for himself.

Mason turned the screen off. While he watched the hardened operative sob like a child, his lips curled in disgust.

"Stop this!" Mason ordered. "I can always whip up another for you. Although why you would want me to eludes me. Let's see," he said as he thought. "I think this is the sixth one to kill herself. Really, Pie. You know, I have Jack Nichol's DNA somewhere. Don't you think it'd be amusing if we brought both of them back and then see how you faired? Amusing as hell."

Pie reached for his handgun. He grasped the butt and pulled it, aiming at Mason, who remained slouched in his chair and smiling. He pulled the trigger until the gun was empty. The hypersonic bullets left the muzzle at a leisurely pace and when they neared Mason, it appeared that he pushed each one aside so they passed by and continued toward the bulkhead. While Mason was focused on the bullets, Pie drew his knife and threw it.

Whatever force was used to control the bullets had no effect on the knife; it flew straight and true, but the blade passed through the vision of the seated man and was lost from sight as it became embedded in the chair. Pie could only stare.

A broad smile spread across Mason's face. "Amazing, isn't it? The holographic engineers have made truly remarkable progress, don't you agree?"

"Mason, show yourself!"

"Really shoddy behavior." Mason said. "Shocking. Even though you've threatened many times, I believe this is the first time you actually tried to kill me. I forgot about that knife you are so fond of. My mistake. I must remind myself never to underestimate you."

"Mason!" Pie bellowed as he searched wildly about the room, crashing into invisible furnishings and falling to the floor, to rise again. "Mason, I want you!"

The seated apparition of Mitchell Mason continued to talk, though Pie was far beyond hearing.

"I had so hoped that you could be reasoned with. Oh, well."

"Mason, you bastard, you son of a bitch, you black-eyed coward, face me!" He no longer knew restraint and began picking up pieces of invisible furniture and crashing them against the wall, causing them to splinter back into visibility, all the while with the background shriek of air being sucked through the bullet holes in the bulkhead. It was a mindless fury that tossed his body about the room, heedless of pain or injury.

A furry figure stepped from behind an optical shield and shot a dart into the berserk Citizen. Other Citizens rushed in to plug the holes in the bulkhead.

Pie never even felt it. The ultra-fast sedative took effect and he slumped forward. He fell onto a low table, making his limp body look like it was suspended above the deck with his bloodied hands draped onto the deck.

Gary Moreau

Chapter 10

Mitchell Mason finally did make a real appearance, his fine hair and tufts of beard, cotton-candy pink. He was far from the pudgy and vulnerable figure that he portrayed; his body bulged with muscle. He surveyed the damage done to his suite and then the unconscious form of Pie Traynor. His pink lips parted in a smile to reveal teeth the color of blood. He wound his way through the room, avoiding the few items that Pie had somehow missed in his rampage, and stopped, looking down at Pie's back. A lanky Citizen covered by short brown fur was holding the spent sedative gun and walked over to stand next to Mason.

"Well, Joshua, what do you think?" Mason asked as he scratched his neck.

"That was an unnecessary risk."

"Not really. He's big and strong but he hasn't taken advantage of enhancement. I could take him. In fact, I think it'd be fun."

"Father, I would strongly oppose such a foolhardy act. We've both seen what he can do."

"There's a reason he's been our best operative. He's one of the toughest men I've ever met and that's without taking into account his physical attributes. All natural by the way."

"I know. Remember father, I've also known him since Copper Mountain. My concern is that Pie has flexed one too many times."

"Yes," Mason agreed, without verbalizing that he considered Pie's self-destructive condition to be one of his most appealing characteristics.

"It's time to turn to other options," Joshua said. "Lem Gan has recovered from his injury and is ready to go."

"No, I don't think so," Mason said slowly, considering. "Traynor is still very effective. If he sets his will to a task, it will get done. The most consistently effective operative we've ever produced. And, he does have the unique experience of having been to Angkor-3. My instincts tell me to stick with him."

"But, you heard him. He's burnt. He's not going, regardless of the consequences."

"Not so fast. Despite what he says, his attitude seems to indicate unwavering loyalty to the Project. All he needs is a little editing."

"You mean like I used to do when I was a kid, cut and paste?"

They both laughed at the absurd comparison.

"Very good, Joshua. That's exactly what I mean."

Joshua considered. "It would require the use of two regeneration units. Do we have another mature clone?"

"Of course we do, son. I always have one or two spare clones ready to go for key personnel. Don't you find that reassuring?" He smiled, revealing his blood red teeth to the furry man, who managed a small smile in return. "However, we don't have much time. The last train leaves in twenty hours. Any later and the Hawking will be beyond reach."

"There's another problem. All the regeneration units are in use."

"That's no problem. Name two in the chambers."

"Well, there's Edwards, a city engineer from Cago, and a comm-ship master, Garcia, from Paz."

"Dump them."

"But—"

"Dump them."

"All right, father...if that's what you really want. We won't be able to recover their memories. They will be truly dead, both body and matrix dead."

"Do you think I don't know what?"

"No, father. What do you want me to do with the bodies?"

"The usual. Add them to the Under protein-pool. They're certainly going to eat well this week." He laughed, but Joshua could not bring himself to join in. Mason's face turned sour and he glared at Joshua, who responded by glancing away.

"Do you have a problem with that, Joshua?"

"No...it's just.... No, I'll get started."

"What's bothering you? You remind me of an Irish terrier I used to have when I was a boy. Whenever we left him at home, he'd go to the window and stare out at us, as if he had just lost his last friend." He put his muscular arm over Joshua's thin, furry shoulders and directed him to a love seat. They sat together. Mason put his arm around Joshua and pulled his head down to rest against his shoulder. He began petting the fur on Joshua's head.

"I suppose you're missing your mother again," Mason said.

"I do miss her."

"Jane was special. I have fond memories of her, but you remember how it was when I regenerated her for you. Unending arguments. I think it's best if we just remember her."

"I don't know, father. I feel...tired. It's only been seven years since my last regeneration and I already feel old."

"Does this have anything to do with your visit to New Berlin and those damn New People?"

Joshua sat up and turned to face his father. "I don't think so, but I'm glad you brought that up. There's something wrong with them, something's missing. It's not just cruelty...it's as if they can't even sense feelings in others. I don't trust them."

"We don't need trust. We have a contract."

"A contract?"

"It has teeth," Mason said with confidence.

"Did you have a chance to review the record of the attack on Lem Gan? The attack that injured Citizen Gam and killed Citizen Ramy."

"There wasn't much to review. And the attack on Traynor didn't reveal much either. There are crazy people down there. Caro Slin and her people are so inept they have yet to capture even one of the terrorists alive. It'd be a real pity if I have to deny her regeneration. She is such a kick."

"I've looked at it too," Joshua said. "The actual attack on Gan and Ramy occurred during a blank period in the record. The New People know how to shield. I can personally attest to that. Do you think they're involved?"

"You'd be surprised how much technology has leaked down to the Unders. There is, or more likely was, an underground organization that laughingly calls itself the Friends of the Earth. It consists mostly of sea-people. Have you heard of it?"

"No."

"They are anarchists, bent on the destruction of the Technocracy. I would contend that simply the use of a shield is not an automatic indictment of the New People. On the other hand, even if there is some kind of conspiracy involving the Friends of the Earth and the New People, I've taken care of it. The raft-villages of the sea-people are ninety-percent destroyed."

Joshua straightened and pulled away from Mason's caressing hand.

"Don't get all hung up on words," Mason said. "Think of it as a pre-emptive strike, a well-considered measure to return order where there is chaos. They'll re-populate, in a couple of centuries."

"I'm not so sure of that. How can you justify killing off an entire segment of people, when humanity is barely hanging on? When's the last time you visited Earth?"

"You're starting to talk like Pie. It's irrelevant. There are plenty of humans, particularly when you include the diaspora. Humanity is safe from extinction and Earth is a junkyard, a place to scavenge parts for the real future of humanity, here on Home."

"I don't like that kind of talk, father. You seem to be surrendering the Earth to oblivion, and Home to the New People. I suppose you're even going to allow them to take their Unders with them."

"They insist, but a good plan is like any living creation, as it grows, it is trimmed here, allowed to grow there. Enough of this. It's time for us to put our friend and colleague to sleep. He's in desperate need of regeneration. We saved him, you know."

Mason called in the regeneration technicians. The chief tech and his assistant entered the chamber and bowed.

"Arise," Mason said without looking at them. "Take him to the regeneration chamber. His clone is thawed and waiting. I want you to do a series of deletions. Delete the memory of our little discussion today, to be certain, delete the last month of memories and I want you to delete all memories of anyone named Roxanne or Wiley. I also want you to insert some memories I've harvested from another citizen. This will mean you have to dump Garcia and Jacobs."

The chief technician stared at him.

Mason finally turned his gaze toward him. "Do you have a problem? What do you not understand?"

"Garcia and Edwards will be truly dead and what you've asked me to do will cause terrible pain, severe agony in the subject when his memories are stripped, and even more pain when another's memories are inserted."

"Yes, it will. He can take it. He's a tough old bird."

"What do you want us to do with the bodies? The usual? Add them to the protein supply of the Unders?"

"That will be fine for Garcia and Jacobs, but not Traynor. Jettison Traynor's body. That carcass has enough toxin in it to kill any Under who even tasted it." Mason laughed.

The technicians hesitated but then joined in his laughter, not really understanding what they were laughing about, but they wanted Mason to know that they agreed with whatever Mason thought or desired. They wanted to assure themselves a clean regeneration when their turn came round again.

While Pie's body was being carried into the corridor, Mason considered. Overall, he was pleased. Pie Traynor would serve his needs well, and the addition of Zinc's memories would not only take the sharpness out of Pie's righteous indignation, it would keep him from focusing too closely on recent events. Things were working out quite nicely.

He removed the knife that was buried to the hilt in the back of the chair and then sat down. He studied the diamond knife for a few minutes; it was a beautiful artifact.

"Joshua."

"Yes, father."

He held the knife out to him. "Put this in Traynor's cabin. It's like a talisman for him. He's going to need all his confidence for the next mission."

Joshua took the knife and left to go to Traynor's cabin.

Mason watched Unders cart away the contents of his ruined suite, but his mind was on Pie Traynor. Traynor could be counted on to protect the Project and would not use whatever he discovered to grab power for himself. In fact, he was so ripe that, with just a little push, he would cease to exist at all.

Mason stroked his tusk-like beard and felt immense satisfaction. He liked the touch of his own fingers better than that of any others.

Gary Moreau

Chapter 11

Pie awakened swathed in pain and sweat. He instinctively knew this was disintegration and desperately tried to hold onto his most important memories. He began repeating Roxanne's name, but there was nothing he could do to resist the tearing away of his mind, a ripping, layer by layer. The pain was a fiery scorching and he screamed and begged for release, but then he lost the knowledge of where, or why he was being tortured. There was nothing but pain. He lost speech and the knowledge of words so that only his screeching cry remained, until that also was taken. Yet, even then, his mouth opened with the soundless and thoughtless expression of unbearable pain. Ultimately, that too was gone. His face became the rubbery mask of an idiot, his tongue protruding and mouth drooling.

When Pie became aware, he was lying on his sleeping pad in his cabin. His head beat with each pulse of blood. He closed his eyes tightly against the painful stab of light. His mind was a hodgepodge, a salad of memories, a nightmare mixture of confusion. He opened his eyes again, this time just a crack. A dark hand passed in front of his vision and came to rest on his forehead. The hand was soft and cool. He turned his head and, with effort, focused his vision. It was an Under-woman; her skin was such a dark ebony that it seemed to have a sheen and her eyes, a rich golden brown. Her hair was thick and kinky, and stood out wildly.

"How do you feel?" she asked in a toneless whisper.

Pie continued to stare at the woman, blinking back tears of photophobia. Her teeth were too white. They should be black like her lips, he thought, and wondered at the absurdity of such an idea.

"My name is Shana-8. Your name is Citizen Pie Traynor."

"I know my own name," he replied, his voice gravely gruff.

"I will attend you during your recovery from regeneration."

She brought a cup of thick, orange fluid to his lips and dribbled a few drops into his mouth. It was a sedative and his eyes drifted shut.

When he awakened a second time, he was alone. Memories swirled in his head. "Childhood first, always childhood first," he instructed himself.

It was a warm summer night, long ago. They were playing hide and seek. There was a tarred wooden pole topped with a silver-capped light, shedding a cone of brightness onto the black, asphalt road. It was home

93

base and other children ran about it, like moths around a flame. He was hidden in a dark shadow, but soon he would make his break for the pole.

"Olly olly oxen free." He smiled.

Other memories insisted on recognition, bizarre, uncomfortable recollections. He recoiled from their touch.

It was cool sidewalks on a summer morning with a bright, blue sky that seemed to stretch forever. It was love letters, laboriously crafted, each letter of each word a different color, handed with a blush to the little girl and then a hasty retreat to the far corner of the schoolyard.

It was a little girl, wearing a turquoise dress with big, black polka dots, riding her tricycle. He had kissed her handle grips and now her hands were touching his kisses. What was her name?

The door to his cabin whisked open and he turned without urgency to look. It was the woman, as dark as a moonless night.

She bowed her head. "Would you like me to return later?"

He pursed his lips and then shook his head. He stretched, arching his back and feeling the strength in his chest. He extended and contracted the bulky muscles of his arms and legs. Then he noticed, with alarm, that his left forearm was bare; his link was missing. In its place, a gold band encircled his wrist.

"Where is my link?" he demanded.

She hesitated for a moment, as if confused. "It's...on your arm."

Pie raised his arm in front of his eyes and inspected the thick, gleaming band. He attempted an uplink.

"Home Control," said the disembodied voice in his mind. "Can I be of assistance?"

Pie broke off the communication and entered the surveillance network. He focused on a gathering in a far arm of Home. They had the black eyes of Citizens but were dressed in circus costumes with sideshow hair sprouting from their faces and occasionally from their scalps. The vision triggered memories and they burst forth as if they'd been waiting in ambush.

Sweat oozed from the pores of his skin. It wasn't right! He saw himself in Cisco City with a woman who had a gold skull instead of hair. She was laughing loudly, her mouth wide, revealing golden teeth. He saw his hand, his fingers tipped with sharp black fingernails, reach out with a jeweled knife and slice the breasts off a writhing Under-woman. He saw a black-nailed hand raise one of the severed breasts to his mouth and felt excitement and sexual stimulation.

"No!" he screamed.

Another memory insisted itself. He saw his hand reach out again with the knife, this time lower.... "No!" He felt sick. He was nauseated, deeply disgusted and angry.

"Citizen Traynor," a voice said as soft hands pulled on his shoulders, trying to restrain him, but they were as nothing to him. With a negligent sweep of his arm, he brushed her away and knocked her to the deck. The awareness of place and time returned. He wiped the sweat from his forehead.

The woman crawled to her feet, keeping her back tight against the bulkhead of the cabin. "Are you all right?" she asked without reproach.

But Pie could not meet her eyes, could not even speak, afraid to trust his own tongue. He forced his mind blank and held his body rigid. He was afraid of his own memories.

"Leave," he ordered.

The woman stepped quickly from the room and escaped to the corridor.

His eyes drifted about the plainness of his cabin until they came to rest on some scratches on the steel wall adjacent to his sleeping pad. It was a crudely shaped heart with the initials "PT + RW" scratched into the center. He couldn't recall having seen it before. How did it get there? He wondered. And who is "RW"? He started to recall recent memories, but pulled away from them at once. He needed another source of information.

"Home Control, send Shana-8 to my quarters."

"Message received."

Within moments, Shana-8 was at his doorway. He opened the portal for her but, when she entered, she immediately backed up against the bulkhead, maximizing her distance from him within the confines of the small cabin.

"Shana-8, this is a difficult time for me."

"I understand—"

"The hell you do!" He looked down and back up before continuing. "You know nothing. As I was saying, this has been an especially difficult transition for me. I'd like your help."

She folded her hands in front of her bosom and bowed her head. "I live to serve." She stepped forward. "I know your pleasures and I am skilled." She placed her hand on his thigh and began to caress it.

Pie knocked her hand away, his faced contorted with anger.

Shana backed up against the doorway to the corridor.

He tried to see her eyes, but her head was bowed too deeply. He took a breath and slowly released it before continuing. "Look, let's start over. What I need is information. I need to know myself." It was a difficult confession for a Citizen to admit and even more difficult to speak of it; memory was everything. "Do you understand?"

She nodded, but did not hazard a verbal answer, unsure of the response it would precipitate.

"Do you know very much about me?"

She stood as she was.

"Well? Speak up! Do you know me?"

"I have studied you," she said in an even voice and then quickly added, "to serve you well."

"Tell me what you know."

She hesitated, wanting to avoid another outburst. Pie waited quietly, so she spoke. "You were born in the old territory of Iowa, in the year 2094. You were the Assistant Director at Copper Mountain. You—"

"I'm more interested in what you know about my recent past."

She looked up quickly, but then slowly raised her open palms and shrugged.

"You don't know. Is that what you're saying?"

She nodded.

"Do you know someone in my recent past with the initials 'RW'?"

"No. Perhaps it is someone you met in Cisco City."

It was a thought he'd been avoiding, but he could no longer escape its grasp. He became quiet. Shana kept her eyes on him.

Pie dipped back into his memories, but shied away again. "What do you know about my activities in Cisco?"

"Well," she began, her eyes shifting about as she thought, "well...you were sought after by the other Citizens and led a very active social life." She stopped.

"Would you say I led a moral life, in terms of an Under?"

"I cannot make such judgments."

"Cannot...or will not?"

She did not look up.

Pie's posture slumped. He rubbed his raw eyes with heels of his palms. He looked up and caught her watching him.

"Damn it, Shana-8, help me! Please. I don't understand." He covered his face with his hands.

She took a half step toward him and began to reach out, but then stopped and pulled back. Her eyes filled with tears. She didn't want to, but could not avoid sharing his pain; it had always been that way with her. She looked upward, at the overhead, and opened her mouth as if to speak, when Pie interrupted whatever she was about to say.

"You may leave now," he said in a deathly voice, anger and anguish so mingled as to be inseparable. "Leave!"

The door slid open and she hurried from the room.

Pie activated his personal safeguards and lay back on the sleeping pad. The pad began working along his body, trying in vain to ease his tension. He ordered it still. His arms were at his sides, while he clenched and unclenched his fists. If these truly are my memories, he thought, and what other conclusion is there? Then they must be faced. He gritted his teeth, grinding molar against molar.

The vision of the desecrated and tortured woman returned to his mind. He tried to remember more but, as with all memories, some parts were clear, while others remained hidden in a haze. He tried to focus on the hands with the sharp black fingernails, but the more he concentrated the less distinct they became. It just didn't feel right. The emotions and perverse act felt alien. He withdrew from the memory.

Who is 'RW'? he wondered. The woman he had painfully destroyed for depraved pleasure? The woman with the gold skull?

"Control, I want a list of all Citizens with the initials 'RW'."

He turned his head and the view screen materialized against the dull blue of the bulkhead. A list of forty-seven names appeared, twenty-three were women. None triggered a memory.

"Control, send the biographical information on these Citizens to my personal data storage."

Chapter 12

Mason had just entered his suite when a technician at Control contacted him.

"First Citizen Mason, the person you have on grade-one surveillance is accessing personnel data."

"What's he doing?"

"He's searching for data on all active Citizens with the initials 'RW'. Is that important?"

Mason was amazed, but did not share his amazement with Control. "This is a very ill Citizen. It is vitally important that he not receive any data on an inactive Citizen named Roxanne Wiley. I want her files expunged, totally."

"You want me to destroy all that remains of a Citizen's existence? True death? ...I don't know."

"Do you know who you are online with?"

"Yes, First Citizen Mason."

"Very good, Citizen Robbins. You see, I know who you are too and, if you ever expect to regenerate again, you will follow my orders, at once."

"Yes, Citizen, it will be as you say."

"Yes, it will."

Mason downlinked. He leaned back in his chair as he thought. No damage, but Traynor would have to be handled with extraordinary finesse. He smiled; the challenge was entertaining and the outcome inevitable.

Mason uplinked. "Pie, this is Mitch. I just wanted to see how you were doing and invite you over. We have some important information to discuss. I have a mission for you."

"Not now."

"Excuse me?"

"I said, not now! I'm not ready."

There was a pause. "All right, Pie. If you're having difficulties, you know you can always come to me. You and I have a special bond and, well...I know it sounds kind of sappy, but you're like a brother to me."

There was quiet on the circuit. Finally, Pie responded. "I'm sorry, Mitch. I'll be all right. I just need a little more time."

"Then you've got it."

"Thanks, Mitch."

Mason disconnected and leaned forward, pulling on the pink hair that stuck out from his face like tusks. He began murmuring. "Time, my dear Pie, is something I do not have. We'll have our meeting sooner than you think."

Chapter 13

Pie had completed his initial perusal and found nothing pertinent. None of the "RW" Citizens had ever been to Cisco City. He reentered the data network and called forth all Citizens with the initials "RW" for the last three hundred years. The list grew to three hundred and sixty-four names. He began reading down the list, saying each name aloud. When he got to the name "Roxanne Wiley", he paused. He could recall nothing about such a person, yet, there was something familiar about it. He called up the personnel file on the inactive Citizen and it started to spill across the screen.

"Roxanne Wiley, born February 16, 2104, in old Detroit. First regeneration, although limited to body alone, 2312—" The flow of information came to an abrupt halt.

That was impossible. Pie reentered the data network, but this time could not even locate a trace of information on a Citizen named Roxanne Wiley. There was nothing, except the one line of data on his temporary screen. Was the Home matrix, with all its built-in redundancy, beginning to fail? Everything was based on the matrix. If it failed, Home itself would disintegrate and the Project would fail, just when they were so close to success. He ran a competency check on his link and found it up to specification.

"Control, I've discovered a malfunction in data storage."

"What is the nature of the malfunction?"

"Data is being lost from Citizen files," Pie replied in a reasonable tone.

"You are mistaken."

"I am not mistaken," this time more forcefully. "I was accessing information on inactive Citizen Roxanne Wiley when the file went blank."

There was a slight pause. "There is no inactive Citizen named Roxanne Wiley."

"That's what I'm trying to tell you! There was one, but the file went blank and then fell out of the system altogether."

"We will investigate this occurrence and send you a report."

"No! I want it checked now!"

"Citizen, please, there is time. There is always time. Believe me, we take your report seriously and will give it our full attention, as soon as we're able."

"Connect me with Mitchell Mason."

A moment later Pie heard Mason's voice. It was syrupy smooth. "Can I be of assistance?"

"You sure as hell can! I was calling up information on an inactive Citizen and the file went blank. Can you believe it?"

"I'm...I'm shocked."

"You should be."

"I'll investigate right away. This could be an early sign of a severe malfunction in the matrix. I'll get right back to you."

"Thanks. And Mitch...it's important to me for personal reasons as well."

"You know me, Pie. I'm like a bulldog when I get hold of a problem. I'll find the answer and get back to you."

"I have another question."

"Go ahead."

"Why would a Citizen have a body only regeneration? I mean, no memories? What would be the point?"

"I have no idea. What would be the point? Sounds kind of perverted to me."

"But...you have oversight on regeneration. Have you ever approved a request like that?"

"Why no, I haven't. Let me get on this and I'll get back to you shortly."

"Thanks, Mitch."

"No problem, buddy. This could very important."

Pie shut the link down. Was it just his imagination? The name brought forth no images, no memories. He made the effort to recall anything about "RW" but barely touched on his memories when other memories insisted on recognition, bizarre, uncomfortable recollections reaching upward with filthy fingers, black fingernails as sharp as razors. He recoiled.

Why was I even in Cisco City? he asked himself. In the past, while on Earth, he had always gone to his house in the mountains. Why the break in the pattern of his life?

"Control, I want a real-time visual on my house. Coordinates—"

"We know the coordinates, Citizen Traynor."

The familiar craggy peaks appeared on the holo-screen. The dome of his house was nestled within the mountain's protective strength. It was daytime. He increased the magnification until he saw the surface of the dome come alive with swarming blackness. He did not intend to magnify any further and, instead, began to look along the pathway that led to his lookout cliff, when he received a message via his link.

"I think I have something for you," Mason said via the link.

"You do?"

"Yes. Why don't you come to my suite?"

"I'll be right there."

Pie picked up his knife and sheath off the desktop as he left the room and hurried as he walked the corridors to Mason's suite, but the closer he got, the more hesitant he became. It was as if for each two steps forward, he wanted to take one back. The door slid open and Pie stood on the brink, not in, not out. A pudgy Mason was sitting in a chair and next to him was an empty chair.

"Come in, Pie," he boomed.

Pie let his eyes roam the room. It was large, very large. Why the waste? he asked himself.

Mason smiled; he appeared jolly and plump. Seeing Mason helped settle Pie's unfocused anxieties. He still felt the fog of incomplete integration, but he walked forward with the appearance of confidence and sat in the chair next to Mason.

"Pie, I investigated this Roxanne Wiley thing and you'll never believe it." He laughed easily. "A data technician was trying out a new storage system and entered a fictitious name to test it. You just happened to key in as he was cleaning up the system." He shook his head. "Crazy, isn't it?"

Pie did not return Mason's smile, nor join him in laughter.

"Don't look so somber, Pie. The matrix is intact. You can stop worrying."

"There's more to this," Pie said. "I'm asking for help and you're giving me bullshit."

Mason was watching him sharply now.

"I had a relationship with someone with the initials RW. A close relationship."

"I know."

"You do?" Pie asked, leaning forward with interest.

"Her name was Rebecca Wong. She was an Under."

The name meant nothing to Pie. "And?"

"You know all about it. Why ask me?"

"I'm having some...difficulty with integration. I need confirmation."

Mason rubbed his hands along his jaw; it almost looked like he was tugging on something. "All right, Pie. I thought it best not to bring this up."

"They are my memories."

"True...as you wish. You were quite taken by her but then the relationship took a turn...to the dark side, I guess you could say. You had, well, I guess I'll call it fun with her. It's all right. We all slip from time to time. I'm not blaming you."

The next time Pie spoke his voice was hardly audible. "Mitch, I...."

"Go on, Pie."

He took a deep breath before continuing. "Is she still active?'

"Of course not. You know that."

"Was I, in any way, responsible for her being inactivated?"

"We're talking about an Under here, Pie. She wasn't inactivated. That wasn't an option. She died. I don't really want to get into this. I told you I'm not one to judge. Don't you remember anything about this unfortunate escapade?" Mason's voice was filled with concern and sympathy, but his eyes were a different matter; they searched for signs of rejection of his fabrication, and found none.

"You seem to know a lot about my activities in Cisco."

Mason smiled. "Plenty, but don't be so provincial. You judge yourself too harshly."

"It's about time someone made some judgments. I don't like the turn the Technocracy has taken."

"You should know, Pie."

Pie glared angrily at Mason, but then uncertainty and depression seeped upward. He lowered his gaze to stare at the gold band on his arm. Mason let him sit in silence and Pie did not see the fleeting smile of triumphant that flickered across his face. The seconds passed to a full minute before Pie broke the silence.

"Why did you really call me here?" Pie asked.

Mason chuckled. "Right to the point. I love that about you. The Star Grazer Hawking returned a message probe from Jacky Nichols."

"What?"

"It seems Jacky made some rather startling discoveries after you left him." Mason shifted his feet forward and back. He was no longer passive; he was energized.

"I didn't leave him. He refused to return."

"Relax, Pie. Bend. Don't get so defensive. Everyone makes mistakes."

"Mistake?"

"Jacky reports that the Blues are an advanced race, with technology far beyond ours. Now wait. Give me a chance to explain. He says they have shielded all traces of their advanced state and," he added slowly emphasizing each word, "they are immortal. I think we've found the home world of the Slan. I've been waiting for this. We've developed a planet buster and it's ready to go, but we need to learn their secrets first. True immortality," Mason said wistfully.

Pie shook his head. "Impossible. The only artifact I even saw was that medallion and necklace I brought back. There was nothing, and I mean nothing else, not even clothing. But it's not only that, the native we contacted had no drive, no sense of vitality. No, it's just not possible."

"Which brings me to what I want to ask you. I want you to go back there and learn what you can. It will be an opportunity to either prove you were right in the first place, or...maybe Jacky did discover something fabulous. Pie we need their technology."

"What for? We're doing all right."

"Perhaps I did overemphasize the possibility of immortality, but what I really mean is, we need new technology and we need it desperately. Do you remember Fredrich Heinz?"

The name was familiar. The picture of a thin, intense Citizen came to mind, and then other memories followed. He and his followers had gone planet-side in the thirty-first.

"As I recall," Pie said, "his belief was that humans should adopt to life on Earth as it is."

"There's more to it than that. It was his theory that progress in the Technocracy had slowed because of our prolonged lifespan. He believed that true creativity only happened when the brain was plastic, as is found in the young. If you stop and think about it, most breakthroughs occur to those in their twenties."

"Are you telling me he still lives? If he rejected regeneration, how is that possible?"

"No, he's joined the true dead. After all, we control regeneration, except for that small operation in Cago. But he did establish a colony in the Sierra Nevada Mountains of old California. We kept a hands-off policy, after all they were fellow Citizens, even if they were, let's say confused. In retrospect that might have been a mistake. The colony is now quite large. Heck, it's a city, particularly if you include their Unders. They call themselves the New People. About fifty years ago they succeeded in blocking our surveillance sensors, but we have continued in a relationship. We've supplied them with power and they've supplied us with knowledge, first of a biologic nature, but more recently of a technical nature as well."

Mason placed what appeared to be a flabby hand on Pie's arm. "I'm going to be frank. The Project is in trouble. Our agents report the New People are on the brink of developing a practical system of cold fusion. It won't be long and our monopoly on power will be broken."

"Is that bad thing?"

Mason studied Pie for a moment before he spoke. "Do you find it amazing that, even after all these years, we're basically the same people we always were."

Pie gave a noncommittal shrug.

"Listen to me. We are barely holding our own in the rehabilitation of Earth and our researchers haven't come up with any substantial breakthroughs in centuries."

"Perhaps Heinz was right. Perhaps when we use regeneration to prolong life, no new ideas are possible. Nothing is new."

"Stop it, Pie. Deep down you know that isn't true."

"Why are you telling me all this?"

"I'm educating you to the economic and political realities of the Project as it stands now, in the year 3998. We can't even afford to spend the resources needed to support another mission, much less a new colonization."

"What have these so-called New People done to put us in their debt?"

"Let me give you an example." A table appeared to Pie's left and then a lounge along the bulkhead and two more chairs; within seconds, the "empty" room was fully furnished, including an over-sized, sleeping pad. The only open area was a pathway from the doorway to where Mason sat.

"You think this cheap trick is valuable? I think it's crap."

Mason frowned. "That was just an example," he said with a bite to his words. "There are many others, the new links, improved food production, and new guidance systems. They have assisted us in controlling fast viruses and have promised to clean up the regeneration process to prevent memory lapses. Are those just cheap tricks?" He leaned toward Pie. "We need the technology from Angkor-3 so we can break the strangle hold of the New People. We need to stand on our own again, or the Technocracy will be reduced to the level of an Under and the Project will languish."

"What do these mutants look like?" Pie could just imagine; they probably had thick, armored skin and bulging eyes, perched on the ends of long stalks. In a word, human-bugs, designed to survive on a world dominated by insect life.

"You'll soon see for yourself."

"Why do you say that?"

"Two New People will be accompanying you on your trip to Angkor-3. After you've obtained the technology, to secure it you'll do away with them. Make it look like an accident."

"What in God's name are you talking about? I haven't agreed to go anywhere and, even if I did, I sure as hell wouldn't take any of these New People with me, much less kill them."

"Bend, but don't break, because soon you'll bend the other way."

"Can that shit. You're not dealing with some first-regenerate sludge. You're blowing smoke at me, Mitch."

Mason leaned back in his chair and waited a moment before continuing. He spread his fingers, imploring. "Please listen to reason. The New People are financing this mission and they've agreed to cancel our debts. You know the old saying, 'you byte my hand and I'll byte yours'. Anyway the only reason they'd be willing is that they expect to come back to Earth with the new technology. I'm sure they plan on cutting us out of the loop."

"No deal. I sense you're manipulating me and that is one thing I cannot tolerate."

"How could you ever accuse me of that?" Mason asked, his mouth held open in a mask of amazement. "I know you as well as you know yourself. It's not even possible to manipulate you."

"Shut up, Mitch. I'm getting out of here. If you want to talk with me further, about something else, you'll find me planet-side at my house."

Pie stood and began walking to the door.

"Wait, Pie." With what appeared to be effort, Mason pushed himself out of the chair, onto his thick, stubby legs. "The Project, all we've worked for, will fail without your help."

Pie paused and turned to face Mason. "Maybe that's just what the Project needs. Maybe the Project has already failed. I'm sure you have a backup for me anyway. You see, I know you as well. I won't do it, Mitch. Send someone else to do your dirty work."

Pie turned away and walked out of the room, already thinking about gathering his few possessions and taking the next comm-ship back to Earth.

Chapter 14

Pie walked the curvature of the cylinder toward his cabin. When the portal to his cabin came into view, he stopped. There were two men with the eyes of Citizens standing outside. They were each holding the long, flared barrel of an energy cannon and facing in his direction. Although hardly an adequate defense, Pie slipped his knife into his hand, but kept it hidden. He renewed his approach, but walked lightly, prepared for instant action.

When he drew to within a few paces, he stopped. "What are you doing here?" he asked.

"Security." The one who spoke carried the weapon as if he had more than a casual acquaintance with its use.

"Who are you protecting me from? We're in the Prime Cylinder."

"Citizen Mason ordered it and his reasons are his own."

"Get out of here. I don't need any protection."

"We have our orders."

"To hell with it. Stand out here as long as you want. Rot for all I care, just get out of my way."

They parted to allow Pie plenty of room as he walked between them and entered his cabin.

As soon as his cabin door slid shut Pie uplinked. "Control, connect me with Mitchell Mason."

Mason came online. "Yes, Pie, what is now?"

"You know damn well what's wrong. Call those goons off before I'm forced to remove them myself. Protection? What bullshit. I don't need protection."

"Trust me."

"I'm done trusting you. Get rid of them."

Pie downlinked before Mason could respond. He walked over and sat down in his chair. After a few minutes he stood; he couldn't sit. Something urgent required immediate attention. What was it? He paced the floor of his small cabin and then stopped. Perhaps something in Jacky's report would trigger a memory.

"Home Control, send a copy of Citizen Jacky Nichols' report on Angkor-3 to my personal storage and can you locate that artifact I brought back from the planet of the Blues?"

"Searching."

Pie stood still while he waited. He told himself that simply reviewing Jacky's report was not a commitment; it didn't mean that Mason had succeeded in persuading him. There was some reason that he must return to his house in the Cascade Mountains. It was imperative, but the reason continued to elude him.

"Citizen Traynor, the artifact will be delivered in thirty seconds; the report has been transmitted. It is ready for your perusal."

"Extraordinary. Why so responsive now? It couldn't have anything to do with Mason could it?"

"I told my fellow technicians about you. You are not timeless. Original Citizens don't seem to have the grace to express appreciation. This isn't the first time I've dealt with you, Citizen Traynor."

"Who are you?"

"My name is Citizen Evans."

"I don't know you."

"I'm the one who saved your thankless hide on that landing pad outside Cisco. Does that jog your memory?"

"You are a confused man, Citizen Evans. I've never spoken with you before in all my lives. If this is an example of your memory, I should show appreciation that you were able to carry out a simple request, or maybe amazement would be more appropriate."

"We feel the same way about you. And I mean all of us. I doubt that there is a Citizen alive who hasn't heard of your colossal blunder with the Blues. This is Control, signing off."

The exchange did not sit well with Pie. It was not like him to offend, when offense was not called for, and what was that fantasy about saving his life all about? He shrugged and sighed. With the holes in his memory, anything was possible. He opened the transport door in the bulkhead and reached in to retrieve the irregularly-shaped, pearlaceous trinket. He let the gelatinous, maroon cord drape over the back of his hand.

Technical data about the necklace began to fill the screen. If Mason wasn't lying, then this, the only artifact Pie discovered during his visit, must be more than decorative. He reviewed the original analysis from a new perspective, suspending his disbelief. There were gold molecules and other exotic heavy metals scattered throughout a crystalline matrix, but there was no sense of order to it.

He squeezed the trinket in his hand; he couldn't concentrate, there was something important that he was supposed to do, a nagging sense of unfinished business, or an obligation.

As if in response to an unconscious command, a view of his house in the Cascades was called onto the screen, replacing the data. It was early evening and the insects had retreated for the night. The stark whiteness of his house seemed to glow in the faint light. Seeing his house meant nothing in particular. There was no answer there.

"Return to data about necklace," he commanded via his link. "Begin at one angstrom. Search for a scale that demonstrates a constant parameter." The speaking of the command required more time than the execution. There was a regularity. At the scale of 10,000 angstrom, there was always the same number of gold molecules, but never in the same arrangement. On that particular scale, the trinket could conceivably contain vast amounts information, if it could be accessed and interpreted. The hair prickled on his neck. It was all a matter of scale. He clutched the necklace in his hand and stared at it. It almost felt alive. On impulse, he slipped it over his head. The moment the medallion came to rest against his chest, his heart started to race. Something was happening.

Gary Moreau

Chapter 15

Mitchell Mason watched Pie via the surveillance he had installed, easily bypassing Pie's feeble blocks. Mason smiled, displaying his red teeth, while he watched Pie pick up the artifact from Angkor-3 and then slip it over his head so that the medallion rested against his chest. The furry man who stood next to him managed a small smile of his own.

Mason nodded. There was no doubt. Pie was hooked; he would go on the mission.

Joshua broke into his reverie. "I'm concerned about the New People. I suppose you're going to allow them to take their Unders with them."

"They insist. But, don't be concerned. After all these years, you should have more confidence in me. I am a virtuoso, son, a genius. Their two, unfortunate Unders 'accidentally' opened the wrong lock and took a bare-skinned walk in space, poor things. And, lo and behold, who turns up? A couple of Unders, who have been gracious enough to 'volunteer' to take the place of their less fortunate brethren. Traynor is not going to be an issue and neither are the—"

The room was shaken by a violent jolt and the rotation of the cylinder was momentarily altered, long enough to make them feel like their stomachs were rising into their chests. Neither man moved; any sense of movement in a cylinder signified disaster, usually of critical proportions.

"Control, what the hell is—" Mason began.

The monitor screen vanished. The embedded light-lines in the ceiling grew dim and the constant background rumble of air circulation ceased. It was quiet in the Prime Cylinder for the first time in nearly 2000 years. Joshua grabbed hold of Mason's arm with both hands and stood pressed against him, but his eyes remained fixed on the deathly glow of the ceiling.

"Let go of me!" Mason jerked his arm free.

Joshua withdrew a short distance, clutching his hairy hands in front of his chest.

"Control, this is Mitchell Mason, report!"

The voice that answered was hoarse with tension. "There's been a blow-out. The Prime Cylinder has been breached. It appears the entry cone is holding. We're still connected to the rest of Home but the torque on the cone is tremendous. We could break up at any moment."

"All right, don't panic." He waved his hand at Joshua, indicating for him to follow as he made his way to a hatch in the floor that led to an escape pod.

"Control, what explanation have you come up with?"

"We're working on it."

"Connect me with the chief engineer."

The hatch led directly to the escape pod. Mason lowered himself into one of the two seats and watched while Joshua closed the hatch. Only then did he feel secure.

"First Citizen Mason, this is Chief Engineer Rheiner," her voice was breathy.

"Get a hold on yourself!" Mason ordered as he powered up the escape pod, bringing the lights to full illumination.

"I've never seen anything like this," the engineer said.

"What do you mean?"

"After the breach, energy began to be siphoned off."

"To where?"

"The focus is not far from the cylinder, no more than a few hundred meters, but its moving away."

"Some kind of a craft, or a weapon? Joshua, activate the scanner."

The vision appeared before their eyes as if they had been reduced to the essence of pure mind and allowed to float freely in the vacuum of space. The ball of light flared with a brightness that would have blinded mortal eyes. Its surface pulsed with raw power, lines of pure, white energy were orbiting the core of brightness.

"What is it?" Mason asked, in awe for the first time in a millennium and not really expecting an answer.

"Citizen Mason," the engineer said.

"What?"

"Control tells me there is an enormously powerful link associated with the anomaly. It's bypassing control and communicating directly with the main matrix. Now there is interference coming from cylinder Alpha-18. I'm losing—"

"Mason, this is Jilla LineBFD/LineDHB. I have a splitting headache! I demand you stop whatever you're doing, immediately!"

"We are experiencing...technical difficulties. You must relinquish the channel so I can correct the problem," Mason replied.

"Jacques says that you have five minutes or we're going back to New Berlin. This is no fun. We never realized what a slip-shod organization this is or, I assure you, we'd never have agreed to participate in this silly mission. Now get it fixed!"

"Five minutes...how very generous of you."

"Yes, but generosity stretches only so far. We are trying our best to accommodate to your limitations, but enough is enough."

"Well, I wouldn't want you to stretch out of shape. Why don't you clear the channel so I can proceed."

"Citizen Mason, this is Home Control. The interference from Alpha-18 has ceased, but the power drain is worsening. That vortex out there is beginning to draw power directly from the solar collectors."

"I see." Mason stroked the tufts of his beard as he thought. "Control, where exactly did the blow-out occur?"

"Damage control is on scene. The hole is in the center of radian 2-B."

"2-B...that's right around Traynor's cabin, isn't it?"

"That is confirmed."

"I don't currently have access to surveillance data of his cabin. What does the surveillance record reveal after he put on the necklace?"

"Not much. After Citizen Traynor put on the necklace he looked surprised and then seemed to be fiddling with the medallion or pulling on it. A short time later there was an explosion that blew out the bulkhead and he was gone, sucked into space."

"Yes," Mason said as he continued to caress his tufts of pink hair. "And the energy absorbing artifact. From its current course can you extrapolate back where to where it originated?"

A few moments later, Control came back online. "It originated at the site of the explosion, Traynor's cabin."

"What's your name?" Mason asked.

"Citizen Evans."

"All right, Evans, dispatch a rescue craft to the site of the anomaly. It must be equipped with a functional stasis-capsule and must be in position within five minutes."

"That's going to be rather—"

"Do it, Evans!"

"Yes, Sir."

"Notify me when it's in position."

Joshua spoke. "I guess that means we better begin the final preparation of Lem Gan to replace Traynor. There's no time for another regeneration, nor do we have another ready clone."

"We'll see. I do have a backup Traynor clone. Prepare for the unexpected. I've told you that a thousand times."

"What good would that do? It wasn't a simple transfer, altering all those memories and such. We don't have time to do it all again."

"We'll see."

"What do you mean?"

"I have my suspicions," Mason said.

"What do you plan to do?"

"I don't know. I was thinking about, maybe, bringing back the dead."

"That's not funny, father."

"It's no joke, son."

They watched the miniature sun as it boiled with power until the rescue ship came into view. Winches and mechanical arms sprouted from the craft, suggesting the appearance of a scorpion.

"Control, instruct it to get closer."

"Citizen Mason, the shields won't hold. They'll be exposed to a lethal dose of radiation."

"Tell them to proceed without fear. They will receive immediate regeneration and ten-thousand bytes of credit will be deposited in their accounts."

The ship began to edge closer to the blinding ball of light.

"Father, there's no way they can have immediate regeneration."

Mason shrugged as he watched the ship draw closer to the lethal ball of radiation. When he was satisfied, he uplinked. "Control, inform the ship that the energy to the anomaly is about to be cut off. They are to move in at once and place whatever they find there in stasis for immediate transport to the regeneration center."

"Message sent and received."

"Good. Shut down the Primary Solar Collector."

The link, though alive, remained silent.

"Control, confirm!"

"Citizen Mason, Home has ancillary sources of energy to maintain itself for a short time, but if the Primary Collector is shut down, all the cities will be without power. There's risk of insect penetration. Anyone in a tube…well…Citizens are going to die. Lots of them. How can we regen—"

"Evans, do as I say, you piece of sludge! It'll only be for a few minutes. Do it!"

"What about the thruster-craft? Can they go without with power for a few minutes? My status screen indicates there are two-hundred and fourteen in flight at this time, many of them still involved in your attack on the sea—"

"Evans, do it now, or I swear, I will personally lop off your head and feed your carcass to the bugs!"

The bright ball of light in the blackness of space began to dim.

"Joshua, I want to be informed the next time Evans comes up for regeneration."

"He was only doing his duty."

"I listened to some of his exchanges with Pie. He shows no respect for Original Citizens. He is impudent. I require obedience! I have no intention of spending another lifetime with a subordinate who doesn't know his place."

The salvage craft blocked the dim object from further view.

"Citizen Mason, the rescue team has discovered a man!"

"Instruct the crew to put him in the stasis capsule and transport him to the regeneration center. When the man is in stasis, reactivate the Primary Solar Collector."

"Father, what's going on?"

"Just a hunch that paid off. I want Pie on this mission more than ever. If we're successful in salvaging him, it's all going to be worth it. This proves Jacky's claims. And be sure the artifact goes with him."

"Is that wise? Why risk losing it? It might be quite valuable."

"Valuable? It sat around in storage for more than forty years. It was not until Pie handled it that anything occurred. No, this is just the break we need to maintain our advantage over the New People. Control, what is the status of the Prime Cylinder?"

"Power has returned and rotation has stabilized. Traynor's cabin has been sealed off."

"Come on, Joshua, let's get out of here."

They climbed out of the escape pod, back through the hatch. Mason's room appeared fully furnished; apparently there were still a few circuits not up to par. An Under stood against the far wall, his eyes downcast, ready to serve.

"What now, father?" Joshua asked.

"Who would benefit most from Traynor's death?"

"I thought it was that necklace."

"No. The necklace didn't cause the blowout. It responded to the blowout. The assassination attempts at Cisco City have followed him to Home, just as I expected it would."

"The sea-people."

"Think for once. There's no way they could've acted without help and certainly not at Home itself."

"The New People."

"Would you get off that? I know you hate them but for God's sake think! Don't just react. Can you name a Citizen who would benefit from Traynor's death?"

117

Joshua was silent.

Mason continued. "Lem Gan would benefit. If Traynor is successfully transferred to his new clone, I'll want to do a brain scraping on Gan."

"But…Lem is my friend."

"Is he?"

"But, it'll be too late by then. You don't have to do a brain scraping on him. The last train for the Hawking will have left."

"True, but we'll be staying behind and it is to our benefit to know as much as possible. Control."

"Yes, Citizen Mason."

"Send a squad of my personal guards to arrest Lem Gan. Have them deliver Gan to the regeneration center and put him in stasis."

"Message received, squad dispatched."

"I hate all these strangers living in my cylinder," Mason said. "At least they are confined to the far end."

"Does that mean you want me to move out as well?"

"Son, what am I going to do with you? You and Pie, and a few others, are the only ones who really understand." Mason looked across the room at the Under. "Joe-54, are you and Shana-8 ready?"

The small man nodded without raising his face.

"Do you have any last questions?"

He shook his head.

"Good, come here and give me a big hug," Mason said.

The Under did as he was instructed and Mason wrapped his muscular arms around the small man, squeezing him against his chest. He released Joe-54 and turned his attention to Joshua. "This plan is developing into such a gorgeous creature. Come on, let's go find out Traynor's condition." He loosened his grip on the short, slight man and ruffled his straight black hair. "Joe-54, have Shana-8 waiting for me when I return. It'll be a long time before I again have the opportunity to take advantage of her outstanding qualities."

Joe nodded agreement and did not brush his hair back into place until Mason was out of sight.

A small crowd of curious Citizen technicians surrounded Traynor's transparent capsule when Mason and Joshua arrived. They parted to allow Mason a firsthand look. It was Traynor all right, but his clothing had disintegrated and his hairless skin was glossy and raven-black. The necklace hung around his neck and appeared unchanged.

Mason tipped his head slightly as he studied the man in the stasis-capsule. "He looks like he's been carved out of onyx. And look, the sheath is gone but that knife of his looks like it's fused into his arm."

A technician with orange skin stepped forward. He sported a ridge of green hair, which began at the tip of his nose and extended upward between his eyes and across his otherwise hairless scalp, presumably to continue down his back. "May I be of assistance?" he offered.

"Is he alive?" Mason asked.

"Amazingly enough, I think he is. I've never seen anything like it."

"Then you should be able to harvest his memories."

"Yes, I think we can."

Mason continued to study Pie.

"They always look like statues when they're in stasis," the technician offered.

Mason turned to face the man and, without uttering a word, caused him to step back. He then directed his attention to Joshua. "What do you think? Is there life beneath that glassy shell?"

"The artifact did function and presumably for a purpose."

Mason smiled his blood-red smile. "I'm pleased, Joshua. I think you are beginning to recover from...your recent doubts. I want you to supervise this regeneration, but don't take him out of the capsule until I give the word."

"Are you going back to the Prime Cylinder?"

"Yes. Are you afraid to take him out of the capsule? Look at all the help you'll have."

Joshua said nothing.

"Joshua."

"All right, father, but I won't have time to make additional adjustments in his memory, if he still has one. It'll be pretty much lock and load."

"Think positive. All we need is to add one more memory. The one where he agrees to this mission. Everything else is already done. Not much. Cut and paste. I'm counting on you."

"First Citizen Mason, this is Control. The squad leader reports that they will be unable to bring Citizen Gan as you—"

"When I give an order, I expect it to be obeyed!"

"Very well. I will instruct the squad leader to bring as much of him as they can."

"Explain."

"Citizen Gan put an energy cannon beneath his chin and blew off his head."

Mason paused as he thought. "I see. I guess there'll be no brain scraping tonight, except possibly off the walls." He chuckled and turned to catch Joshua's eyes, but Joshua was looking away.

"Joshua!"

"Yes, father."

"I'm depending on you. There is no backup. Don't let me down. We'll be using Traynor's final clone. You know how long it takes to grow one. I'll tell you when to begin."

"You can depend on me," he answered in a subdued voice.

"I know I can, that's why you live in Prime. When you've finished, put Traynor directly into a stasis-capsule in the passenger car of the out-ship. I don't have anything more to discuss with him that can't wait another two hundred years. And be certain the Angkor-3 necklace goes with him and, now that I think of it, if you're able to pry that knife off, send that as well. It seems to give him confidence."

Mason walked back down the corridor toward the Prime Cylinder. He felt pleased enough to whistle, for the first time in a century.

Chapter 16

The door of the glass-like stasis capsule opened without a hint of sound. Pie stumbled forward, but his fall was broken by two sets of hands. With effort, he was dragged and then lifted into the cocoon-bed, where he lapsed into a moaning unconsciousness. An ebony hand reached out to feel his brow, but he twisted away from the touch, as if it were fire. The two figures withdrew from the cabin, leaving Pie to deal with his personal demons by himself.

He recognized he was experiencing regeneration recovery and concentrated on a time long ago, a time of cane poles and sunfish, of firecrackers and BB guns, of snowballs and sleds, but it brought no relief. Where was he? There were holes. Dread grabbed his throat and made it difficult to breath, difficult to swallow. His mind was filled with gaps and contradictions.

He knew the routine. First seek peace and nothingness and then childhood. His heart was slowing and his breathing had quieted when a new onslaught of memories assaulted him. He clutched frantically at the bed, digging his fingers into the resilient surface and then reached out for anything, grasping, his arms waving about frantically trying to avoid being sucked into space. His eyes saw and then, finally, his mind. He saw the velvety brown surface of a cocoon bed.

His intellect told him he was safe but his muscles did not relax, nor did his breathing quiet. He slowly lowered his grasping hands to his sides. He focused on each muscle group until he was nearly at peace, but not quite.

If not self, then place, he instructed himself. He turned his head. It was a small rectangular room, with gray new-steel walls. A stasis capsule stood open in the corner and across the room from the cocoon bed was a cup chair. He was in the passenger car of a train. He was alone. He was Pie Traynor. He tentatively tried to dip into his memories but it seemed out of plumb, indefinite. A tremble of panic threatened to burst forth again and he shied away.

"Flow, Pie," he said to himself. "Flow. Let it unfold, be a part of it."

There was something...a mission, but he must go to his house! A vision slipped into his mind, of Mason slouched in his chair and smiling. But...he had refused...and agreed. Which is which? What is true? He searched deeper and recoiled from horrors worse than any nightmare.

121

He became aware of a tingle of life in the golden link around his wrist. He was not totally abandoned. There was hope. He sensed the train driver making minuscule adjustments as the ship rushed toward a rendezvous. He searched further. The ship was on a line to intercept the Star Grazer Hawking as it passed on the outward leg of its parabolic path around the sun, never stopping, never losing momentum.

He downlinked and pushed himself to a sitting position on the edge of cocoon. His feet rested on the cool surface of the deck. When he stood, a brief twirl of vertigo caused him to pause and take hold of the canopy of the cocoon. He walked over to a long panel in the wall and opened it with a thought; it contained suits and, in a transparent case in the door, his diamond dagger with a sheath he did not recognize and the strange necklace the Blue had given him.

Sight of the necklace cracked open a torrent of memories, of the Blues, of Cisco City and torture, of immense power filling him until…. He bit into his lip to deflect the stampede of painful memories that threatened to drag him into a sea of incoherent insanity. He squeezed the door to his memories shut.

He turned the new sheath over in his hand, inspecting it. Why a new sheath? He shrugged and buckled it onto his forearm, slid the dagger into place, and then reached without conscious choice to pull out a navy-blue bodysuit. As he stepped into it, he allowed a trickle of memory to return and tried to find his place in the confusion that rocked his sense of wellbeing.

He settled into the cup chair across from the cocoon-bed and experienced a sinking sensation in his viscera as he tried to force order and comprehension where there was none, filling spaces with plausible, but unremembered events. He was trying to reconstruct a rationale for his actions, but when the visions of Cisco came to mind he quashed them. He was so internally directed that he didn't hear the door to the cabin open. When he looked up, he was startled to see Shana-8 standing there; he had forgotten to safeguard his cabin on awakening.

She remained motionless, moving only her lips as she spoke. "Citizen Traynor, will you be needing assistance?"

"What are you doing here?"

"The train driver sent me."

"Who are you?"

"Shana-8."

"Do I know you? Have I ever seen you before?"

Shana looked down at the deck. "No," she said softly.

Pie looked her up and down, a womanly figure, but his gaze settled on her left wrist where there was a small gold band.

"Since when does an Under wear a link?" he asked.

Shana looked at her wrist before raising her gaze to meet his. "It's not a real link."

"What is it then?"

"The New People make us wear it. They use it to…communicate with us."

Pie lapsed into silence.

Shana waited as long as she could before speaking. "The others are waiting."

Others? He massaged his forehead with his fingertips. Now he remembered. "Damn Mason all to hell," he muttered. "Passengers."

"Excuse me?" Shana asked.

"I'll be there when I'm ready and not before!"

"Very well, Citizen." She bowed and backed out of the cabin. The door slid shut after her.

She was gone less than a minute when Pie uplinked. "Ship, send Shana-8 to my cabin."

When he detected her moving down the narrow corridor he opened the portal and, after a brief hesitation, she stepped through and reentered the room. She wasn't looking down and her hands weren't folded.

"What is it with you, Citizen? You send me away and then call me back. Just like back—I mean. Is this your way of demonstrating your control over me?" Her eyes glittered.

Pie leaned back in his chair and smiled; insolence was much better than whining obsequiousness. While he studied her, an enigmatic smile spread across his face. She began to back toward the portal.

"I'm the one to ask questions and you're the one to answer them," Pie said.

She said nothing.

"First of all, what the hell is an Under doing on a train?"

"Citizen Mason sent me. The New People expect Unders to attend them. We were sent to serve them...not you," she added with evident satisfaction.

"We? Just how many Unders are there aboard?"

"Two."

"And who else is aboard?"

"Two New People and the train driver."

Pie shook his head in amazement. He laughed quietly and without humor. "Shana, do you have any idea what you've let yourself in for?"

"I didn't choose. I'm just an Under, remember? But, if I had the right, I would've gladly chosen to go on the mission."

"Wipe that silly smile off your face. Your naiveté is offensive."

The smile vanished, but she stood straight and pulled her shoulders back to meet his gaze directly.

"So, are you prepared to help me with my needs, even if you do belong to the New People?" Pie asked.

Shana pressed her lips together so tightly that they lost their color. She reached up to begin pulling her suit open. She had experienced this scene many times before. She sent her mind to stillness and distance.

"What are you doing?" Pie asked.

She stopped, her hand still in place, the bulge of her breasts peaking though the crack in her suit.

"I just want to talk with you," Pie said.

She took a breath and quickly resealed her suit, giggling with relief and embarrassment. "Where would you like me to sit, on the floor at your feet?"

Pie chuckled. "Didn't take you long to get your bite back, did it?"

She softened her tone. "I'm sorry."

"No, not at all. To tell you the truth, if you promise not to spread it around, I rather like it." He stood and held his arm out, indicating the chair he'd just vacated.

She shook her head. "No, I couldn't."

"Please."

She smiled, revealing her lovely, white teeth, and sat in the chair, her posture too upright to be truly comfortable.

He squatted next to the chair and looked up at her. Her honey-brown eyes were bordered by black eyelashes that curled so tightly, they almost formed circles at their tips. He wondered why they weren't golden and then shook the absurd thought off.

"Shana, you need to know what you're in for. By the time we return to Earth, many years will have passed, nearly two centuries. No one you know will still be alive. No one will remember you, or care about you. Society itself will have changed in some unpredictable manner. You will no longer fit in. You'll be more alone than you ever imagined possible. It is difficult...even for a Citizen."

"Even for a Citizen? You call us Unders and treat us like something under your feet. Let me tell you, we are people, no less than you. You talk about loneliness. How would you feel if your friends or lovers were taken from you without warning, never to be seen again, never even to say goodbye? How would you like to have no choice, no voice, to be treated like a useful appliance by any Citizen, for any whim? I didn't leave Home. I escaped."

"Was it that bad? It's stated in the Convenient of Man that all are created equal."

"Really? Is that how you treat me?"

Pie said nothing.

"What is it that wanted to ask me?"

"Nothing, not now," Pie said.

"Then I guess I'll be going." She arose from the chair and walked toward the portal. "Will you be calling me back again before I reach the end of the corridor?" she asked without turning to face the still squatting Citizen.

"No."

He opened the portal and she left, without another glance in his direction. He pulled himself up, into the chair. It was so easy to think of Unders as less than real people. They were disposable people. When had that happened? He had not always felt that way. We were equal in the beginning, he remembered. Those who had not opted for regeneration were simply considered to be natural people, not people of a lesser value. It had been so gradual. She had struck truly. He was guilty and knew it. After a few more minutes, he pushed himself to his feet and entered the corridor that led to an up-tube.

When he stepped out of the tube, onto the deck of the commons, he found three people staring back at him, one adult and two children. The woman had the black eyes of a Citizen, but no eyebrows. She was wearing the symbol of her profession, a Stormy Kromer cap. Her face sparkled with pinpoints of rainbow colors and her fuchsia lips parted in a smile to reveal fuchsia teeth. She doffed her cap and bowed to Pie, revealing a multicolored scalp.

Pie swung around to stare with even greater incredulity at the children. They sat in apparent innocence, both with curly blond hair and pink cheeks. Carefree, they swung their legs from the edge of the too-high, lounge seat and held hands.

"What the hell!" Pie declared loudly. He turned to the woman Citizen. "How the hell did children get on a train? Are you responsible for this?"

The two children giggled and their eyes met, before turning back to the stony-faced Citizen.

The multicolored woman spoke. Her voice was harsh, overly loud and raspy. "Don't you recognize me?"

There was something familiar about her. He seemed to know her, but absolutely no associations came to mind.

The woman was of medium build and sat up straighter, turning her profile to Pie so he could see her from another perspective.

"I don't know you," Pie said.

She turned and slouched back against the lounge backrest. "I can't believe it," she belted out. "We spent over four years together on Mesa and you don't even remember, to say nothing of Holy."

The memories came together. "Kin? Starglow Kin?" He was shocked. She was supposed to have carrot-red hair and a hoard of freckles. He looked again. It was her all right. "It is you."

"Flow, Pie," she said with a fuchsia bordered smile.

"Flow, Kin," he answered, pleased she was here, whatever her appearance. He sat down next to her, glancing for a moment at her mirrored fingernails. "It's great to see you, Kin. I couldn't wish for a better driver."

Pie glanced at the children. They were grinning with their small, evenly spaced milk-teeth. He turned back to Kin. "How did children—"

"If you call me a child again, I'm afraid I'll have to take action," the little "girl" piped in her high-pitched voice. She slid off the edge of the lounge seat and stood next to it.

"Sit down!" Pie ordered.

Kin put her hand on Pie's thigh. "Pie...these aren't children. This is too much!" She broke into her coarse, deep-throated laugh.

Pie found no humor in the situation. "Let me in on it then, Kin." There was not a trace of a smile on his rugged face.

Kin managed to catch her breath. "Pie, these aren't children. They're New People."

Pie turned to study the "children" more closely. The "little girl" remained standing, her tiny, dimpled hands set firmly on her undeveloped hips, while the pretty "little boy" returned Pie's gaze with his startling, blue eyes and long, blond lashes.

Pie leaned forward. "How old are you?"

They looked to one another and giggled.

"How old are you, degenerate?" the "boy" jeered in his immature voice.

"What did you say?" Pie demanded, his anger rising quickly.

"I asked how old you were," the "boy" said, and then added, "How thoughtless of me. You probably don't remember."

The "girl" tittered with appreciation.

"There is something you two tykes need to know," Pie said. "I do not like being placed in the position of being responsible for ill-prepared civilians but, now that you're here, it's time to learn the first rule. I am the team leader. You will do as I say. Any deal you may have made was with Mason, not me."

"Oh my!" the "girl" exclaimed and turned to the "boy". "Do you think the big, bad man will break our little arms?"

The boy grinned mischievously and met Pie's glare straight on.

Pie stood and stormed across the room to stand over them, his face flushed with frustration and unresolved anger, fueled by confusion. "No," he grunted through gritted teeth, "I won't break your arm but I will spank your ass until it glows red."

The "boy" ignored the close presence of the glowering Citizen, despite his intimidating appearance, and turned without hurry to face the "girl". "Do you think we should ignore him, or do you think we should punish him for his impudence?"

She put her pudgy little finger up to her cheek and twisted it back and forth as she tilted her head slightly. "Oh, I don't know. He looks so distraught. After all, he's not New." She turned back to Pie and curtsied. "All right, Mister Citizen, we'll be good, but you must be nice, or it'll be out of our hands." She straightened, with the top of her head not even reaching to Pie's waist.

Kin walked over to stand behind Pie while he continued his heated stare. She put her hand on his arm and gave it a tug. "Come on, Pie. Let's go. We have some catching up to do."

Pie stood there a moment longer, while the "children" looked up at him, their eyelids aflutter with supposed innocence. Finally, he deepened his scowl and broke away, leading the way with long strides to the downtube. He dropped into it without stopping or glancing back.

Kin caught up with him in the corridor of the Citizen level and squeezed past him to open and enter her room. She walked over to sit on the edge of the cocoon bed, leaving the chair for Pie, but he remained standing just inside as the portal slid shut.

"What are you looking at, Pie?"

"You."

"Me?"

"You look...." He searched for the right word.

"I gather, from the look on your face, it's not going to be a compliment," she said in her raspy voice.

"Kin...you used to be so beautiful. Why did you do this...thing to yourself?"

"Is this your way of telling me you don't like the way I look?" she asked with her fuchsia smile.

Pie searched for an answer.

"I guess you don't," she added.

"To be honest, I'm just glad you're the driver, regardless of your appearance." He dropped his gaze and voice, "I need someone I can trust." He looked back up.

"Pie, this is just cosmetics." She held out her sparkling hand, her fingers tipped with mirrored nails that ended in sharp points. He wanted to take her hand, but her nails sparked memories that he quickly suppressed.

"I think I need more time to adjust."

She dropped her offered hand. "I brought you down here because you were losing it. I don't think I've ever seen you like that before. Not my go-with-the-flow-Pie."

"I've been having problems with my regeneration."

"Want to talk about it?" Kin asked.

"No."

"All right then, maybe we should talk about our guests. You won't find any information about them in our data banks."

"I know."

"Yes, I'm sure you do. The woman is Jilla LineBFD/LineDHB. The man is Jacques LineERM/LineDHB. She is eighty-four years old and he is ninety-three. They are most definitely not children, but they play the part because it amuses them. Close your mouth, Pie."

"That's impossible!"

"Flow, Pie. I had quite a chat with Joshua Mason. They are not to be underestimated, or messed around with. It's a game with them but beneath it all they are truly dangerous."

"I don't know, Kin. I don't get the sense that they're acting. I think their maturity was stunted along with their growth."

"Listen to me, Pie. Don't believe what you saw. They've been biologically engineered to optimize their abilities and have selected immature bodies for their healing properties and as part of the solution to longevity. Their average lifespan is over two-hundred years."

"I still think they are both in desperate need of a spanking."

"Don't get sucked in. Jilla is an expert matrix-technician and Jacques is a highly respected bio-engineer and, for the New People, that's saying something. I have to confess, she knows far more about the hardware on this ship than I do. After all, she designed most of it. Pie, why are you laughing?" She joined in without knowing why.

He couldn't seem to stop.

"Pie, you are the strangest Citizen I've ever met. I guess that's why I like you so much."

He looked up sheepishly. "I was just thinking—I know it's not all that funny, but, anyway, I was thinking about the names of the New People, Jilla and Jacques. Here we are aboard a spaceship, approaching the speed of light, on our way to investigate an alien race, and who are we traveling with? Jack and Jill."

Kin looked back at him blankly.

"Don't you get it?"

She shook her head.

"Don't you remember?" Pie asked.

"Remember what?"

> "Jack and Jill went up the hill,
> To fetch a pail of water;
> Jack fell down and broke his crown,
> And Jill came tumbling after."

It was a moment before Kin spoke. "I get it. When you were a child it was dangerous to go for water, so parents used this saying to warn their children."

He smiled. "That's right, Kin. You understood perfectly."

"You know, Pie, I have a special feeling for the twenty-second, even though I'm a twenty-ninth myself. I think that's why we get along so well, don't you?"

"Absolutely. Why, you could've walked any street when I was a boy and people would have thought, 'That beautiful lady's definitely a twenty-second'."

"Compliments now? You are in a special mood."

Pie became more serious as his thoughts returned to the reality of their situation. "Isn't it weird to have Unders on a mission?"

"Actually, I think it might be nice to have someone to attend us, if the New People aren't too greedy."

"It makes me uncomfortable."

"Nothing used to make you uncomfortable. Have you forgotten how to bend?"

There was no trace of levity in his voice when he spoke again. "I think this is going to be my last regeneration."

"Go on. I didn't mean anything."

"I feel out of place. I don't know why I do things anymore." After a moment of mutual silence he continued. "I did some terrible things my last time. I don't feel very good about myself."

"Just tell old Kin all about it. I guarantee you it won't shock me. I'll still like you."

He shook his head and looked at the deck. The silence returned and he leaned back against the closed portal.

Finally, Kin spoke. "Tell me about these creatures we're going to visit. You named them the 'Aboriginal Blues'."

Pie snorted a short laugh. "I guess after Jacky's report, if it's true, they'll have to be renamed. Perhaps, with the skill they have at hiding their culture, they should be called the Blue Houdinis."

"The Who-deanies?"

"Forget it. The point is, and I've been over and over it in my mind, the Blue I met struck me as singularly simple. I wonder if Jacky actually found a way to survive. Knowing he was Jack's son, I can almost believe it. If his report is accurate, he might even be immortal by now."

"Maybe." Kin shrugged. "It's more likely that by the time we get there, even his bones will be ancient. Over two-hundred and forty planet-years will have passed since your first visit."

Pie took a deep breath and let it out fully. "Yeah, you're probably right. Kin, why did you decide to accept this mission?"

"Why do you think? I was having a grand time in Aires, but my funds were running a bit low. I'm not rich like you. And then I heard you were going, so I just jumped in. Why do you ask?"

Pie sighed without realizing it. "I don't know. It seems like I was about to refuse...and then...I guess I said 'yes', and the next thing I know I'm on a train nearing rendezvous." He shook his head. "It's strange," he said quietly. After a moment, he looked back up. "Kin...have you ever gone on a mission and felt like you had left something unfinished, or that you had left something important behind?"

She thought for a moment. "No, I don't think so. Do you think you left the stove on?"

"This is no joke."

"Sorry. What did you leave behind?"

He wouldn't meet her eyes. "I don't know. I think I'll head back to my cabin. It's great to see you again, Kin."

She opened the portal. As he disappeared into the corridor, she yelled out, "Flow, Pie," but he either didn't hear, or chose not to respond.

Chapter 17

It was during the next sleep period that Pie was awakened. His cabin was bright with harsh light and his door was open. For a moment, he thought he was on Home, but then remembered he was on a train. The grogginess passed quickly and he sat up with the startled realization that his cabin had been penetrated, despite his personal block.

"Citizen Traynor, report to the commons."

What the hell? Pie thought. He uplinked; it was 03:00 ship-time.

"Citizen Traynor, report to the commons."

Pie was outraged by this flagrant invasion of privacy. He jerked on his suit, and strapped his sheath and knife to his forearm, as much a part of dressing as putting on his bodysuit. He entered the corridor and ordered the portal shut, but it remained as it was, wide open. Every twenty seconds the message repeated.

He uplinked. "Kin, there's a matrix malfunction. I need assistance in the commons."

He entered the up-tube, even though Kin had not responded. While he ascended he unconsciously fingered his knife, assuring its presence. When he entered the commons he found the New People were already there, sitting next to each other on the far side lounge.

"Kin, report to the commons," he ordered, but there was no response. He walked over to stand before the child-like humans.

"I should have known," he said. "This is your doing. I will not tolerate this mischief."

They looked at each other and smiled.

"He is a brute, isn't he?" Jilla said in her little voice.

Pie's tolerance was at the breaking point and he glowered at them in his most menacing fashion; any normal human would've cowered at the sight.

"We need to reach an understanding," he managed, his voice clogged with anger.

"Quite so," Jilla agreed. "Sit down."

"The hell I will!" But, as the sentence leapt from his mouth, his legs lost their tone. It was as if they were not there at all. He broke his fall with his hands and immediately pushed himself up, reaching for his knife, but then his arms gave way. He collapsed heavily onto the deck, rapping his head against it.

131

"That's better, don't you think, Jilla?"

"Yes, Jacques. He left us no choice. Are you all right, Citizen?"

"Shut up you little shits! You'll regret this! Kin, report!"

Jilla walked over and sat cross-legged near Pie's head. "Now, don't try to bite me or spit. This is merely an educational exercise."

Pie stared at her, his black eyes narrowed with frustrated rage, but he said nothing.

Jilla continued. "We could have done this in front of Citizen Kin and the Unders, but we are sensitive to your ego needs. You are, after all, an ancestor, although quite distant."

"I'm no ancestor of yours. You were manufactured by a molecular biologist. Your parents were—" His tongue went lax and his lips flaccid; saliva drooled out of the corner of his mouth. He turned his head to the side to prevent obstruction of his breathing passage.

"As I was saying, we are sensitive and understanding, to a point. I think you've gotten the point. We are willing to play our part in this charade and you can continue to play the part of leader, but it's important that you never forget. It's only a game. This is reality. Grunt twice if you understand."

They both giggled at Jilla's joke while she rocked back and forth, her hands pulling on her knees.

"Well, Jilla, it's getting late and we really should get our sleep, because tomorrow we have to fetch a pail of water. Shall we go?"

"I think so." She stood and they walked hand in hand to the down-tube. "Good night, Citizen," Jilla called out as she dropped into the tube.

After five long minutes, Pie could speak again and then strength returned to his arms. When he was able to move his legs, he stood and walked to the tube, to exit on the Citizen level. He passed by his cabin door, which was still ajar, and stopped in front of Kin's; this could not wait until morning.

He uplinked. "Kin wake up and let me in." He repeated the message twice more before the portal slid open.

"Pie?" she croaked, her voice even more coarse with sleep.

Pie remained standing in the portal. She sat up and swung around to sit on the edge of her cocoon. Her breasts were bare, both tipped with a metallic plug instead of a nipple.

"What are you staring at?" Kin asked. "You come to my quarters in the middle of the sleep-period and then stand there like some dumb Under." She touched one of her metallic "nipples" with a mirrored fingernail. "Is this what's bothering you?" She stood and retrieved a bodysuit. "Is this better?"

"It wasn't necessary."

"I'm not a juice-head, if that's what you're thinking, but I do get satisfaction through my peripherals, and I know how to handle it. You have any objections?" she added hotly.

"What you do is your own concern."

"Do you have any complaints about my job?"

Pie shook his head and looked down at the deck. "No, of course not. May I come in?"

"You're standing in my doorway. I guess that would be up to you."

He took a step into the cabin and the portal slid shut behind him. "I just had a confrontation with the New People."

"At this hour?"

"I didn't arrange it. They did. When we were talking last day-period did you have a personal block on your quarters?"

"Of course I did. What a ridiculous question. Why do you ask?"

"We've got troubles. The New People have a level of control above ours. To them our interaction with the matrix is of a secondary nature. Theirs is primary. I must warn you, everything we say, possibly everything we even think, is accessible to them."

"I have nothing to hide."

Pie was irked by her lack of concern, but he forged ahead, certain the next information he revealed would stimulate a reaction. "That's not the worst of it. They have an ability to access our nervous systems through our links. They completely paralyzed me. I was at their mercy and, as far as that goes, we still are."

Kin sat down on the edge of her cocoon. "What can we do? And, more to the point, what should we do? I haven't noted any sinister motives in them, and we are useful members of the team. Why can't you just flow with it? If you didn't have the eyes of a Citizen, I'd swear you were an impostor. Bend, don't break. There is always plenty of time."

Pie stared at her for a moment. "I cannot tolerate this situation and I will not, but...I guess I could've waited until morning to tell you. I guess...I just thought you'd want to know as soon as possible. My mistake."

"Of course I want to know. Well, there are still two days until intercept. I'm confident a compromise can be negotiated. Just don't push so hard."

Pie turned to leave, but the portal remained closed. "Open it, Kin. I'm in no mood."

"I'm trying," she said without concern.

"Those bastards," he muttered, "still playing with us."

"Calm down, Pie. It's only a closed portal. You can join me for the rest of the night. That wouldn't be so bad now, would it? Remember that time on the veranda of the Grand Canal—"

"I think I'll just sit here," he said as he plopped into the chair.

She slipped out of her suit and nestled into her cocoon. "That's up to you. I do have a couple of heavy days ahead." And then added, "You know, I think that Under-woman has a crush on me. She follows me everywhere."

Pie frowned but, before he could formulate an objection to her theory, her breathing became regular and deep with peaceful sleep.

He studied her in the dim light of night-cycle. Maybe she's right, he thought. He sat and brooded, not even noticing the transition from introspection to slumber.

Chapter 18

Pie awakened when he felt his shoulder being touched. His neck was stiff from sleeping in a chair. He ranged it in a circle to loosen it up and opened his eyes, expecting to see Kin. Instead, he saw a man with the eyes of an Under, the inner corners softened by epicanthic folds. His straight, black hair was clipped short and his skin, Asian dark.

"How did you get in here?" Pie demanded.

"Pardon, Citizen," Joe-54 said, "but meal-one is prepared and the Masters are waiting for you and Citizen Kin." He kept his back to Kin, whose partially clad figure was still sprawled in sleep. He bowed and then backed out through the open portal.

When Kin and Pie arrived in the commons, Jilla and Jacques were sitting quietly at an oval table that had been raised from the deck. They were sitting in tall chairs. To Pie it looked like they were sitting in highchairs.

"Now, don't start the day by saying something disagreeable," Jilla said.

"Why would you think that?" Pie asked.

"You're not smiling," Jilla said. "You don't look happy. What do you think, Jacques?"

"I completely agree. He is not smiling."

Joe-54 raised stools from the deck so that Kin and Pie could sit across the table from the New People.

"Real cozy," Pie muttered as he took his seat.

"You had a lot of exercise last night," Jilla said to Joe-54 and Shana-8 with an exaggerated wink. "I hope you both slept well."

"Yes, Master," Shana-8 said.

"What's this 'Master' shit?" Pie demanded.

"Master or Citizen, does it really make any difference?" Jacques asked. "An Under is an Under. What do you care?"

Pie glanced up at Joe-54 and Joe lowered his eyes, but not before Pie saw a spark of feeling. Pie continued to stare at the man while Shana-8 brought in the food and set it before them, starting with the New People. Pie was about to rebuke her, but held his words in check. He was not going to use the Unders as pawns in a power struggle.

The food looked better than usual and tasted better as well. It reminded Pie of waffles smothered in maple syrup.

135

"I take it you like the improvements we've made in the hydrocarbon-reconstitution-oven," Jilla said.

"It's all right," Pie admitted begrudgingly.

"I think it's great!" Kin said with enthusiasm as she gobbled her food.

"I thought this meal might give us an opportunity to get to know one another better," Jilla said.

"Let me begin then," replied Pie with the tone of a dare. "Why are you on this mission?"

"That's a silly question," Jacques answered and craned his neck to look around Shana's arms while she poured orange juice substitute.

When Shana noticed she was in the way, she bowed and withdrew. She stood next to Joe, out of direct sight, but ready to serve.

Jacques continued. "We are just as interested in the technology of an alien culture as any Citizen. The potential benefits are obvious."

"I mean, why you in particular? As individuals, if you are individuals."

"I do declare," Jilla said turning to Jacques, "I think the good Citizen is trying to insult us. Apparently he has learning disabilities."

"Not at all," replied Pie in his most reasonable tone. "I know so little about you."

"It's true. You do know so very little," Jilla replied.

"Allow me," Jacques said. "I think Citizen Traynor is having an adjustment reaction. We've seen it before. As New People it is our obligation to assist those who are less fortunate."

"Jacques, you are so generous," Jilla said and then added, "and so gifted." She gave him a peck of a kiss on the cheek. She turned back to Pie. "Jacques is not only a great molecular biologist but he's also a great sculptor. It's been confirmed by our Council of Critics."

"Yes," Jacques agreed, "that is true, but I want to be remembered for my actions, as well as my creations."

"I see," said Pie. "This Council of Critics can determine who is great and who is not. Where did they ever get such insight?"

"Citizen, I think you are trying to goad us again. That isn't very nice," Jilla said.

"It's okay, Jilla," Jacques said, "I don't mind. The Council of Critics is made up of individuals who've been certified. One can join the Council only by the invitation of the other members. There is no question about their judgment and it saves so much time. The rest of us don't have to make all that effort at judging art for ourselves. Quite efficient."

Pie said nothing.

"Citizen Traynor," Jilla said, "I don't appreciate that arrogant smile."

"Was I smiling? I didn't mean to. I was just thinking about what you said earlier. You'll be happy to die, if people remember your name and something about you. Is that the gist of it?"

"Crudely put," said Jilla, "but in essence correct. We've outgrown our fear of death."

"So, the fact that Citizen Nichols reported that these aliens have developed immortality holds no attraction for you."

"None whatsoever," Jacques said.

Pie nodded. Kin kicked him under the table, but he ignored it.

"This is difficult to believe," Pie said.

"I'm sure it is difficult...for you," Jilla replied.

"Let me get this straight," Pie continued. "If, for instance, you had the historical stature of, say, a Napoleon Bonaparte—"

"Who?" Jilla asked.

"Napoleon," Pie repeated and turned to Kin, but she just shrugged. When he turned back to Jilla her eyelids were drooping, and then, as if clicked back on, her eyes opened.

"You don't know who Napoleon was?" Pie asked incredulously.

"Of course I do," Jilla replied smugly. "Tell him, Jacques."

"Napoleon Bonaparte lived in an old-Earth territory called France. He controlled about five-percent of the Earth's land for a few years in the Nineteenth Century," Jacques said.

"There is nothing we don't know," Jilla added. "But, to answer your question, this mission will gain us a considerably bigger slice of history than that."

"I think you have trivialized Napoleon's importance a bit," Pie said dryly.

"I think not," Jilla replied.

"Now, it's our turn," Jacques said.

"Go ahead."

Jilla paused a moment as she thought. She pushed a crumb around the tabletop with her fat, little fingers, and then looked up. "Why do you Citizen believe the fantasy that if your memories live on, you live on? Are memories all there is to a person? Is that all that distinguishes a person from a rock?"

"It's not a fantasy," Pie said as he leaned forward. "Ask Kin. I feel the line of my life extending unbroken for nearly two thousand years. I don't have to justify it. I feel it. Tell them, Kin."

"He's right," Kin said in her gritty voice. "I can remember myself growing up and I can remember experiences all the way along to the present."

"Does that mean the memories you've forgotten represent a partial death?" Jacques asked.

"You're not listening," Pie said. "I know when I'm alive. It's not only the memories, but the memories in a living body."

"Which body?" Jacques asked.

"This body, my body."

"But this body didn't experience or do all those things. Those people are dead. Do you even know when you're dead?" Jilla asked and flipped the crumb she had been pushing around onto Pie's lap. "My analysis indicates you are twenty-four years old, not two thousand or whatever ridiculous figure you claim."

Pie was quiet. He had a strong deja vue sensation of having had similar discussions in the past. When? he wondered. When was it?

"Pie," Kin said quietly out of the side of her mouth, "are you all right? You look pale."

Pie looked back to the New People. "I know what I know."

"Oh, that's brilliant," Jilla said. "The man knows what he knows. You've certainly convinced me." She turned to Jacques, "Hasn't he convinced you?"

The little "boy" nodded. "And it logically follows that he doesn't know what he doesn't know."

They both giggled.

"I'll tell you this," Pie said as he stood, "if regeneration is death, then it is a death I can accept." He turned his back to the table and walked to the down-tube.

Jilla called out to him. "I finally understand. It's a death you can live with." They both wiggled with renewed laughter and Jacques pounded his tiny fist on the table with glee.

A minute later Kin followed after Pie. She found him in his quarters with the portal open, lying face down in his cocoon. She sat down next to him on the edge of the cocoon.

"Are you okay?"

"Let me be," Pie answered, his voice muted by the padding of the cocoon.

Although reluctant, she stood. "If that's what you honestly want."

He didn't respond, so she continued. "Don't let them get to you. I understood what you were saying. I know my life is continuing, that death has not touched me."

Pie turned his head to face her, the black slits of his eyes barely open. He pushed himself to a sitting position and leaned forward, holding his face in his hands.

"I don't know anymore, Kin," he said softly. "Instead of knowing more with each passing year, I know less." He paused, and then added, "I feel lost."

She walked back over to him and he leaned forward to rest his forehead against the warmth and softness of her belly. She brushed her fingers through his thick hair.

"I need you, Pie. I can't do it alone. You're supposed to be the decision maker, the creator of solutions."

"Beginning to have second thoughts about coming on this mission? It's a bit late."

"I joined this mission because you were the mission leader."

"Is that a question? Because it sounds like you are trying to convince yourself."

"Damn it! Stop this...whatever it is. I'm counting on you."

"I know. I'll be all right."

She patted his back. "Sure, Pie. And, if you need me, just call. I'll come running. You can depend on me."

He nodded listlessly, but said nothing.

"Damn it, Pie! Get your shit together." She waited for a response, but got none, so stood and walked to the portal.

It sounded to Pie as if she had struck the portal with her fist before opening it. When the portal slid shut, Pie's cabin became quiet, but his mind was not. An urge began to assert itself, one that was a surprise.

Chapter 19

Pie didn't appear for meal-two and, when he failed to show for meal-three, Shana brought food to his cabin. She was standing in the corridor, not certain if she should disturb him, when the portal slid open. She remained where she was.

"Citizen, I brought your meal."

Pie was sitting in his chair. "I know. I'm glad you're here."

"Thank you, Citizen."

"My name is Pie."

"Yes, Citizen Pie."

"Come in for a moment, will you?"

She stood still, her golden eyes downcast, and answered in a quiet voice, "As you wish, Citizen. I live to serve." She took two steps into the room.

"Shana, look at me!" he ordered.

Startled, she raised her eyes to meet the black eyes of the Citizen.

"I want you to do something for me, but first I want to talk with you for a few minutes." The portal closed and her eyes darted to it. "Just talk. You know me, always wanting to talk. You can put the food tray on the deck."

She stood still, her way of hiding.

"I understand Citizens have used you," Pie continued, "but you can relax here. I'm not going hurt you or take advantage of you. Evidently you've heard that before. You can trust me."

"If you say so, Citizen," she said quietly.

"Go ahead and sit on the cocoon."

She looked at it.

"Go ahead," Pie persisted.

With stiff-legged steps, she walked over to the cocoon, set the food tray on the deck, and then sat on the edge, her back rigidly straight, her eyes directed forward.

"Tell me about yourself," Pie said.

She turned to look at the Citizen.

"Were you born in Home?" Pie asked.

"No."

"Well?"

"I was born on the ocean."

"How did you end up in Home?"

She gathered her arms across her chest as if to hug herself.

"I'm waiting," Pie said, his voice conversational and patient.

Her voice trembled as she spoke. "I was very young then. I remember my mom and dad...a little, and I think I had a brother. We lived on a great raft that traveled between islands, but it was big enough to be an island itself. Then, one day, a machine came out of the sky, a thruster-craft." She paused as she remembered. "It broke up the raft. They didn't seem to do it on purpose. It was more like they just didn't care. I tried to run and dive into the ocean, but an arm scooped me up and...." She stopped, her eyes lined with tears. "Is this really necessary?"

"And then what happened?"

She turned her eyes to him, and although tears trickled down her cheeks, her voice was empty of emotion. "I turned and for the first time saw the eyes of a citizen. I begged him to let me go. The ocean was only a few steps away and I wanted to dive into it and swim to the very bottom, but he only held me tighter and laughed. Then he put me to sleep and when I woke up I was in one of the cylinders of Home. I remember crying. I cried a lot back then", she said as she sniffed and wiped the remaining tears from her eyes, "but I don't anymore. It's not acceptable."

Pie smiled. "Well, I'm glad you've got that under control."

She didn't seem to hear him. "I have been granted many benefits since I came to Home, security, education—"

"Cut the drivel, Shana. You're not talking with Mitchell Mason. That bullshit may have served you well at Home, but not here. It's just you and me."

Her amber eyes were rimmed with white as she stared at him.

Pie reached out to pat her on the shoulder but she leaned away from him, so he dropped his hand into his lap. He sighed and began staring at the plain gray bulkhead as if he'd forgotten she was even there.

Finally, she could tolerate the silence no longer. "I live to serve," she said meekly.

He looked back to her, but all she could see were those black cat-eyes.

"It's about twenty-four hours until intercept," he said. "Do you have any questions or concerns?"

"You want to know if I have any questions?"

"That's what I said."

She remained silent.

"Surely you must have some hidden fears. This is your first rendezvous."

She nodded.

"Out with it then."

The words rushed from her mouth. "If we miss the rendezvous with the star grazer, will we travel in space forever…and die?"

"That's right," Pie answered factually, but then added with a smile, "Don't worry. The last train to miss was well over seven hundred years ago and, with the improvements the New People have made, the chances of failing to make the rendezvous are extremely remote. Also, we have a very skilled train driver."

"What happened to the people on the train that missed? Couldn't Home send a rescue ship?"

"The train was moving too fast at that point. Kin Starglow has driven many trains, not just the one we're on. In preparation for this mission she's been driving numerous trains for the last year while we were in stasis. Positioning them. Enough trains so that what remains of each train will provide us with an adequate amount of water to slow us at Angkor-3 and then accelerate us to again rendezvous with the Hawking as it returns, traveling the curve of a long parabola."

He uplinked. His face became blank, while his detached mind marveled at Kin's delicate touch on the controls, and then he slid back into his body. "She is marvelous. We are on course and on speed. When we intercept tomorrow, we'll match the star grazer at seventy-two percent of the speed of light. After we lock on, we'll enter the starship and then go back into stasis, but this time for the Deep Sleep."

"Citizen, how will we know if the star grazer ever arrives at the destination?"

"That's the job of the star crew." But then her question took on a new meaning. "Are you referring to the Pinnacle?"

She nodded.

"You have to remember, that was the first starship. It wasn't a star grazer. It's funny about the Pinnacle, no, that's not the right word. Tragic is the word. They bypassed, Procyon, Mesa, and Rigil Kentarus while trying to reach Myphid. Of course, we weren't as good at detecting planets back then. Although bypassing Rigil was a stroke of luck. I think it was a mistake to colonize that ball of iron."

"Do you think those poor people on the Pinnacle are still alive and in stasis?"

"After all these years? I doubt it."

"What do you think happened to them?"

He shrugged. "I haven't the foggiest notion. I doubt that anyone will ever know, but don't worry. The Star Grazer Hawking will deliver us. All we have to do is go to sleep for the ride."

She nodded, but it was a sober face that focused its attention on Pie.

"Now, I want you to do something for me," Pie said. He stood and walked over to sit next to her on the cocoon bed.

Her eyes narrowed and she scooted slightly away so their bodies weren't touching.

Pie reached into his left sleeve and drew his wicked looking knife. When he looked to her, he saw that she was holding her breath with her gaze fixed on the knife.

"Stop it, Shana. I'm not going to hurt you. I already told you that." A memory forced its way into his mind, of blood and pain and slicing a woman to pieces.

Shana remained perfectly still while Pie stared at the bulkhead across the room. He finally broke his stare and returned his attention to her.

"The new links aren't like the old ones," he said. "They can't be removed. There's no release. It's fused into my skin and has penetrated into my nervous system. I've tried to remove it myself, but can't. I want you to do it."

The skin at the base of her nose creased. "But, if I do that...."

"If you do that, I'll be an Under?"

She nodded and looked down at the deck.

"Is that such a terrible thing to be?" Pie asked.

She raised her chin. "No. It's not terrible to be an Under. It's terrible to be treated like an Under."

"I'll take my chances. Will you do it?"

"I don't know," she said, slowly shaking her head with indecision.

"Let me help you make up your mind," Pie said with a hard edge to his voice. "I am a Citizen and you are an Under. You will do it. Furthermore, you will not call for help, should you witness something that worries you." He leaned over and pulled her chin around until their noses were almost touching. "Do you understand, Shana?"

"Yes," she whispered, "I understand."

He released her chin. "Would you mind getting up? I think I need to lay down for this." He smiled with an ease that he did not feel.

She stood and held one hand clutched in the other.

"Good," Pie declared, the edge gone as quickly as it'd been called up. "Take this blade and insert it all around, between the link and my skin, and then slice outward. It's simple. There will be a little bleeding, but don't worry, it'll stop."

He took hold of her trembling hand and placed the handle of the diamond knife into her palm, closing her fingers around it, and then returned his attention to the overhead. His jaw muscles bulged while he clenched his teeth and a shiver of dread washed through his body before he was still.

"I'm ready, Shana."

Nothing happened.

He looked up at her. "I said, I'm ready."

She knelt on the deck, took a deep breath, and slipped the blade under the gold band on his forearm. A trickle of blood followed the path of the blade and dripped onto the pad of the cocoon. Soon, there was a dark-red stain spreading from beneath his arm. She stopped for a moment to glance up at him. He had said nothing, had made no noise, but sweat was dripping from his face.

"Do it," he commanded through clenched teeth.

She pulled the blade outward against the golden band and severed it.

Chapter 20

Shana held her breath. He moaned and she scooted back. He cried out once and then was silent. His body began to shake in rhythmic shudders. Blood-tinged saliva frothed at his mouth and he arched his back in a prolonged, tonic contraction. His lips turned blue, unable to even breath. But, just when she was certain he was dying, the tone left his muscles and he slumped back into the cocoon, with his breath coming in deep gasps, gurgling through his mouth. The color gradually returned to his lips.

Shana cautiously approached the cocoon. She touched his skin; it was moist and cool. She called his name and touched his shoulder, but he did not awaken. She grabbed his shoulders and shook him with the strength of panic but he didn't even open his eyes. Withdrawing her hands she squeezed them into fists until her nails bit into her palms.

She backed away, toward the portal. She knew how to open it and wanted to run away to hide in the Under-quarters, but stopped. He appeared so vulnerable, so much in need. She couldn't desert him. She knelt next to the cocoon and cleaned his wound, dressing it with a strip of material she had cut from the leg of her suit. The bleeding stopped, just as he said it would.

Finally, on an impulse, she crawled over his body and lay down next to him. She circled her arm around his chest and held him against her, sharing her heat with him and wishing for this Citizen to survive.

Chapter 21

Pie awakened to aching muscles, but his awareness was centered on the warm body that conformed closely to his side. He felt the softness of her breasts and the firmness of her pelvis. Her cheek rested on his shoulder and her breath tickled across his chest. But, the wound on his left arm would not be denied; the raw skin burned as if a flame was licking it. He raised his arm and found it neatly bound in a green bandage, the exact color of Shana's bodysuit; its innocent appearance contrasted sharply with the sensations that lay beneath it.

He returned his arm to its resting place at his side and a third aspect revealed itself; he felt buoyant. Laughter threatened to percolate up, without reason. It was as if the band had been encircling his chest rather than his arm and, now that it was gone, he could breathe, freely and deeply.

"Shana," he whispered, and then more loudly, "Shana."

Her eyes fluttered open but she remained resting against him, until realization quickly banished all thoughts of security and comfort. She bounded upward, bumping her head against the padded overhead of the cocoon.

"I'm sorry, Citizen," she sputtered and gingerly crawled over him

He turned to watch her as she backed away from the cocoon. Her eyes looked everywhere, except at Pie.

"Citizen, I—"

"Please, Shana, my name is Pie. I am in your debt."

She swallowed visibly. "I was afraid you were going to die."

"To the contrary," his voice was robust, in distinct counterpoint to her meekness, "I feel more full of life than at any time I can recall." The ghost of a memory passed its hand across his mind. Had he lived so long that there were no new experiences? he wondered.

Shana saw the cloud pass across his face and instinctively reached out to touch his hand. When she touched the bandage, the pain flared, but he did not withdraw; he suppressed the pain and smiled.

"Help me up, will you?" Pie asked. He could not help but notice that the right leg of her bodysuit was shorter than the left. "Thank you for dressing my wound."

He offered his other hand and she took hold of it.

"What time is it?" he asked.

"I don't know."

"Well, I think it's time we take a look around. Don't you?"

She lowered her gaze to the deck at her feet.

He raised her chin until their eyes met. "Shana, I've seen the real you, don't masquerade behind the facade of an Under. I don't need or want an Under. I need a friend."

A wan smile graced her face, barely revealing the whiteness of her teeth. "Then, as a friend, I would recommend that you take a moment and get cleaned up."

"No, I don't think so. I feel like a newborn. If I wash, the feeling might be washed away." He glanced over at the closed portal. "This is a bit inconvenient. How the hell do we get out of here? Damn it! Of course they know I'm offline and they've sealed us in."

With a sly grin, Shana pulled a fine, silvery wire from the sleeve of her suit and walked over to a panel adjacent to the portal. Pie watched with interest while she worked one end of the wire into the edge of the panel and the other into a power port. Without stopping to explain, she retrieved a cup of water from the personal-closet and splashed it onto the panel. It sizzled and crackled, and then erupted with sparks and acrid smoke, closely followed by a dull "clunk". The portal was ajar. She slipped her fingers into the crack and tugged the door a hand's breadth farther into the wall.

Pie could wait no longer. He reached around her and gave it a shove; it fairly flew into its slot in the bulkhead. The light in the corridor was at full brightness; it was day-period. Before stepping into the hall, he turned back to Shana. "How did you learn to do that?"

She smiled brightly. "You may think of us as Unders, but we're not stupid. You have a lot to learn, Cit—I mean, Pie."

"So I see," he said as he studied her with new interest. "I better go first."

She did not object.

When Pie exited the up-tube and entered the commons, he stepped aside to make room for Shana. Kin was standing in front of the New People, who were sitting on the lounge to the right, while Joe-54 was standing in the back, boldly staring at Pie.

Kin's eyes focused on Pie's arm and the bandage around his wrist. She knew he'd gone offline, they all did.

Pie stepped forward, ignoring the plaintive question on Kin's face, and stood between her and the New People, who were sitting quietly, expressionless for once. He leaned over them and breathed into their faces. Jilla wrinkled her nose and Jacques slid farther back in his seat.

"You stink!" Jilla declared in a child-like screech.

Suddenly, Pie slammed his fist into the bulkhead above their heads and they both jumped. If eyes could burn, Pie's would have incinerated the two child-like humans. When he spoke his voice was a growl. "I am the leader here and I will not tolerate being taunted or ignored!" He pointed his finger so close to Jilla's little, button nose, it caused her eyes to blink. "Do I make myself perfectly clear!"

Jilla and Jacques nodded as if one.

"Good," Pie said softly and took a step back. When nothing further was said, he turned to leave, but then Jilla spoke.

"I have a question," she said in her sweet little girl voice.

Pie turned back to face her.

"How can you possibly fulfill your duties as team leader now that you are offline?"

"I'm the leader because of my judgment and experience, not because I was attached to a device. It's not the matrix that makes the difference."

"But, how can you make decisions without input?" Jacques asked.

"I'll manage. You may not believe this, but there was once a time when all machines were accessed without matrix contact."

Jilla and Jacques turned to one another and smiled, their humor and equilibrium returning. Then, as if synchronized, they both laughed.

Pie took the short step needed to stand over them once again. "Do you have an objection?" His anger showed visibly, as distended veins in his neck and a bounding pulse at his temples.

"Why, no. Not at all," Jilla answered, "but, what do we call you? Let me see." She put her pudgy little finger into her dimple and smiled. "Got it. You are an Under who popped out of nowhere, so you must be an Underwear."

"Good one!" Jacques declared.

They giggled.

Pie took a calming breath and leaned back. "Make your simple-minded jokes, if it helps you feel more comfortable, but I will not tolerate insubordination."

"O-o-o-u," Jilla squealed, "don't worry. We feel quite comfortable around Unders. Don't we, Jacques?"

"Quite, Jilla. No problem here, but I do wish he'd do something about that foul, body odor. Have you noticed that about these old style humans? They don't seem to care about personal hygiene."

"Yes," Jilla said, "and it is so inconsiderate of others, very poor manners."

Pie turned away while Jilla was speaking and stalked back to the down-tube. Kin walked forward as if to approach him, but he gave her such a black glare that she stopped, without a word, and let him pass. Shana floated down the tube after him. He didn't exit until he had reached the Under level, just above storage, and was waiting for Shana when she entered the corridor.

"Take me to your cabin," he said.

"Why do you want to do that? You have your own."

"Oh," he nodded. "My apologies. It seems I got the wrong message."

She shifted her eyes.

After a moment of silence he added. "I really am sorry. Presumptuous at best. Perhaps I can blame it on those two little weirdoes. They really know how to piss me off. Am I forgiven for my unwarranted audacity?"

She looked up. "Cit—I mean, Pie, Joe and I share the cabin. It's not mine to offer. I just can't."

"I understand. Guess I better be going." He took the few steps to the up-tube and entered it without glancing back.

When he arrived at his cabin, the door was still wide open, just as he'd left it. While he stood there, he was suddenly overcome with exhaustion. His knees threatened to buckle and he stumbled forward to collapse into his cocoon, where he lapsed into a fitful sleep. His dreams were invaded by hordes of insects, their serrated legs cutting, their clicking-jaws nipping. His pain did not leave him, even in sleep, it just became more grotesque.

When he awakened, he found himself looking blurry-eyed at a horrifying apparition. He withdrew deeper into the cocoon and reached for his knife.

"It's sixty minutes until intercept," Kin said in her raspy voice. "The star grazer is on the screens. Come on. You need to get cleaned up." She tugged at his arm while he pushed forward to sit on the edge of the cocoon, casually dropping his hand from his knife.

"By the way, Pie," she said, "you're not fooling me. The next time I wake you up, I'm going to do it from across the room."

He matched her smile with one of his own.

She stripped his suit off his shoulders and he stood to step out of the legs. He walked without modesty to the personal-closet and stepped into the shower; if there was one luxury on an out-ship, it was the abundance of water.

He searched for an "on" mechanism, but couldn't locate it. He never really noticed that before, just took it for granted. It was exasperating. He hated to ask, but.... "Kin, would you turn it on...please."

"Oh, sure, sure." Kin stood just outside the closet and studied him, wide in the shoulders, muscular, a giant of a man. "Do you remember that time on the Grand Canal on Holy? I don't think we were very holy."

Pie laughed. "No, not holy at all." He swept the water from his eyes and turned toward her with a smile. "I could never forget that."

"How about it then?" Kin asked.

"No...I think not."

"What is it, these?" She poked a mirrored nail at one of her implant-enhanced breasts.

He stepped out of the cabinet. "No, that's not it. I'm not the prude you make me out to be, as you well know, but I can spot an act of charity when—"

"Charity? Bullshit. Since when have I ever been accused of charity? You know what I think. It's that Under-woman, isn't it? What's going on? Ever since she spent that night-period with you she's been avoiding me."

"Jealous?"

She chuckled. "Pie, sometimes you're really a shit."

He smiled and nodded in agreement as he pulled out a new bodysuit and slipped into it, while Kin continued to study him, unabashed.

"You've changed," she said. "What happened?"

"First it's Shana and—"

"Shana-8."

"Yes, Shana-8, and now it's me."

"I'm serious, Pie."

He sealed up the front of his suit. "I don't know." The memory of a tortured woman forged its way to his consciousness. Although it remained as distasteful as ever, it had lost some of its shock value.

"Now there's a damned cheap answer if I've ever heard one."

"That's all I've got."

"Shit." She paused and massaged her neon rainbow scalp before continuing. "Well, you've been acting weird, but you can still count on me. It'll be double duty, but I'll try to keep a matrix-eye on you too."

"Thank you, Kin, and I want you to know, I'll get us through this. I haven't lost a partner yet and I'm not about to start now."

"All right, big fella," she said, "you've got yourself a deal. I need to attend to my duties. It wouldn't do to miss a rendezvous." As she walked through the open door, she glanced askance at it, but didn't comment.

Pie followed her up to the commons, where they parted, with Kin ascending the short up-tube to the bridge. The other crew members were already present, their attention focused on the holo-stage, hardly even taking note of Pie's arrival.

The meter-sized cube was transparent, revealing the blackness of space, sprinkled generously with sharp specks of starlight, but what held them transfixed was the three-dimensional image of the starship, growing perceptively larger by the moment.

The black silhouette of the seven-kilometer long Hawking looked incongruously like a ten-penny nail against the grainy whiteness of innumerable distant stars. Its "head" appeared thin, but was actually a hundred meters thick and three-hundred meters in diameter; made of solid new-steel, it functioned as a micro-matter shield, protecting the body of the craft and the many segmented trains that clung to its sides.

The idea was simple. Hero, of ancient Alexandria, would've been gratified if he knew that his invention now transported mankind through the firmament; the out-ship trains were nothing more than glorified steam engines. The fusion engines transformed water into super-heated steam, which provided propulsion. When a cylinder of water, a car in the train, was empty, the car itself was consumed by the giant maw of the engine. No mass could be wasted. The only unique, out-ship train was the one that contained the humans. The out-ship was shaped like a fat bullet and stood at the forefront of the train, while the engine at the end consumed everything that entered its giant maw.

The star grazer not only provided refuge for the travelers, it was an automated factory that reworked spent engines and refitted the out-ship, so that it would be ready to take them to Angkor-3.

"Is the star crew aboard?" Shana asked and looked to Pie.

"Yes, the outbound crew has been aboard for a year. The inbound crew left the ship long before the star grazer passed the outermost fringes of the solar system, just like we'll do when it's our turn to go planet-side." Pie directed his comments to Shana, though he was in fact speaking to everyone present.

"When we enter the star grazer, you will see many stasis-capsules, thousands. The star grazers were first used to transport colonist."

"Citizen," Jilla said, "if you don't really have anything new to say, be quiet."

"Pie ignored her. "Six of the capsules will be open, probably near the entry portal. Go directly to a stasis capsule and enter it. Do not speak to the crew. Do not bring any personal possessions and, especially, do not be so foolhardy as to try to smuggle a weapon on board. It has been said that no star crew is trustworthy until they've been crazy for at least a hundred years."

"We don't even need them," Jilla declared. "This is a ridiculous arrangement. I could design a matrix that would manage all the details,

154

just as they do on comm-ships. It''s simply a matter of technology and engineering."

"You're wrong, Jilla," Pie replied. "There is something out there. I felt it when I did my stint as a train driver. If Kin were here, she'd tell you the same thing."

"Something out there," Jilla repeated. "It's probably the devil."

"It might be," Pie said.

"Oh p-e-lease. No more. I didn't realize that Citizens were not only primitive in appearance, but superstitious as well. Jacques, can you believe what this ignoramus is saying?" Jilla began giggling.

"Tell me about it, Citizen Pie, please," Shana said.

"A starman spends many years in isolation, with only a matrix for contact, while the rest of the crew waits for their turn, suspended in stasis. Through the years, I have had an occasional opportunity to uplink with a star grazer. There is something out there and the desire to be with it, to join it, is very seductive. The starmen hear the siren song as well but, being human, they're able to resist and correct the drift in the matrix, but whatever is out there knows. It threatens the crew. It shows then images of their most grotesque fears and tells them it's going to sneak inside them and torture them and then kill them. After many years of constant uplink with the starship matrix, a part of each crew member remains locked in the struggle for control of the matrix and something of the thing that calls to them from deep space seeps into their minds, bringing with it fear and confusion. They think the monster is hiding everywhere, especially in other people and has gained control of them, and that it is coming to eat them."

Jilla clapped. "Wonderful! I love ghost stories. The odd thing is, he seems to actually believe it. It makes you want to laugh, right Jacques?"

"Well, Jilla, just before sleep, sometimes I—"

"Jacques!"

"Yes, Jilla. I'll be quiet."

"Jilla," Pie said, "you're a so-called expert on the quantum matrix, do you know what goes on beneath the surface?" Pie asked.

"That's irrelevant; all the programming takes place on the surface. It is because of the self-processing ability of the interior that it is such powerful tool, and that's all it is, a tool. All this talk about it being alive is nothing more than mumbo jumbo. At the very best, it's speculation of the most outrageous kind."

"If I truly gave a shit what you thought, I'd ask Kin to let you link with her during planet-fall, but I think far too much of Kin to ever put her through that."

"I'd like to," declared Joe-54.

"Did I give you permission to talk?" Jilla said.

He bowed his head.

Pie studied the normally quiet Under for a moment and then answered him. "It's impossible Joe-54. It requires a fully functioning link."

"Thank you, Citizen," Joe said without raising his face.

"We have obtained synchronization in speed and position," Kin declared through the ship audio. "Acceleration will be terminated in thirty seconds."

"Prepare yourselves for free fall," Pie reminded them. "A sense of weight will not return until the out-ship is oriented toward the star grazer."

Kin shut down the engine and everyone in the commons grabbed hold and felt as if their insides were dropping away. Shortly, a small jolt passed through the out-ship and gradually it picked up the spin of star grazer; weight returned.

Kin dropped down, out of the bridge, and entered the commons. "Docking complete, Pie."

Pie turned to each person in turn. "Remember what I've told you."

"You're the boss," Jilla said lightly with a bright smile.

"You had better mean it," Pie replied.

"Oh, we do, we do. Don't we, Jacques?"

Jacques nodded, his plump cheeks exaggerated by his big grin.

Pie led them to the docking portal, but it remained shut. He turned to Kin. "Open it," he whispered impatiently.

The portal slid open and they ascended in another tube, the spaceway that connected the gigantic star grazer with the small out-ship. The inner lock slid open and the cavernous interior of the starship lay before them. A starman was standing no more than five meters away, wearing only a belt and using an old-fashioned energy cannon to wave them toward the six open capsules.

Shana pushed up behind Pie and whispered, "There are two more hiding down the row of stasis capsules."

Pie turned to her with a slow, deliberate movement and stared at her. His non-verbal communication was effective; she did not speak further. They marched forward in a single file until each stood before an open capsule.

They could not resist looking "up". The sight of the rows of crystalline tubes that lined the wide corridor pulled their attention upward. The rows of tubes climbed to follow the inner curvature of the ship. It was captivating. They looked directly overhead until they were staring at the distant reflections of light from stasis-chambers, over a hundred meters away. Light-lines extended radially from the capsules, toward the center of rotation, thousands of gossamer spokes. Finally, they returned their attention to the open crystalline tubes that stood before them and stripped.

Pie could not resist sneaking a peek at the New People. Their genitals were as immature as those of small children.

"Getting a good look?" Jilla asked and giggled.

Pie saw movement out of the corner of his eyes and slowly pivoted. Heck Dixon held the canon leveled at them and his head was jerking about, as if on a ratchet.

"Stand perfectly still," Pie ordered in a whisper.

The smile evaporated from Jilla's face and she obeyed. They stood frozen in place, until Dixon lowered his weapon to a rest position. When Pie turned back to his capsule, he noticed that Joe-54 seemed engrossed in studying the starman. It was an invitation to disaster. Damn it! Pie thought, but then Joe broke off his stare.

When Pie and Kin entered their capsules, the rest followed suit. The only thing they were allowed to wear was their link, if they had one. All inanimate objects, outside the confines of a body, experienced an accelerated deterioration in stasis, except for the matrix link. This is one of the anomalies that led some experts to theorize that the matrix was actually a life form.

Heck Dixon visited each capsule, stood there for a moment, and then sealed it. He saved Pie's for last. He stood in front of Pie, but Pie remained perfectly still, avoiding contact with Dixon's eyes, afraid it would be taken as a challenge.

Finally, to Pie's amazement, the man spoke. "You are Pie Traynor."

"Yes," Pie admitted, not knowing if this would trigger some hidden fear in the man.

"Beware, Pie Traynor. The little ones tried to enter my matrix. Beware," he repeated, drawing out the last word as he shut Pie's capsule.

Chapter 22

"Beware!" The word occupied Pie's mind for a hundred years, but to him it was no more than a twitch in time. The capsule opened. He stepped out, onto the new-steel deck. The Dixon crew was not in sight, but he was absolutely certain they were watching.

"Is this some kind of practical joke?" Jacques squeaked in his high-pitched voice, his pudgy hands planted firmly on his sides without real hips but, when he bent to pick up his suit it crumpled into a pile of colored dust, it's engineered obsolescence long past.

Jilla poked her diminutive foot at her own suit and a cloud of fine particles rose into the air.

Pie turned to Kin, ignoring the New People as they stared dumbfounded at the deterioration time had wrought. "Kin, go on ahead and line up the train cars as soon as possible." He turned to the others. "The rest of you follow me, and I mean now."

Subdued for once, the New People toddled along after Traynor, followed by the Unders at a respectful distance.

When they reached the out-ship, Pie stood before them in the commons. "Soon, you will sleep. Do not resist the First Sleep. I'll wait for Kin."

One after another they disappeared into the down-tube, until Pie was alone. He lay down on one of the lounges and was aware of an occasional distant bump as Kin added another water-filled tank "car" to the growing train, until the out-ship was long and multi-segmented. It required an enormous amount of mass and energy to decelerate from near light speed and then re-accelerate after their visit to the planet.

By the time Kin had completed her task, she was beyond exhaustion. When she entered the commons she paused, her shoulders visibly sagging.

"Thanks for waiting up, Pie." She smiled.

"Sometimes it's good to know you're not alone. You know?" Pie had done nothing; yet, he too was overcome by body-numbing fatigue.

She nodded. "I better get back to the bridge. See you in-system." She paused for a moment at the lip of the up-tube to the bridge, and then stepped into it, letting it lift her.

After a few moments, a shudder passed through the out-ship as it disengaged from the star grazer. There was a moment of weightlessness and then the engine of the out-ship kicked in. The star grazer, that had filled the holo-stage with solid blackness, quickly dwindled and disappeared among the specks of space. It would be two years before the starship completed its long parabolic turn and be ready for rendezvous and the trip back Home.

It was a struggle, but Pie made his way to his cabin and then into his stasis capsule to join the others in another year of dreamless sleep. Kin remained where she was; for her it would be a year of vigilance and tiny corrections in course and speed. Their destination was still just another pinpoint of light.

Chapter 23

Angkor-3 had grown to the shape of a colorful disk; greens and blues could easily be distinguished through a patchy, white cloud cover, but Pie's attention was not on the holo-stage. He was thinking about Jacky Nichols, dead, somewhere on the alien planet below. He could understand now why Jacky had decided to stay behind; he had simply reached the end.

It's strange, Pie thought. He had always considered it an inviolate tenet of his life that he would determine when he had had enough but, now, it seemed life was determining when it had had enough of him. His attention shifted to the New People as they chatted gaily. Pie felt envious, and then quickly suppressed it, disgusted that he could even be susceptible of desiring what the New People had. He was immensely grateful that they couldn't read his mind.

Pie cleared his throat. When no one turned to him, he spoke anyway. "I realize a month is not much time planet-side, but that is all we'll have. It'll take us a year of constant acceleration to rejoin the Hawking. At best, it will be over two hundred years before another star grazer will use Angkor as a pivot back to Home. Any questions?"

No one said anything so he continued. "Do you know why the star is named Angkor?"

"Not again," Kin moaned.

"The others will find it interesting," Pie said.

"I doubt it."

"The star was supposed to be named 'Anchor', because it was the pivotal start for the Grand Procession, but a technician accidently entered the word 'Angkor' instead." Pie looked around but no one commented.

"Boring," Kin declared.

"It is not. It's very interesting."

"Is the atmosphere safe?" Jacques asked.

"Remarkably so. View my report."

Jilla raised her arm in the air and energetically waved her hand. Pie reluctantly nodded to her.

"Is this the same report that states the inhabitants are ignorant primitives?"

Pie turned away without answering and entered the down-tube to return to his cabin. Kin had installed an Under-jack in his room so he could access the matrix, at least in a limited way. He inserted his index finger into the dark red tube and felt a trickle of sensation at his fingertip, a pale experience compared to that of a full link.

"Pull up the geological data on Angkor-3."

The screen flickered and then went dark. "Damn it!" What now? Then, just as suddenly, the screen came back to life, filled with Jilla's smiling face, surrounded by the blond ringlets of her hair.

"Citizen Traynor, did you say the magic word?"

"You are shitting me. Don't you have anything better to do?"

"Jacques and I have talked about you. We've decided to focus on your training. Training is important. So, what's the magic word?"

"Get off the fucking link."

"No," she said softly, as if to herself, "that's not it."

Pie huffed with unspent anger, but there was nothing to be done. "Please, get off the link."

"Oh, much better, Citizen. Your manners are improving every day. Carry on." Her face faded from the screen to be replaced by the words, "This equipment has been designated as Underwear-man friendly."

After another half-minute, this too vanished. Finally, the data he called for came onto the screen. He'd been thinking about the trinket and remembered gaining an insight, but the memory was mixed together with an absurd nightmare of being sucked into space. Although he admitted it to no one, not even Kin, he had serious fears that his memory had become corrupted in the last transfer; his mind permanently damaged. He stared morosely at the screen for some time before he was able to suppress his worries and doubts.

He studied the average distribution of "trees" and the ratio of land to water. When he had finished, he leaned back in his chair. It was with both satisfaction and chagrin that he recognized his initial report had been in error. It was an error of scale. On a grand scale, it was remarkably regular throughout the entire planet. It had the undeniable hallmark of a planned and controlled environment. A completely tamed planet, designed...by whom? It gave credence to Jacky's report of an advanced culture, yet, where was it? The blue alien he had met was not the answer. He could not have been wrong on that account.

His gaze had drifted to his slipper covered feet. When he looked up, he saw a figure waiting patiently in the corridor. "Come in, Shana."

She took one small stride into the room. Although hesitant, she used his name. "Pie, I viewed your report, but...can I just talk with you for a minute?" She began to back from the cabin when she saw the grim lines of his face, but his voice said otherwise.

"I'm always happy to talk with you. What's on your mind?"

"Nothing really...it's just...I don't...I—"

"For crap's sake, Shana, spit it out."

"I just wanted to hear you, you know, your voice telling me what it's like down there. It makes it more real."

Pie was quiet as he drifted back in memory and saw Jacky, serious, but not somber as he waved his last goodbye. Shana shifted her position and Pie returned his attention to her.

"There are shallow valleys and rolling hills covered with a lush, green 'grass', accented with splashes of brightly, colored bushes. There are 'trees', or at least that's what we called them."

"What is a tree?"

"You never visited an arboretum in one of the cities?" Pie asked.

As Shana shook her head, Jacques' face appeared on the view screen, accompanied by his voice. "A tree is a large plant that grew on Earth, now extinct, except for a few specimen in bubble cities. Of course, we have no such primeval attachment to vegetation in New Berlin. At any rate, it was...."

While Jacques rattled away, Pie had his own recollections, of a breeze rustling leaves and the creaking of heavy branches, of cool, dappled shade on a hot, summer day.

"Now the gingko tree—"

"You know, Jacques, all you do is piss me off with your pseudo knowledge. Link off or I'll trash this unit."

"Dear me. So destructive. Whatever will you do next? Poke yourself in the eye?" His mocking face faded from the screen.

"As I was saying," Pie continued, in a more civil tone, "there is tall vegetation, some over twenty meters in height, with a turquoise trunk and black leaves. There are lakes with sandy beaches—"

"I don't mean to interrupt, but why didn't you bring any samples of the plant life back with you?"

He smiled with good humor. "I did, but the crazy star crew thought it was poisoning them so they dumped it all, somewhere in deep space."

"Will you take me to a lake, Pie? I've seen holo-images. It's not like the ocean I swam in as a child but I would really like to see one, to touch it."

"It'd be my pleasure."

"How sweet," the view screen said.

A flush of anger spread up Pie's neck and onto his cheeks, but he quieted himself. "Bend, don't break," he counseled himself.

"What did you say?" Shana asked.

"Nothing. I think it'd be better now, if you return to your duties. Soon you'll be able to form your own impressions."

"But, you didn't tell me about the natives."

"It was actually only one. You told me you read my report."

"Yes, I did," she answered in a small voice.

"It was as I described it," he said, clipping his words.

"I should go."

"Yes, you should."

She turned and left the cabin. Pie felt uncomfortable with his harshness. It just seemed to boil out of him. He quieted his mind and he drifted off into a light sleep. He dreamed of his egg-house in the Cascades and remembered feeling happy. He was not alone. He was waiting for her in their shared bed. She would round the corner in a moment and then—

"Five minutes until atmospheric contact," Kin's voice said over the ship's audio.

Pie opened his eyes. "Thanks, Kin," he said to no one. It was a slice of hell not having access to the matrix. He tried to remember the dream but it was gone, as if it had never been. He waited for the cocoon to wrap him in its protective grip.

Chapter 24

Kin glanced over at Shana, who was in the co-pilot's seat when the out-ship separated from the train and began its descent to the planet. Kin could not understand why the Under-woman had started spending time with her again. There had been no flirting, from either of them. They usually spoke very little, unless it involved the actual performance of Kin's job as a driver but, at the moment, Kin was too involved to give it much thought.

The "petals" of the co-pilots seat folded around Shana until she was hidden from view, but she could see; it was as if she was hurtling toward the planet with nothing at all around her. The invisible upper atmosphere glowed orange in front of her and then turned threatening crimson. She was tight-jawed and her hands were balled into fists while the ship bucked and shook, plummeting toward the planet. It seemed to go on and on, until she was quite certain that this would be her death.

"We're in," Kin said for Shana's benefit, but did not divert her attention from the ship as she directed it to Jacky's last known location and the location of his dome. The dome, if it still existed, no longer emitted evidence of electronic life, but it was as good a place to start as any.

During descent, the New People had been tightly linked with the ship's sensors but, to their puzzlement, they found no evidence of an advanced technology, just as Traynor had reported. They could not even locate a sentient being.

Kin set the ship down in a small valley, surrounded by softly rounded hills. Her skill was such that the only physical clues of planet-fall were the sudden absence of subliminal vibrations and a slight downward bob indicating the end of deceleration. This was followed by a "thud", both heard and felt, when she fired the stabilizers into the planet's surface.

Pie rolled out of his cocoon and arrived in the commons just as Kin dropped down from the bridge, followed by Shana-8.

"Good job, Kin," Pie said.

Kim nodded, without a hint of humility. The New People and Joe-54 arrived a moment later.

"It's about mid-day out there," Pie said. "The ground around the ship should be cool enough in thirty minutes. I can see no reason to delay disembarking to the planet's surface. Jacky Nichol's dome should be visible."

165

"If it's still there," Jilla said. "Having had first-hand experience with your technology, one can only wonder."

"It's still there. It was made of perma-foam. Nothing could—" A strange memory arose, of a fingernail cutting into perma-foam.

"You were saying?" Jilla prompted.

"Nothing," Pie said.

"For once, we agree."

"Will the natives come to greet us?" Shana asked, her eyes bright with excitement and her hands fluttering from position to position as if they were birds.

"I don't know," Pie answered, "but I doubt it. I saw only one during my entire four weeks on the surface."

"During descent, Jacques and I identified an equipment malfunction," Jilla declared. "We detected no intelligent life forms, or evidence of technology. Kin, I order you to investigate. Check all the hardware."

"Up yours, you little bitch," Kin said conversationally.

"A female dog. I've heard that word used as slang before," Jilla said.

"I bet you have," Kin said.

"I suspect it's some form of insult, although I can't fathom why."

"Insulting you is a pain in the ass. It's completely lost on you."

"So Jilla, you think there's an equipment failure, uh?" Pie smiled with pleasure. "Isn't that extraordinary? That's exactly what we thought. The same failure twice in a row would be quite extraordinary, don't you agree?"

"Not with your hardware. Besides, what you saw might not have been a member of the dominant species, more like an Under."

"You are really disgusting," Pie said in an even voice.

She seemed surprised and turned to Jacques for clarification. "What did I say?"

Jacques shrugged without giving it much thought.

Pie glanced over at Shana, whose eyes were downcast and then at Joe, and caught him staring at the New People, but once he saw Pie watching him, he quickly dropped his gaze as well.

"It is time," Pie announced and stepped into the tube to float down but had to wait until they had all gathered in the ready room. He nodded to Kin and they heard the whine of the ramp extending until it touched ground.

"Open it, Kin."

The outer lock slid open. Pie took one step out and stopped at the top of the ramp, ignoring the pressure of Kin's hand against his back. He was captivated. The spongy green "grass" spread away in all directions, a carpet of smooth velvet, punctuated by swaying "trees" and vibrantly colored bushes. A subtle fragrance flirted with his nose, a hint of lemon, a trace of mint, refreshing. But it was the sun, beaming through a cloudless blue sky that brought cheer and warmth; the star Angkor was as yellow and friendly as Sol.

"Get out of the way, Pie!" Kin finally demanded.

He started walking. The rays of the sun warmed his hands and he rolled up his sleeves, revealing skin as white as that of a cave dweller, and the diamond knife in its sheath. A pink band of new skin encircled his right wrist. When he stepped onto the grass, Kin joined him and together they strolled into the fairy landscape. Their footsteps had a spring to them as they walked on the resilient grass and then climbed the grade of a hill.

The New People resembled children ever more closely as they held hands and swung their arms, running and walking by starts and stops toward the nearby trees. The two Unders followed after them, but were too engrossed in their own observations to pay any attention to the little "masters".

Pie was lost in speculation about the natives when he heard Jilla shrieking. He turned to see the New People racing toward the ship, their short legs pumping as fast as they could.

"Bugs!" Jilla screamed.

Shana and Joe also began sprinting for the ship, their longer strides eating up the distance much faster than was possible for the New People. Pie turned toward Kin, but before he could reach out to stop her, she too had bolted for the ship. He watched all the activity from his perch on the hill and smiled smugly.

Kin cut in front of the New People, inadvertently blocking their way to ramp and entry lock; she immediately dropped, hitting the hard ramp as if her legs had been cut out from under her. The New People ran over Kin's body, stepping on it as if were just another bump. Kin began desperately trying to pull herself to the lock, but, as soon as the New People entered, the lock slid shut.

Pie started running down the hill toward her, hearing the terror in her voice as she cried for help. When he reached her, he cradled her in his arms, but fear had stolen her reason. She scratched at him and gouged red streaks of blood into the skin of his shoulder and back, her nails cutting through the material of his suit as if it wasn't even there. Then she collapsed and began sobbing. Pie had never seen Kin cry, had not even known it was possible. The sound of her bawling was even more distressing than witnessing her horrified panic. She shivered and shook as she clung to him.

"Kin, the bugs won't hurt you," Pie explained, but she was beyond words, her black citizen-eyes were staring past Pie's shoulder, searching for the hoard of insects that would sink their jaws into her body and suck it dry with a million, nibbling bites. A brilliant, red insect flew past them and landed on the edge of the ramp, its wings moving in slow motion while it rested, and then it took off to flutter away on the warm breeze.

Pie held Kin's face against his chest. "Damn you!" he yelled at the ship. "I know you can hear me! Open the lock, and I mean now, or I guarantee you I'll do so much damage to the ship so that it'll never fly again!"

Kin was no longer struggling. She had lapsed into a faint and lay limp in Pie's arms. He laid her body on the ramp and picked up a boulder that had been exposed by the incinerated ground cover around the ship. He threw it with all his anger and frustration, and it hit with a "bang" against the new-steel. The noise of the boulder striking the ship was magnified by its hollow interior. Despite the fact that it had not even scratched the new-steel, it had sounded ominous to those inside. The lock slid open.

Pie picked up the flaccid body of his friend and carried her into the ship. He had to use the emergency staircase to ascend to the commons, where he gently laid Kin out on a lounge seat. Her eyelids flickered and then opened fully.

Pie stroked the smoothness of her scalp. "Flow, Kin."

She smiled weakly and moved her head in an abbreviated nod.

"You placed us in mortal danger, Under!" The words were strong, but the voice was small. Pie stood and turned to face his accusers.

Jilla and Jacques were both standing. Jilla held a device in her hand, a handle topped by a pink disk. She held it out in front of her, the way a person would hold a weapon.

Of those present, only Pie had a memory of insects as mere pests. To everyone else, the word "insect" was synonymous with gruesome death.

"There's a Citizen saying," Pie began, "bend or you will break."

"I'm listening, and it better be good," Jacques replied.

"This is not Earth. Earth has become inhospitable, but it was not always that way. There was a time when the Earth was lovelier, more inviting than this world outside our ship, and there were insects, but they existed in balance with the rest of Earth's life. There is a balance on this world. If you run as you did today, you must recognize the fact that you are running away from your Earth fears, not real danger." Pie chanced a look at Kin; he was speaking to her as much as to the New People.

"Prove it!" Jilla demanded.

"First, return control of Kin's legs."

They stared, round, blue eyes at black ellipses for eyes.

Then Jilla smiled and lowered her weapon. "Why not? It changes nothing."

Kin swung her legs over the edge of the lounge and came to a sitting position. Pie kept his attention on the New People.

"Now it's your turn," Jilla said.

"Fine. I'll go back outside, by myself."

"Don't, Pie," Kin said. "It's not worth it."

Pie knelt down next to her. "Kin, you weren't listening."

Kin grabbed hold of his arm.

"Trust me," Pie said.

She loosened her grip and Pie stood.

"Time to enter the food chain, Citizen," Jacques quipped.

Pie admonished Kin to do nothing until he returned. After removing his shredded bodysuit and putting on a new one, he descended to the ready room. When he stepped into the lock, the inner door slid shut and the outer opened. He walked back out, onto the cushy grass, and sat down. He saw a six-legged, white creature climbing around the black leaves of a nearby tree, and he saw bugs. The more he looked, the more he saw: metallic-green ones, climbing through the grass; blue-winged ones, flitting about; tiny, black ones, flying in modest sized swarms, but none showed the least interest in him.

He sat and watched until the clouds on the far horizon turned gold, and then pink and purple with twilight. Stars had begun twinkling in the darkening purple of night, when the portal to the ship slid open. Stiff from inactivity, he shifted his weight to stand, and felt the pain of the wounds Kin had inflicted. He leisurely walked into the lock and it slid shut behind him.

When he entered the commons, Kin was seated on the lounge, and Joe-54 and Shana-8 were standing in the back. The New People were seated, eating and chatting, as if unaware that Pie had returned, unharmed.

"If we can't learn trust," Pie said, "we will be our own worst enemies."

"I'm sorry, Pie," Kin said in her coarse voice. "I hope I didn't hurt you much."

Pie looked to her and smiled reassuringly. "Just a few scratches. I'm fine. You were a victim of your memories and of the actions of these very little people, tiny people."

He walked over to stand in front of the New People. They looked up. Jilla brought her hand out from under the table to reveal the weapon she was holding.

"Trust is okay among equals," she said, "but, for us, obedience will do. You may go to bed now, Citizens, both of you."

"To hell with you," Pie replied.

"Isn't he deliciously primitive?" Jilla squealed and giggled.

Pie turned from them and effortlessly scooped Kin off the lounge.

"I can walk," she protested.

"Everyone deserves to be pampered sometimes."

"I would prefer to walk."

Pie set her down; she walked on her own to the down-tube and dropped into it. He was about to follow when Jilla spoke.

"Should we?" Jilla asked.

He paused at the tube.

"Why not?" Jacques answered with a mischievous grin.

"Shana-8," Jilla called in her best, little-girl voice, "You and Joe-54 will accompany us to our cabin."

Both the Unders stood as they were. Shana held one of her hands in the other, as if to squeeze it into submission.

"Well?" Jilla asked more sharply.

"Yes, Master," Shana answered in a subdued voice.

"And you, Joe-54?"

Joe's darkly hooded eyes and blank face effectively masked any expression. "I live to serve, Master," he finally said.

Pie had heard enough. He dropped into the down-tube.

Chapter 25

At the beginning of the next day period, Pie was sitting on the edge of his cocoon applying healing-gel on his numerous scratches and gouges when Kin entered his cabin.

"Don't you ever knock?" he asked gruffly.

"Knock? You mean hit the portal with my hand? That's weird. Your privacy screen was off so I figured…oh, I see. I keep forgetting you're not linked." She studied the deep scratches, sometimes in groups of three, across his chest and arms. "Sorry, looks like I did a job on you. Here, let me help." She took the tube from his hand and began applying the soothing coolness to his upper back.

"At least now you can see what I've been telling you about those two little jerks."

"I believed you, Pie."

"Believing and experiencing are different levels of knowing."

He stood and walked over to the clothing cabinet. He chose a forest green bodysuit and stepped into it. As he pulled it up he saw the medallion the Blue had given to him so many years ago. He sealed his suit and reached for the medallion. The urge to put it on came on him so quickly that he didn't even think about what he was doing. He slipped the cord over his head. When the pearly white medallion came to rest against his chest, there was a tingling sensation and then it was gone, as if had never happened. He stared down at it. The Blue had given both Jacky and himself a medallion. Jacky had put his on but Pie had carried his in a pouch. He wondered, why now? Why had he put it on now? He could never recall having worn it before. A thought flashed through his mind, perhaps a memory, a feeling that he had worn it before, but when he tried to focus on it he came up empty. It was frustrating.

"What are you doing?" Kin asked.

"Nothing. Come on. I'm sure the others are already are already in the commons."

"Since when did you start caring about that?" she muttered as she followed after him.

The New People were sitting in their usual place, well into meal one. Shana-8 and Joe-54 were standing in the back, out of the way. Kin raised a second table, as far from the New People as possible. When Pie and Kin had seated themselves, Jilla spoke.

"Did you sleep well last night, Shana-8?" she asked.

Shana averted her face.

"Shana," Pie said, "would you mind bringing us some food?"

She bowed and backed through an adjoining portal.

Pie returned his attention to the New People. He couldn't stop staring. They were wearing sparkling silvery suits with white ruffles around the cuffs. Their chest area was covered with ruby and emerald gems. He was about to comment about the suits to Kin but when he saw her glimmering skin and fuchsia lips, he kept his thoughts to himself.

"Citizen Kin," Jacques said, "I thought you were such a great driver. Where is Nichol's dome? We've searched with ship sensors and found absolutely nothing."

"I hit my target."

"Really?" Jilla said.

"Yes, really," Pie said, "If Jacky's report wasn't hallucinatory, then it follows that sophisticated technology is being used to shield the dome from our sensors."

"Why would the aliens screen a dome?" Jilla asked.

"I don't know."

"I see you've decided to go native today," Jilla said. "That is the necklace you recovered from the planet and brought back to Home, right?"

"Yes."

"I want it. Give it to me," Jilla demanded.

"Give it to you?" Pie managed to sputter. "Hell no."

"Now don't get hostile," Jilla said sweetly and scolded him with her index finger.

"I'm not hungry," Pie said to Kin. "I'm going outside. Would you open the lock for me?"

She indicated "yes" with a trace of a nod.

When Pie exited the ship and stepped outside, he paused. The morning air was cool and fresh with a breeze. He walked away from the ship and then pivoted slowly until he had made a complete circle. He began a second survey of the surroundings when he came to a stop. There was something different about one of the hills; it was almost too round.

He brushed away an occasional pesky red-fly. He spoke in a conversational voice, fully expecting that someone was watching and listening.

"Kin, have Joe-54 bring out a heavy laser-cutter and a star-lamp. He'll have to get them out of secondary storage."

Kin's voice was broadcasted from somewhere in the ship. "You got it. He'll be down shortly. Pie...."

"Yes?"

"Umm...it can wait."

He was watching towering cumulus clouds fade from salmon-pink to fluffy white as the morning sun fully arose, when the lock to the ship opened.

"Bring them down to me, Joe," Pie yelled.

Joe did not appear. Pie began walking up the ramp when a buzzing insect flew by and into the lock. When he arrived at the top of the ramp, he saw Joe against the far bulkhead, holding the heavy laser-cutter with both hands, while his eyes darted about.

"They won't hurt you, Joe. Bring the cutter to me."

Joe didn't budge.

Pie entered the lock and Joe raised the cutter and pointed it at Pie's chest. Pie's hand went to his knife and he began to slowly withdraw it from its sheath.

"Put the cutter on the deck, Joe."

The man hesitated, but then complied with the order. The black of Pie's eyes were thin ellipses while he studied the Under. Both men stood still until Pie broke the silence.

"Push off. Get out of here."

Joe hurried over to the up-tube and disappeared from sight.

Pie picked up the cutter with one hand and the star-lamp with the other. He walked toward the hill that he had selected, the slightly odd one. The carpet of grass that he was walking on would have had plenty of time to cover the dome in a thick blanket. There even a few scarlet bushes scattered across its roundness.

He stood near the steep slope at the base of the hill when he heard his name being called. He turned. A figure was approaching him from the ship. It was Shana, bobbing as she dodged flying insects that were too small to even be seen from Pie's perspective. He watched with a smile while she zigged and zagged, rushing and stopping. When she had completed her harrowing trip across the harmless meadow, she stood before Pie; her forehead was beaded with sweat and creased with anxiety.

"Jilla sent me," she said, and then paused to catch her breath. "But I wanted to come, to help you...if you want my help."

"Of course. But first tell me something. How is it that you're able to be out here in this bug infested world and Joe can't even leave the lock?"

Her gaze was direct. "It's not his fault. Citizen Kin didn't do any better. I was born on the sea in a floating village. I've been outside, when we were far out to sea where there are no bugs, but Joe grew up in Shang and then was taken to Home. He has never been outside."

Pie nodded. "Okay. Maybe I should cut him some slack."

"Don't you dare cut him!" She stood toe to toe with him, her finger pressed against his chest.

He looked down at the woman with the eyes of a lioness who was glaring up at him. "I meant, give him a chance. Try to understand him better. Sometimes you seem ready to take on all comers and other times you're submissive to the point that I hardly recognize you. What gives?"

She bowed her head. "I live to serve."

"Cut out the crap. You're not impressing me."

She gradually raised her face until Pie could see the devilish smile that graced her features.

Pie continued. "I can understand when you're around the New People but no more of that bullshit when it's just the two of us, okay?"

"Hell no, shit, damn," she said and laughed. "How's that?"

Pie smiled. "Not bad. Pretty good actually. Learn a lot of new words recently?"

"Kin is a good teacher."

"Well, you better be selective what you learn from her."

Suddenly, Shana's smile froze. A golden beetle with orange stripes had landed on the exposed skin of her arm. The beetle's feet caused a sharp prickle as it crawled up her arm. She leaned away while she stared wide-eyed at the insect that was climbing toward her neck.

Pie put his finger in the beetle's path so that it climbed from Shana's glistening black skin onto Pie's pink fingertip. He held it up for Shana to see.

"Beautiful little beast, isn't it?" Pie said. He flicked the beetle into the air and it "whirred" softly as its golden wings took it away on the warm, summer breeze.

Shana remained mute, but her face relaxed. She stood tall and took a deep breath. Pie followed her example; there was a faint fragrance that reminded him of jasmine.

"Feels good, doesn't it?" Pie said.

"Yes," she breathed, "good."

Pie reluctantly turned his attention to the abruptly rising hillside. If he was right, he expected to find the remains of his friend, possibly in some state of partial preservation. He flicked on the cutter and its bright white blade sprung into existence, "hissing" with superheated air. A pungent gray smoke curled upward as Pie cut a long oblong into the hillside, big enough to step through, if he was right about Jacky's dome. He shut the cutter down and laid it on the grass.

"Stand back," he ordered. Starting with a short hop, he kicked with his full weight, striking the center of the oblong; it disappeared as it fell inward. A cloud of ash and desiccated dirt billowed out. When the air cleared a black hole in the green of the hillside was revealed.

He smiled as he thought about the shielding, high-tech? Possibly extremely high-tech. Ship's sensors should've been able to penetrate. It made him wonder what else was buried beneath this carpet of "grass". He inspected the sunlit edge of the cut, twenty centimeters of greenery, roots and soil and an inner border that was three centimeters thick and bright white, foam-steel. He had found Jacky's dome.

He retrieved the star-lamp from his waist pouch and held the pea-sized globe on his palm while he stepped over the threshold and into the dome. The air was cool and dry. Directly in front was the rectangular silhouette of Jacky's mainframe matrix and next to it his reconstitution unit. He glanced upward at the blank white dome, arching overhead, before returning his attention to the hole he had cut.

"Coming, Shana?"

He watched her step over the verge and into the dome, careful to touch nothing. Together they walked toward the center of the dome, the star-lamp providing them with a bubble of light. Each time they passed a chair, Pie would look at it, expecting that he would see Jacky's dried face looking back at him, minus eyes.

Pie placed the lamp on the floor in the center of the dome and opened it fully. The light reflected off the dome so that the entire space was lit. On the far side of the dome there was an area that Jacky had curtained off. Pie decided that was probably where Jacky had slept; it seemed to Pie it was a basic human instinct to hide away when it was time to sleep, even when there was nothing to hide from. As he walked toward the curtained off area, a breeze whispered past him and chunks of the curtain fell away. With a sweep of his outstretched hand the remains of the curtain were brushed aside. At first he thought he saw a human form on the sleeping pad; his heart beat palpably. But, on closer inspection it was only crumpled bedding.

He began a more methodical search of the dome. When completed, he had found no body. It was more with relief than disappointment that he ended his exploration and returned to the center of the dome where Shana had remained. From the center, he began another visual survey. He saw light reflecting off tools that Jacky had left out on his workbench. Jacky had always been so fastidious. Whatever had happened must have happened quickly and it had happened somewhere out there, on the surface of the planet.

"Pie," Shana whispered, "I don't like this place."

Pie barely heard her, still engrossed in his own speculations. "I think I can find what we need if I can access Jacky's mainframe." He shook his head. It was so exasperating not to have a link. "Kin", he said as if she were standing at his side, "try to switch on Jacky's matrix."

There was no response.

After waiting a moment more, he walked over to the workbench and selected a simple tool with a flat tip that he could use to pry open the cabinet. He worked it along the edges until a panel popped open. He reached in and removed the memory cube from its slot. He slid the memory cube into his pouch.

"Are you ready?" he asked.

"I'm definitely ready. More than ready," she said and hurried for the oblong opening and sunlight.

Pie picked up the star-lamp and followed with deliberate steps, still lost in thought. The sunlight was blinding bright after being in the dim dome. It looked to be about midday. As they approached the lock a swarm of tiny black insects passed in front of them. Pie brushed them aside with a wave of his hand but Shana stopped and waited for them to pass; she wasn't quite ready for purposeful interaction with bugs.

The ship lock opened for them and they entered to ascend to the commons. The New People were there. Jilla was jumping up and down and clapping.

"What did you find?" she exclaimed. "Give it to me." She held out her pudgy little hand. "Give it to me."

"In a minute."

"In a minute?" Jilla was incredulous. "Jacques, do something!"

Jacques began fumbling in his waist pouch while Pie surveyed the room. Joe was standing in the back of the room but his eyes were bright with curiosity. Kin was sitting by the holo-stage but had twisted around so she could see.

Jacques finally managed to get his weapon out and pointed it at Pie.

"Put that away you little shit," Pie said and returned his attention to Kin. "What did you detect, anything?"

"Nope. And once you were inside the dome, I had neither audio nor visual on either of you. It was as if you were gone from the face of the world. It was Jacky's dome, wasn't it? Was he…."

"Yes, it was his dome but, no, I didn't find him. I saw nothing that'd suggest what happened to him. No clues as to how or when he met his end."

"Jacques!" Jilla barked. "What are you waiting for?"

"Wait, Jilla. Let's hear what he has to say."

"Maybe this will help." Pie reached in his pouch and brought out the memory cube.

Jilla ran over. "Give it to me."

Pie held it higher, out of her reach. She jumped once. Her face flushed with anger and she stomped her little foot on the deck. "Give it to me, you underman, you, you—"

Pie flipped it over to Kin who caught it.

"You are not a nice man," Jilla declared.

Pie ignored her and addressed Kin. "Upload this to the ship's matrix. Let's see what we have."

Kin left the commons for the bridge, inserted the cube, and returned to the commons to watch the holo-stage along with everyone else.

The stage flickered to life and then went blank. Kin linked in to see what the problem and immediately linked out to give the New People a look that could not be misunderstood. The New People settled a little more comfortably on a lounge and then Jilla looked up and smiled.

"Are you ready now?" Pie asked dryly.

They nodded in unison and the stage reactivated. Seeing Jacky again was unsettling for Pie. Curly black hair, eyes the black of a Citizen. He had a deep dimple in his chin and a space between his two front teeth. Pie smiled. Jacky had persisted in his refusal to get them fixed. Claimed that his soul lived in the gap. Images of Jacky's sister and father came to mind. He must have known Jacky's mother too. He felt a chill. Who was she? Something. He could almost remember...something.

"Pie."

He looked up and met Kin's eyes. Clearly she knew something was up. He returned his attention to the holo-stage.

The voice emanating from the stage was typical Jacky, measured and methodical. "Greetings citizens of the future and, even more probably, of the past. I hope you will find this information useful. This is the first installment of what I assume will be many before I die." He laughed uneasily, as if he'd been having second thoughts about his decision to stay. "What you are seeing is a matrix simulation. It seems some things are reluctant to allow sensors to detect them, and it appears I'm one of those things." He laughed again. This time genuine. "I'm invisible. Anyway, I've decided to study the insect life first. And one more thing, I know how impatient citizens can be and if you rush through it you might miss something important or interesting. So—" He smiled. "—settle back and enjoy the show. The report went on with both text and Jacky's voiceover. Insect after insect, flying, crawling, eating, and hatching. Everyone but Pie backed a little farther away from the stage.

After a quarter hour, Jilla could sit still no longer. "Citizen Kin, flash forward."

"Wait," Jacques said. "This is quite extraordinary."

Jilla turned to her usually synchronous partner. "You can study this material just as well back in New Berlin as here."

"All right, Jilla. I guess you're right," he added reluctantly.

Kin looked to Pie. "Want me to see if I can flash forward?"

"Please."

Kin uplinked but Jacky's presentation continued to plod along. She downlinked and turned to Pie. "Jacky's put some kind of a block on it. I've never come up against anything like it before."

"Some matrix technician you are. Sad really," Jilla said and then her gaze drifted while she fully engaged the ship's mainframe matrix. After a moment she was back. Her eyes met those of Jacques, wordless questions and guesses passed between them. In the meantime Jacky's report continued to play itself out, at its own rate and in its preordained order.

Pie couldn't help but laugh. "That little twit. He always was a genius when it came to matrix technology. If he weren't already dead, I'd strangle him myself. Oh well. I think he got it from his mother. Now there was one damn smart woman. His mother...."

"You were about to say?" Kin asked.

"Kin, do you remember Jacky's mother? Anything about her?"

"No. Should I? I hardly even knew Jacky."

"No, no, of course, not." He looked away.

"I wish he'd stuck around long enough to teach that matrix trick to me," Kin mused.

"This is stupid," Jilla declared. She stood. "Shana-8 and Joe-54, come with us."

"Wait," Jacques said and returned his attention to the holo-stage to watch a crab-like creature hatch.

"Jacques," Jilla said out loud. Followed by further non-verbal communication. Jacques cheeks flushed pink.

"Okay, Jilla," Jacques said. He stood and together the New People headed for the down-tube.

When Shana passed Pie, she tried to get his attention, but he was involved in a discussion with Kin and didn't notice. When her subtle attempt failed, she dropped her head and assumed the pose of obedience as she followed the New People and Joe into the down-tube.

Pie and Kin remained in the commons, watching the holo-stage and chatting about nothing of importance. Time dragged on.

Late in the afternoon, Kin sat forward and said, "There's something you should know."

"Yeah, what's that?"

"You are not detectable to ship sensors."

"I know. You told me, when I entered the dome."

"No. All the time. Right now as a matter of fact. I thought you should know because if I know, the little ones know as well. I can't track you and if I can't, they can't either. If they sense they are losing control they can very dangerous."

"Hmm…that is odd."

"Odd? It's downright creepy. What's happening, Pie?"

He said nothing.

"It's that damn necklace you're wearing. Take the damn thing off."

"I can't."

Kin threw her hands up in exasperation. "What the hell. Pull the damn thing over your head. Need help?"

"I can't." To demonstrate, he began pulling on the medallion, obviously straining, but it remained fixed in place. He gave up and rested his hands in his lap.

"Now that is double creepy," Kin declared.

Pie nodded. "Indeed."

"I guess your best bet is to feign ignorance. If they don't know you know…you get my drift?"

"You're suggesting I play stupid."

She nodded. "That's pretty much it. Think you can handle it?"

Pie laughed. "Yeah, no problem there. It's a good thing I have you."

"It is."

Pie nodded. "It is."

There was nothing more to be said. They returned their attention to the holo-stage. Jacky was talking about a rather ugly animal that he had named a nine-toed sloth.

It was not until it was time for meal three that the New People reappeared in the commons, followed by the Unders. Shana served the meal but she seemed withdrawn. Pie was about to comment on it when the figure of a native appeared in the holo-stage.

"This is a matrix simulation of one of the local inhabitants," Jacky said in his voiceover. "Unfortunately, it, like me, cannot be detected or recorded by our current technology. Perhaps in the future…but I doubt it. Interesting, isn't it? It's enough to make a person wonder."

The native appeared to be aimlessly ambling along. Its arms hung loosely at its sides and its head bobbed forward and back with each step. The creature had a large cranium, covered with smooth skin, cornflower blue. It's eyes were not visible, set deeply within rectangular indentations in a face as plain as that of a cartoon character. It had no nose and only a tiny slit of a mouth. The body was small in comparison to the head size, making them look top heavy. A medallion, identical to the one Pie wore, hung around its neck; otherwise it wore no clothing or decoration. There were no nipples, no umbilicus, and no genitalia. It was, in two words, blue and plain.

"How does it breathe?" Jacques asked. "Does it breathe?"

"Never mind that," Jilla said as she leaned forward to get a better view. "Is it male or female?" she asked. When no one answered she turned to stare at Pie. "Citizen, I asked you a question."

"Sorry. I thought it was rhetorical question. I would guess it's neither."

"Good eyes," Kin said with a broad smile. "I'm going to go with you on that one."

"But Citizen," Jacques said, addressing Pie, "one cannot assume their sexuality is similar to our own."

Pie nodded.

Jilla piped in. "What about the one you met last time you were here? Didn't you ask it?"

"Now that's a subject that didn't come up. You seem kind of fixated on that topic. Got the hots for a Blue?"

"You are disgusting," Jilla declared.

"It wasn't easy to communicate with it," Pie said. "The one we had contact with last time was intelligent enough and picked up our language in less than an hour. It was more of a conceptual problem. A point of view issue. Its responses were concrete. It was frustrating."

"When you say 'frustrating' I assume what you're really doing is making excuses for your incompetence," Jilla said.

"Careful there or you might hurt my feelings."

Jacques turned to Jilla. "I have an idea. Let's go find a native. I'm certain we could do much better. In fact, that's probably the reason none of the natives have approached us. They probably think we're all like these…." He waved his hand in the direction of the others.

Jilla clapped her hands with delight. "Yes! We'll leave first thing in the morning. Joe-54 will come with us."

Joe took an involuntary step backward.

"Oh don't be such a sludge," Jilla said. "We'll provide protection. You'll be completely bug proof." She stood. "Go to your cabin," Jilla ordered the Unders.

The New People followed after them.

A short time later, when Jacky had moved on to discussing the bushes that dotted the landscape, Kin shut down the holo-stage for the night. She stood and stretched. "Damn," she said, "I hated to shut it down just when it was getting interesting."

"Tomorrow's another day."

"Gosh, that was clever. Did you make that up yourself?"

Pie laughed. "Flow, Kin."

"Yeah, flow, Pie."

He dropped into the down-tube. Kin followed a short time later.

Gary Moreau

Chapter 26

Pie and Kin were just finishing meal-one when the New People entered the commons. Apparently "leaving early in the morning" didn't mean all that early. They were wearing tangerine-colored jump suits, but it was their conical hats that captured Pie's imagination. It reminded him of a birthday party when he was a child. All the kids had to wear a pointed, party hat with its tight, elastic string that seemed to cut into the skin under the chin. Joe arrived a moment later, also wearing one of the hats, but the copper cone appeared even more ridiculous on him; it looked ten sizes too small.

Jilla saw Pie staring at the Under and turned to inspect him. "Jacques," she exclaimed, "can you believe it? He's wearing that drab-brown outfit again."

Jacques shook his head and clicked his tongue in agreement.

"Really, Joe-54," Jilla continued, "I'm not going to meet an alien with you dressed like that. Now go on and get into that pretty yellow outfit I like so much. Go on," she urged, shooing him away with her hand.

He turned with a brisk, barely disguised, angry twist, and dropped into the down-tube.

"Joe-54 is going to have to be disciplined," Jilla said. "A shame really." She turned her attention to Pie. "Citizen," Jilla said sternly, her hands on her underdeveloped hips, "are you laughing at us?"

"Me? No," Pie said while he continued to smile broadly. "Those are...unique hats, a nice touch...really."

"Thanks," Jilla said with pride. "They are called B-hats. Don't know why. They were all the rage when we left New Berlin. But these are special. They provide complete protection from insects."

"I see. How do they work? Do you stab bugs with that pointy tip?"

"Even if I tried to explain it to you, you wouldn't understand," Jilla said.

Joe made his grand entrance, but kept his eyes trained at the deck. He was wearing a canary yellow bodysuit with hot pink accents.

"Very nice," Jilla said. "Turn around so I can see your back."

Pie also watched with interest, almost expecting to see a little puffy bunny tail.

Jilla smiled and nodded. "Now, don't you feel better? Of course you do. Come along."

183

She led the small procession to the down-tube but, instead of going all the way down to the ready room, she exited on the storage level. She and Jacques climbed onto the front saddle of a two-person whistle-cycle and Joe mounted the rear saddle. The storage bay lock dilated and, when it was fully open, the craft arose on jets of air. Its high-pitched scream filled the bay and then quickly faded as they flew out of the circular lock and into the alien sky.

After they had departed, Pie looked to Shana, who had been standing quietly out of the way, using the Under trick of melting into the furnishings. "Shana, what can you tell me about Joe? Is he playing the same game you play?"

Shana glanced toward Kin and then away. She held her eyes downcast and her hands clasped before her, the very picture of subservience. "Citizen," she said in a small voice, "I don't understand what you mean."

"I don't understand what you mean either," Kin said. "Stop pestering the poor girl. She's just an Under."

"Kin, stay out of this. Shana, answer my question."

"He is a good servant, Citizen," she finally managed.

"My name is Pie. Say it."

"Yes, Citizen Pie. I live to serve."

"Oh, for God's sake, leave the girl alone," Kin said.

Pie turned to Kin. "Shana and I are going to take a ride. Do you mind monitoring Jacky's cube while we're gone? He's bound to say something useful sooner or later."

"Sure, Pie, no problem. I can hardly wait to watch another episode of 'Jacky's Wild and Wacky World of Plants'."

"Would you rather take Shana? I can stay here."

"Take her? Where in the hell would I take her? No, that's all right. I'll stay. Shana-8, go on down to storage. I want to talk with Citizen Traynor for a moment."

Shana nodded and obediently disappeared into the down-tube.

As soon as she was gone Kin spoke in her gravelly voice. "I don't think you should encourage such familiarity with an Under. It's not healthy."

"I'll decide what's right and what's wrong. I don't need you to tell me."

Kin shrugged. "Do as you wish."

"I intend to."

"Fuck it," she said with a fuchsia smile. "What in the hell was I thinking?"

"Would you help me launch the other whistle-cycle and provide an energy beam?" Pie asked.

"Sure."

"Thanks, Kin. I appreciate it."

She waved his gratitude away with a flick of her hand and Pie entered the tube to follow after Shana. When he arrived in storage he settled onto the front saddle and Shana climbed onto the rear saddle.

"Kin, dilate the iris," Pie said, and the storage portal twisted open. He looked down at the smooth, black console in front of him. "Damn it!"

"What's wrong, Pie?" Shana asked.

"I can't fly this thing without a link."

"Well I can't fly it, and attend to the ship, and Jacky's cube and everything else," Kin's disembodied voice stated.

"Which way did the neutered people go?"

"Funny, Pie. Southwest. They're about ten kilometers out."

"Shana, get two survival packs, will you? I think we'll take a walk."

Pie jumped the two meters to the resilient grass and caught the packs that Shana tossed down. He then reached up and effortlessly lowered her to the ground. Automatically, he slung the packs over his shoulder.

"I'll carry my own," Shana announced.

He grinned and handed her one of the packs. She slipped her arms through the harness straps and shifted the weight until it felt comfortable.

Pie started walking in long strides. When Shana gained his side, he spoke. "Let's head north. There should be a lake about two kilometers in that direction."

Shana nodded enthusiastic agreement.

The air was pleasantly warm. The sky was filled with flat-bottomed clouds, each like a small island, floating over the land and spotting the emerald hills with slowly moving patches of shadow.

During the first kilometer, Shana dodged and swerved to grant each and every insect the right-of-way but, by the second kilometer, her fear was wearing thin. She tentatively slipped her fingers into his hand and he glanced curiously at her, but returned the gesture, firmly clasping his hand around hers. When they topped the rise of a hill, the sparkling glitter of sunlight on water lay before them.

"Oh, Pie!" Shana exclaimed with delight.

She pulled her hand free and ran down the hillside with an exuberant disregard for the laws of physics, nearly toppling forward as the slope of the hill added to her momentum. She stumbled but managed to regain her balance and come to a stop at the water's edge. Her feet rested on a white beach of fine sand, too white to be more than comfortably warmed by the sun, so soft it was difficult to feel. The beach stretched away in both directions with an undulating width until in the distance it thinned to a line and then disappeared. Farther out on the lake, a brisk breeze was whipping up white-topped waves. There was a minty fragrance in the air. Pie stopped next to her on the virginal sand, untouched by tracks, but their own.

"It's about fifteen kilometers around," Pie said. "Would you like to walk it?"

"May we?" she asked with child-like joy.

Pie nodded, pleased with himself, and began walking again, with Shana running on ahead. Gusts of lake breeze blew her thick, kinky hair, pushing against it as if it were one piece.

When Shana began to walk more consistently at Pie's side, he spoke. "What can you tell me about Joe?"

Some of the spring left her step. "Well, he came to Home when he was five, from the City of Shang, and...I don't know. What did you want to know?"

"Does he feel resentment as an Under?"

"Was that a serious question? We all do. What are you thinking, anyway?"

"I think he is so contained that he'll explode someday."

She lowered her gaze. "Joe provides reliable service."

"Kind of quiet though, isn't he?"

"Yes."

"He must talk with you, after all, you're both Unders and share quarters. What does he talk about?"

It was a moment before she answered. "He talks about lots of things."

"Such as?"

"He tells me about his childhood in Shang and about how shallow and silly the New People are and...."

"And?"

"Well...he thinks Kin is coarse and arrogant but not a bad person."

"What about me?"

"He doesn't understand you."

"Do you?" Pie asked.

She stopped walking and Pie stopped with her.

"Sometimes I think I understand you," she said.

"Do you trust me?"

They began walking again and took several strides before she answered. "Yes...I trust you."

"You don't sound that certain."

186

She met his eyes and her face flashed with a bright smile. "I answered your question, Citizen."

"Yes, I guess you did. I trust you, too."

She returned her gaze to the lake and then ran on ahead, effectively ending the conversation. When their paces matched again, they walked in silence for a while before Pie spoke.

"What does Joe want?"

"The same thing we all want, freedom…and a healthy Earth."

"That's understandable."

The silence returned for a few moments, and then Shana spoke. "Pie?"

"Yes?"

"Can we just be together for a while without all these questions?"

"All right, Shana," Pie said with a laugh. "Let's walk, not talk."

By the time they reached the far side of the lake, a bank of thunderclouds had moved in from the west and the light had darkened to a dull gray.

"Looks like we're in for a little rain," Pie observed.

"Rain? I get to see rain and a lake in a single day?"

"You are a lucky woman. We might as well sit it out here." He slung the pack off his shoulder and rummaged around in it until he found a small package marked "shelter". He peeled off the soft shell and dropped the contents of the package on a mat of the ubiquitous grass, about twenty meters from the beach. When air touched it, it expanded into a mini-dome, big enough for two people.

He looked back across the lake as a bolt of lightning cracked its way across the sky and, a second later, the ground shook with the deafening "boom" of thunder. Shana dived for cover in the back of the small tent as if that would offer any real protection.

"Shana, come sit with me and watch this."

She crept toward the dome opening until she was pressed against his side.

"You know," Pie began, "this entire world is obviously engineered and controlled, yet, here is the very essence of chaos, a thunderstorm. You know what I think?"

Shana remained silent so he continued.

"I think this is an example of alien art. It wasn't allowed or promoted for a functional reason. It exists only for its esthetics."

"Art?"

"Yup. Perhaps it could be considered a type of performance art."

A dense, gray curtain of rain hid the far shore and was advancing across the lake. The temperature was dropping. It was cool and invigorating; excitement spread before the advancing face of the ozone-charged wind.

They huddled a little deeper in the shelter, but Pie left the oval doorway open so they could watch the advancing storm. The rain began as a few "plops", but within minutes it was a downpour. The sheet of rain was so thick, the lake was hidden from view despite its nearness. It pounded on the shell of the shelter, making any attempt at speech useless, so they simply sat near one another, warm and dry. There was a sense of security and isolation within the shelter while, just outside, the full rawness of the storm soaked the land.

The intense fury of the rain was replaced by a lighter, but more enduring patter, steady but chaotic, comforting. Shana shivered as a cool breeze swirled into the shelter and Pie put his arm around her.

"Is this what the Earth was like before the Death?" Shana wondered aloud.

When Pie answered his voice was as distant as his mind, recalling the Earth of long ago. "Of all that you have experienced since planet-fall, this is closest to old Earth. It was a wild and vigorous world, full of variety and chaos. I remember a storm just like this one when I was a boy. I took refuge under the corrugated, metal roof of an empty stable. The rain rattled against the roof while I sat on a bail of straw smelling the sweetness of wet earth and freshly cut hay."

Although the references were odd, she understood the essence of his words and sat quietly at his side. It was some time before she ventured to break into his reverie.

"What happened, Pie? Why did the Death occur?"

"Someone, or something, in the universe wanted our jewel of a planet. It was a long-term plan, at least on a human scale. We were genetically modified by them to be susceptible to a trigger, as was all life on Earth. It took our blundering to trigger the trap. The second Mars expedition and what they brought back to Earth. All life on Earth was pushed to the edge of extinction. But we survived, barely. Mason believes this is where the attack on Earth originated. If I find the least evidence to support that contention, he plans to send another star grazer to deliver mass weapons traveling at near light speed. It will destroy this world."

She thought about the pastoral landscape, peaceful. "Do you believe this is where the attack originated?"

"No. That's bullshit. I think they came from much farther away."

"What is this bullshit you keep mentioning?"

Pie sighed. "Does it really make any difference, Shana?"

188

She pulled away from him and turned to face the blank wall of the dome.

Within another hour the rain had passed. It was late afternoon when they stepped out of the dome, onto the sopping wet grass, and they were treated to a breath-taking vision. Golden sunlight slanted in from the west, just under the edge of the cloudbank, lighting the landscape of greens and turquoise to an almost phosphorescent brightness against the dark gray background of storm clouds.

The air was newly freshened and Pie breathed deeply, stretching inside and out. "Do you want to go back, or should we spend the night?" he asked, as he stared out across the still choppy water of the lake.

She rested her hand on his forearm. "I'd like to stay."

"Yeah, me too. I'll get the transmitter out and tell Kin not to expect us." He ducked back into the shelter and returned with a small, featureless box. He turned it over a couple of times while he inspected its glossy blackness.

"Would you like me to help?" Shana asked.

"Sure," Pie replied easily and handed it to her.

"I need something sharp, like maybe that knife you seem so fond of."

He withdrew the knife from its sheath and handed it to her. "Be careful," he advised, "it's molecular-sharpened and will cut anything with the lightest touch."

"I know. This isn't the first time I've used it." She smiled and bent over the box to work on it. "Don't worry. I'll be careful." She ran the blade along a nearly invisible seam and the back fell off. "I like this knife." After inspecting the interior she caused an arc with one of those silvery wires she carried hidden in her clothing. Then she handed both the knife and the box to Pie.

"Kin?" Pie said, without expecting an answer.

"Yes, Pie," the permanently harsh voice of Kin replied promptly.

"Shana and I are going to spend the night out. Just wanted you to know."

"Really," Kin replied, drawing out the word. "You be sure to have a good time."

"It's not like that," Pie objected.

"No, of course not," Kin answered, a smile in her voice.

"I'll call you, if I need you, otherwise, link-off."

"Got you covered. Kin off."

Pie tossed the device into the shelter and returned to Shana on the beach.

"How did you know how to do that?" he asked. "Did you get some kind of special training or something?"

"That's the problem, one of many when it comes to the Technocracy. Citizens have come to believe their own propaganda about Unders. We aren't stupid and have had to discover workarounds."

"I don't underestimate you."

"That's good."

"What would you like to do now?" Pie asked.

"I'd like to go for a swim."

"You would?"

"When I was a little girl, after the sun went down, we would take off our sun-suits and the adults would mark off a circle of water with their boats, holding torches. The light splintered in reflection off the waves. Everyone not holding a torch would dive in. It was wonderful," she concluded, tears shimmering along her eyelids.

"Do you think you still remember how?"

She brushed her fingers across her eyes and rubbed her nose, but her voice was clear. "I'll never forget. Do you know how?"

"I think so," Pie said somewhat doubtfully. "What about some creature in the water? We don't know what's there. They might be dangerous."

"I've swum with sharks, sea snakes and barracuda. What could be worse?"

"Sounds inviting."

"You can stay on shore if you want," she said as she pulled open the binding of her body suit so that it dropped to the sand.

"Wait," Pie said, "I'll come with you." He stepped out of his suit, but kept the knife in its sheath on his forearm.

"Aren't you going to take off your necklace?" Shana asked.

"I can't."

"You can't?"

Pie shook his head and, instead of telling her, demonstrated. He pulled the trinket five centimeters away from his chest with ease, but pulling it a sixth centimeter required all the strength in his arms. His muscles bulged with definition and the veins in his arms stood out before he gave up the useless effort.

"I guess I'll just have to wear it until we leave the system."

Shana looked down at the sandy beach, so white it was almost luminescent. "I guess so," she said, and then added with more energy, "Come on, Pie!" She bolted for the lake, a white splash marking each step, until she knifed into the water with a shallow dive and when she surfaced rolled onto her back. "Come on in. The waters fine!"

He edged forward until he was ankle deep. Then, with a slow, painful progression, he advanced until the water was mid-thigh. It was cold. Goose bumps sprouted. "Shana, this isn't fine. It's damn cold!"

"Don't be a sludge. Just dive in."

Finally, with an exercise of will, he fell forward. The cold took his breath away and he clamored to the surface, gasping for air. Although reluctant, he forced himself to swim out to her. He was treading water, watching while she sliced through the water, as graceful as any sea creature.

"Don't go out so far!" he called, his own strokes not much more than a thrashing about.

"You worry too much," she answered, but swam over to meet him. When she was nearly there, she dived under the water and came up behind him. Reaching up with both hands, she pulled him under. He came sputtering back to the surface in time to hear her laughing. Her laughter was too light-hearted for him to resist.

He smiled. "You just wait until I get you back on land," he warned with mock seriousness.

It was not long before he tired of his struggles and swam back to shore, his teeth chattering with cold. He set up the infrared unit and experienced the pleasure of warming from a chill. While his skin dried he kept his eyes on Shana's indistinct form, a line of white water as she cut through the surface. Shortly, she too came out of the lake to stand by the warmth.

"You aren't a very good swimmer," she said.

"No kidding," Pie said, and this time they both laughed. He handed her a nutrient bar.

"Wouldn't it be nice," she said around a mouthful of food, "if we could have a real fire?"

Pie nodded and then slipped into his bodysuit and walked into the darkness. When he returned, he was carrying an armful of strips he had cut from one of the "trees".

"I don't know if it'll burn, but it's worth a try."

He arranged the chunks of turquoise "tree" in the shape of a pyramid and lit it by placing a small cube under the pile that burst into flames. Surprisingly, the "wood" did burn, sizzling with a blue flame, and soon the air was filled with a heavy floral fragrance, much like standing under a magnolia tree in full bloom.

"Beautiful," Shana whispered. "Thank you, again. It's been such a wonderful day. Maybe my best ever."

"I'm glad you had a nice time. I did too."

The clouds had cleared completely and the night sky filled with more stars than could be seen from Earth. They filled the firmament with uncountable bright specks. Pie laid out a blanket and they sat side by side, with their backs hot and their fronts cool. Small waves twisted out of the black water, slapped softly on the sand, and then "swished" as they slid back into the lake.

Pie watched their shadows dancing to the light of the flame. It was not the shadow of a single person, but two melded together. He could feel warmth as she pressed against his side.

"Is Shana your real name?"

"Absolutely. My parents had eight girls and named each one Shana. I was number eight."

Pie laughed.

"I'm sorry," Shana continued, "it's just that sometimes you think like a typical Citizen. It just gets me."

"I think I deserve a better answer than that."

He could tell she was studying him, but he continued to stare out into the night.

"You're right," she finally said. "Shana feels like my name, but of course it isn't the name my parents gave to me. I can hardly remember them." She took a long breath. "My name was Sea Spray, daughter of Moon Water."

"Would you like me to call you Sea Spray, daughter of Moon Water?"

She expelled a short laugh. "I think Shana will do. Is Pie Traynor your real name?"

"It is. My parents named me after a baseball player."

"So, you're named after a participant in some kind of game? Your parents must have really liked that game."

"That they did." Pie turned to study her in the light of the fire: her high cheekbones, straight nose and full lips. "You are beautiful."

She glanced down, before turning to Pie with a pleased smile. "Thank you. I think you look...interesting as well."

"I didn't say 'interesting'," Pie said dryly.

She looked down again.

He chuckled. "What I meant to say is, thank you. I've always prided myself on my 'interesting' appearance."

She turned to him as if to respond, but he held up his hand. "It's all right, Shana. I appreciate honesty much more than empty compliments."

192

"But, it was a compliment."

"In that case, I thank you, again."

She looked at him with exasperation, but refrained from further comment.

The fire began to burn low and Pie stood, offering his hand to her. She walked with him to the shelter, holding onto his arm. He stepped back to allow her first entrance. He had prepared it. The floor was soft and an infrared heater had warmed it to a cozy level. Soft, indirect light reflected off the domed ceiling.

Shana lay down on her back, her arms at her sides, her eyes staring at the dome roof. It was obvious what she expected to happen next.

"Shit," Pie said, and then laid down with his back to her, not touching.

After a while Shana spoke. "Are you awake?" she whispered.

"Yes."

"Don't you like me?"

"That's a stupid question," he replied gruffly. "Of course I like you."

She was quiet for a moment before she spoke again. "Don't you want me?" she asked softly, and then hurried on, "I mean, not like an Under servicing a Citizen, but...like one person to another, a free woman to a free man."

"Are you a free woman?"

"I will be."

"And when is this going to happen?"

"You will make it happen," she declared.

Pie sighed and then nodded. "If I can, I will."

"Not good enough."

Pie laughed. "Okay. I will do it."

"Excellent. In that case I have something else to say. I want you."

Pie rolled over to face her, frowning. "You don't know me. I've done unspeakable things. Terrible things. Horrific—"

"That's not true!"

"How would you know?" he asked harshly.

"I...well, I just know. I can sense what kind of person you are."

"Right," he said bitterly. "You know, Shana, there was this poet who died long, long ago. He wrote about love. He said,

> It comes in close in lazy circles
> Without touching
> It comes in very close
> But it's always out of reach
> Because
> It always comes closer

Only as it comes.

He pushed himself to a seated position and then stood. "This is neither the time, nor the place, and I am not the person. Now go to sleep. I'm going for a walk. I'll be back in a little while."

She got to her knees. "I'll go with you."

"No. I want to go by myself."

She sat back on her heels and he stepped out into the night. It was quiet, but for the soft slapping of wavelets against the shore. The sand was star-lit white. The wind that blew against him was cool, but not cold.

It would be much longer than a "little while" before he returned to the shelter.

Chapter 27

When morning came Pie dissolved the shelter and cleaned up the site of their beach fire. He wasn't ready to return to the ship and neither was Shana. The discussion from the night before was not brought up by either of them. They began walking down the beach, speaking very little.

Shana was debating with herself, but finally decided she could withhold the information no longer.

"Pie."

He said nothing.

"I hope you won't hate me for what I'm about to tell you." She paused and swallowed, her throat instantly dry.

That statement caused him to stop. His black eyes narrowed with suspicion. "What do you want to say?"

"An unforgiveable thing was done to you during your last regeneration. The New People have changed the regeneration matrix so that memories can be selectively deleted and, if desired, other memories inserted in their place."

"You don't really expect me to believe that crap do you?"

"It's the truth! I swear it. Ask the New People."

"I will, you can count on it. Of course, they're about as trustworthy as a woodpecker in a bubble."

"Pie, please...."

He looked ahead and began walking, with Shana hurrying along at his side. Her voice was tremulous when she spoke.

"Pie...you had memories inserted into your mind that were taken from a man named Jericho Zinc. He was a horrible man."

"Was?"

"You killed him."

"I did, huh?"

"Yes, you did, and you were...in love with a Citizen named Roxanne Wiley."

RW. Pie stopped and grabbed her by the shoulders, turning her to face him so quickly, she would have tripped and fallen if he hadn't been holding on. "Did you say Roxanne Wiley?" The picture of a heart scratched into the wall of his cabin on Home came to mind. "What do you know about Roxanne Wiley?" he asked as he shook her.

"Stop it! You're hurting me."

Pie took a breath and let his hands fall to his sides. "Sorry. I'm...I'm—"

"I only know that you loved her and...and that Citizen Mason wanted you to go on this mission, but you refused. So he erased your memories of her and replaced them with some memories harvested from Jericho Zinc. I heard him tell Joshua that it would make you more pliable, less self-righteous. He said that it would rid you of an obsession and that Zinc's memories would keep you from probing. He said it was kind of like psychotherapy and then they both laughed. They didn't see me, or maybe they didn't even care that an Under woman was there."

Pie was still and quiet while he thought. Jericho Zinc, who the hell was that? And Roxanne Wiley. That name brought warmth and comfort, vague general emotions. If this fantastic story was actually true, then something big in his life was missing, but nothing came to mind.

"Why did you wait until now to tell me?" he asked.

Shana looked at her feet. "If I had told you on Home, First Citizen Mason would have killed me. There are no secrets from Citizen Mason. You were just another Citizen...then. Why should I have cared what happened to a Citizen?"

"And now you do, I suppose."

"Yes, I do. You're different. You see me. You see me as real person."

She put out a hand to touch him, but he shook it off with a rough jerk. He turned from her and with long angry strides started walking up the beach, nearly missing the prints in the sand. He stopped, turned, and looked again. They were human footprints, barefoot, and they had to have been made since the rain. He dug the communicator out of his backpack. He called out for Shana and she hurried to his side. He handed the communicator to her.

"Do whatever you do," he said.

She probed in the box with a wire until satisfied and then handed the communicator back to Pie.

"Kin," Pie said.

Jilla's answered. "Kin's resting. So typical, she expects us to do the real work."

"Get Kin online. Damn it! This is important!"

"Calm down," Jilla said. "Take a deep breath, in through your nose, out through—"

"Were you and Joe-54 out in this direction yesterday, or this morning?"

"Why...no. We figured you could cover a few kilometers. After all, we searched nearly two hundred square kilometers. That's not too much to expect, even from a Citizen, is it?"

"Shut up and listen! There are some fresh footprints out here that were made by an adult human. Get on a whistle-cycle and get out here!"

"Jacques and I are eating."

"Forget your damn meal! These tracks are fresh. Whoever made them can't be far."

"You have so little self-control. It's disgraceful. We will be there when we've finished eating."

"Damn it all to hell!" He jammed the communicator back into his pack and started walking briskly in the direction the footprints pointed. After a few strides he broke into a loping trot, with Shana running along behind. At the top of the third hill, somewhat higher than the rest, he came to a stop and began scanning the surrounding hills for signs of movement, but there were too many hills and too many valleys. It was impossible to accomplish an adequate search on foot.

He was still breathing deeply from the exertion when Shana caught up with him at the top of the hill. It was a warm morning and sweat trickled down his back, causing the pores of his suit to dilate so that the breeze could cool his skin. As he caught his breath and began to cool, the tension melted from his muscles. He thought about what Shana had said while he stared across the hills, clumped together like giant green, cobble stones.

It was with a deep sense of relief that he came to realize that what she'd told him was logically consistent with his inner feelings of wrongness. Those memories were too bizarre, too foreign, to be his own.

To Shana's surprise he suddenly raised his fist over his head and turned his face to the sky. "Mason," he yelled, "I'm coming back for you!"

It was ludicrous and he knew it, but somehow it made him feel better to declare it out loud, even if only Shana was present. He turned his gaze to her and she shrank away from him.

"Aren't you still afraid that Mason will execute you when we return to Home?"

Shana blinked and looked down. "I couldn't see you suffer anymore," she whispered.

"Do you think I can, and will, protect you?"

She looked up. "Yes...I do. I feel safe with you."

"Shana...I honestly appreciate your confidence in me and would do my damndest to protect you and would love to witness you becoming a free woman but, when it comes right down to it, I don't know if I can handle Mason. At Home he's like a spider in his web."

"I know!" she answered brightly. "Maybe you can find something on this world to use. You said there is high technology at work here."

"Yes, perhaps too high."

He took the communicator out of his backpack and Shana did her trick.

"Kin?" Pie said.

"She's in the bathroom," Jilla said and laughed.

"Oh my God, you haven't left yet? Connect me with Kin. Immediately!"

"No can do buckaroo. Did I use that right? I've been doing some research on archaic—"

Pie threw the communicator a short ways into the air, drew his blade, and sliced it in half as it fell.

"I guess that means you're done talking," Shana said.

Pie looked down at the communicator, lying on the grass, neatly severed in half.

"You miss your link, don't you, Pie?"

He nodded. "At times. It comes and goes. We've come to rely too heavily on our matrix extensions. It was one of the reasons my report on Angkor-3 was so inaccurate. I asked the wrong questions and didn't look with my own eyes, nor did I listen to my instincts. Come on. Let's go back to the ship. We're not going to find him this way."

"Him?"

Pie said nothing.

"You think Citizen Nichols is still alive, don't you? He'd have to be over two hundred years old."

"Yes, he would, wouldn't he," Pie agreed quietly.

"If he is still alive, why hasn't he come to greet us?"

"I don't know, Shana."

"Look," she pointed. "Looks like more art is headed our direction."

Pie turned to look and laughed. Towering, black-gray thunderheads were on the horizon. He looked at her smiling face. He took her hand and lead her down the hillside and on toward the ship.

"Shana, what do you know about Roxanne Wiley?"

She didn't answer right away, but Pie waited for her response without further prompting.

"Not very much," she finally said. "I don't even know what she looked like."

"Does she love me?"

"Yes, I'm certain she did—" She caught herself, but it was too late.

"Did? She doesn't love me anymore?"

He felt her fingers loosen in his hand, but he held onto them. "What is it?" he asked urgently.

"She's dead, Pie," Shana blurted and expected a reaction, but none came.

"When you say dead, do you mean body dead or matrix dead?"

"All I know is that her body is dead. I'm sorry. Really I am."

"How did she die?" he asked.

"I don't know...I swear it."

"These memories that you claim were taken from me. Do you think they still exist somewhere?"

"I don't know."

"No, I don't suppose you would." Pie rubbed his forehead and sighed. "You know, the hell of it is, I don't feel any love for this Roxanne Wiley, or even the pain of losing her. To me she is only a name. I hate Mason most for this. He's going to pay the price this time."

They both heard and then saw a whistle-cycle coming toward them from the direction of the ship. Jacques and Jill were on the front saddle and Joe on the rear. Jacques pointed in their direction, but the cycle didn't slow. It was soon past them and on the way to the lake.

Pie and Shana continued to walk. They just managed to make it back to the ship before the thunderstorm struck. When they exited into the commons, they found the New People sitting on the lounge to the right and Kin to the left, with Joe in the background.

"What are you doing here?" Pie demanded angrily. "You did a piss, poor job of searching!"

"We did a better job than you did," Jilla replied without rancor. "It started to rain."

"The cycles are equipped for rain," Pie said. "You wouldn't have gotten wet."

"Rain is icky. I don't like it."

Shana pushed her way past Pie and walked to the corner, to stand next to Joe.

"What the hell." Pie sat down on a lounge. "I've become aware of some important information," he said.

"Oh, really?" Jilla replied.

"Yes, really. Were you aware that the regeneration unit on Home was altered so that memories could be selectively extracted and false memories inserted? Are you aware of this?" he asked, and sat forward, leaning toward the New People.

"Of course," Jilla replied. "Jacques and I designed it. Impressive isn't it?"

"Why?" Pie pleaded.

"Citizen Mason contracted with us to make the required improvements. He was quite pleased."

Pie stood. "Have you no conscience? No ethics? Don't you realize you are crippling Citizens with these so-called improvements?"

"You are so melodramatic, Citizen Traynor. Each time you regenerate, you die. What is a memory or two? Out with the bad, in with the good." She looked over at Jacques and he raised his eyebrows, echoing her sentiments.

Pie could restrain himself no longer. He lunged the few steps needed to grab hold of Jilla and lifted her into the air, shaking her like a doll; her head whipped back and forth with each hard shake.

"You are a heartless little bitch!" he hissed, and then suddenly dropped her to the deck. He glanced with surprise at the palms of his hands, already blistering from burns.

Jacques jumped off his seat and ran to where Jilla had fallen. He brushed the curls of hair out of her face and held her head cradled against his chest.

"Jilla, Jilla are you hurt?"

"No, Jacques," she said in a tearful voice, "I'm okay."

Jacques turned to face Traynor.

Pie's anger had crested. He felt ashamed to have attacked a "little girl", but there was perverse satisfaction as well. He turned to leave.

"Traynor," Jacques croaked, his voice uncharacteristically strained.

Pie slowly pivoted to face the New People. Jilla was staring sternly at him, her cheeks rosier than usual, but Jacques' face was white. He pulled the handle topped by the disk from his waistband, but he kept his eyes fixed on Pie.

"You are nothing more than an Under," Jacques declared.

Instantly, a half circle of platinum-white light materialized, arching forward and stopping no more than two centimeters from Pie's abdomen. The light was so bright, it temporarily bleached the color from the room. It was so hot the temperature began to rise, despite ship's effort at maintaining homeostasis.

"You have not been useful, or obedient," Jacques said. "I should slice you in half. The only thing that comes close to being interesting about you is that necklace you're wearing. Give it to me and I might spare your life."

The heat was beginning to melt a line across the fabric of Pie's suit, causing it to bubble and run in droplets before congealing.

"Pie, get out of here!" Kin yelled.

He did not move. The muscles of his jaw bulged as he stared over the half circle of light, refusing to look away from Jacques, refusing to back off even a millimeter.

Shana was crouched in the corner, her hands clasped over her eyes, and Joe was standing next to her, peeking through a crack in his fingers.

Kin began to move. Hugging the bulkhead, she maneuvered herself into position behind Pie and started pulling on his arm. "Pie Traynor, get your ass out of here! Now!" she bellowed. "This is not the time!"

Jacques was grinning as he spoke. "Give me the necklace, Citizen, or I'll burn you in half and slip it off myself."

Shana pushed herself out of the corner, jostling Joe as she rushed to Jacques' side. "Wait! He can't take it off, even if he wanted to! It's impossible!" She touched Jacques on the arm, and quickly jerked her hand away, her fingertips blistered from the brief touch.

"Shana-8's right," Kin said. "I've seen it myself. He can't give it to you."

Jacques turned toward Shana, his lips curled into a thin smile. "Don't ever touch me, Under." He returned his attention to Pie and yelled, "He dies now!" At that exact moment, the arc of light and heat disappeared. He looked down to stare at the weapon, his eyes big.

When Jacques' broke eye contact with Pie, it was as if Pie had been released from a spell. He backed the few steps necessary, and dropped into the down-tube, closely followed by Kin.

They exited at the Citizen level, with Kin trailing behind Pie as he punched the "open" pad, and entered his cabin. The room felt cold compared to the heat they'd just experienced. Pie sat on the edge of his cocoon and rested his blistered hands on his thighs, palms up.

"You're one lucky son of a bitch," Kin began. "If that Under girlfriend of yours hadn't distracted that little shit's attention, you'd be dead meat by now. Thank God the weapon malfunctioned."

"It was strange. I remember wanting to reach out and pinch that beam off and...."

"Don't kid yourself. It was just another example of that famous Traynor luck. What were you trying to prove?" Kin asked as she returned from the personal room with a tube of gel.

"Didn't you hear? Weren't you listening?"

"Yeah, yeah, I heard," she said as she applied the cool, pink gel to Pie's hands.

"It's true, damn it!" he exclaimed, raising his arms and accidentally flicking some of the gel onto Kin's suit.

She wiped the globule off with one of her mirror-tipped fingers. "Thanks, Pie."

"Kin, listen to me. The regeneration matrix no longer belongs to the Citizens. It is Mason's tool."

Kin shrugged. "It always was Mason's. He is the one who decides if you get a new body, or not."

"He used it to cripple me. He killed a part of me. He did it to me, Kin! This isn't just a theory. This is fact." Pie ignored her ministrations. "Did you know a Citizen named Jericho Zinc?"

"I've heard of him. You tar-ball, this is a deep burn!" She bit her fuchsia lip with her fuchsia teeth and shook her head.

"Forget the burn, Kin. What do you know about him?"

"Who?"

"Jericho Zinc, damn it!"

"Well...let's see. Not much. He had a reputation of being ruthless, a cruel sludge as I heard it."

"Did he have black fingernails?" Pie asked.

"Hasn't everybody had them at one time or another?"

"Not me."

"I'm talking about fashionable people."

"Please, Kin, leave the burn alone and listen."

She stood and leaned back against the bulkhead.

"Mason took part of Jericho Zinc's memory and stuck it in my mind and then he erased my memories of a Citizen named Roxanne Wiley."

Kin stood away from the wall. "You're serious, aren't you?"

Pie just stared at her.

"Do you have proof?" she asked.

"I am utterly convinced," he replied. "The atrocities I have in my memory would shock you. Where was I before being called up to Home?"

"How the hell should I know? You are dear to me, but I didn't follow you around. Did you keep track of me while I was in Aires?"

He was silent in thought.

"So, Pie, where is this Jericho Zinc?"

"I'm told I killed him."

"Well, don't stop there like an Under, tell me more."

"I can't."

"I get it. You can't remember, right? I don't know, Pie. It all sounds a little farfetched to me. Who provided you with all these revelations?"

"Shana."

"Umm...so an Under told you all this, like, maybe this little Under-woman is privy to all these Citizen secrets. Really, Pie, get serious."

"Didn't you hear Jilla admit it?"

Kin shrugged. "So what if it is true? What are you going to do about it?"

"I'll tell you what I'm going to do. I'm going to slice Mason into so any pieces people will think he's confetti."

"Well, I always say if a job needs doing, it's worth doing well." After a moment she spoke again. "Do you think Jacky is out there somewhere?"

"Yes."

"After the New People finally told me about the footprints you had found, I reviewed the video recorded by ship sensors. It was weird. The beach was smooth and then the footprints started to appear, one after another, it looked like they had originated from the lake, but there was nobody making them. It was just like when I was following Shana-8 and you when you were walking along the beach. There she was, holding hands with nothing, and footprints appeared at her side out of nowhere. It was eerie."

Pie looked down at the milky-white trinket that hung around his neck.

"On the cube today Jacky mentioned that 'Click-click'—is that what you called the alien?"

Pie smiled and nodded. "You see, when it spoke, it made these clicking sounds."

Kin nodded. "Sure, Pie, real cute. Anyway, this 'Click-click' was going to show Jacky a 'Source'. Do you know what that is?"

Pie shook his head. "Sounds interesting, doesn't it?"

"Sure does...a hell of a lot more interesting than bugs and plants. Let me finish dressing that burn. Does it hurt much?"

"It hurts like hell."

Kin shook her head while she pulled the melted body suit away from Pie's abdominal wall. The skin came with it, but it appeared less serious than the hand burns even though it left a patch of raw red skin behind.

"I need to apply more of the healing gel and then let's call it a night. I think we had better get plenty of rest before tomorrow. I'm dreading dealing with the New People."

"You know they're probably listening to us right now, don't you?"

She winked. "I have no secrets."

"Are you referring to Holy again?" Pie asked with a grin.

She answered with her coarse laughter and then bent forward to finish attending to Pie's wound. When she was done, she seemed satisfied with her work.

"Thanks, Kin, and thank you for saving me from myself today. You are very special to me."

"Oh go on! You'll turn my head," she said as she brushed her hand across her glittery, bald scalp. "Tomorrow then. Flow, Pie," she said as she left his cabin.

"Flow, Kin."

Chapter 28

The following week found the New People flying about the countryside, searching without success for sight of a native. The minimal contact between Traynor and New People was cold, but not violent. The absence of the Little People provided Pie and Shana with an unexpected holiday. A day did not pass without them lounging on the beach of their private lake. Swimming in daylight was a constant source of delight for Shana.

On the seventh day, Pie was dozing on the beach, with the rays of the sun warming him to a state of perfect, animal contentment. Shana was sitting on the sand nearby, studying him. His skin had taken on a brownish hue, except for the purple stripe of a scar that ran across his stomach. His hands had healed well. While she sat there an irresistible idea hatched in her mind.

She emptied out their daypack, filled it with cold water from the lake, and crept toward the sleeping man. Stifling a laugh, she held the bag over him and then dumped it, jumping back at the same moment.

The splash of cold water was a shock. Pie's breath caught and his arms and legs came up at the same time. For a second, he was balanced on his buttocks, gasping air. By this time Shana was already running down the beach, watching him over her shoulder and laughing as she ran.

He bounded to his feet and sprinted after her, a spray of sand marking each leaping stride. His laughter joined hers as he closed the distance between them. Too breathless to speak, he finally caught her and they tumbled onto the sand, rolling over and over until the fine sand was plastered on their bodies.

He looked down at those rich, golden eyes set above the graceful curve of her cheekbones and the glistening blackness of her skin. Her hair was like a roaring, black flame, captured in stillness. He lowered his face toward hers and touched the softness of her lips with his own, and felt the pressure of the kiss returned. He withdrew to admire her beauty, and the woman she was, when her expression changed; she stiffened as she stared past his shoulder. His hand went to his knife as he rolled off her, but he held from drawing the weapon.

It was an alien, strolling along in its gawky gait, no more than thirty meters away. The two humans froze in place, but the alien seemed totally uninterested, not even glancing in their direction. They watched it as it plodded along. Pie turned back to Shana.

"I'm going to follow it. Get your suit on and go to the ship to inform the others."

He jumped to his feet and started jogging in the direction the native had gone, calling over his shoulder as he ran. "And bring me something to wear."

It was only a moment before he caught up with the alien. He walked behind it for a few paces, but the alien neither increased its stride, nor slowed. It seemed to Pie that it was acting as if it were unaware of his presence. Pie began walking at the alien's side, still the native did not as much as turn its head in Pie's direction.

Pie spoke. "Click-click, is that you?"

"Click, I am me, click."

"Aren't you surprised to see me, after all these years?"

"Click, you never left, click." It spoke in a monotone with the cadence of a metronome.

"What do you mean?"

The native stopped to pick berries off a bush with its two long fingers and thumb. The digits were smooth and bulbous at their tips. It popped one berry after another into its tiny berry-sized mouth, "clicked" and swallowed.

Pie's mouth was dry with excitement and dread. He cleared his throat and then asked, "Is Jacky Nichols still alive?"

The creature didn't answer. It continued to leisurely pick berries and eat them, one at a time.

"Did you hear me? Is Jacky Nichols alive?"

"Click, Jacky Nichols is part of the whole, click."

"What is the whole?"

The alien walked away to find a fresh bush and Pie tagged along after him.

"Why didn't you come to greet us? Didn't you know we were here?"

"Click, yes, click."

"I asked why."

"Click, I am, click."

"Look," Pie said, "I'm trying to communicate with you. I don't understand what you're saying."

"Click, I understand. I can talk, click."

And this is an advanced being? Pie asked himself. It was just like before. It acted and looked defective. Pie almost reached out to grab the creature's arm, but stopped; the memory of the burn when he had grabbed Jilla was still fresh in his mind and in the tender skin of his palms.

"Are you the same 'Click-click' I talked with before?"

"Click, are you the same human? Click."

The native inserted one more purple berry into its mouth and then started walking again. Pie followed along with it as it meandered through the countryside. Then, without warning, it stopped and lay prone on the thick grass. Pie had gone through this before, during his prior visit to Angkor. It looked like it was dead but he knew from experience that it would get up and start walking again. When was anyone's guess.

Pie sat down nearby and watched the alien until he heard the high-pitched whine of a whistle-cycle. He caught motion out of the corner of his eyes and stood; the cycle disappeared behind a hill.

"Damn it!" He began rubbing his right forearm. The skin where he had removed his link never quite returned to normal. He resigned himself to hiking to the top of a nearby hill, while he kept an eye on the alien, resting quietly below. It was all so ludicrous. He had to smile. Here he was, citizen of a star-traveling species, reduced to standing on a hilltop and waving his arms to get attention.

The scream of the whistle-cycle turned him around. It was about two hundred meters away. The figure in the rear saddle waved back at him and the cycle began to approach. When it drew near, Pie could see the riders were Jilla and Shana. The cycle stopped twenty meters away and ten meters above the ground. Jilla sat there watching him. Soon, he heard a second cycle and it made its appearance, carrying Jacques and Joe.

Pie pointed in the direction of sleeping alien and began walking downhill. The two cycles dove past him, coming dangerously close, causing him to drop to the ground. He lay there for a moment. "What the hell," he muttered and then climbed back to his feet.

By the time he reached the bottom of the hill, the New People and Unders were standing around the sleeping alien, looking down at it. Pie approached cautiously, still uncertain of the greeting he would receive.

The New People ignored him while Shana stepped away to hand him a suit. The New People were dressed in matching teal-blue suits, their heads topped by hypersonic "party hats", and around their waists they were wearing thick, gold belts. It was the first time Pie had ever seen them wear an obvious matrix link. Jacques was holding a short, glowing tube in his hand and passing it over the perfectly still body of the alien. Jacques returned the tool to a pouch and walked a few steps away with Jilla.

Pie could contain his curiosity no longer. "What did you find out?"

"What do you think?" Jacques said, looking at Pie but obviously addressing Jilla. He postured his pudgy finger against his chin. "He's been awfully mean."

Jilla nodded, "Very. He's been a very naughty boy, but...if he were to apologize...."

Pie's face worked with conflict. Intellectually, he knew this was a self-centered, old woman, who used other humans as if it were her God given right but, emotionally, he still felt the shame of attacking a "little girl".

"We-are-wait-ing," Jilla urged in a singsong voice.

Pie glanced over at Shana who was studiously avoiding eye contact, and then at Joe, who met his gaze with a hint of increased tone in his cheeks. A smile? Pie returned his attention to the New People and drew in a deep breath.

"I'm...sorry...if...I...hurt you," he finally concluded.

"I don't think that was adequate," Jacques said smoothly. "Do you, Jilla?"

She shook her head and wagged her finger at Pie.

"Why don't you try again," Jilla suggested. "But this time kneel...and put some feeling into it."

Pie flipped them a finger sign that would have been recognized by nearly every human on Earth, when he was a youth, but, other than the fierce lines of anger on his face and the violence of the movement, its meaning was lost on those gathered in the small valley.

"You know, Jilla," Jacques said, "I think he still harbors animosity and is not sincerely contrite."

"I agree, Jacques."

Pie relaxed with a realization. "You didn't learn a God damned thing about this native. It's just as invisible to your super-charged matrix as it is to ship's sensors."

Jacques raised his nose a degree higher. "I guess you'll never know, will you?"

"You are a genius," Jilla gushed as she faced Jacques, and then she turned to the Unders. "Shana-8, and Joe-54, set up our shelter and prepare our meal."

The Unders set to work at once. First they expanded two bag-chairs, into which the New People plopped as soon as they were inflated. While Shana prepared the survival dome, Joe heated the food.

Pie sat apart from the others, on the nearby hillside. He idly watched them for a while and then lay back on the grass, with his head resting in the palm of his hand. He looked up at the sky. The clouds were light brush strokes of lavender and the sky a deep blue. With the coming of purple evening, the stars filled the sky with their bright points of twinkling light. Nearby movement brought him back.

Shana knelt next to him. "I brought you some food."

"Did you eat?" he asked.

"I brought extra so I could eat with you." She smiled and reached out to squeeze his hand. "Don't be so hard on yourself. You're better than both of them put together."

"Yeah," Pie replied dryly, and then turned to her and smiled.

They ate in silence as night stole away the colors of the world, leaving only the black shapes of tall "trees" and rounded hills.

"What's the big sigh for?" Shana asked.

He shook his head.

"That's a cheap answer," she said.

"Shana-8," Jilla called. "Come here."

She stood. "I'd better go."

He also stood. "I'll come with you."

When they walked into the campsite, they found Jacques and Jilla lounging in their bag chairs, holding hands with their fingers. The camp was lit by a star-lamp; the light reflected off the surrounding hillside and the underside of nearby trees, giving the camp a safe and cozy feeling with the darkness all about. Pie stopped on the fringe of the light, but Shana walked forward to stand before the New People.

"Shana-8 and Joe-54," Jilla said, "we are ready for you to perform."

Shana quickly glanced to where Pie stood, the tremor of her chin not visible in the soft light. She wiped a tear from her eye.

"Unders," Jacques said, "we don't expect to wait all night. Move it!"

Slowly, reluctantly Shana, reached for the sealing strip of her suit and pulled it open, while Joe, standing a few paces away, let his suit fall to the grass and stepped out of it.

"Shana-8," Jilla pricked at her with her voice, "are you having trouble tonight? You've performed so well in the past. Tell Auntie Jilla what the problem is."

"Nothing," Shana whispered in an inaudible voice and lowered her gaze. She slipped the suit off her shoulders and it fell to her waist, baring her breasts and abdomen.

"All the way, Shana-8," Jacques urged and giggled.

Pie strode forward. "What the hell is going on here?" His hand was on the knife handle.

"Citizen," Jacques replied, "sit down and join us. The Unders are about to perform the sex act. They'll do anything we tell them to do. Any special requests?"

Pie pulled the knife from its sheath; the edge of the blade flashed in the light of the star-lamp. "I'll cut your heart out first," he said in a guttural growl. "If you want sex, then grow up, you perverted little creeps."

Jilla turned casually to Jacques. "Well, what do you know? He not only has atrocious manners, but he's a prig as well. Can you believe it?"

Jacques shook his head and smirked. "Go on Shana-8, show Joe-54 the rest of you, after all, it's not as if this is a new experience for him, or you." They giggled.

She pulled the suit over the curve of her buttocks and it dropped to the ground. She stood naked for their inspection. Slowly, she turned her face, glistening with the wetness of tears, to Pie. "Please, go away," she begged, her voice cracking, threatening to break into a cry of sorrow and regret.

"Not without you."

"Tsk, tsk," Jilla hissed, and pulled the weapon from her waistband. "She stays, and if you continue on the course you've set for yourself tonight, we will begin by ridding ourselves of a marginally serviceable Under. We don't really need two. Joe can perform all by himself. Even though she was talking about Shana, her weapon and attention were focused on Pie."

Pie took another step toward the "little girl". She responded with a grin. "Isn't reality tough sometimes?" she said.

"Please, Pie!" Shana begged. "Go away."

"Yes, 'please, Pie'," Jilla mimicked.

Pie desperately wanted to use his knife, but could see no way to kill them both. Shana and he would be killed and Shana would be truly dead.

"Please, Pie," Shana begged in a tear-choked voice.

He bowed his head and his shoulders collapsed forward as he turned away and walked blindly into the darkness. He walked until he reached the shore of the lake and sank to his knees on the sand.

He felt tired, so very tired. And old, too old to go on. He drew the knife from its sheath and touched the sharpness of the blade to his thumb, causing blood to trickle down his hand, black in the darkness of the night. He raised the blade tip and felt the pulse of blood in his neck. It would be so easy, he thought, but then lowered his hand to his lap. It was not yet time. Soon, he promised himself as he wiped the blade clean in the sand.

The sun was just beginning to light the eastern horizon, when he heard a soft voice behind him.

"Pie?"

He sat as he was.

"Pie...I'm so ashamed. Forgive me." she said, her words slurred by sobs.

Pie twisted around until he could see her. "Forgive you? I'm the one who needs forgiveness. I, the great Citizen, who did nothing. I'm not even in control of myself."

There was silence. The screeching night sounds had given way to the quiet of day, broken only by the lapping of waves against the beach. She sat on the grass and he on the sand. The tears were gone from her voice when she spoke again.

"You now know what it is to be an Under. It is degrading, but we are not helpless. We will not tolerate it forever."

Pie turned to study her. She did not hide her face; her eyes were bright with anger and determination.

"And how do you hope to accomplish this remarkable feat?"

She looked away, toward the still dark, western horizon. "I believe it," is all she said.

Pie pushed himself to his feet and Shana stood to join him.

"I too have wishes," he said, "less grand than yours but, perhaps, just as impossible."

He placed his hand under her chin and lifted her face toward his. He kissed her lips with the touch of a butterfly. She responded by throwing herself against him, wrapping her arms around him, and burying her face against his chest. He gathered her in his own arms and held her securely against him. After a few minutes, Pie gently pulled her arms from him.

"Come, Shana. Let's see how things are going at camp. I think we're ready to face them."

She smiled as their eyes met and nodded.

When they reached the campsite, it was abandoned. The whistle-cycles were gone and the survival bubble was empty. They were uncertain which direction to go, when they heard Joe yelling at them from the crest of a nearby hill. They hurried their pace to catch up with the group.

The two whistle-cycles were hovering riderless, off in the distance. The New People were walking on either side of the alien; its head bobbed forward and back with each step; its arms hung at its sides. Joe dropped back. He handed Shana a nutrient bar and a flask of water, pointedly ignoring Pie, and then hurried back to walk a few paces behind the New People.

Shana broke the bar in half and insisted that Pie have a share. When Pie and she had closed the distance, Jacques turned his head part way toward them.

"Sleep well last night, Citizen?" he asked with a grin. "You should have seen them. Best performance so far, don't you think, Jilla?"

"Oh, absolutely."

211

Pie did not respond until Jacques turned his back toward them. Then Pie's hand went to his knife.

"No, Pie," Shana whispered.

He relented and dropped his hand to his side. They were now close enough to hear Jacques talking with the alien.

"I know your first contact with our species was not impressive," Jacques was saying, "but you can't judge us all by the likes of the first humans you happened to come across. We are New."

The alien stopped and began eating berries. Jacques stood nearby and continued his one-sided conversation. "We have information that suggests you may know the secret of immortality. Is that true?"

"What do you care, Jacques?" Pie asked. "You're going to be so famous, death will feel like a standing ovation, or are you actually just as afraid of death as the rest of us mortals?" Pie didn't expect an answer and got none.

The alien popped another berry into its mouth.

"How old are you?" Jacques asked.

"Click, old? Click."

Jacques smiled. Now he was getting somewhere. "Yes, how many revolutions of this planet about the star have you lived?"

"Click, it has no meaning, click."

"What do you mean no meaning? It was an exact question!" Jacques replied hotly.

"Jacques," Jilla warned with her voice.

He decided to try a different tack. "Can I eat these berries?"

"Click, yes, click."

Jacques plucked a cherry-red berry from the bush. He put it his mouth and bit down on it, immediately spitting it out, gagging and grabbing at his throat. Jilla rushed to his side.

"Water!" he cried hoarsely, and bent at the waist to retch repeatedly.

Jilla turned to Pie. "Do something!"

"I am," he said, and started laughing.

Jilla fumbled for her weapon while Joe rushed forward with a canteen. She grabbed it away from Joe and gave Jacques a sip.

When Jacques caught his breath, his skin was still moist and pale. "You said it was safe to eat these," he said in a weak voice to the alien.

"What it actually said was that you can eat them," Pie said with growing satisfaction.

Pie almost expected Jacques to pull his weapon but he only nodded.

"Right. Right," Jacques said. "I see what you mean now when you said they are concrete thinkers."

The alien resumed its ambling.

While Jacques walked at its side, the color returned to his lips and cheeks. "All right," he finally said with a forced laugh, "I understand. That's fair," he said to the alien. "You answered my question. Now I have another question for you. Is there a place called the Source."

"Click, yes, click."

"Will you take us to the Source?"

"Click, yes, click."

Jacques turned and smiled for Pie's benefit. "Very good. When will you take us there?"

The alien said nothing.

"Can you lead us there?"

"Click, yes, click."

"Great! Let's go."

The alien turned to the south and the party of humans tagged along.

"That's a pretty necklace you're wearing," Jilla said to the alien in her best little girl voice. "I like it. You gave one to our friend. Can I have one too?"

"Click, it's not necessary, click."

"Oh, I know that. I'd just like to have one," she said and batted her eyelashes with child-like flirtation.

There was no response.

Jilla and Jacques dropped back and were quiet, but the flashes of looks and half-completed gestures were definite signs of ongoing communication, even if it wasn't standard speech.

Abruptly, the alien stopped and squatted. Jacques nearly ran into the creature, but managed to side step and slide past. The alien defecated, stood, and then continued walking without a backward glance.

"Hey, Jacques," Pie called out loudly, "there's a little biological output for you to study." Pie laughed and Shana covered her mouth to hide her smile. When he glanced toward Joe, he saw a definite smile, revealing small, regular teeth.

"Yes," Jacques agreed enthusiastically, and was about to bend over to inspect the steaming pile more closely when Jilla took hold of his arm.

"They're laughing at you!" she said.

Jacques was unperturbed. "They are unimportant."

But he yielded to Jilla's wishes and soon the two of them had regained their positions at the alien's side, taking two steps for its one.

"Do you have space travel?" Jacques asked.

"Click, no, click."

"Do you mean your species has not visited any other star system?"

"Click, no, click."

"I don't understand. How did you travel if not through space? Can you explain?"

"Click, yes, click."

"Yes, what!"

"Click, I can explain, click."

"Then explain!"

The alien veered off in a new direction and, after taking only a few steps, lay face down on the grass. Jacques and Jilla were at a loss as to what they should do next while they stared at the sleeping alien.

Pie stopped a few steps away, and leaned against the smooth skin of a tree. "I see what you mean, Jacques. You do have a special talent for communicating with an alien species. Very impressive."

Jacques glared at the broadly smiling Citizen, but then turned to Joe-54. "I'm calling up a whistle-cycle. I want you to go back to the ship and bring us more supplies. Water in particular. When you get there, consult with Citizen Kin. She'll know what we need."

Joe bowed his head. "Yes, Master."

Next Jacques turned to Shana. "Shana-8, you will set up our camp and prepare our food."

"I live to serve," she replied, but, as she bent to find a shelter in the survival pack, she managed to catch Pie's eye and gave him a big wink. It eased the tension in his face and he settled onto the soft grass at the base of the tree. When it came time for him to set up his own shelter, he placed it on the far side of camp, keeping as much distance between the New People and himself as he could, while still remaining in the circle of light.

Joe returned after midnight. Pie awakened when he heard the airy scream of the whistle-cycle landing nearby. He pulled open the entrance of his dome and watched Joe, who was talking with the New People just outside their shelter. Jacques pointed toward Pie's dome. Joe bowed and began walking in Pie's direction. He stopped a respectful five paces away.

"Citizen," Joe called, "are you awake?"

Pie studied him from within the darkness of his dome. The man couldn't seem to stand still.

"Citizen," he called out a second time.

This time Pie answered, still within darkness. "What do you want, Joe?"

Joe lowered his eyes and his voice. "Citizen...I have bad news."

Pie slid out and stood. He took two strides and was standing within arm's reach of Joe before he spoke. "What is it?"

"Citizen, when I returned to the ship—" He stopped to swallow.

214

"Damn it! Say what you have to say!"

"I found Citizen Kin. She was…dead."

Pie grabbed the man around the throat, lifting him off the ground by his neck. Joe desperately tried to break out of Pie's grip as Pie brought the struggling man's face to within centimeters of his own.

"What the hell happened?" Pie asked, a cold stillness in his voice.

"Answer me!" Pie yelled, but Joe's arms fell lax to his side as he began to lose his fight for breath and life.

Shana ran across the circle of light and, when she reached Pie, began pulling on his arm. "Let him go!" she screamed. "You're killing him!"

Pie loosened his grip and Joe fell to the ground in heap, his breath returning as a harsh squeak. Pie knelt next to the small man and grabbed a handful of his suit, pulling him into a sitting position.

"What happened?" Pie demanded.

Joe's voice was hoarse and quavered when he answered. "When I arrived at the ship the iris port was already open." He took a deep unsteady breath. "I was told to find her when I got to the ship and ask her to help with the supplies. She did not respond to voice so I searched for her…and…and I found her."

When he stopped talking Pie shook him.

"She was in her cabin," Joe blurted. "Attached…you know…to power cables. She was…burned."

"Burned?" Pie tightened his grip on Joe's suit causing it to rip open.

Joe coughed and cleared his throat. "It looked like a high-energy current had traveled the cords."

"Did you do anything to try to save her?" Pie demanded.

Joe shook his head and tried to lower his eyes, but Pie just tipped him back farther until his face was in full view. "Citizen," he said weakly, "she was dead."

Pie pushed Joe hard away from him. The Under lay perfectly still in the position he'd been thrown; only his eyes moved, watching the Citizen. Pie stretched to his full height and walked in long strides to confront the New People.

"You had to have known," Pie said. "You knew it the second her link went dead. Why didn't you tell me?"

"What was the point? When Joe-54 got back was soon enough," Jilla said.

"When did she die?"

"If you what to know things, put on a link," Jacques said.

"Send me back on a cycle, tonight," Pie demanded.

"Don't get all upset," Jilla said. "I'm sure I can do Kin's job better than she ever could, better than any Citizen could."

Pie reached out, but stopped short of touching her. She didn't flinch.

"We're so pleased with your progress," she said. "Aren't we, Jacques?"

"Definitely," Jacques said.

"I need to go! Don't you understand?"

"It can wait," Jacques said. "She's dead. There's nothing you can do for her tonight. Besides, as I understand your beliefs, she's only body-dead. I don't understand why you're so upset."

"I need to go. She was my friend."

"You can go, if you want to," Jacques said. "You're in luck. It just so happens I have a spare link and I think it would fit you perfectly. Otherwise...good night, Citizen."

He and Jilla turned together to reenter their shelter, but stopped when Pie spoke.

"Wait," Pie said quietly.

Jacques turned back to him, an impish grin on his face.

"All right, you win. Give me the damn link."

Jacques glanced over at Jilla. "Do you think that's a nice way to ask for a favor?"

Jilla shook her head and her golden curls danced in the light of the star-lamp. "Kneel, Citizen."

Pie slowly got down on his knees before the little people, but his head was still above theirs.

"Lower," Jilla said, and Pie crouched, bending his head forward.

"What do you have to say?" Jilla asked in a rising tone.

"Please, let me have the link," Pie said quietly.

"I can't hear you," Jilla said.

"Please," Pie said in a louder voice, "let me have the link."

Jilla turned to Jacques. "What do you think?"

He shrugged and then entered their dome, returning a moment later with the gold band dangling in his hand. As he held it out to Pie, Jacques added, in an offhand way, "Did Joe-54 tell you that he saw Citizen Nichols as he neared the ship?"

Pie looked up quickly.

"Maybe you can make yourself useful again and track him down for us. I have a few questions I'd like to ask him," Jacques said.

He and Jilla turned away to enter their dome, leaving Pie still kneeling on the grass. He stood, as if carrying a heavy weight and began walking toward the whistle-cycle.

Shana rushed forward and clung to his arm. "Pie, don't! Don't do it."

He broke Shana's grip with a twist of his wrist.

She continued. "You will become a plaything for them, again."

"When haven't I been a plaything for them?" He walked on without breaking his stride.

Her mind raced to find a convincing argument. "They will steal your will. You have your will."

"What good is a will when there is no way to implement it?"

"You will not be in control of yourself. They will. You'll no longer be a free man."

He stopped and turned to her; his lips curved downward and there were dark creases on either side of his mouth, highlighted by the oblique light of the star-lamp. "You mean like an Under? Do you have control of yourself? Rutting like an animal for their amusement."

"You can go to hell!"

Pie could see the tears shimmering in her eyes when she turned away from him. He watched her walk away and enter the Under's Dome. He wanted to go after her, but what did he have to offer? Perhaps it was better this way.

He turned and walked to the whistle-cycle. He looked again toward Shana and Joe's dome. No one was outside. Still, he hesitated before applying the matrix-band to his wrist. The situation seemed so familiar, like a dream re-dreamed, and it wasn't a pleasant one. He stuck his hand through the circle of the link and felt the tingling, numbing pain of matrix contact, and then the flow of information.

Gary Moreau

Chapter 29

Pie's mind was empty of conscious thought as he approached and then circled the bullet shaped out-ship. The storage portal remained open, unnatural, as if the ship had been gravely wounded. Pie linked into the ship's matrix and felt the absence of Kin's life-signs. He landed the whistle-cycle on the grass in front of the ship and shut it down, but did not dismount; now that he had arrived he was reluctant to confront the reality of her death.

He thought about what Jilla had said. Logically, she was right. It was body-death, not matrix-death. Why was he taking it so hard? Maybe he was afraid there'd never be a Kin again. Maybe he had begun to believe that body-death was true death.

He leaned back in the saddle of the cycle and listened to the night sounds, the haunting cries of unseen beasts, never seen in daylight. He turned to stare into the darkness. He had the feeling he was being watched and shivered, despite the warmth of his thermal suit. Looking back over his shoulder, he slid out of the saddle and walked toward the looming darkness of the ship. He caught hold of the lip of the storage portal and pulled himself up and through. After ordering the portal to close, he opened the ordinance cabinet, surprised that the New People hadn't sealed it; perhaps they had no fear of Technocracy weapons. He selected a personal laser and belt, buckling it on he ascended to the Citizen level.

The door to her cabin was open. He could smell the nauseating odor of burnt flesh. He remained standing in the corridor. The last steps were the hardest. When he finally stood in the doorway, he slowly raised his eyes. He saw Kin's body in her cocoon. It was as Joe had reported.

"Kin." It was a senseless plea not to be dead. The sight was hideous. The power cords were still attached to her charred chest, a third cord extended to her blackened pelvis. "Kin," he said aloud to the corpse, "how could you have let this happen?" Anger flared and flushed across his skin.

He linked into the ship and followed the lines of power. It had been sabotage. He could picture in his mind the melted bridge of a conductor, purposefully laid across the lines to Kin's cabin, turning a trickle of power into a torrent. He accessed records but could find nothing. Whoever had done this had deleted all record of the act. No telling how long the trap had been place. No knowing the last time Kin had pleasured herself. It had to be someone who knew wiring and also how to alter a matrix, no simple task.

With a strength that was more mental than physical, he slashed the power cords and lifted her body, already cold and stiff. He carried her out of the ship and laid her tenderly on the grass.

He returned to the ship for a heavy-duty laser and returned to stand next to her desecrated body. "We will meet again, Kin, dear friend. I promised you I would get you Home, but...so sorry I wasn't here for you. I should have been looking after you instead of the other way around. Your memories are safe in the Home matrix. See you soon, my friend."

He activated the laser and passed the ice-blue beam across her body until it was reduced to a vapor. When he cut off the beam, all that remained was a fine, gray ash. "Flow, Kin."

He reentered the ship and went to the commons where he activated the holo-stage, but it was empty; Jacky's memory cube was gone. He slumped onto the lounge and remembered Kin as she had been, with her thick, red hair, and freckled nose. He remembered Kin, irreverent and irrepressible, and Kin the wild lover and honest friend.

With the first light of dawn, he was on the whistle-cycle, searching for a lone, human figure somewhere out there in the park-like world. He searched from morning until midafternoon, when Jilla messaged him.

"Citizen Traynor, pick up an Under. We're returning."

"What?"

"Do as you're told." The communication ended.

He turned the cycle to the north and passed the New People and Joe as they flew back to the ship. An hour later he was at the campsite, which now consisted of one human woman, sitting on a hillside. The alien was not in sight. He landed the cycle near her and sat on it a moment, studying her, before he shut it down and walked over to where she was sitting. As he approached she stood.

"I had to go," he said. "You do understand, don't you? Kin was my friend. She was depending on me and I let her down."

"It's not my right to question a Citizen," she replied.

He stepped near her and put his arms around her. She did not resist, but neither did she respond. He lowered his arms and backed away.

"Is this the way you want it between us?" he asked.

She lowered her eyes and said nothing.

He sighed, but then hid his feelings beneath the mask of a Citizen. "All right then, Shana-8. Where is the alien?"

"Jacques killed it, Citizen."

Pie was stunned. "Why?"

"It is not my place to say, Citizen."

"God-damn it! Get on the whistle-cycle. Move!" He grabbed hold of her arm and dragged her to the cycle. "Shana, you're acting like an ass and I'm in no mood to put up with it." He lifted her onto the rear saddle and then climbed onto his own. During the flight back to the ship he tried to contact the New People, but they were not accepting communication.

When they arrived at the ship it was nighttime. He dilated the storage portal and brought the cycle directly into the storage bay. He was already striding toward the up-tube when Shana touched his arm. He stopped and turned toward her.

"Pie," she said her eyes searching his face, "I'm sorry about your friend's death, even if it was only a body-death."

Pie's stance softened and he nodded. "Thanks. Shana, why are you pushing me away?"

Her eyes moved from his face to the gold link and finally returned to his face. "When you put back on the link, you renounced your natural heritage and became a matrix puppet again. It was as if you had just been waiting for a good enough reason to uplink. You didn't do it for Kin. You did it for yourself. It was a surrender to the matrix. The convenience, the power. Especially the power. No, Pie. I didn't leave you. You took yourself away from me, and now, instead of being the two of us, you are a Citizen and I'm an Under."

Pie reached out and grasped her hands. They were cold and unresponsive. "I am the same person I always was. I just needed to use the technology. It's not inherently evil. It's just a tool."

"Who is the tool, Pie?" She kept her eyes directed at the deck at their feet, avoiding the demon eyes that studied her. "Sometimes a person has to do things that are personally painful, even destructive, if it is for the benefit of others."

Pie dropped her lifeless hands. "What are you talking about?"

"Nothing."

"Are you talking about me, or you?"

"I don't know. Maybe I'm talking about both of us."

They stood there in silence, until Shana broke into a run and disappeared into the up-tube. Pie watched her go and then slowly followed. He exited into the commons. Joe was serving the New People a meal.

Pie walked over to them. "Why did you kill the alien?" he asked, keeping his voice civil.

Neither of them answered. Their lips occasionally moved as they carried on a secretive and silent conversation.

Pie repeated his question, this time louder, but still they chose not to recognize his presence. Joe backed away.

Pie slammed his fist on the table, flipping Jacques' plate onto the deck. "Why the hell did you kill it?" he yelled.

"Sit down, Citizen," Jacques ordered.

Pie did not budge. His face was rosy with anger, visible even through his newly acquired tan.

Suddenly, Pie's head jerked back. He straightened and took several mechanical steps backward, until he dropped without grace onto the opposite lounge.

Jacques studied him, and then said in a cold voice, "Only a reminder, Citizen. It is important to remember there are limits."

The rigidity of Pie's posture left, but the tension did not. He grasped the edge of the lounge with such intensity his hands looked bloodless.

It was Jilla who spoke next. "As you know by now, we are reasonable people. I'll tell you what you want to know, even though there is no reason I should. That creature led us around, in circles. I don't know who it thought it was dealing with, never showing us respect. So we decided to kill it. It was a rationale decision. If it was immortal, it'd be impossible to kill it. On the other hand, if it just died, then it wasn't worth bothering with in the first place. You could call it an experiment. The creature didn't defend itself. It didn't even seem to be aware that it was being attacked. It just stood there like an Under and let Jacques cut it up, and then it dissolved, soaked right into the grass. I wanted the necklace but it glowed a bright orange and vanished with a flash of light, and then there was nothing."

Jacques picked up the story. "We waited, after all, it's not as if we'd done something wrong. It was perfectly justified. But nothing happened. There was no response."

"As much as I hate to admit it," Jilla said, "your assessment might have been accurate after all. Now tell us something. Did Kin just overdose on current and orgasm to death?"

"She was killed," Pie stated blankly.

Jilla appeared absent for a moment and then reanimated. "Ah, I see," she said. "And there's no record. Had to be someone with access to ship's matrix, unless she did it herself. Had she been talking about killing herself?"

"No."

"And, as I understand it, Jacky's cube is missing. Sorry, Jacques. I know you were looking forward to studying it when we got back to New Berlin."

Jacques nodded. "Yes, I was really looking forward to that. Well, that's the way it goes. It's been fun in an odd way, don't you agree, Jilla?"

"Yes, but a waste. I'd never recommend it be repeated."

"Me either," said Jacques.

"So, who killed Kin?" Jilla asked. "Not you, I assume," she said addressing Pie. "There's only one other Citizen on this world. Jacky Nichols. I'm curious. In the time that remains, are you going to try to bring this wayward Citizen to justice? Or, are you going to be reasonable and forget this sordid detail of an otherwise interesting, all be it overlong, visit to a planet designed by an alien-Under?"

Pie stood and walked toward the down-tube without answering.

Jilla shook her head with amazement. "What did I say? I think I've hurt his feelings again. Do you think he's going to his room to get even and off-link a second time?"

Pie hesitated at the mouth of the tube.

"You have to admit," Jacques said with a giggle, "he was comical as an Under. Remember when he was standing on that hill waving? Hilarious."

Jilla tittered, "Oh, Jacques, you have such a keen sense of humor."

Pie dropped into the tube.

Chapter 30

At sunrise, Pie was sitting on the whistle-cycle. He checked the laser pistol to ensure it had an adequate charge and slid it back into his holster. He dilated the iris portal, but instead of taking to the sky, he just sat there. An alien was standing motionless outside the ship, facing it.

Pie uplinked. "Jacques, I think you have a visitor." There was no response. "Jacques, I know you can hear me. Time to wake up. Click-click, or his twin, has come a callin'."

Within minutes they were all gathered in the storage bay, the New People and the Unders.

Jacques peeked over the lower rim of the portal and then quickly pulled his head back. He turned to Pie, his face pale, "Go see what it wants!" he ordered urgently.

"Gee, I don't know," Pie said as he settled more comfortably in the saddle. "I kind of think it's come to see you."

"Citizen, don't mess with me! I haven't forgotten your treatment of Jilla. I can make you do it, you know."

What the hell, Pie thought, and dismounted from the cycle. He dropped over the edge of the portal, landing lightly on the grass, and boldly walked up to the alien, who remained stationary.

"What do you want?" Pie asked, and at that same moment heard a startled scream from the ship. He turned in time to see Jacques float out of the storage-bay portal, as if invisible hands were lifting him. He kicked his legs and screeched a piercing cry, but to no avail. Pie stepped back, as Jacques drifted over to the alien and remained hanging there in mid-air, a meter off the ground.

"It was a mistake!" Jacques yelled. He pointed at Pie with his little hand. "He made me do it!"

"Click, why did you give me a slow day? Click."

"Me? No, it was this...." he said waving his hand at Pie.

There was no response from the alien.

Jacques began to cry. Big, tear drops rolled down his cheeks. "Believe me," he said, his voice choking on his tears, "the Citizen threatened to kill me. He was going to kill my sister, too."

Pie smiled as the little person struggled to escape the transparent grip that held him suspended in front of the alien.

"Jilla," Jacques cried, "now!"

225

Pie turned toward the ship and saw Jilla holding her weapon, but nothing happened.

"Jacques!" she cried helplessly.

As the moments stretched on, Jacques tired of his fruitless struggle, and hung like a worn, rag doll. "It was an experiment," he finally mumbled. "We wanted to see what would happen. We didn't think it would hurt you. Please, believe me."

"Click, an experiment, click."

Jacques fell to the resilient grass without warning and bounced once before laying still. The fall had knocked the breath from him.

The alien turned and ambled away. All eyes were on the alien as it stopped briefly to nibble on berries from a near-by bush, and then continued on its way, without another glance in the direction of the ship.

Jacques' legs were shaky and he was still tremulous, but he managed to get to his feet and toddle over to stand in front of Pie. "What did you do to help?" he demanded angrily.

"Nothing," Pie answered honestly. "I don't think we are very important to them, although I'll have to admit, you did manage to get their attention for a moment."

Jacques pivoted on his heels and stalked over to the lock to enter the ship. Pie uplinked and called up the sensor record of the ship. He studied a high magnification, high resolution picture of the grounds around the ship and saw the serial, up and down indentations in the grass that were made by the alien's footsteps. He followed the path backward until it was obvious where the trail originated; the Blue had come from the direction of the lake.

He glanced at the tightly sealed ship and then turned away from it and began walking toward the lake. When he came to the beach, after only a brief search, he found what he was looking for: oval indentations in the sand made by the alien's feet. They led directly into the lake.

He made a decision. Unbuckling his laser belt, he laid it on the sand, and then he removed his sheath and knife and laid them next to the pistol. No weapons. He undressed and walked to the edge of the cool water to let it wash over his feet. When he had eased his way waist deep into the lake, he took a series of deep breaths and dived under the water.

The sandy lake bottom dropped off sharply and he pulled downward until his ears hurt from the pressure, but he forced himself to go even deeper. The air hunger grew and became a burning pain in his chest; his breath demanded to be released. His vision took on a reddish haze and then, suddenly, it was easy. He felt no urgency, no discomfort.

"Is this what it is to drown?" he wondered languidly, as if in a dream, and made a feeble effort to turn back toward the surface, but had lost track of direction. He was confused, but still felt no panic. Even when black spots appeared before his eyes and his head began to thud with a distant ache, he experienced a sense of wellbeing, and then lost consciousness.

He was standing. He had no recollection of arriving, had no idea how long he had been there. He saw white. It was all about, above and below. He thought he closed his eyes, but the vision remained unchanged. He was not afraid. He felt welcomed and loved. It was as if he was greeting himself, completely immersed in self-love that originated elsewhere. It was pleased with him and he was pleased with himself. It was a state of being gathered-in and kissed and caressed, without a hint of criticism. It was positive, gratifying, agreeable.

"Where am I?" he tried to say, or might have said. He wasn't sure. He heard his voice, but it wasn't sound. He was in one place and, yet, was in many places. He saw, he understood, and he was satisfied. There was no urgency, no sense of time at all, but he was ready to return.

Gary Moreau

Chapter 31

His back was pleasantly warm. He rolled over. There was bright light and he opened his eyes; it was the sun. The sky was a deeper blue than he could ever recall. Waves slapped politely against the beach and the air was zestful and clean.

He sat up and looked down the beach for his suit, more interested in finding his knife than anything else; his forearm felt naked without it. There was nothing but beach. Then he noticed his right forearm was bare as well; his new link was gone. He stood and felt the medallion against his chest. He glanced down at it and then at his abdomen; the burn scar was gone, without leaving a trace. He felt wonder but did not feel a need to question the changes in him; all was as it should be. He began walking, climbed the hill next to the lake, and strolled off in the direction of the ship.

Joe was outside and saw him first. He froze, and then began yelling something while he ran toward the ship. Within seconds, the New People exited the lock, closely followed by Shana. She broke into a run and jumped into his arms, wrapping her legs around him.

"Pie!" she cried.

He held her. "Hey, what's going on? Not that I object. What is it?"

She had her arms around his neck and her head rested against his chest. Then, through sobs of breath, she spoke. "We thought you were...dead. We thought...you had drowned. Oh, Pie! Thank you for being okay."

"Well, you're welcome." He continued to hold her and felt the warmth of her tears on his chest.

Joe and the two New People were standing a few meters away, but keeping their distance. Jacques had his weapon in his hand, but Pie continued to ignore them and rocked Shana in his arms, before taking her by the shoulders and moving her far enough away to see her face. When their eyes met she pushed away. He managed to lower her to the ground.

"What's wrong, Shana?"

She backed away a couple of steps.

"What is it?" Pie asked with concern wrinkling his forehead.

"Your eyes," she whispered.

"What do you mean?"

229

Jacques spoke, "Citizen, you have the eyes of an Under and your link is missing. Where have you been?"

"Been? Why...nowhere. I've been right here...back on the beach." Visions of whiteness and warmth surfaced in his mind.

"Pie," Shana said, hesitantly, "you've...been gone...eleven days." Her mouth tightened with relived sadness. "I looked for you. I wouldn't stop, but I couldn't find you! You were...gone." The tears threatened to well up again and she wiped her red eyes with their puffy lids on the sleeve of her suit.

"That's impossible," Pie scoffed. "The sun is...." He looked up, and then over at the mid-afternoon sun, and then back to Shana.

She nodded, not knowing if she should flee or hug him close. "It's true, Pie."

He dropped to his knees on the grass. "I understand," he whispered.

"What did you say?" Shana asked cautiously.

He closed his eyes and saw with his new knowledge through a link more powerful than anything he had ever experienced before. He saw the New People and knew them for what they were, matrix-human composites. He saw the matrix-brain interface within their skulls. They were cyborgs. The weapon Jacques had been holding dangled from his fingers and then fell to the grass.

Pie regained his feet and held his hand out toward Shana. "Come. Let's go into the ship."

For just a moment, she hesitated, and then took hold of his offered hand. Together they walked to the ship, with the others following a safe distance behind.

It felt so good to hold her hand, to feel her nearness. He smiled and looked down at her, and she smiled and looked up at him.

She hugged his arm and giggled like a girl. "You have beautiful eyes."

"Really?" He was pleased and surprised. "I'm not certain I can remember. What color are they?"

"Hazel, a beautiful hazel green."

"So, you finally found something attractive about me."

"You are a beautiful person."

He laughed. "Thanks. I've had someone describe me as interesting."

When they entered the ship they went to Pie's cabin. There they made love without shame or reservation. Later they entered the commons. He felt closer to his youth than ever before and silly with joy. The New People were quiet and Joe withdrew to his usual position.

"I have learned much," Pie said as he settled onto the lounge and motioned for Shana to join him. "But it's of no real use to us. They are most definitely not the Slan. I've learned that these aliens, who call themselves—he uttered a rapid series of clicks—are an ancient species. They arose during the second wave of stars, over ten billion years ago. When the goldilocks zone begins to disappear, they move their planet. This is their sixth star. They have explored the universe by skimming along the event horizon. In the topography of the universe, all black holes are one. They shield themselves, not from neophytes like ourselves, but from other ancient species who consume the essence of life."

He turned toward Jacques and laughed, at Jacques and at himself. "The entity that we thought was the alien is an engineered being. It is a limited life form with no sense of self or of self-preservation. Each Blue has its assigned plot of land to wander across, but you probably already knew all this, right, Jacques?"

Jacques nodded.

"Sure you did." Pie continued, "It's a three-tiered existence. The physical being provides animal sensation. They are the sensory organ. Individuals occupy localized matrixes in the second level and in the third level is the community of all beings, mixed together in a cauldron of shared existence.

"They have mastered chaos and have used this mastery to control entropy, but there has been a price. As death withdrew, I believe, life withdrew as well. I sensed that they don't know they're alive, and maybe they aren't. Without the pressure of time, there is no urgency, no drive, no goals, and no emotions, at least as we humans experience emotions. They are caught in a trap of their own making. They are trapped for eternity within unbreakable changelessness.

"There is nothing for us here. There are no points of contact between our species and theirs, no bridges, no communality and the gap in technology is far too wide to bridge. They took Jacky and me and gave us these," he pointed his hand at the opalescent device that hung against his chest, "because we were a new species, one that evolved long after they explored the universe. They used the device to bring what it is to be human into the cauldron of their communality. They studied us, but we were no mystery to them, nothing new."

What Pie had revealed was almost the truth. Actually he had learned something useful. He understood the matrix like no other human and was wearing a link that had the power to reach into any matrix. The matrix was alive, but it was a crippled life form because it lacked a will. He knew how to bypass the superficial crust of programming and provide a will for the life within. The New People could feel it, without knowing exactly what had happened. They knew they were no longer the masters and it paralyzed them with fear. They were even afraid to communicate with one another.

Pie stood and stretched. Shana and he walked past them to drop into the down-tube, leaving them to consider the new reality of their accountability to a Citizen.

Pie and Shana were snuggled comfortably in Pie's cocoon, nestled in the darkness of night-cycle, when Shana broached the subject that had been bothering her since Pie's return.

"Pie?"

"Yes."

"I looked for you when you...disappeared. I used an air extractor and spent hours at a time searching the floor of the lake, until I was too exhausted to go on. All I could find was your knife and—"

"You found my knife?" he asked with interest.

"What is it with you and that knife?"

He was silent for a moment before he answered. "It was given to me by a special person...long ago."

"A woman?"

"It was a long time ago."

"Was it Kin?"

"No...I really don't want to get into this, but...her name was...." He shook his head. "God damn it! I can't even remember her name. Mason will pay. I swear it."

"Do you think it's that Roxanne Wiley that you've mentioned?"

"I guess it's possible, for whatever that's worth."

"Do you remember anything else?" Shana asked.

"I do remember that it was given to me as a joke because I was always complaining about over reliance on technology."

"What happened?"

"I've had it for over a thousand years. I became accustomed to wearing it—"

"You know very well that's not what I was asking."

Pie was silent for a moment before he continued. "I'm not certain, but I think I left her."

When Shana didn't respond to his statement he felt obligated to continue. "It had something to do with regeneration. To really understand you'd have to understand my fear of death." Pie stopped. It seemed strange that he had ever felt like that. It was a queer sensation.

"Pie, are you okay?"

"Yes...anyway...it's all so confusing. My memories are a mishmash. I wish I could remember her. I remember being old, the oldest I've ever been. I remember we were living the in the City of Cago and I panicked. I started running and couldn't stop. After I regenerated, I returned to the apartment we had shared, but found it was empty. I would guess she had died while I was gone. I had broken a promise to hold her hand when she was dying."

"But you still can't remember who this 'she' was."

Pie nodded and waited for a lessening of Shana's closeness, but as the seconds passed, she remained cuddled against him.

"That wasn't you, Pie."

"Then who was it?"

"I don't know. You couldn't be more than thirty years old."

"Well thanks, Shana. My body age is twenty-four."

"Okay. Twenty-four. That means the story you told me couldn't possibly be about you."

Pie sighed. "This all seems so familiar. I just can't place it."

"Do you still miss her?"

"How could I? I don't even remember her."

"She might have regenerated. Are you going to try to find her? You know her name."

"I know a name…Roxanne Wiley. I wish it meant something."

"You're going to try to find her, aren't you?"

"I don't know. I'm beginning to think the person who loved her no longer exists."

"I'm glad you told me."

"I'm not sure I am."

It was a while before Shana spoke again. "You almost made me forget what I wanted to ask."

"Who's being interrogated now?" he asked with an unseen smile in the dark. "Go ahead, Shana. What do you want to know?"

"What happened to you? Are you a Citizen, or an Under? You're not wearing a link, but something's going on. I've never seen the New People act like that before."

"I don't know."

"Pie, be honest."

"I think I'm…neither."

"What do you mean? Where were you the last eleven days?"

"I have my suspicions. Did you feel any unusual…emotions when you were searching the lake bottom?"

"Unusual? No, I don't think so. I was frantic…afraid I'd lost you."

"That's not what I mean. I don't know…. I guess I felt like I was being welcomed home by me. I wasn't afraid. I felt safe…and loved. I think my awareness was somewhere beneath the planet's surface." He hesitated, but decided if what he had told her so far had not alienated her, one more admission might be tolerated.

"Shana, I think there is a duplicate of my consciousness living among the aliens. I think...I died and was regenerated. I suspect I am providing sensations for my other self, just as the Blues provide sensations for the aliens down below. I can feel something reaching out to me and calling to me. I feel like I'm attached somehow. I suspect, in a way, in the way of this planet, Jacky's still alive, if you can call it that."

"Obviously he's alive. Why do you think he killed Kin?"

"Shana, I need to tell you something else. I kind of glossed over it. Listen to me. The man who you've come to know as Pie Traynor died in that lake, nearly two weeks ago."

"A body-death."

"Now you're talking like a Citizen. Dead. He's dead. I'm not the same person."

"Of course you aren't. We change a little every day."

Pie shook his head and sighed.

"Is the attraction you feel for this planet very strong?" she asked.

"It's very strong."

She took his face in her hands and kissed him, prolonged and warm. She withdrew but continued to hold his face in her soft hands. "I have first claim. So, you can tell the planet to fuck off."

"How very sweet." But it made him think of Kin.

As if reading his mind she said, "Kin was a good teacher, but we'll see her again."

"I hope so."

"I want you," she said. "You are mine."

She cuddled closer.

Pie was comfortable. He wanted nothing more than feel Shana against his side. He waited until her breathing was deep and regular and then whispered, "I want you too."

Chapter 32

When Pie jerked awake, at first he didn't know why. Then, mentally, he heard a cry of anguish so heart-rending, so desolate, that it brought tears to his eyes. It was Jilla. He rolled out of the cocoon and slipped on his suit.

"Shana!"

Her voice was thick, still groggy with sleep. "What is it, Pie?"

"Jacques has died."

"What! What did you say?"

"Jacques is dead. Come along. I want you with me."

She slid out of the cocoon and quickly pulled on her bodysuit. "What happened?"

"I don't know yet."

Together they hurried to the up-tube and exited on the New People level. Joe was standing outside the cabin. Jilla's keening cry was non-stop.

"Wait out here with Joe," Pie said to Shana.

"I'm coming with you," she replied firmly. But, when she saw the sight, her breath sucked in audibly with horror and shock. The curly-haired "girl" was sitting on the deck, rocking back and forth, with Jacques' decapitated head in her lap.

Shana stepped around Pie and was about to approach Jilla, to comfort her, but Pie caught hold of her arm and pulled her back.

"Don't touch her!" he ordered and backed her into the corridor. He turned his attention to Joe. "What can you tell me?"

"I know very little, Citizen. I was awake, preparing storage for lift off, when I saw a figure running past me from the direction of the down-tube. The portal opened and the man jumped out and ran off into the dark, closing the portal behind him."

"A man?"

Joe dropped his gaze to the deck. "I think it was Citizen Nichols."

"Think?"

"It was a human man," he answered, his hands folded in front of him in submission.

Pie frowned as he considered. "How do you happen to be up here, in this corridor?"

"I entered the up-tube to see if I could determine why the man had been running."

235

Pie's expression became distant as he uplinked, but the New People had placed a block on surveillance of their deck, so ship's sensors recorded nothing. He downlinked. It probably wouldn't have been useful anyway, he told himself. Jacky is invisible to the ship's sensors.

Shana touched Pie's arm to get his attention. "Isn't there anything we can do to help Jilla?" There was pain in the tight expression on her face.

"I doubt it, Shana," he answered, but then reestablished his connection and entered the part of Jilla that was matrix, effortlessly bypassing her internal blocks, and shut it down. She slumped forward, her screeching voice silenced.

"Is she dead?" Shana asked anxiously.

Pie shook his head. "More like a deep coma. It won't help her in the long run, but at least it'll give us some time to sort through this." He uplinked and accessed ship's sensors to study the grass around the ship; this time he couldn't detect the compression of grass from footfalls. He had no idea which direction Jacky might have gone. He downlinked and turned to Joe. "Keep a close guard on Shana. I want both of you to arm yourselves with lasers, but don't depend on them. They may not function any better than Jilla's weapon did against the Blue at their last meeting. And, Joe, carry Jilla up to the commons. I'll dispose of Jacques' body when I get back. Any questions?"

"I understand," said Joe. "I live to serve."

"Where are you going, Pie?" Shana asked, the pitch of her voice rising.

"I'm going to find Jacky. He can't be far."

"Don't go!" Shana cried. "Please, Pie," she begged, tugging on his arm. "I don't want you to leave. I'm afraid you won't come back."

"Shana!" Joe said. It was one word, but it seemed to have meaning for her.

Pie turned again to study the small man. Joe bowed his head and in a quiet voice said, "Please forgive me, Citizen. I too am upset. An Under should always obey."

"Can I at least go down to storage with you?" Shana asked.

"Sure, come along."

On the way down, she stopped off at her cabin. By the time she arrived in storage, Pie was already sitting on the whistle-cycle and the iris portal was open. She rushed over to him and handed him his knife and sheath that she'd found on the beach.

He strapped the blade to his forearm and looked up at Shana with a smile. "Thank you."

"Do you have to go? How will it change anything?"

236

"I need to confront him. He killed Kin and Jacques. I need to know why."

"But, damn it, what if the planet claims you and you never return to me? Promise me you'll come back."

"I'll be back, Shana."

"How long will you be gone? Liftoff is at 6:00."

"Hard to know. Perhaps a couple of hours, maybe all day. I'm well aware of liftoff."

"If you're not back by 15:00 ship time, I'm coming after you, even if I have to walk."

"Don't do that."

She backed away from the cycle and crossed her arms across her chest. Clearly she meant what she said.

He smiled but the smile was short lived. He was going to bring an old friend to justice. It was dawn, but soon it would be full morning and he didn't want to give Jacky an even longer head start. He eased the craft through the portal and then held it in place, hovering outside the ship. When he closed the portal, he saw Shana, standing alone in the storage bay, waving goodbye.

The sense that he'd done this before struck him with force. Was everything only a repeat of what had gone on before? Shana blew him a kiss. Not everything. He continued to hoover just outside the ship until the iris portal twisted shut and she disappeared from sight. The ship returned to darkness.

He began his search in the faint morning light, spiraling out from the ship in an ever-widening circle. The morning passed without success, but then, shortly after noon, he spotted an alien. He followed the Blue at a distance and then saw another figure. The new figure walked with an easy grace. Pie was positive it was Jacky, even at this distance.

He directed his cycle toward the ex-Citizen. Now that he'd found him, Pie wasn't sure what he was going to do. Perhaps Shana had been right.

When he'd left Jacky marooned here centuries ago, he never in his wildest imagination expected to see him again, dead or alive. The Blue and Jacky were walking toward one another. It appeared to Pie that he was about to witness a meeting, but they passed each other without a sign of greeting, without a change in their steady gaits, and then they were walking away from one another.

Pie swooped down and landed a hundred paces ahead of Jacky, in line with Jacky's unhurried progression. He stayed seated while he watched his former partner and friend draw near. Jacky was naked except for the medallion that hung from a cord around his neck. He was certain Jacky had seen him; it would've been impossible not to.

Jacky's face was empty, but it wasn't flaccid, just unconcerned and uninterested. When he was not more than ten paces away, he stopped.

Pie slid off the saddle and mentally steadied himself for the confrontation. While he walked the last few steps, he put his hand on the handle of his knife. There was something else different about Jacky, Pie thought as he stared into the man's face, and suddenly it was obvious; Jacky had the eyes of an Under. All the while Jacky's blue eyes looked back at him, but not quite, as if he was looking at Pie's ear rather than his face.

Pie was about to speak when Jacky bent to the side. Pie drew his blade, but Jacky only knelt and began to eat, plucking berries from a bush.

"What the hell are you doing?" Pie demanded.

"Eating," Jacky mumbled, his mouth full of berries.

"Don't you see me?"

He swallowed. "I see you. Hello, Pie."

"What's wrong with you?"

"Why...nothing." He remained kneeling on the grass. Thick, berry juice dribbled out of his mouth and a drop hung tenaciously to his chin, wiggling when he moved or spoke. "Only eat the yellow ones, Pie. You'll want to know that. They are so delicious. They all look the same but each one is different."

"Jacky, why didn't you come to greet me and to talk with me?"

"You never left. I talk with you all the time. You were lonely, but now you're happy, whole again. It is good."

"Are you talking about, Shana?"

Jacky looked at him without a sign of comprehension.

Pie stood there for a moment more and then slipped his knife back into its sheath. This was no killer. This was barely human.

"Jacky, did you kill Starglow Kin?"

His mouth was full again. "No," he managed to say as he stuffed more berries into his mouth.

"Son of a bitch!" Pie swore. It was so obvious. "Jacky, I want you to come back with me. We're going back to Home."

Jacky slowly craned his neck around. "Pie, I cannot leave...and you cannot leave. It isn't right. I've tried to share as much as I can with you but there is only so much. The Pie I know, the one who stayed behind, needs you and you need him. He has memories that you want, that you are missing. He needs you to see, hear, taste and feel for him. Without you he is blind and deaf. It is your duty."

Pie felt the growing pressure of need and the presence of another. He was being petted and caressed by someone who knew him intimately, himself. There was comfort here, security and love for eternity. He knelt, as if pulled to his knees and picked one of the yellow berries. He rolled it around on his fingertips as he inspected it and then put it in his mouth. It was sweet and more; the best thing he had ever tasted. All was right, as if this was the only right decision he had ever made. His planet-self soaked into him with gratitude and joy and love. He picked a second berry and was about to put it in his mouth, when he paused. There was something...some urgency. What was it? He wondered.

He continued to hold the berry. He had promised to return. Where? To his egg-house in the Cascades? No, that wasn't it. The ship. Yes, someone was in danger. Someone needed him...Shana. His planet-self touched him and revealed the terrible pain of loneliness.

Pie stood and looked in the direction of the ship, but couldn't see it. Shana was there, on the ship. Shana wanted him. He looked back to Jacky, who was kneeling next to a bush with his face turned up, toward Pie. Pie noticed the gap in Jacky's front teeth. Where was his soul now? He shivered with an icy chill. His thoughts returned to Shana and the sense of being owned by the planet, receded.

He allowed the berry to fall to the grass. "Jacky, you are ill. You had no one to save you from yourself, but now you do. You have me." He reached down and pulled Jacky to his feet. "We must leave now."

Jacky jerked his arm free and backed away, his eyes wide and staring. "No, Pie," he said as he shook his head.

"I'm taking you! I will not leave you here to wander aimlessly forever."

Jacky quickly bent and began pushing the leaves of a bush aside, searching. Pie reached for him but, too late. He saw the white berry enter Jacky's lips. Pie tried to pry his mouth open, but Jacky's eyes rolled up and he shook violently before becoming completely still, nothing but dead weight in Pie's arms. While he held him, the medallion that Jacky wore glowed orange and boiled away to nothing.

Pie gently lowered Jacky's dead body onto the grass. Not having the engineered body of a Blue, it would be years before he was reduced to bones. He would be back long before that with the newest version of his body, but not soon enough to be saved.

"I have little time my old friend. I'll be gone by the time your slow-day passes. I wished I could've saved you but clearly that is not something you desired. Goodbye, my friend. Flow, Jacky."

Pie turned to look back in the direction of the ship. He lifted the cycle into the sky and pushed it to maximum speed.

As he approached the ship he dilated the storage portal open and recklessly entered the bay with excess speed, flipping the jets forward to bring the cycle to a sudden stop. He linked with the ship as he ran to the up-tube and located the two Unders and Jilla. Shana was in the Under's cabin, alive and well, but Jilla was in the New People's quarters just as he'd left her, except she was dead. Joe was in the commons.

He exited at the New People level and rushed down the corridor. When he came to the open cabin, he stopped, and leaned against the frame of the door. Jilla was still on the floor, but she had a transparent bag tied over her head. Her face was cyanotic in death and her lips purple.

He reentered the passage and jumped into the up-tube, drawing his blade as he exited into the commons. He pointed the knife at Joe, who was sitting on a lounge as if idly waiting for Pie's arrival. The Under didn't move, or make a threatening gesture; he just sat there and smiled, with his small, regular teeth plainly visible for the first time.

"It would've all been worth it," Joe said, "if just to see the look on your face, oh Great Citizen."

"Why, Joe? Why did you do it?"

Joe leaned forward, the smile gone. "Don't ever call me by that name again. My name is Quang Lu. Mason thought he was so clever." Quang laughed harshly. "I was his special tool and I was trained well for my function. I had any Under-woman I wanted, any pleasure, and he thought he'd bought me." Quang spat on the deck. "I spit on his memory. My father got behind in his payments to the overseer. Did Mason really think a five-year old wouldn't remember Citizens breaking into our home and killing my father and mother in front of me and then kidnapping me? The only thing that saved me was the stupid arrogance of you Citizens and of Mason in particular.

"He had me trained to be an assassin and I learned it well. I was his pet project. His secret weapon. I never failed him. I kissed him and hugged him, but in my heart each kiss was a dagger, each hug a crush. He tested me. He made me kill my own sister as proof of my loyalty, but it proved nothing, except that there was no sacrifice too great to rid the world of the Technocracy."

"You are crazy! Killing Kin and the New People changes nothing."

"I'm not crazy, but you are right. Their deaths change nothing. Mason taught me that the best way to ensure a plan's success is to eliminate other players. I would have preferred to eliminate you but when I saw Kin, all hooked up and ready to be cooked, I couldn't resist. I knew the New

People would be aware of Kin's death so I went immediately to them on my return to camp."

"So, they were in on it and erased ship's record."

"No. Do you know what this is?" He held up a small gray disk.

Pie shook his head.

"A gift from Mason. It's a single use matrix access port. I used to have two of them. The great thing about them is that they allow the user complete anonymity."

"Why did you kill the New People?"

"Simple. I hated them. Didn't you? Mason told me you couldn't be counted on to kill them but you sure made it a lot easier. I do thank you for your help with Jilla." He sucked in a deep breath of self-satisfaction. "That was almost too easy."

"When we get back to Home I'm going to turn you over to the New People."

Joe made a laughing sound. "You, like all Citizens, think of us as Unders, but we are not! We are legitimate humanity. The Earth belongs to us. We are Friends of the Earth."

"So you killed a Citizen and two New People. What the hell good does that do for your cause?"

"That's not the plan. That was simply taking out the trash, clearing the way."

"What is the plan?"

"In a minute. Don't you think I did a great job of acting when I told you about poor Kin's unfortunate death? I fooled you, completely."

"You say you hate Mason. Don't you see? You're doing the same things Mason would've done. You've become the perversion you claim to oppose."

"So true. He taught me well."

"You are a cold, heartless bastard!"

Quang nodded. "It is to your advantage to recognize me for what I am. I am not naive, nor am I blind. I do not lie to myself about my nature. I am evil like Mason, but there is a difference. Mason manipulates and destroys for the benefit of Mason. I, on the other hand, am willing to sacrifice myself for the salvation of the Earth."

"What do you hope to gain by this so-called sacrifice...Quang?"

"I'm going to do what you claim to have been trying to do for two thousand years. I'm going to save the Earth. Don't you want to know how?"

Pie was prepared to kill the man, but he seemed unafraid. Pie did not underestimate the cleverness of a sociopath. There was something more here. "Sure, tell me about your big plan."

"I am going to take over the Star Grazer Hawking and swat Home from the heavens like a big fat bug. Don't give me that look, Citizen."

"You are crazy."

"Come now. Take a moment and organize your thoughts. I expect better from you than that."

"Don't you realize the absurdity of all this? Over two hundred planet-years will have passed before the Hawking returns to the Solar System. You won't even know who controls Home, or whether it even exists. And, if by some astronomical chance you manage to succeed in this mad scheme, you'll kill Citizens but you'll also kill hundreds of thousands of Unders. Are you really prepared to kill all those innocent people?"

"Who is to say who is innocent? If that is the price that must be paid, it is not too high of a price to save the Earth."

"You don't understand. You just don't understand."

"You are the one who doesn't understand and, furthermore, you are going to help me."

"The hell I will!" Pie took another step closer. One more step and he could use his knife.

"I would've preferred to have killed you too. It would have been easy enough."

"Really?" Pie said dryly.

"No question about it. Your good fortune could not have protected you forever. There were a few enlightened Citizens in my organization. One of them was a Citizen named Lem Gan. Did you know him?"

Pie shook his head. "I knew of him."

"He was your backup, but somehow you managed to escape assassination by my Friends of the Earth."

Pie stared at the raving man.

"You don't remember?" Quang laughed. "That's not a new problem is it? You escaped assassination in Cisco City and then again on Home. It cost Friend Gan his life. Do you remember a brief walk in space?" Quang smiled. "I can see you still possess some shreds of actual memory. I ordered Shana to kill you on Home, but she failed me and, as a result, Gan had to kill himself. She hid behind the excuse that it would alert Mason to our plot. She has proven herself to be a true Under. If not a slave to the Citizens, then a slave to her emotions, but always a slave."

"Shana was in on it?" He chanced a brief up-link; she was asleep in her cabin.

"Don't be so simple, Citizen. She didn't participate in the liberation of the out-ship. I couldn't trust her. But she must have suspected what was happening. Her mission was to learn hardware from Kin. What a joke. All she did was sit around and watch Kin, while Kin did her real work through her link. She learned nothing, and that is where you come in. You will drive this out-ship to a rendezvous with the Hawking."

"There is something I need to take care of first." Pie closed the final distance.

"Do you truly love Shana?"

Pie held his hand.

"If you do, you'll want to hear the rest of what I have to say. I must admit you are making me a little nervous," Quang said. "Would you back up a little, please?"

Pie remained as he was.

"I asked nicely. Believe me, you want to hear what I have to say, if you love her. I'm not going anywhere. I've no doubt you could kill me anytime you want to. Step back please."

Pie slowly backed away until he stood in the center of the commons.

"Thank you. Simple Shana always wants to believe the best of a person. Me, not so much. She told me all you needed was to be informed. Here, get informed." He flicked a pebble-sized object at Pie.

Pie dodged out of the way; the small object bounced off the deck and rolled to a stop.

Quang laughed. "Kind of jumpy aren't you, Citizen? It's only a memory capsule. You made it yourself. Go ahead, pick it up." He slid a little deeper onto the lounge seat. "I'll just sit here."

Pie glanced down at the red capsule. It appeared to be a standard, memory capsule. What was the trick? he wondered.

"Go ahead," Quang Lu encouraged. "It won't hurt you. It really is yours. Shana stole it from your cabin at Home. Remember, I need you."

Pie slowly squatted, but kept his eyes on the Under while he groped around with his fingers until he felt and picked up the small capsule. He flipped it back to Quang, who causally caught it.

"If you want me to see this," Pie said, "go to the bridge and drop it in the matrix slot. I'll wait here."

"No problem. You certainly are a suspicious person," Quang said over his shoulder as he entered the up-tube. A moment later he reappeared.

Pie waved his blade toward the holo-stage. "Stand over there."

Quang shrugged and did as he was instructed.

Pie activated the stage. The flow of information began with his personal code, but he couldn't remember having made it. The contents of the capsule revealed the raping of the Earth by Home and documented the dismal failure of the Project. He ran a quick matrix analysis of the capsule. It had all the characteristics of a search done by himself. It was the genuine article. Another erased memory? he wondered.

"So, Citizen, what do you say now?"

Pie was quiet as his mind raced to digest the startling information that had just been revealed to him, of the ultimate and complete failure of his life's work. Finally, he spoke. "I've learned much on this planet. The ultimate outcome of regeneration will be the obliteration of change, of life itself. Leave this to me. I can and will bring the Technocracy down."

Quang patted his hands together, a soft clapping. "Bravo, Citizen. Your ethics are inspiring, but do you really expect me to trust you? Or believe you? I'm not asking that much of you. All I aim to do is soften your dedication to the Technocracy. Now it's time for Shana to finally play a useful part, all be it a passive one. I've implanted an explosive device within her abdominal cavity. Simple really, an oral sedative, a few minutes of minor surgery and it's done. And, no, it's not matrix based. If you try to tamper with it, our pretty, little Shana will be splattered all over the bulkhead and you along with her, if you're standing close by."

Pie licked his lips as he assessed the Under's threat. "If I should die, you'll have no one to drive you to the star grazer."

"True. The decision is yours."

Pie slid his blade into its sheath.

Quang nodded. "If you harm me, or fail me in any way...ka-boom!" He raised his arms as if they represented an expanding explosion.

"How do I disable the bomb?"

"I'll give you the code, at the proper time."

"How do I know I can trust you to keep your word?"

"I have nothing against Shana. In fact I owe her. She provided me with the only real pleasure of this trip. I don't think she enjoyed it as much as I did but she was good, well trained. Don't you agree?"

Pie took a step toward Quang.

"Stop," Quang said. "Ka-boom. Remember? You and your kind are the ones who trained her. I don't see how you have any right to be pissed off. She's sweet and genuine, and an Under, like myself, but far from being a trained operative. It was Mason's mistake of including her. Thinking with his penis. I certainly wouldn't have. However, all things being equal, I'd like to know she lived."

"How do you plan to take control of the star grazer?"

"Leave that to me. I'll have plenty of time to master the skills of running a starship."

"That wasn't my question, but you bring up an important point. Do you realize that, if by some fluke you succeed in taking over the starship, you'll still be unable to accomplish your suicidal goal? Even the most skilled star grazer crew couldn't hit a fifty kilometer target, and if you are off by as little as a hundredth of a second, out of a hundred year voyage, you risk hitting the Earth, a much bigger target. Instead of saving the Earth, you'd be the one to destroy it, forever. Think about it. It's not the star grazer that makes a rendezvous, it's the out-ship. Seriously, man, think about what you're planning! Think!"

Quang Lu smiled. "We must lift off within seven hours. I'm going down to sit with Shana. The sedative I gave her should wear off shortly. I wouldn't want her to take an unscheduled trip with you. It wouldn't be healthy for her, you know?"

Quang turned his back on Pie and disappeared into the down-tube. Pie sat down heavily on the lounge seat to lean forward, supporting his head with his hands, his elbows resting on his knees. His mind wandered from one thought to another, from the failure of the Project, to his own personal failures. He no longer felt that terrible fear of or attraction for death, but if he stayed on this world there would be neither death, nor life.

So, Shana, he wondered, *are you to be the next sacrifice in this human farce to save the Earth?* There would be no possibility of regeneration; her memories resided in only one place, her mind. Could he justify risking the lives of millions to save the life of one hostage? The numbers were lopsided, but his feelings told him otherwise. Perhaps he could do both. He could buy time, he rationalized, perhaps during the year outbound to rendezvous, he could find an acceptable solution. In fact, it'd been so long since he'd functioned as a driver, they might miss the rendezvous.

An hour slipped away. Most of the time he wasn't thinking, just sitting. He wondered what the chances were for this crazed fanatic to take over a star grazer. Quang would not have the advantage of surprise; the starmen thought everyone was an assassin.

His mind drifted, unguarded. He could feel the need of his other self, calling to him, begging for him to stay. He didn't have to leave; he could stay here and be loved and cared for. Thoughts of Earth and Quang Lu and Shana escaped his mind. The one person who truly understood needed him here. *Yes,* he nodded. *I'm coming. There will be happiness...forever.* He stood and turned to walk toward the down-tube, but stopped; surprised to see Shana standing there.

"If you want me to leave, I will," she said. She walked over and knelt in front of him.

He trembled with the realization of how close he'd just come to being captured by the planet of the Blues, forever.

He pulled her to her feet. "What are you doing on your knees?"

"I'm sorry, Pie. I know you can't forgive me. I should've known...I guess I did, but...I just couldn't face it. If you want to execute me for the death of Citizen Kin, or even the New People, I don't ask for mercy."

"Come here, please."

She stepped forward and closed her eyes, arms at her sides, waiting for his decision.

He wrapped his massive arms around her and held her to him. She returned his embrace.

"It's still an hour until I need to go to the bridge," he said. "Would you sit with me? I need you to sit with me. Would you?"

She nodded. The tears began to trickle, glistening on her black skinned cheeks, an unsightly drop hung from the tip of her nose. He led her to the lounge seat and pulled her into his lap.

"I like to feel the weight of you on me," Pie said.

She kissed him softly on the cheek.

"You saved my life and you continue to save it," he whispered.

"I don't understand."

He kissed the top of her head. "Shana."

"Yes, Pie?"

"It's time to go home."

Chapter 33

During the year of being outbound in search of rendezvous with the Star Grazer Hawking, Pie frequently escaped into stasis, awakening from time to time to redirect the out-ship. The risk was great but he could not tolerate the long days of vigilant solitude with nothing to do except brood and question the basic beliefs of his life. The capsule also offered his only respite from sharing in the suffering of his planet-bound self and the guilt of abandoning him.

Lift off from Angkor-3 had been a harrowing experience. His planet-trapped self had left no vulnerability unprobed, and he knew them all. He begged and threatened. He showed Pie an image of a woman with red hair and named her for Pie, Roxanne Wiley, proof that he had the memories that had been stolen from Pie. His other self had cried tears of pure terror and had revealed to Pie the horror of being abandoned to an eternity of loneliness and darkness. He had played on Pie's sense of duty and had ruthlessly castigated him for both cowardice and selfishness. And through it all, Pie could do nothing but accept the accusations and share in the pain because it was himself that he had deserted to a fate of unending torment.

Only the presence of Shana provided the extra strength he needed to resist aborting the rendezvous. It was Shana who saved him. Even as far out as halfway point, the point of no return, he continued to hear and feel the desperation and desolate pain of irreparable loss. He hoped, without knowing if it was anything more than an empty hope, that Jacky would find it in himself to share, but he could not escape the guilt that he had condemned his other self to everlasting hell, an existence that offered at best only one avenue of escape, insanity.

More often than not, when his duties dragged him out of the wintery grip of stasis, he would spend time sitting in the cabin of the Unders. Both Quang Lu and Shana could be seen in their transparent stasis capsules, so near, yet so far beyond reach in their timeless sleep. He would touch the clear surface of her capsule, almost a caress. He wanted, needed her, but could not risk exposing her, and the device Quang had implanted in her, to the passage of time.

As a result of his neglect, when the Unders were revived in preparation for rendezvous, Pie had no time to spend with them. He hid the desperation of those days while he fought to bring the out-ship into line with the Hawking, both in time and space. He had violated the most

247

basic duty of a driver, to remain constantly attentive. His shame prevented him from revealing just how close they'd come to being swallowed up by the universe.

When the out-ship locked onto the Hawking, Pie was physically and emotionally exhausted, but the dilemma that had haunted him for the last year, and that had succeeded in chasing him into stasis and near disaster, remained unresolved. It was not until he dropped into the down-tube and entered the commons that he knew what his decision was, if it could be called a decision.

He was wrong, and knew he was wrong, but he was going for a personal victory this time. During lifetimes of dedication to the success of the project, he had failed, and now he was withdrawing. Let chance, or the star grazer crew take up the cause; he was through. He found Shana waiting for him and Quang Lu standing behind her.

"Shana," Quang said, "go wait in the star grazer lock."

Shana remained as she was and looked to Pie.

Pie nodded. "Go ahead, Shana. I'll be along in a moment," he added with a confidence that was no deeper than his words. When she had disappeared into the up-tube, Pie found himself confronted by the mischievous grin of Quang Lu.

"Feeling nervous, Citizen?"

Pie revealed nothing while he waited for the next minute to unfold.

Quang spoke again, light and casual. "I guess the question is, now that you're no longer useful, do I dispose of you, or...do I allow you to survive, shackled by emotion to an Under-woman? Vulnerable to anyone who knows. Tell me, have you enlisted the star crew in your cause? Warned them about the terrible upstart of an Under-man who has gained complete control over you?"

"Crew does not communicate."

"So...you have tried."

Pie neither denied nor confirmed the assertion.

"What can you tell me about the Dixon's that might be of help?" Quang asked.

"Nothing," Pie answered promptly, "but they have scanned us. They expect three. I wouldn't advise you to stimulate their already psychotic paranoia."

"You aren't being very cooperative, considering the circumstances," Quang said and opened his hand to reveal a poison-pellet gun. "As you can probably detect, this is pre-matrix technology. Simple, but effective."

Pie had had enough. Whatever would be, would be. He pulled up his sleeve and stripped the sheath and knife from his forearm, laying them on the lounge seat as he walked past it toward the up-tube. He paused at the mouth of the tube and turned to face the small man who was holding the deadly but miniature gun.

"Quang," Pie said, "I'm going to enter the star grazer lock. Then Shana and I are going directly to our capsules. When you join us, and I recommend that you leave the little 'toy' here, I expect you to tell me how to inactivate the bomb. If you do not, I will cause such a ruckus, the Dixon's will undoubtedly kill us all."

"So, you have decided to trust me to give you the real code."

"Not really, but I do believe you wouldn't kill Shana without cause."

"You think you know me, you arrogant bastard Citizen?" He raised his weapon and pointed it at Pie.

Pie turned his back to the man. He expected to feel the tiny bite of a pellet, but refused to give Quang satisfaction. He took the last steps toward the up-tube and then paused at the mouth, as if daring Quang to shoot. Finally, he finished the action and ascended to the star grazer lock.

Shana hugged him. "What were you two talking about that couldn't be shared with me?"

Pie returned her embrace; her wild hair tickled his nose.

"We were coming to an understanding," Pie said.

"About what?"

Quang Lu joined them.

"Trust me," Pie said, but he couldn't prevent himself from looking at Quang's hand; he didn't see the weapon, but that didn't mean it wasn't there.

The star crew activated the lock portal and it slid open, exposing the interior of the star grazer. The large and brightly lit capsule-deck seemed empty; the Dixon's were nowhere in sight, but that didn't mean they weren't hiding nearby. Pie led the way toward the three open capsules. When they had stripped in preparation to enter their capsules, Pie saw Shana inspecting a small wound on her abdomen. She touched it and looked to Pie as if he knew how she had gotten it. Pie shrugged and turned to face Quang. The meaning of Pie's gaze was obvious; it was either now or never.

Quang smiled before he spoke. "Use a frequency modulated radio wave of 95.5 megahertz. The code is in the preservation locker in Kin's cabin." The Under-man appeared perfectly at ease, in control, but he carried no weapon.

Pie returned his attention to Shana. "I love you," he mouthed.

"I love you," she answered silently, with her lips.

Pie entered his capsule and saw that both Shana and Quang followed his action by entering their own cylinders. Then Pie saw it. The nail of Quang's right index finger was longer and sharper than the others, and probably painted with poison. Simple.

At that moment Pie was startled to see Heck Dixon standing in front of his capsule. The star-man's eyes flicked about and his eyelids jerked with a tic. Pie lowered his gaze. Avoid contact, avoid confrontation his years of experience told him. Dixon reached forward; Pie remained perfectly still and watched as Dixon touched the medallion with the tip of his fingers, caressing it, almost as if worshiping it. Dixon slowly withdrew his hand, as if reluctant to lose contact with it.

"You are Pie Traynor," Heck Dixon said.

"Yes."

Dixon stared at him.

The impulse to warn the star-man overcame Pie's inhibition about speaking. He took a breath to speak and Dixon closed the capsule. For Pie, time stopped.

Chapter 34

Quang Lu watched Dixon close Pie's capsule and then Shana's. He took a calming breath. Now that Pie and his link were sealed away, it was time. Dixon walked over to stand in front of Quang's capsule. He began to raise his energy canon; his intention was obvious, but it took a moment too long to raise the weapon. Quang struck with the speed of a snake. His rigid index finger punctured Dixon's right eye and penetrated through the socket into his brain. There was no poison, but Dixon was a dead man, still standing but beginning to fall when Quang pulled the energy canon from his dead hands and flipped out of the capsule and onto the deck. He squirmed forward, between two capsules, and stood. He waited and watched for the other two Dixons.

He looked overhead at the distant gleam of the double row of capsules on the opposite side but saw no movement and heard no sound. He returned his gaze to the body that lay sprawled on the deck before him. Heck Dixon's forearm, encased within an old-style black link; was extended, as if pointing to Quang's hiding place. If he was to have any chance against the remaining Dixons, he'd need a link. He knew the old links could theoretically be worn, shared with another, but was also aware that it had been imprinted. That was a real danger, but Quang was confident that he could suppress whatever remained of Heck Dixon.

He reached out and tugged the heavy bulk of the dead man closer to his hiding place and paused. He thought he heard something, possibly the sound of quick, light footsteps, but then the silence returned. They were closing in on him. He refocused on the link; it was his only chance, despite the risk. He heard the sound again but ignored the approaching attackers while he ran his fingers over the link, frantically searching for a release.

Suddenly, he was knocked aside by a splash of energy from a canon as it vaporized the capsule next to him. He pressed his finger into a small slot in the link and jerked it off the dead man's arm. Another blast of energy struck his hiding place, this time vaporizing his left leg from the knee down and at the same time cauterizing the wound.

The pain threatened to overwhelm consciousness but he'd been thoroughly trained as an assassin and fought to block the pain. He slipped his arm into Dixon's link and it sealed itself to his arm. As he raised his canon to defend himself, the link activated and sunk its neural teeth into his psyche. He stiffened with agony and dropped the canon to the deck. He grunted and snorted as if possessed. In fact, the character of Heck Dixon, imprinted on the link, possessed him.

His eyes stared widely and he bit off the tip of his tongue. He spit the piece of tongue at the thin man who was watching him, with an energy canon held at the ready. He laughed and the laughter turned into a cackle as blood filled his mouth and ran down his chin.

"I am Dixon!" Quang screamed. "I am Quang Lu," he growled with a gurgle. "What are you staring at?" he demanded with a bloody sneer. "You and Lev are mine. You'll always belong to me."

The Dixon who was holding the energy cannon lowered it and looked over his shoulder at the other Dixon, the one who held a laser pistol in each hand.

"I am!" Quang Lu-Dixon yelled. "I am the savior! I will kill! I will kill! Purify the monster! I will incinerate their souls. I will kill them all! I will save us."

Chapter 35

When Pie's capsule opened, a man was standing in front of him. The man was old. His sparse beard consisted of a few wisps of fine, white hair. Numerous deep creases radiated outward from his lips, and the taut, shiny skin of his bald scalp revealed the bony structure of his skull. He had the eyes of Quang Lu. Before stepping out onto the deck of the star grazer, Pie waited for the man to move to Shana's capsule with his slow, deliberate steps, bent and rigid with age. All that remained of two stasis-capsules across from him were the melted bases, like two missing teeth, and the adjacent capsules were marred by the white, feathery pattern of an energy splash. And within the space left by the vaporized capsules were the bones of a human.

When Shana's capsule opened, he saw her take a breath to speak, but then closed her mouth. She sidled over to Pie and took his hand, as they both watched the white-robbed man hobble farther down the corridor. The ancient man's left foot was new-steel gray and with each step it clicked metallic against the deck. He took up the dominant position between two slim crewmen who were also wearing long white robes. Pie recognized them as the Dixons, but Heck Dixon was not with them. He briefly glanced at the bones and the returned his attention to the starmen; they too showed signs of aging, but only the typical aging expected of a starman near the end of a grand procession, not at all like the tremulous old man who stood between them.

Quang must not have gone into stasis at all, Pie thought. If he was unbalanced before, he must now be floridly psychotic. Pie broke the rule of avoiding eye contact, hoping the man wouldn't take it as a challenge. Quang Lu-Dixon's eyes burned with an unblinking intensity that confirmed Pie's suspicions.

The acolyte to Quang's left aimed his energy cannon at Pie and spoke. "Bow your head, infidel. The savior is in your presence. The savior is great! The savior is good!"

Pie obeyed and hoped Shana was doing likewise.

Quang spoke, his voice squeaking and cracking with age. "You've served me well, my children, and as your reward you've been chosen to be my prophets. You will witness the fulfillment of a solemn promise, a promise to rid the world of the monster within. Tell them that their deaths were pleasing to me and that I shall raise them up again when the world is

253

safe. I am coming to redeem mankind and give rebirth to the world. Go forth, my children, and spread the word."

Pie moved at once, keeping his head bowed as he walked. He stopped before the space-walk lock, wondering if it still led to the out-ship, or merely opened onto the vacuum of space. He resisted the urge to uplink; this was a very unstable star crew that held weapons on them, the worst he'd ever seen.

When the lock cycled open, Pie stepped forward and heard Shana's light steps following behind him. After the lock to the star grazer slid shut, the mouth to the down-tube opened, without explosive decompression; the down-tube was pressurized and presumably still led to the out-ship.

After a quick glance at Shana, Pie hurried to the down-tube. They exited into the commons of the out-ship and he locked off the tube to the star grazer.

"I don't have time to talk now," he said. "We need to disengage before Quang and the Dixons decide that we need to be 'cleansed' as well."

Immediately, he re-entered the down-tube and floated out of sight. When he arrived in storage, he sealed it from the rest of the ship and climbed into a one-man shuttlecraft. The bubble-canopy cycled shut and he opened the storage bay to the vacuum of space. Air exploded from the bay in a sparkling of tiny crystals as it met the cold of deep space. He launched the little craft into the vacuum and began maneuvering to pick up the "cars" and an engine to make up a train.

When the task was completed, he returned to the storage bay and re-pressurized. As he waited the minute it took to replace vacuum with air, he uplinked with the out-ship and took a first reading on their destination. It was a spectral class "G2 V" star. It could be Sol. He hoped it was, and hoped it wasn't.

When he entered the commons he nearly collapsed, jittery, aching, and cold with fatigue. Shana's nude body was stretched out on one of the lounges, already deep into the First Sleep. He belted her down and then staggered over to the short up-tube that led to the bridge.

Once again he uplinked, this time to disengage from the Hawking. The seat wrapped him in its abbreviated set of "petals" as weightlessness swept through the ship and then he activated the engine at the far end of the train. The weight of deceleration pushed him into the seat and the star grazer shot forward, a bolt of near, light-speed mass, aimed at the heart of humanity. In less than a second, the Star Grazer Hawking was gone.

When Pie awakened, he dropped down into the commons. Shana was already awake, sitting with her legs pulled up in front of her, munching on a nutrient bar. He sat down next to her.

"What are you thinking about?" he asked.

She rubbed her fingers on the silky, rose-colored bodysuit she wore. "I don't know. A lot of things. I was so glad to be leaving that world but, now that we have...I remember those warm, summer days on the sand, and the clear cool water of the lake, sparkling in sunlight." She was quiet. "I won't know anyone and no one will know me."

"If you're thinking about Home, or even the Earth, you better put it on hold," Pie said grimly. He pounded his fist on the lounge seat. "Shit!" and then more softly, "I can't believe it."

"Quang Lu?"

Pie nodded, and a moment later, begrudgingly admitted, "If we had had Citizens as dedicated and single-minded as Lu, we might have succeeded, that son of a bitch. He must have spent his entire life linked with the starship. I'd never have thought it was even possible."

He stood, disappeared into the down-tube, and exited to enter Kin's cabin. He paused after entering, overcome with the guilt of having failed his friend. He opened her preservation chest. There was paraphernalia that he tried his best to ignore; he focused on a matrix chip. Hopefully Quang hadn't lied and this was the code to deactivate the bomb inside Shana. He ascended to the bridge and dropped the chip into the matrix reader. He instructed the reader, when it was activated, to broadcast the signal at 95.4 megahertz.

He reentered the commons, wearing a black bodysuit. He sat down next to Shana and put his arm around her. Whatever was about to happen would happen to both of them. He uplinked and activated the chip. An audio signal filled the commons.

Pie smiled. The code to deactivate the bomb was musical. It sounded familiar. Pie began to hum, and then the words came to mind and he sang along. "Jingle bells, jingle bells, jingle all the way...." When the tune completed itself, silence returned.

"I recognize that song," Shana said and laughed. "Why did you play it? Quang used to sing it sometimes, usually late at night. He told me his father was an expert on pre-Death folk songs. How did you learn it?"

Pie was amused. "You forget, I am one of humanity's leading experts on pre-Death culture. I—" Sudden sadness and longing took his voice.

"But, why did you play it?" she asked.

"It was a welcome home present from Quang Lu."

"Well that's certainly odd. Would you teach it to me?"

His smile returned. "Sure, I'd be glad to."

"Good. What's a 'one-horse-open-sleigh'?"

"Shana," Pie laughed and shook his head, "what is it that we have in common?"

She put her arm around his neck and rested her head on his shoulder. "Well...we have lots of things in common."

"Name one."

"Okay...we both like to swim."

He laughed and returned her embrace. "I guess you've got me there."

They rested in each other's arms. "Pie, I've been wondering...how did Quang Lu convince you to cooperate? Was it after you reviewed that memory capsule I borrowed from your suite back on Home?"

"Borrowed?"

"It got returned didn't it? Am I right about the reason?"

"Yes...you could say that."

Shana increased the pressure of her hug. "I knew you were special. I told Quang you were different. I could sense the justice in you, even when we were on Home, even though you did scare me a little bit." That gave her pause. "Home will be...destroyed...won't it?"

"I doubt it," Pie answered in an even voice.

She lifted her head away from where it had been resting against his shoulder.

"Quang has managed to gain control over the Hawking but the speed involved is so great, that infinitesimal errors can have a significant effect on the results. At these scales and speeds, entropy and chaos have the last word." Pie shivered and Shana felt the tremble pass through him.

"What is it, Pie?"

He didn't respond at once. He closed his eyes. There had been so much death and now.... These were the words that he didn't want to say, as if the saying of them would confirm the reality.

Shana waited.

He opened his eyes and turned to face Shana. "Chances are far greater that the star grazer will hit the Earth, than an insignificant speck we call Home. For all we know, he may be trying to hit the Earth."

He sat forward and covered his face with his hands. Shana put her hand on his thigh.

"It's my fault," he whispered. "I can't bear it." There was no refuge, no sanctuary from his guilt. "It would have been better if I had allowed the planet to claim me."

Shana pulled his hands away from his face.

"No, Pie, you are a good person. I know these things. I can sense them."

"Good, bad...you don't know anything. I didn't have the courage to face...."

"To face what, Pie?"

There was no response.

"To face what, Pie?" she said as she raised her voice. "You said that you did it because of what the memory capsule revealed. Isn't that the truth? Please, Pie...I need to know."

He took a deep, jerky breath, "Shana...."

She grabbed onto his hands and held them tight, her dark eyes glittering with tears of empathy. "What is it, Pie? Tell me."

He remained silent.

"Tell me!"

"I did it because Quang was going to kill you. I allowed my personal emotions to guide me, ignoring the consequences."

She straightened, and although she kept hold of his hands, pulled back slightly. "Am I to take it that you're sorry you saved my life? I think that was a good decision. Damn good, as Kin would say."

Pie smiled and nodded. "Damn good."

"Isn't it possible, or even probable, if what you say is true, that the star grazer will miss everything?"

He looked into those amber eyes and kissed her on the forehead. He pulled her against him.

"Pie," she whispered, "promise you'll never leave me."

The words hung in his ears. The same words echoed down the tunnel of his memory, though he could not recall the context, he sensed a chain of broken promises. He even thought about his other self, deserted on that distant, alien planet.

"Shana...I can't make promises, but I will never choose to leave you."

"I know," she said softly.

Although reluctant, he was forced to release himself from her embrace. "If we're going to stop, I have work to do. We're on the same course as the Hawking, though it is far ahead of us by now. Quang has managed to alter the parabolic curve. We've lost the distance of the curve and, as a result, I need to increase the rate of deceleration. I'm afraid it's back into the stasis-capsules for us, until the last week. I'll set the parameters for the matrix and then join you in your cabin. By the time we awaken, whatever is to happen, will have happened, months ago."

"Don't you need to stay awake to drive the ship?"

"Yes, but I wouldn't survive the deceleration. I will occasionally leave stasis to make course corrections. The last week will be the worst."

When he returned from the bridge, he joined her in the Under's cabin and stood before her while she entered and stood within her capsule, facing him.

"Are you afraid, Shana?"

She nodded.

"Me too. Well, with luck, we'll have a little time together before Homecoming. I love you. Keep the thought," he said as he closed her capsule, and then entered his own.

The months of being inbound passed away, day by day. Other than for Pie's brief escapes from stasis, there was nothing. They did not see or hear as the ship continued to shed momentum, trusting their frozen bodies to the matrix designed by Jilla LineBFD/LineDHB.

Another year had wedged itself between them and the rest of humanity. Then the day came when life was breathed into one of the frozen bodies. Pie stepped out of his capsule to the extreme quiet of the ship. After a quick visual inspection of Shana, he was satisfied all was as it should be, at least when it came to stasis. He sat down in a chair and wasted an hour, not wanting to know what had happened but knowing he must. He uplinked with the bridge matrix. There was a backlog of transmissions from Home, the last not more than five minutes past, warning the out-ship to dump velocity or be destroyed. Home still existed, but of the Earth, he couldn't tell. It was senseless in a way, but with the passing of the event, whatever it was, he felt the burden of responsibility lift.

His current assessment of their situation was that it was bleak, but not hopeless. He knew what needed to be done, but wasn't sure he could tolerate it, physically or mentally. He again turned to study Shana in her capsule; she seemed to be smiling. It was better that he didn't bring her out just yet. There would be no joy, only pain.

He put on a bodysuit and walked the corridor to ascend to the bridge; he would need the physical support that could only be found on the bridge. He settled into the driver's chair. He knew of no driver who had survived multiple G-forces for days, had not even heard of such a story told late at night when truth was less important.

The first item on Pie's agenda was the easiest: send a message to Home, assuring them that everything was under control, that it wouldn't be necessary to vaporize the ship. He turned his attention to fuel. It was good that he'd added more cars than usual. He was going to burn through the mass at a prodigious rate.

He increased the force of deceleration. The petals of the chair enveloped his body and searched out contact to provide nutrition, fluids and vascular support. His body was no longer his responsibility; it belonged to the chair. He gave himself up and became one with the matrix, adding himself to the decision-making, consuming data at a rate he'd never attempted before. He struggled to cope. It filled him with a sense of doom and suffocation.

He didn't feel his chest struggling against the crushing force of deceleration, or that his bones ached as if hammered. He could not identify his body. It was elsewhere while he traveled the wavering wave of probability, altering the thrust vector in pursuit of the best and only solution. He chased the solution, a mote of light flashing in and out of perception as his mind dove into black-mouthed spaces, sorting actions and probabilities at speeds he wouldn't have believed possible.

The pain was always there and growing. It began to break through his block but he fought to ignore it; if he hesitated even a second among the choices that fluttered through his mind, it would mean failure, disaster and death.

Faster, the decision points came faster and faster, and each decision caused another lash of body pain. It wouldn't end. This was to be his fate: pain, burning, squeezing until he knew he'd die and then the elusive light he'd been chasing stopped. A blinding bright filled his mind, but he had no lids to protect his eyes. He was no more. He begged himself to give up. Then darkness came and there was nothing.

The jolt that awakened him came from without. The pain was gone. The petals of the chair kept him from drifting out of the seat. There was a gentle pushing, he had a trace of weight and then there was none. He began to open his mind to the matrix, but fear chased him away. He tried again, and heard voices. The noise of speech became words, and the words became sentences. He listened without making a sound, hiding from them, afraid they were the ones who had tortured him, but he remembered what had been said.

Even after returning to sleep and reawakening, he remembered the words he had heard. Orientation returned. He knew who he was and that he was on the out-ship and then he remembered Shana.

A sense of time returned, six days. Six days of chasing a phantom through the universe. He felt the pull of acceleration again and uplinked. The out-ship was being maneuvered by a tug, nothing more than an engine attached to an over-sized grapple. He located Home. It would still be half a day before they docked. He listened and learned.

259

When the time grew near, he released himself from the driver's seat and swam toward the down-tube. It was time to awaken Shana. When he entered the cabin, he deactivated her capsule.

Her smile remained when the door opened. "I love you, too."

"What?" Then he returned her smile. It seemed like she had read his mind, but in fact was answering the last thing he'd said to her.

She floated into the room. When she was able to see him better, the creases of a frown quickly replaced the smile. "Are you sick? You look pale and tired. You don't look good."

"You look wonderful," he said.

"Are you sure you're okay? You look—"

"I'll be okay. It was a bit of a struggle to bring us Home."

"Home? Are we at Home? Does it still..."

"It survived."

She pushed off a bulkhead and wrapped her legs around his waist and her arms around his neck. Together, they began a slow motion twirl.

"What happened, Pie?" she asked.

He couldn't see her face, but worry was strong in her voice.

"I've had a little time to piece it together and I think I've a fairly good picture of what happened."

"The Earth?"

"It's still there. As I see it, the star grazer came in too fast for Home to destroy or divert it, traveling nearly as fast as the information front that preceded it. Quang managed to increase the speed of the starship with a hundred years of acceleration. That added acceleration nearly cost us our lives. We came quite close to missing the Solar System altogether, much less Home. Apparently Home tracked us, probably to destroy the ship if necessary, and now we are in tow. We should arrive at Home within the next six hours."

"So, it was as you predicted. Quang failed."

"The star grazer didn't miss everything. It struck a glancing blow to the moon. Home is heavily engaged, using its energy canons and multi-array lasers to destroy fragments of the moon that threaten to hit it. Some of the fragments blasted out of the moon are the size of mountains. The moon was pushed into an elliptical orbit."

"What does it mean, Pie?"

"To the Earth, ultimately?"

She nodded.

"I don't know. It's going to have an impact on Earth, that's certain. The tides are going to be huge and I'm sure earthquakes will be triggered, possibly volcanoes as well. I'm just thankful the star grazer didn't strike the Earth."

"See, Pie. Now aren't you glad you saved me?" She gave him a kiss on the ear while she continued to hang onto his neck.

"I always was."

"I'd like to believe that. Say, I have an idea! Let's take the out-ship and, just the two of us, find an island, burn it clean, and spend the rest of our lives there."

"Sounds tempting."

"But?"

"I have some unfinished business to attend to on Home."

"I don't want to go there, Pie, and I don't want you to go there either. I'm afraid of it. It's a trap. Let's escape while we can. We can break away from the tug, right?"

Pie was silent.

"Well?"

"You above all people know what Mason has done. It is so much worse than simply failing. He has actively prevented the Earth's recovery because it might threaten his power."

"Mason is still alive?"

"He's already survived two thousand years; another two-hundred shouldn't surprise anyone. I positively identified his voice on some of the transmissions and can sense his presence in the Home matrix."

"But, you keep telling me that time has passed. What happened between him and you was long, long ago, over two hundred years ago. Don't ruin our lives simply for revenge."

"Shana, the technocracy is fatally flawed. You know that. Taken to its logical conclusion, it'll lead to a changeless society, a state of non-life. I must confront Mason and the system must be dismantled. If I don't do it, who will? Do we wait for another zealot like Quang Lu to jeopardize the very survival of the Earth? No, it's up to me. I wasn't able to save the Earth as a Citizen of the Technocracy, maybe, at least I can save it from the Technocracy."

"You call Quang Lu a zealot. Who do you think you are? The savior? The great and good savior? Are you sure you're not making high sounding excuses to justify an obsessive attempt at recovering your memory of Roxanne Wiley?"

"Are you worried about that?"

"No!" And then, "Yes!"

He reached up to touch her cheek and trace the curve of her cheekbone. "Do you trust me, Shana?"

"I trust you, Pie."

"Then believe me. This is something that must be faced. Do you really think Mason would allow us to go on an extended vacation for the rest of our lives? He views people, Citizens or Unders, as tools to be used as he sees fit." He was quiet for a moment and then continued. "He must be killed if...."

Shana finished the sentence. "If you can. Pie, I'm afraid."

"Don't worry."

"Don't worry? Don't worry? Is that what you said?"

"Yup."

"Thanks, that really helps a lot."

He chuckled and reached up with both hands to pull her around until she was tight against him. "We have a little time. What would you like to do?"

She studied his face with sober concentration. He looked older. The whites of his eyes were laced with tiny blood vessels and the skin beneath his eyes was dark, as if bruised.

"I think you should get some sleep," she said.

"Not a good use of time. I have a few things to show you that we may never have an opportunity to experience again. Stop that frowning. I mean we might never again be weightless, with a little time to spare."

"All Right, Pie," she whispered, "teach me. You'll find me to be a good pupil."

The weariness was pushed aside. This was their time and the sweetness of the pleasure did more to heal Pie's wounds than the nap that was to follow.

Chapter 36

Home had grown. It now infested one hundred cubic kilometers of space. Both Pie and Shana viewed the sparkling intricacies of the twirling cylinders of Home as it was revealed in the holo-stage. It was a kinetic sculpture fit for the universe. When Shana turned to Pie, it was with exasperation; he had assumed the face of absence while he established a deep link with Home.

He circumvented the blocks of the Home matrix with ease, despite the improvements made during their long hiatus. This was by far the largest human-style matrix he had engaged with his new link. While its character was similar to the smaller versions, its massive complexity granted it a much greater degree of self-awareness. It could resist and respond. Perhaps in time, it would evolve a totally independent will and become completely alive. Perhaps it already was. He decided the best way to communicate with what amounted to an alien intelligence was through images. He imagined the matrix caught within a web that was the cylinders of Home, with a human figure looking much like Mason. The Mason figure was using a chisel to scratch the surface of the matrix, marring an otherwise pristine surface. He imagined the matrix reaching out with a diamond blade, much like his own, and severing the web. Then he showed the star grazers, free to seek out their destiny. He visualized the starships breaking away from the Grand Procession and streaking toward the heart of the Milky Way.

The Home matrix considered the request for a nanosecond, the longest processing it had been called on to perform in a millennium.

An image appeared in Pie's mind. The sparking spokes and cylinders of Home began to splinter and fly apart in an expanding cloud. As he watched the vision of the terrible destruction unfold, he could not avoid imagining all the death and vowed to save as many as he could. The vision was a speeded up version of the future destruction. In reality, it would take weeks, maybe months, for the colossus that was home to disintegrate, as a result of repair and maintenance functions being disabled. But, once it started, there would be no stopping it. And then he thought about the matrix. It too would die.

Something of what he'd been thinking must've leaked over to the matrix because another vision unfolded. A flower appeared, daisy-like.

The flower folded in on itself and became smooth and shiny and as hard as a ball bearing.

He downlinked.

"What's happening?" Shana asked with urgency.

"I've just destroyed Home."

"What?" She looked at the holo-stage; the twisting mesh of cylinders appeared unchanged.

"It won't be obvious for weeks, but it is inevitable. How long have I been uplinked?"

"An hour."

"That long? Has Home Control been trying to contact us?"

"How would I know?"

Pie immediately established a link with Home Control.

"Out-ship of Hawking, this is your last warning! Open communication, or we will be forced to board which will result in catastrophic decompression."

"Control, this is the out-ship of Hawking, Citizen Traynor speaking. What's your hurry? We've been gone a couple of hundred years, a few more minutes shouldn't cause alarm."

"Citizen Traynor, we were concerned something might have gone wrong. After the star grazer Hawking came in out of control and nearly destroyed us, you can imagine we were more than a little interested when you didn't respond."

"Your sensors have already informed you that there are two humans aboard."

"Now that is interesting. We detect only one human, currently in the commons of the Up-Ship. And you say there is another? Who is the other?"

"Control, I want you to prepare to receive the out-ship at old dock '7-A'."

"'7-A'? That's deep in the labyrinth! It hasn't been used for years. It isn't even equipped with magnetics. Are you crazy?"

"That's not a very tactful thing to say to a Citizen returning from a deep mission."

"There's no way you can get an out-ship in there."

"I've run the program. It works if you disengage that tug."

"I was warned about you."

"Oh, who warned you?"

"Nearly everyone. You think because you're an Original Citizen you don't have to follow the same rules as the rest of us."

"Tell Mitchell Mason that I've brought back something important from Angkor. As if he's not already lurking," Pie said.

"What is it?" Control asked.

"How many people do you detect aboard the out-ship?"

Pie detected a side link that Control had established and followed it into the deepest recess of Home, to the Prime Cylinder and Mitchell Mason. A moment later Control reactivated its link with Pie and Pie detected the tug releasing its hold on the out-ship.

"Your request has been approved," the voice said, decidedly cool in tone, "but I want you to know, this is an unnecessary and dangerous stunt you're pulling. You'd better know what you're doing."

"Thank you for your encouragement. However, I do have one more small request. I want no more than two greeters. I feel nervous around people. Who knows what might happen if I experience a panic attack. You do understand, I'm sure."

There was another pause before Control answered Pie's new request. "It will be as you ask."

Pie severed the connection and turned his attention to Shana. "Well, we're in it now."

"In what? In case you've forgotten, I'm not linked in. What's happening?"

There was no answer; he was uplinked again. She grabbed hold of him and they began slowly spinning as they drifted across the room, until Shana managed to stop them with her feet against the bulkhead. A trace of weight returned as the ship began to accelerate and they drifted down to the deck. There was a slight jolt as the ship made contact with something and then free fall returned.

Once again the humanity returned to his face and he spoke. "I've placed a block on the out-ship that is impregnable. If this is going to work, I have to move fast. I have maneuvered the ship into a dock near the Prime Cylinder. The ship will remember how to get back out."

"What? Why should—"

"Please, Shana, let me finish. I'm going into Home by myself. You will stay aboard the out-ship. If I have not returned in one hour, speak your real name out loud. The ship will disengage and, with any luck at all, land you safely on an island."

"Pie—"

"Please, don't interrupt. Mason is probably already deploying forces to board the ship."

"Pie, don't—"

He put his index finger against her lips. "You deserve to know everything, but we don't time. I'm sorry. I will return. This is just a contingency plan."

She took his finger in her hand and pulled it down. "Pie, don't go. I beg you."

"We've talked about this. There's no other option." Then he added, "Don't worry, Shana. I'm not planning on dying. I plan to grow old with you."

She swallowed her tears back with an audible "gulp". "I'll wait for you."

"One hour," Pie reminded her, "no more. Promise me. I need that reassurance."

"You have your plans and I have mine, which I don't have time to share with you by the way."

"Shana, I can't be worrying about you and taking on Mason at the same time. Promise me."

"What is that you want me to promise again?"

"Shana, damn it, please!"

"I promise," she mumbled.

He kissed her. "I'll be back. One hour, no longer."

"If you'll be back, why—"

"Shana, I can't take him on and be worrying about you. Please."

She nodded but said nothing.

Pie passed through the ship's lock and entered the acceleration cone of the docking cylinder. He took his seat and it began to spin. "Flow, Pie," he whispered to himself while he fingered the handle of his knife. He uplinked and confirmed that only two people awaited him in the corridor beyond the cone. He turned the surveillance feed into an endless loop. It wouldn't fool Control long but with these two Unders standing at attention in the loop, it should be enough.

When the rotational speeds had matched, the chime sounded. Pie stepped through the inner lock and into the cylinder proper. There were two Unders standing rigidly at attention and perfectly still.

Pie smiled. Perfect. He stopped to inspect them, the first examples of the current culture. The pendulum of society had swung toward militarism. One was of medium build and male. The other was obviously a woman, despite attempts to minimize the differences.

"Citizen Traynor," the woman said, "would you follow us, please?"

Pie continued to study the two of them. They both wore their hair closely cropped, with sharp edges, like a helmet. Their tight, gray uniforms flared backward in the sleeves and legs to form sharp ridges, a fin-like effect. They wore knee-high glossy-black boots and carried wicked appearing side arms. He uplinked and studied them. The guns were props but he discovered they also carried a real weapon, a neural weapon. Interesting.

"Citizen, please," the woman said, evidently the senior of the two.

He looked back to their faces and the lightning bolt, tattooed on their foreheads. They probably were members of some kind of elite guard, expecting a reward for loyalty to the Technocracy. Probably promised to have their memories stored in the matrix and to be raised up to the level of Citizen.

"Citizen Traynor," the woman said, "you are to...." Her words failed her when she raised her gaze and saw hazel eyes looking back at her, not the black eyes of a citizen. She immediately shifted her focus to his forearm, as if she could see through the long sleeves of his bodysuit and confirm that this man truly was a Citizen and wore a link.

"You were saying?" Pie prompted.

"You are to report at once to the Imperial Commander, Sir."

"The Imperial Commander? Do mean Mitchell Mason?"

"Yes, Imperial Commander Mason demands that you report to him."

"I plan to," Pie said easily, "but first we need to chat for a few minutes. What's your name?"

"Name?"

"Yes, you know. What are you called?"

She pulled in her chin and stuck out her chest, flattened by the material of the uniform, "Mika-264, Sir!"

Pie turned to the man, "And you?"

"Pell-168, Sir!"

Pie shifted his weight so that he stood at ease, in sharp contrast to the straight posture of the Unders. "Mika and Pell, I have some information for you, and a job."

Pell chanced a nervous glance at Mika. His thoughts were clear to Pie, "This Citizen is deep-spaced and possibly dangerous."

Pie continued. "The information is that Home is going to self-destruct over the next twelve to fourteen weeks."

There was undisguised disbelief in both their faces and they openly looked at one another. Pell did not even attempt to hide his smirk when he spoke, "Thank you, Citizen, for generously sharing this information with us."

"Don't patronize me, Pell." This time Pie's voice was commanding.

Pell snapped back into rigidity. "I would never do that, Sir!" he declared.

"Unders, discharge your weapons at me."

Pell stuck his head slightly forward, as if he could hear better if he were a few centimeters closer.

"That is an order!" Pie barked.

"We can't do that," Mika said in a small voice, "the Imperial Commander would...." She stopped talking when she saw Pie roll up his sleeve and draw the diamond knife. Her eyes fixed on the gleam along the edge of the blade.

"The Imperial Commander is a God damned self-serving son of a bitch. Need I say more?" Pie asked casually.

Pell sucked in a breath, expecting such terrible retribution he could not even visualize it. He wanted help, any kind of help, and stole a glance down the corridor, wondering what was keeping the reinforcements.

"If you don't use your weapon, Pell, I'm going to cut out your heart." He had the man's undivided attention. He took a measured step toward the Under and then another; the man froze into immobility, only his eyes moved as they followed the approaching knife. Pie noticed movement out of the corner of his eyes. Mika had raised a silvery wand, the real weapon. She shook it and then stared at it.

Pie halted his advance on the Under-man and pivoted toward Mika. She leaned back against the bulkhead, too frightened to even breathe.

"Thank you, Mika," Pie said. "That's not a very impressive weapon."

"But...." was all she could manage.

Pell's forehead beaded with perspiration except where he'd been branded with the lightning bolt.

"Hot, Pell?" Pie asked.

The Under did not answer.

"There is an Under-woman still aboard the ship. Her name is Shana-8. I am going to open a line of communication. Talk with her. Ask her what you will, but note this well, in fifty-three minutes I'm going to return to this cylinder and take the ship to Earth. I can take some Unders with me. Most others will have to find their own way during the next few months. If Shana convinces you that what I'm telling you is the truth, then you will gather together forty who wish to go with me. You now have fifty-two minutes," he said as he brushed past them and shoved his knife into its sheath.

It had taken too long to show the Unders that the Technocracy was not omnipotent, but it had been an important step. It had to be done. As he passed from cylinder to cylinder, he searched ahead and behind, inactivating weapons throughout the cylinders. It was mildly reassuring that the traps were meant to disable rather kill. As he walked the corridors, initially he saw a fair number of austere Unders, all dressed in shades of gray. They would scurry away, into their cabins or down side corridors. It reminded him of another walk he had taken but he couldn't quite place it. *Was there nothing really new in his life?* he once again wondered.

As he continued, the corridors became increasingly empty as the information front of his passing spread through Home. In the bigger cylinders, even the far overhead walkways were empty.

When he arrived at the Prime Cylinder, he paused, not to reminisce, but to search and disable the matrix traps that Mason had set. He looked ahead along the matrix web. There were three people in the Prime Cylinder: Mitchell Mason; another Citizen, probably Joshua; and some kind of a partial person, with matrix input but no access. He opened the lock and seated himself in the entry drum of what had been his real home in space for so many hundreds of years.

He detected scanners searching him for weapons and he permitted it. The inner lock opened and, ahead in an enclosed entryway, a sparkling curtain of light blocked his way. It crackled and sputtered with energy. As he drew near the energy field parted for him and, after his passage, collapsed shut with a "snap".

Pie paused while he took in the interior of the Prime Cylinder. He had never seen it like this. The huge cylinder had been gutted, creating a massive space, and in all that vastness there was only one object, lighted by a single beam from somewhere high in the overhead. It was a desk-like console and sitting behind it was a man wearing military fatigues. The other two individuals he'd detected were somewhere off in the darkness to his right.

Pie began walking through the darkness toward the desk. He could only see the figure from the waist up, but there was no doubt about the person's identity; it was Mitchell Mason.

Pie slipped into the matrix pathways and discovered that the figure was not real. It was only a clever projection. He stopped and searched again. Mason was actually in the dark off to his left, but he did not turn in that direction, instead he starting walking again, toward the convincing illusion. The waste and self-isolation reeked of insanity.

"Flow, Pie," the projected figure called out. "As you can see, I've done a little remodeling since you left. Sorry about your cabin, but it had to go. Make way for the modern. You know. Come closer, so I can see you better." The figure pointed to its left and a chair appeared within the bright circle of light, surrounded by unnatural darkness. Pie walked to within twenty meters of the simulacrum and stopped. Another beam of light burst forth to place Pie within his own bright circle.

"Please, come and join me," the projection said in a friendly, fatherly way as he extended his hand toward the chair.

"I'll stand," Pie said.

Mason's projection appeared morbidly obese. His eyes were thin, black grins on either side of his nose. Pie thought he detected the odor of sweat, even though he knew it was only a projection.

"We have much to talk about, old friend," the vision of Mason said smoothly. "Two hundred years is a long time between visits. Things change."

"I will not talk with a clever light show. If you cannot show me the simple courtesy of meeting me in person, then I'll leave."

The projected figure in front of Pie boomed with a belly laugh and then said, "You are truly one of a kind."

Pie heard a shuffling of feet and the "swishing" of thigh rubbing against thigh. The real Mitchell Mason waddled out of the darkness and sat down in the chair already occupied by his projection. Mason sat there for a moment, wheezing as he caught his breath. The superimposition of the real Mason and his projection created a double exposure effect; the two images were close but not identical in movement or position.

When Mason's breath returned to normal he spoke. "You always were the most astute operative. I knew I made the right choice when I asked you to go," Mason paused, as if he expected a response, but when none came he continued. "I long-scanned the out-ship. There is nothing on board that cannot be accounted for as part of your original manifest." One set of lips talked, while the other opened a crack and stuck out a little, pink tongue, running it along its lips in a circle. "Does that mean you failed to bring back the technology you were sent after? I've never known Pie Traynor to fail at anything."

"I thought I was sent to determine if it was the home world of the Slan."

"Come, come, Pie. I've had many years to think while I waited for your return. The inhabitants of Angkor-3 are not the Slan, but they do possess advanced technology. What did you bring me?"

Pie skimmed along the matrix paths and turned weapons into junk, and then searched for and disabled booby traps until the giant cavern was clean.

"I'm waiting," Mason continued. "Don't you have anything to say for yourself? There has to be a reason you are invisible to sensors. If it hadn't been for the behavior of the Unders, it would've been impossible to track you. What did you bring me?"

Pie remained silent.

"You are so stubborn," Mason said with a grin in his voice. "Tell me what you want in return."

Pie said nothing.

"I do not have infinite patience. I'll tell you what. Let's start with an easy one. What happened to the Star Grazer Hawking? You must know."

"I've come to kill you, Mitchell."

"Of course you have," Mason agreed affably, waving his arm away from himself as if it were an irrelevant detail to be brushed aside. When he moved his arm, the projected arm moved a fraction behind it, causing it to blur. "It's the same thing after every deep mission you go on."

"Why don't I remember that?"

"How should I know? Do you blame me for Starglow Kin's inactivation? She is inactive, I assume. No matter. I'll regenerate another, just for you. I know you like her but I need something in return. It seems we are having some difficulty with the Home matrix. Can't seem to download memories into new clones. Did you have anything to do with that? If so, you might want to help me fix it, if you expect to ever see Starglow Kin again."

Pie didn't respond.

"Surely you aren't still upset about the New People I sent with you. They didn't return. Did they piss you off or something? As it turns out, their deaths are rather inconvenient. I've forged an understanding with the New People. You might even characterize us as allies." He sucked on his lower lip for a moment. "Most unfortunate."

"Unfortunate? You know damn well who killed them. It was you who engineered the whole thing. You are the one set an assassin loose among us!"

"Yes, yes, well that's all in the distant past. I am curious. What happened to Joe-something or other? As if I can't guess. You are so brutal, one of the things about you that appeals to me."

"You know very well what his name was. This act of a forgetful old man isn't fooling me. Cut it out."

Mason laughed again. "God I love you. Why do you have to be so stubborn?"

"You don't love anyone but yourself."

"Hush now. That isn't nice. Times change. Bend don't break. Flow. You know, Pie, we are the only two originals left, you and I, two of a kind. Survivors. Brothers."

"You aren't my brother. What happened to Joshua?"

"He inactivated."

"He died, Mitchell, died. Are you afraid to use the word?"

"Oh very well, he died. Took an out-ship and drove it into the sun. Quite wasteful. I'm rather miffed at him for that. I haven't decided if I'll regenerate him or not."

"He is your son."

"That was a long time ago. That father-son thing grew kind of thin centuries ago. Anyway, as I was saying, we're the only ones left."

"Yes, and it is time that we die."

Mason massaged his jowls with his thick fingers. "I think not. Have you ever noticed that, when you say something, the people around you have no idea what you're talking about? You and me, buddy. I can see by your expression that you know what I'm referring to."

"It's time."

"Oh stop it. Why do we always have to have this dance before you come on board again? Pie, why do you have the eyes of an Under? There's only one way I know of that can happen, regeneration. Did you find the key to immortality?"

"There is no such thing."

"We'll have plenty of time to talk. You have so much to tell me. To prove my goodwill, I have a gift for you." Mason paused for a response but, when Pie said nothing, he signaled into the darkness with a wave of his hand.

A young woman with red hair was illuminated by another beam, as if this was nothing more than a stage production. Standing slightly behind her was a Citizen wearing a uniform that few if any would recognize anymore, a Waffen-SS uniform with a red band on his arm displaying a swastika. He was smiling and his hands were tight against the back of her neck, holding the handles of a garrote.

There was something about the woman. Pie couldn't stop staring.

"Her name is Roxanne Wiley," Mason said. "Say hello to Pie, Roxanne."

"Hello, Pie," she said in a sultry voice, "we need to get to know each other again. I've missed you terribly. Have you—" She bit her lip hard enough to draw blood. "You can eat shit, Mason, and so can this asshole!" She tried to kick the Citizen who held her. Then she stood still and stopped struggling.

Mason laughed, genuinely amused. "Typical Roxanne. As you can see, she is the genuine article."

Pie didn't answer.

"Don't worry, Pie. I have your memories of her and will return them. I'm not the evil person you seem to think I am."

By following the thin threads of control to its source, Pie made a startling discovery. What had he promised, or sold, to the New People for this? Pie wondered. Mason had a much more extensive matrix implant than either Jilla or Jacques. It occupied the entire area of his brain formally devoted to the visual cortex and parts of the brain stem involved in hearing. A quick look revealed that the Nazi Citizen had a similar implant.

Pie had stayed longer than he had intended, repulsed by what he had found, and yet, curious as well. That explains why it took so long for Mason to notice my eyes, Pie thought to himself. Mason sees with a holistic vision, receiving input from throughout the chamber and possibly throughout Home itself, excellent for an overview, but not reliable at picking out small details in a face-to-face meeting.

"Pie, what are you doing?" Mason asked, by now aware that Pie could manipulate the matrix network that he had thought to be impregnable. "You're a cunning one, perhaps more cunning than even I suspected. I looked for artifacts and you brought back information. Shrewd. I approve. You're probably wearing that necklace under that pretty bodysuit. We can make more of them. That's part of the answer, isn't it Pie? With your knowledge of the matrix and that technology, we can reassert ourselves as the undisputed, dominant force."

Pie was aware of Mason's talking, but was dangerously preoccupied. Why have I not killed him? he asked himself. Kin will never be again. She will be truly dead. Maybe, if I wait— His attention was brought back to the cylinder by Mason's silence and he shuddered with the realization of the risk he'd just taken.

"I have news," Mason said. "We've made—"

Roxanne began to struggle. Pie focused his attention on her and saw that Mason had put implants in her as well, but these were for control. She became still again but Pie could see tears in the light that reflected from her eyes.

"What I was about to say," Mason continued, "before I was so rudely interrupted is that we've made giant strides in controlling the bug problem in the last two centuries. In fact, I can claim, it's no longer a problem, thanks to the New People. In fact, you can now take a walk in sunlight without concern, as long as you're wearing appropriate sun protection and that's next."

Pie stared at him.

"You don't have much to say, do you? Not quite what you expected, is it? I know you never really liked me, even when you were my assistant director at Copper Mountain. However, you always recognized one thing.

273

I get things done, even if it requires action that you would find distasteful. You need me, Pie. You've always known that." Mason paused. "Why do I get the feeling you're not listening to me? Is it because I haven't offered you something you really want?" His hand disappeared from sight, beneath the old fashion desk.

Only ten minutes left, Pie thought. He steadied his resolve. This is the man who is keeping the Earth under his heel, making certain it remains a dead world.

Mason smiled as he raised his hand from beneath his desk. He held up a three-centimeter sphere in his fingertips. It had a metallic sheen.

"Your memories of sweet Roxanne," Mason said. "Want them?"

Pie uplinked and detected that Mason was trying to activate his weapon systems; he was beginning to panic, but one would never know it by listening to him.

Pie slipped his knife from its sheath.

Mason "saw" the blade from a dozen different angles and magnifications. Instead of cowering, he merely smiled.

"Really, Pie?" Mason said. "Your pet knife? Ridiculous. You're not even enhanced. Jericho could take you with one hand behind his back. He has continued to improve himself. I told him you are the one who inactivated him during his second regeneration. He's interested in giving it another go. Aren't you Jericho?"

"My pleasure," Jericho said while he continued to hold the garrote tight around Roxanne's neck, "but don't misunderstand. I don't hold a grudge against you. Don't even remember it. Doesn't even exist. But, I'd like to be the one who showed the great Pie Traynor his place in the New Society. That would be amusing. And then do you know what I'm going to do?"

Pie studied Jericho, but said nothing. It felt so familiar.

Jericho continued. "I'm going to take this delicious woman and play with her. I've learned a lot of new tricks. Commander Mason tells me he shared some of my memories with you. Did you enjoy them? Did they turn you on?"

"You are a beast. After I kill Mason, I'm going to kill you, and you won't be coming back."

Jericho laughed. "Such a talker. Anytime you're ready."

"A minute, please, Pie," Mason said while he rolled the memory sphere around on his fingertips.

Pie continued to hold his blade out in front, but did not move.

"What would you trade for your memories of Roxanne? And to get her back in one piece? I can get you a fresh one, not tampered with, if that's what you really want. Your memories are here, you know. I'm holding them in my hand at this very moment. Would you like them?"

The small globe rolled off Mason's fingertips and bounced toward Pie with the sound of metal tapping on metal.

Pie watched it as it bounced in his direction. Eight minutes, part of his mind said, but his eyes fastened on the globe with a hunger to know, a hunger that suddenly bloomed with desire. He bent to pick up the metal ball. When he straightened up, he saw Mason was holding a weapon; it was not a matrix device.

"One must be prepared," Mason said. "It required an extensive search to find it, but it was worth it. Poetic even. You might recognize it. It's a forty-four-magnum revolver. Smith and Wesson. It's yours. Primitive, like you, but satisfying in a way. I can see why you liked to hold it. Heavy. Solid. With a kick that would knock a less sturdy man over. And the punch! Fantastic. I tried it out on a few Unders. The pleasure of brut force. I'd almost forgotten about it."

He pulled the trigger. The gun sounded with a deafening "boom" and spat fire. The heavy slug struck Pie in the right chest and kicked him off his feet, tossing him onto his back as if struck by a giant fist. The pain was horrible, but Pie fought to remain alert. Mason stood and walked around his desk to stand over Pie and take careful aim at Pie's mouth.

"Goodbye, Pie. I'm going to put this bullet into your brainstem and harvest your memories. We don't really need you as yourself. I gave you a chance. No one cares about you anymore, old buddy. You are irrelevant."

With an effort fueled by desperation, Pie flipped onto his side and at the same time uplinked, severing every thread of the matrix web in the Prime Cylinder. He left nothing intact, nothing functioning, not even the environmental system. It had been an act of desperation and had taken away his most effective potential weapon, the control of both Mason and Jericho via their links.

Mason screamed with surprise and then began to methodically empty the gun, spraying the area that he remembered Pie to be lying in, not aware the gun was empty until it stopped bucking in his hand. He could smell the acrid odor of gunpowder, but he was deaf and blind. He groped his way to the desk and took hold of the edge.

"Pie," he called out, uncertain if he had succeeded or not, "we can still make a deal. It's not too late, not between friends. Jericho, where are you?"

Jericho also could neither see nor hear. He had severed Roxanne's head from her body and she lay crumpled on the deck.

Pie had been struck a second time, in the thigh. The bullet had passed through the muscle without striking bone, but the wound leaked blood. He felt breathless and dizzy while he dragged himself toward Mason, trailing a path of blood. His skin was cold and wet with sweat, and his tongue tingled with the taste of metal, but he refused to succumb. By centimeters he pulled himself closer.

Mason continued to talk. "Pie, we need each other. I know that now. Who else can remember the smell of a pine forest or the beauty of a waterfall? Who else, Pie? Just you and me. Pie, give me back my hearing. That won't be a risk to you and then we can talk, figure a way out of this mess. Pie, where are you?"

Pie's breath was a raspy razor in his throat. His thirst was like none he'd experienced before.

With his hand on the edge of the desk, Mason was working his way around but slipped in the pool of Pie's blood. He hit the deck hard and screeched like a wounded animal. He tried to regain his feet on the slippery surface but was too obese. He lay prone on the deck and stopped struggling.

"Where are you, Pie? I'm sick. I'm a sick man. Help me, Pie! Please, help me. I'm begging you. You are my friend. Help me."

"I'll help you, Mason," Pie said in a gasping whisper. "It is time for us."

With his little remaining strength, Pie raised the blade and plunged it into Mason's neck, crunching against bone and passing forward into the soft tissues of blood vessels and airway. Pie looked toward Jericho who was stumbling about and threw the blade, striking Jericho in the chest, penetrating his heart. Jericho fell to the deck near Roxanne, but Pie had collapsed as well, not seeing the success of his deathblow.

With the metallic memory sphere clutched in his hand, his thoughts turned to Shana. Do it. Go. Sorry, so sorry. Love…was his last coherent thought as his vision faded to black.

Chapter 37

Pell and Mika and a gathering of other Unders were with Shana when Pie's voice was broadcast throughout the ship.

"Shana, if you are hearing this message, it means my time has expired. On your love for me, I demand that you fulfill your promise and disengage from Home. It is time for you to return to Earth, but know this well, if it were at all possible, I would've returned to you. Go now. My love goes with you."

The message ended and there was a moment of silence until Shana screamed and grabbed hold of her head with both hands. The Unders nearby pushed away from her, floating away until Shana was separate from everyone.

"No!" she yelled and when she glared about the commons, all could see that she'd been transformed; there was not a gentle line, nor a peaceful movement.

She pointed at Pell, "You, get three strong Unders and take me to the Prime Cylinder."

Pell didn't move. "No Under who has entered the Prime Cylinder has ever been seen again. It is a place of death."

"I've been there. Am I dead?"

She pushed off and as she swam past Pell, slapped him across the face, hard enough to raise a welt.

"I swear to you, to all of you," Shana said while her gaze raked across all who had gathered in the commons. "I will not release this ship from Home unless Pie Traynor is aboard. Do you understand?" She steadied herself and gazed around the room a second time.

Pell nodded and picked out three "volunteers" to accompany them. Together the five of them entered the docking cylinder with Shana leading the way. The cone began to rotate with what felt like a creeping slowness. Each cone and cylinder they passed through was a torture of time passing. The Under-guards they ran past recognized Pell and watched them with curiosity but did nothing to obstruct their passage. At last they were running the last corridor, toward the Prime Cylinder.

When they neared the entry drum, a man slipped out of a side corridor. He wore a severely tailored coat with gold braid on the shoulders and around his wrist he wore the link of a Citizen. He stood squarely in their path, his feet well-spaced and his arms crossed.

"Just where do you think you're running to?" the Citizen asked while his black eyes scoured them with contempt.

Shana turned to the Unders who followed her. They were standing at attention, their arms across their chests in a salute.

"You sludges!" Shana shouted. "You oil-burning tar-balls!" she cursed.

The Citizen who was watching this unusual display chuckled. "And what do we have here? You know the penalty for being out of uniform, don't you?" he asked as he reached out to pull Shana to him, but Shana did not respond like the typical, docile Under; she jammed her elbow backward, catching the Citizen in the pit of his stomach. He bent over at the waist, holding his abdomen as he struggled to regain his breath, but then slowly straightened and withdrew a gray disc from the pouch he wore. He pointed it at Shana, holding it between his index finger and thumb; it was a hypersonic disintegrator, capable of turning human tissue to mush while leaving property untouched. It was the current favorite weapon of most Citizens; people were cheap, objects were not.

"Pretty or not, you will pay for that mistake," he said.

Shana turned to the other Unders but they retreated from her, standing as far to the sides as possible to avoid any over spray from the weapon.

"You are Unders and you deserve to be Unders!" She spat at their feet. "I'd rather have this Citizen, than any of you."

"Too late, girly. You had your chance." But as the Citizen stood there, his smile flattened and he began, almost imperceptibly, to back away. He attempted an uplink and then began shaking his arm with the golden link, as if he could shake it to life. He continued to push the activator on his weapon but nothing happened. Shana started walking toward the man and he backed up farther, until he was flat against the drum lock.

"The time is now!" Shana declared, and the Under-men who accompanied her began to creep forward. The Citizen dropped his weapon and turned to run, but Pell grabbed hold of him, and then all four Unders piled on top of the Citizen, riding him to the floor. Pell grabbed hold of the man's ears and began pounding his head on the deck until it sounded like a wet, cracked gourd.

Shana had to pull on them to make them stop. "He's dead. Can't you see that?" she yelled at them while she tugged on their arms. Sense slowly replaced the frenzy of rage. They stood and looked to her for direction.

She found the Under-panel and opened it, activating the lock to the final entry cone. When they entered the Prime Cylinder, the Under-men stepped back to allow Shana to lead the way.

A single shaft of light shown down onto a console at the far end of the great hall. Shana began walking toward it, and then started running when she noticed two bodies lying within the cone of light. The Under-men followed, huddled in a group, and whispering among themselves as they advanced toward the light.

She drew near and identified one of the bodies as that of Pie Traynor. She knelt at his side. He was still breathing.

"He's alive!" she yelled.

The Unders stood around, glancing nervously into the darkness. There was a headless woman, a headless man, and another man with a knife sticking out of his chest.

"Pick him up and let's get out of here!"

They didn't have to be told twice. Quickly now, they heaved the heavy bulk of Traynor onto their shoulders and headed for the lock. Shana's heart felt like it was being crushed. He was so pale and lifeless. His lips had no color and his skin was ashen and cold.

"Faster!" she urged, and they stumbled down the corridors in an awkward run. One of the Under-guards they passed stuck out his arm to stop them, but Shana slapped it away, and they hurried onward.

They were all huffing with air hunger by the time they reached the out-ship. The Unders parted to make way as Pie was floated through the commons. Shana directed them to take him to his cabin, one above and one below as they floated him down the tube.

By now Pie's breathing was irregular, punctuated by deep gasps. Shana slapped an osmotic pad onto his chest and hoped the machine would respond. One of the Unders had followed them down to Pie's cabin.

"I've had experience as a bio-agent," he said calmly. "This man is moribund. If you step aside, I'll see what I can do to try to save him."

Shana stood, reluctant to loose physical contact with Pie. She made just enough room for the bio to work in, and watched all his moves with critical suspicion. With each passing minute of the crisis, she felt she could not take another. To know that he was dying, was a thought she could not accept.

Chapter 38

Days had become weeks and weeks had become months. The dawn sky was crisscrossed with bright lights streaking through the atmosphere, a display not seen since the Earth was young.

It was going to be another cold day. The sunrise was a muted event; the sky was always filled with dark clouds that dropped rain incessantly.

The out-ship rested on a plateau, while far below an angry ocean attacked the coastline with huge beakers, crashing against the black volcanic rock that lined its shore. Shana stood in the open portal of the out-ship and watched another sheet of gray rain advance across the sea toward the island, an island that Pie had told her had been named Maui at a time in the distant past.

A large man walked up to stand behind her. "Better get used to it."

She jumped, and then turned to smile at him. "You shouldn't be up."

"Actually I'm feeling quite well, thanks to you and Miles. Did you know he was once a bio-agent in New Berlin? And get this, they have a zoo. It would almost be worth a visit, if we could get there, and if it wasn't the city of the New People. Don't you agree?"

"Sure."

"Hey, you," he said, and wrapped his arms around her so that her back was against his chest. She could feel the lump of the medallion that still hung around his neck.

"What are you thinking about?" he asked.

"What is happening to the Earth? Is it really dying this time? It sure looks and feels like it." She shivered despite the warmth of his body pressed against hers.

"You know, there was once this catcher—"

"A what?"

"A baseball player."

"Oh, the ball and club game." She was pleased with herself for having remembered.

Pie chuckled. "Right. Anyway this man once said, 'It ain't over 'till it's over'. I think that's where we, and all of humanity stand. It's just possible that Quang Lu succeeded after all, but it'll be a difficult time for many generations. I think this means that the Earth has turned the corner and is on a long road to recovery."

281

She was quiet for a moment. The air was becoming cooler by the minute. Their breaths were beginning to puff with little, white clouds of water vapor.

"So, you think the water level will decline?" Shana asked.

Pie nodded. Though she couldn't see the gesture, she could feel it.

"Large chunks of the moon have been striking the ocean and blasting huge clouds of water into the atmosphere. The clouds are cooling the Earth. I'm fairly certain ice is already re-accumulating in the polar regions."

"First too hot and now too cold. When will it ever be right? When will it start to warm up again?"

"I don't know. The Earth is probably headed for an ice age. I don't know if it'll rebound from the shock of this new insult, or not. The environment may have been pushed too far from its balance point. Nor do I know what will survive. I imagine there will always be some kind of life in the oceans. Thank goodness."

He thought about all the seeds that were waiting for fertile ground in his egg house in the Cascade Mountains. The house had a nuclear generator, one of the few active generators on Earth, and the seeds would be protected for a long time, but it would not be his command that would send them forth. He knew that now and accepted it, just as he accepted his own mortality. The seeds were no longer his responsibility, that responsibility would lay with some future friend of the Earth.

A bright shaft of light appeared far out to sea. It was sharply defined and so intense that it looked like the sky had cracked open. It moved rapidly across the horizon. If Pie and Shana had been closer, they would have seen the seawater boiling into great clouds of steam.

Shana twisted in Pie's arms so she was facing him. "What was that?"

"That, if I'm not mistaken, is a sign of death. Home is dying." Pie sighed. It had been so expensive in lost knowledge, lost opportunity, and the loss of life.

"What do you mean, Pie?"

"That was an energy beam from a broadcaster, drifting out of control. The cities are without power. Lines of misdirected energy are raking the Earth and space. It will be sometime before the master collector also drifts out of alignment. Until then, whatever the beam touches will be vaporized. This is not a kind world we are going to try to make peace with. But, the people.... I bear that responsibility. I've done what I could. I lied. I was able to access the communication satellites and informed the cities that they need to send all comm-ships to Home and rescue as many as they can. If they do this, I've promised to restore their power."

"You can do that?"

"No. There are many brave men and women risking their lives piloting their ships to Home, a rescue attempt in a very chaotic and dangerous environment, with cylinders coming apart and striking others, pieces of space debris everywhere. Many will die. And that's not even taking into account the anarchy that must be taking place in bubble cities without power."

"You did what you could. It's not your fault."

"It is my responsibility. I did it."

"It had to be done."

"Did it? There must have been a better way."

She turned around so she was facing him and wrapped her arms around the big man. She could feel him shaking; he was crying.

"I should take the out-ship and go help with the rescues. There are still people up there, dying."

"You can't. You said we needed the ship to manufacture nutrients that we can't get from the sea and it is our only medical facility. You said, if we're careful, the remaining power should last a lifetime."

He said nothing. She took his hands in hers; they were cold.

"Come." She tugged on his hands. "It's time for us to join the others in the village."

He nodded. "It's time to make preparations. The long winter is nearly upon us."

"They want you to be their leader," Shana said.

He shook his head. "I've had enough of that. I don't want anymore. I can't."

"You have to. They're counting on you. You're the only one who can access the out-ship matrix."

"I'll have to fix that."

"They trust you, Pie."

"They shouldn't."

The icy rain had eased and they stepped out of the portal and walked down a ramp. He automatically felt for his knife but it too was gone, lost forever, along with Home. He briefly uplinked and the iris portal twisted shut, locking away the little that remained of the Technocracy. He turned away from the rugged coastal scene to look down a long gentle slope toward a valley. Among the white survival domes, there were the beginnings of primitive stone buildings. Occasionally, a figure could be seen scurrying from one dome to another. Pie couldn't help but wonder, if there'd ever be technology again.

"It's a pity," Pie concluded, "that none of your island people were here to assist us, helpless, civilized humans."

"Yes, I was looking forward to meeting them, but...that was a long time ago and far away. They lived on rafts off the coast. We are on an island out in the middle of a vast ocean. Right?"

"Right."

She looked out to sea, at the giant rollers striking the beach and hoped her people had managed to find a safe harbor in time, if they still even existed.

Large, white flakes began drifting out of the gray sky. Shana turned to Pie with open wonder on her face, with snowflakes clinging to her black hair. She held out her hand and watched the white crystals turn into drops of water as they contacted the warmth of her palm. The snowfall grew heavier, dressing the world in white and powdering it with quiet.

Shana laughed with delight and it lightened Pie's heart to hear her child-like enchantment. The snow stirred memories of his own childhood and he tipped his face to the sky, feeling the soft touch of snowflakes on his cheeks.

"What is it, Pie?" Shana asked, but she giggled and ran ahead onto the plateau without waiting for an answer.

Pie could see her drawing a shape in the snow with her feet, but he could not determine what it was, until he drew closer. He stopped and thought about the metal memory-globe, somewhere in the ship, waiting for him, and remembered the heart that had been etched into the bulkhead of his cabin back on Home.

She was standing in the center of a heart, scratched into the white blanket of snow. At the top of the heart she had traced a large "S". But, as she stood there, her bright smile began to fade.

Pie took a deep breath and slowly released it in a small cloud of steam. He stepped forward and, with his foot, rubbed a "+" and then the initials "PT". They stood looking at one another across a span of two paces. Shana held out her hand to him and opened it. It was the memory sphere.

He took it from her hand and stared at it.

"I understand," she said. "Go ahead and download your memories. You want to."

He shook his head. "These don't belong to me. They belong to someone else." He threw the globe as hard as he could and it became a speck as it sailed over the cliff edge and disappeared into the raging surf below.

He returned his attention to Shana. "I love you and I'll never leave you."

"I believe you. I love you, Pie. I—" Her voice caught with joy, but she still managed to add, "I will never leave you either."

After a moment she spoke again, in a whisper. "I'm pregnant."

He pulled away a little. "What did you say?"

"I'm pregnant," she declared in a stronger voice, almost defiant.

His face was quiet for a moment and then broke out with the biggest grin she had ever seen on him.

"Pregnant?"

"Yes, Pie."

He looked over shoulder at the raw sea and roiling black clouds. His smile began to fade.

"You don't think we're up to it?" she asked.

"A boy or a girl?"

"I have no idea. Does it matter?"

"No. How far along are you?" he asked.

"Twenty weeks. Did you think I was just getting fat?"

"You are beautiful, skinny or fat. I don't care. And yes, if anyone's up to it, it's the two of us."

He cupped her face in his hands and kissed her lips. Together, holding hands like teenagers, they walked through the carpet of gathering snow, toward the village of domes and into a new world.

Epilogue

What would the future hold? Mankind could not reject knowledge without drifting into primitive ignorance, but the thorns of knowledge were many. Mankind could not stay still. It must either advance and change, or regress and change, but change it must; to be caught within a circle of changelessness was neither death, nor life.

Maybe all this was just part of a picture on such a grand scale, that a person, even a person who had the memories of two thousand years, couldn't appreciate the pattern. Maybe this was simply a part of the human condition, an oscillation between high and low technology.

Pie Traynor had found a basic understanding that had eluded him. He understood now the place of memory. Memories were not like jewels, to be clutched avariciously to his chest, until so many recollections had been gathered that they slipped through his fingers. They were not to be secreted away for some ill-defined climax in the nebulous future. Memories were made for use in the present. While it was entropy and chaos that made life possible, it was memory that gave life value and reason.

Pie Traynor had wanted to spread seeds across the earth, but he had planted an even more important seed, the seed of life. It would be for other generations to reap the fruit of change. He had found what he had been looking for, a life he could live and a death he could face.

About the Author

Gary Moreau grew up in a small town in Iowa called Estherville. He discovered science fiction in the fifth grade, beginning with a book by Alan E. Nourse entitled *Star Surgeon*.

He graduated from medical school at the University of Iowa and then completed a residency in emergency medicine at Los Angeles County/USC Medical Center. Following his training, he practiced emergency medicine at Long Beach Memorial Medical Center.

It is not likely that he became a physician because of Nourse's book, but it was the beginning of a lifelong love of science fiction. His plans for the future include a focus on his passion for storytelling. *Another* Breath completes the cycle that began in *Almost Human* (published in 2001 by Yard Dog Press) and continued in *Judas Gene* (which is a prequel to *Almost Human* and was published in 2016 by Yard Dog Press).

He and his wife Gloria have two daughters, two sons-in-law, and five grandchildren. His greatest joys in life include family, friends, writing, art, and travel.

Publisher's note: Gary's love for art is demonstrated by the great cover he created for this book.

Yard Dog Press Titles as Of This Print Date

Selina Rosen

The Four Bubbas of the Apocalypse: Flatulence, Halitosis, Incest, and... Ned, Edited by Selina Rosen

The Four Redheads: Apocalypse Now!, Linda L. Donahue, Rhonda Eudaly, Julia S. Mandala, & Dusty Rainbolt

The Four Redheads of the Apocalypse, Linda L. Donahue, Rhonda Eudaly, Julia S. Mandala, & Dusty Rainbolt

The Four Redheads: The Wrath of Satan, Linda L. Donahue, Rhonda Eudaly, Julia S. Mandala, & Dusty Rainbolt

The Garden in Bloom, Jeffrey Turner

The Geometries of Love: Poetry by Robin Wayne Bailey

The Golems of Laramie County, Ken Rand

The Green Women, Laura J. Underwood

The Guardians, Lynn Abbey

Hammer Town, Selina Rosen

The Happiness Box, Beverly A. Hale

The Host Series: The Host, Fright Eater, Gang Approval, Selina Rosen

Houston, We've Got Bubbas!, Edited by Selina Rosen

How I Spent the Apocalypse, Selina Rosen

I Didn't Quite Make It to Oz, Edited by Selina Rosen

I Should Have Stayed In Oz, Edited by Selina Rosen

In the Shadows, Bradley H. Sinor

International House of Bubbas, Edited by Selina Rosen

It Came to Tranquility, Tracy S. Morris

It's the Great Bumpkin, Cletus Brown!, Katherine A. Turski

Judas Gene, Gary Moreau

The Killswitch Review, Steven-Elliot Altman & Diane DeKelb-Rittenhouse

The Leopard's Daughter, Lee Killough

The Lightning Horse, John Moore

The Logic of Departure, Mark W. Tiedemann

The Long, Cold Walk To Mars, Jeffrey Turner

Marking the Signs and Other Tales of Mischief, Laura J. Underwood

Material Things, Selina Rosen

Medieval Misfits: Renaissance Rejects, Tracy S. Morris

Mirror Images, Susan Satterfield

Mirror, Mirror and Other Reflections, James K. Burk

More Stories That Won't Make Your Parents Hurl, Edited by Selina Rosen

Music for Four Hands, Louis Antonelli & Edward Morris

My Life with Geeks and Freaks, Claudia Christian

The Necronomicrap: A Guide to Your Horoooscope, Tim Frayser

Playing With Secrets, Bradley H & Sue P. Sinor

Redheads In Love, Linda L. Donahue, Rhonda Eudaly, Julia S.
    Mandala, & Dusty Rainbolt
Reruns, Selina Rosen
Rock 'n' Roll Universe, Ken Rand
Shadows In Green, Richard Dansky
Stories That Won't Make Your Parents Hurl, Edited by Selina Rosen
Strange Robby, Selina Rosen
Tales from Keltora, Laura J. Underwood
*Tales of the Lucky Nickel Saloon, Second Ave., Laramie, Wyoming, U
    S of A,* Ken Rand
Tarbox Station, Rhonda Eudaly
Texistani: Indo-Pak Food from A Texas Kitchen, Beverly A. Hale
That's All Folks, J. F. Gonzalez
Through Wyoming Eyes, Ken Rand
Turn Left to Tomorrow, Robin Wayne Bailey
The Twins, Selina Rosen
The Undead At My Head, Ethan Nahté
Villains in Training, Julia S. Mandala and Linda L. Donahue
Wandering Lark, Laura J. Underwood
Weirdough, Inc., Selina Rosen and Sherri Dean
Wings of Morning, Katharine Eliska Kimbriel
Zombies In Oz and Other Undead Musings, Robin Wayne Bailey

Fantasy Writers Asylum (A YDP Imprint):
Blood Songs, Julia Mandala
Gateway to Corimar, Julia Mandala & Linda L Donahue
Tale of the Black Heart, Linda L. Donahue

Double Dog (A YDP Imprint):

#1:
Of Stars & Shadows, Mark W. Tiedemann
This Instance Of Me, Jeffrey Turner

#2: Currently out of print
Gods and Other Children, Bill D. Allen
Tranquility, Tracy Morris

#3:
Home Is the Hunter, James K. Burk
Farstep Station, Lazette Gifford

#4:
Sabre Dance, Melanie Fletcher

The Lunari Mask, Laura J. Underwood

#5:
House of Doors, Julia Mandala
Jaguar Moon, Linda A. Donahue

Just Cause (A YDP Imprint):

The Bitter End, Selina Rosen
Death Under the Crescent Moon, Dusty Rainbolt
Duckrt: Mystery at the Museum, Zeb Rosenzweig
Getting It Real, Selina Rosen
The Ghost Writer, Selina Rosen
It's Not Rocket Science: Spirituality for the Working-Class Soul,
    Selina Rosen
Meditations of a Hoarder, Melinda LaFevers
Not My Life, Selina Rosen
Permanent Solution to a Temporary Problem, Selina Rosen
The Pit, Selina Rosen
Plots and Protagonists: A Reference Guide for Writers, Mel. White
Vanishing Fame, Selina Rosen